Make Strange

Also by Niamh Campbell

This Happy
We Were Young

Make Strange

Niamh Campbell

W&N
WEIDENFELD & NICOLSON

First published in Great Britain in 2026 by Weidenfeld & Nicolson,
an imprint of The Orion Publishing Group Ltd
Carmelite House, 50 Victoria Embankment
London EC4Y 0DZ

An Hachette UK Company

The authorised representative in the EEA is Hachette Ireland,
8 Castlecourt Centre, Dublin 15, D15 XTP3, Ireland
(email: info@hbgi.ie)

1 3 5 7 9 10 8 6 4 2

A CIP catalogue record for this book is
available from the British Library.

ISBN (Hardback) 978 1 3996 3179 2
ISBN (Export Trade Paperback) 978 1 3996 3180 8
ISBN (Ebook) 978 1 3996 3182 2
ISBN (Audio) 978 1 3996 3183 9

Typeset by CC Book Production
Printed in Great Britain by Clays Ltd, Elcograf S.p.A.

MIX
Paper | Supporting
responsible forestry
FSC® C104740

www.weidenfeldandnicolson.co.uk
www.orionbooks.co.uk

For Matt Packer, with love

Everyone knows what the female complaint is. Women live for love, and love is the gift that keeps on taking.

Lauren Berlant

I

It was a Sunday in October and Sunny had been feverish all day. In the morning, she came loping into her parents' room, confused, then spent the afternoon lying on the couch. She sat up at twelve, and again at dinnertime, to vomit a watery stream.

Sunny was three and lived on the fifth floor of a build-for-rent apartment block – a nice one, with hundreds of windows.

That Sunday her parents, Lena and Odhran, took advantage of the relative peace to read newspapers and make adult conversation. But around seven o'clock, when darkness had come and the ambient mundanity of Monday loomed, they became afraid. The cough she'd had for days seemed suddenly wetter and worse.

'A&E,' Lena said.

'Do we think it's that bad?'

'Probably not, but the out-of-hours clinic is chaos.'

'Chaos,' Odhran agreed.

Odhran brought the car around and Lena waited on the pavement outside their block with Sunny, standing under a drumming umbrella.

There was little traffic and the units they passed – a churning laundrette, an off-licence with a light pulsing over the door – seemed to represent bleaker versions of life in the city; stakes they did not subscribe to personally.

Odhran turned in the front and asked, phatically since they'd discussed it already, 'James's or Temple Street?'

'Oh James's,' Lena replied from the back seat. 'Stay on this side of the river.'

Odhran was thirty-eight, and Lena thirty-four. Sunny was their only child. Her plush face, hot and framed by clammy curls, lay against the side of her bumper seat. Lena pressed her hand across the brow and felt captive heat.

'First thing tomorrow is that difficult woman. The Dutch one,' Odhran announced suddenly.

He spoke blandly and over the rain. He was talking about work, about his job. The blandness was intended as a balm: there would be tomorrows, frustrations, but never the tomorrow of loss or deformation of life as it was. Hospital just happened as a comical precaution sometimes.

'If we get stuck in the waiting room you can leave and go back to sleep for a bit,' Lena offered. They both knew this would not happen.

'I'll stay with you. Do you think she'll be admitted?'

Lena looked at the little girl, who just then took a breath and sighed.

'No,' she said.

When this kind of thing happened, a small dash to the doctor or a fright, Lena felt contained and borne forth, ineluctably, in a mode reminiscent of all the times she'd been borne forth by her father's car and by other men, in other cars, at earlier stages of life. It wasn't just that she never drove: sitting in the back, and not shotgun, where she might stretch her legs out and flirt, returned her to the state of vulnerability she'd been in on the day she'd left the maternity hospital, and in this state she was more than typically willing to be led.

There was a script, for instance, for A&E. Sunny simplified the sum of her mother's parts. Whenever Lena presented at A&E, or any other health appointment, she was received as credible, legible; met with a respect and ease never afforded to earlier, single, childless or just socially opaque versions of herself.

'Hi there, I am here with my daughter,' she declared.

Odhran was parking. Sunny had been woken and wanted to walk. The place was vast. Plexi panes and pillaged boxes that had once held paper face masks lay about everywhere. The light was bright and, even in this atrium, a number of people with children waited, watching, mutinously.

'Sunniva,' Lena said slowly to the receptionist. As she spoke, she stood on her toes and lifted her chin while lowering her eyes, trying to catch a sight of the data onscreen. 'Marley Flynn. S-u-n-n-i-v-a.' She gave them Sunny's date and place of birth. She said *the Coombe*, to sound local. She told them: 'Flu symptoms, and fever, not going away. Since last night. Some vomiting. But a spike, around seven this evening, to forty degrees.' They directed her down a corridor, with Sunny trailing after, cardigan hanging off her shoulder in picturesque.

'I have headache, Mama,' she whispered. Her voice was slight but rang, always, like an altar bell in Lena's head.

'You can have a nap on my knee.' Lena found a seat. She was lifting Sunny into her lap when Odhran arrived.

He entered at once into the hectic affect of the busy man – matter-of-fact, speaking quickly but low, looking for somewhere to sweep down his coat that would not result in it trailing to the floor. He established that Sunny would soon be called to triage before sitting down next to them on a plastic chair and sinking with relief.

'We could be out in an hour,' he reasoned.

Lena looked at him with tenderness. Just yesterday, they had argued about something familiar, something domestic, or else an old erotic wound, forgotten now – and she'd called him an asshole. He'd said, 'Don't call me that,' and she had retorted that asshole was a soft and minor and even affectionate word, and anyway accurate. 'Don't call me that,' he'd commanded again, robotically. The composure made her want to throw something at a wall. She did not – she could not anymore, ever again, because they had a child together now.

But in this moment, in the waiting room, she looked at

her husband, who was always calm and direct in a crisis, with tenderness.

Sunny lay in Lena's arms and dropped her head against her collarbone. The crown of her head smelt vaguely of vomit, but the almondy warmth of her original, infant odour was always detectable underneath.

It might be hours, Lena thought. It might be brutal.

The waiting room was windowless, its air gelatinous with food-smelling heat. There were television sets mounted at either end. These showed Sky News, and at the bottom of the screen a ticker tape of AI subtitles struggled into sentences uglily and, each time, one clause would pause and seem to accumulate force before spilling out into subsequent clauses, ellipses and redundancies. Lena found herself focusing on it as Sunny fell asleep. Odhran was scanning emails on his phone.

The room was full, though not to capacity: a couple with a baby in an earth-tone onesie paced fretfully. A gaunt woman with three children, none of whom seemed actively ill, ignored them to scroll Instagram reels that let out shrieking, shorted tunes. Her children came back and forth from the vending machines. A teenager with obliterative acne sat straight-backed by her father, expressionless.

Lena allowed a painful hour to pass without complaining, banking karma, and then stepped up to the desk. She slung Sunny, too heavy and still entirely asleep, onto one shoulder.

'My daughter has been waiting,' she said. She did not say sepsis, Covid or RSV; she did not say croup. All of these alarms and their potential were implied.

'We are sorry.' Lena felt the two staff, young women, seemed energised by what they told her next. They assumed looks of sad wonder. They had been waiting for somebody to lose patience and properly ask. 'Everyone is waiting, but I'm afraid we have a child just now in resuscitation. This child is in the resuscitation room.'

This was why, they explained, everybody was waiting.

Lena returned to her seat with a grievous and immediate

feeling. There were images in her mind that had been close to the surface for some years now – images of busses crushing prams, of seizures, eyes rolling inhumanly in heads. Images of defibrillator paddles and the soft, puppyish matter of a body being shocked. Memories of slow ambulances drawing away from accident sites as viewed from the passenger seat of a car. After Sunny was born, she used to advance, dreadfully, on the crib after a nap and believe, in the half-light, that the baby was dead. Every time she stepped off a pavement onto the road, she saw a van crashing around the corner, saw the small body sail through the air like an object, pictured the poppy bruise and open-coffin horror show.

Her own child: she could picture it. The image came in a single wretched strobe.

Lena wanted to tell Odhran what the nurses said but couldn't find the words to whisper it. It was the kind of thing that demanded response, but response could only mean speculation, the shaming luxury of pity, a touch of the void, and something stupid to be added – something like, *God help them*, or *imagine the mother*.

But Lena imagined the mother. She sat there, tense with empathy, and imagined being the mother of that child. She looked at the pale or drawn faces of everyone in the waiting room, everyone hot and rotten in the artificial heat, the TV subtitles glitching and flinching with insect autonomy. Did they know, did anyone else know, about the child in resuscitation?

Odhran tried to stretch in the uncomfortable chair. He began to talk about work in a listless voice while gazing into the distance.

The Dutch woman he disliked was based in Nijmegen. Lena knew this was a town of beerhalls and clocktowers, with a post-Corbusier university campus, and that the Dutch woman was one part of a large, collaborative, trans-European and multidisciplinary research project. She was a professor of archaeology and highly emotional; she phoned or Zoomed or emailed Odhran to lament with great, and greatly inappropriate, feeling about the merits and moral imperatives of her side of the project, of her team of furry archaeology interns, because Odhran was the contact for the administration of their funding grant. It was, he told Lena again, a fucking huge grant, co-funded by several unwieldly continental stakeholders, and the idea that Odhran, or anyone, would convey this woman's complaints to these funders and co-researchers was absurd, completely absurd, she had been told as much, and still she wished to speak to him first thing about something.

'How do you deal with it?' Lena asked mechanically.

'I used to answer emails covertly, you know,' he mimed tapping keys, 'while she was talking. Now I try to count backwards from one hundred, things like that.'

When they'd first met Odhran was mad for Lena – longed for her, impatient between dates, sent her gifts in the post even though they lived in the same city. He was proud to introduce her to everyone, as if she proved something about him people had failed until that point to see or appreciate properly. Now they interacted with the pragmatism of parents, or at least of parents with children under ten, but his command, his calm, even his self-absorption, were useful in such moments as this.

She smiled at him tensely. It seemed impossible to bring up the child in resuscitation now and Lena felt absolved of it.

She was surprised to hear Sunny summoned from a side room suddenly. Her daughter woke up. Lena let Sunny cross the room herself, holding Lena's hand, sensing faces turn to them – women calculating whether or not they'd arrived first, before her, with their own children.

'Now.' The nurse was young and Filipino.

'I'm not seeing the doctor yet?' Lena asked.

'This is just to assess,' smiled the nurse, 'if we need to admit Sunniva.'

They did not. Heart rate was only slightly elevated, by pain; fever was falling, due to Calpol, and there was no sign of anything wrong. Sunny looked miserably at the woman as she scratched things onto a clipboard and asked about medical history.

'In my opinion,' the nurse said, 'this is a virus. It's bad, but she is not dehydrated and we are not seeing any problems with the kidneys, we are not seeing anything to too much worry about. But if you still want to see the doctor, you can wait. You will be waiting maybe,' her eyes flew up, then down, 'it is maybe all night.'

'Oh no,' said Lena. 'I'm happy with that.' The clipboard, she saw, had a box reading *reason for presentation* in which was written 'MOTHER CONCERN'.

She was grateful to return to the waiting room.

Odhran lifted Sunny and they left, emerging into darkness in which the rain had so recently ceased. There was an empty, silken space where it had been. Lena felt giddy. The hospital block of yellow windows looked like a prison or a submarine, a place in which the glamour of urgency gave, as she knew, all the time, every day, into death. She thought of the resuscitation room, of gurneys and frightening wires and machines, and lingered on it morbidly as she watched Sunny's curls bobbing like a bouquet of flowers over Odhran's shoulder.

And here was the lonely poetic moment of Dublin at night – wet and fragrant, dirty and depressingly suburban, eternally trolling her somehow.

In the early months of motherhood, Lena had dreamt vividly. In one of these recurring dreams, she passed through a blasted, blackened arch to a scene of burning fuel and desert chaos, holding the severed foot of a child.

The family drove home. The streets were mute and glazed with rain. Riding the lift to their apartment, Sunny woke up and asked for a snack.

'You'll be asleep again soon,' Odhran said.

'I won't be *asweep*.' Sunny sounded offended, and more like herself. She asked for Paddington Bear and buttered toast then ate none of it, lying achily against the arm of the couch, and was carried to bed.

'Are you worried about tomorrow?' Lena asked Odhran when he returned. She was sitting in lamplight, on the couch before the showstopping windows of city lights and sliding headlamps, staring at a potted money plant. It was bulging from her other houseplants searchingly, like a plasma ball. She could not remember choosing or potting it.

'No.' Odhran yawned widely. 'It is just another day.'

Happily, after this, they slipped between their bedsheets, which Lena had cleaned and dried and flashed up over the bed and tucked in tightly and pleasantly at some industrious point in the weekend. The city's buzz always felt like a jungle, the bush, a waterfall, a chasm of activity as awesome as death and as tame as a screensaver, and it helped them sleep.

2

It began, then, two weeks later, on an orange afternoon, cool but ruminant, and close to Halloween. On this afternoon, Sunny looked up from the terrarium-sized tub of toys in the living room and asked, 'Mama, do you remember when I died?'

'Cried?' Lena had been scrolling on her phone.

'No died,' Sunny said.

'You mean you fell?' Lena sat forward and slipped the phone behind a cushion. 'You mean,' she continued, 'do I remember when you fell last week?'

'No, when I was alive before, and I died.'

'You were in hospital when you had a fever.' Lena smiled. 'You were in hospital, you mean? Maybe you are remembering the hospital.'

In the living room there was a standing lamp like a big basket-headed person, propositional or just humanoid, and in this moment – of orange afternoon sedation, TV low and entropy of content on the phone – Lena became eerily aware of this presence, of this quality of thinking, intentional presence emanating from the lamp. It was as though a priest or witness had just joined them in the room.

Beyond it: a wall of windows and a wooden balcony. Within: a kitchenette from which cream film veneers were coming loose and slicing, sometimes, to the floor.

'You didn't die, love,' Lena told Sunny gently. 'You were fine.'

'Yes but I died another time, and I was sad, and you weren't there.'

'Was this in a dream?' Lena frowned.

'No.' The child gave up. She picked up a doll and said, 'Turn dolly on.'

Lena parted the matted Velcro of the doll's back and pushed a switch to one side, which made it laugh and whoop, tinnily but sweetly, before commencing a looped track of crying. The only way to stop it was to place a plastic bottle before a pink machine-appliquéd mouth, where it connected with a magnet.

Sunny, however, did not go scouting for the bottle; she pressed her index finger into the mouth bluntly, stopping the cry. She performed this short circuit of the doll's major conceit so casually, and for the first time, that Lena felt extra unease.

'We make dolly feel better,' Lena said.

Sunny smiled angrily.

Later – sometime later, but the same day – she insisted, 'Mama doesn't remember when I died.'

After that, often. Practically every day.

At Montessori the following week, they asked, has there been a death in the family? The older woman, narrow and always wearing a tracksuit, ushered Sunny and Lena into the corridor that smelt daintily of poster paint and standing damp and asked, 'Has there been a funeral recently?'

'Oh – no.' Lena was taken aback and also assumed an expression of somewhat overdone or explicit surprise. 'Nothing like that.'

'Sunny has been talking' – the woman mouthed this second part – 'about dying.'

There was a tone for this, for such things as these.

'Yes, that.' Lena looked away. 'Yes, there's been a few days of that.' She smiled. 'We don't know where she got it from, perhaps something she saw. I mean, we were in A&E there the other week, I told you. She had a fever, but she was fine.'

'Has she been OK since then?' Fever was a red flag at Montessori.

'Oh the best. She eats rings around herself,' Lena promised, in local mother mode. This was important because some distracting elements, of dress and micro-expression, could turn women against her easily, she'd always found.

'She ate all of her lunch today,' the woman offered, then, in corroboration. 'We'll keep an eye. She's always sunny, our Sunny.'

Sunny perked up, smiling to attention.

When confronted at home however she said, affronted, 'I not *like* Montessori.'

'Sunny is being silly and funny,' Odhran opined. He was just in from work. 'Spooky and cute.' He picked Sunny up and flipped her over, banding his arms around her waist and *brushing the floor* with her hair, saying, 'Spooky and cute! Cutey and spook!'

Sunny shrieked with delight and then objection, shouting, 'I not *like* Dada.'

'It was awkward,' Lena told Odhran when Sunny had gone to bed. 'I felt embarrassed at the Montessori.'

This was not, of course, the first embarrassment – more than once she'd dropped Sunny off artificially cooled by paracetamol and winced, returning penitent, when phoned. Also, at the playschool where they'd sent her first, childcare workers had variously informed Lena that Sunny required new shoes, bigger nappies, had contracted slapped cheek not eczema, had contracted hand-foot-and-mouth not impetigo, and then needed new shoes again. In these pinched moments of exposé she wondered if other mothers were worse. She thought of the kid whose Montessori kitbag was simply a bag-for-life dropped onto the coat hook every day.

That night, Lena was taking a bath, gazing plainly at the steam glazing into vapour by the jumpy light of a candle, when a thought occurred to her. She remembered a day when Sunny was, oh, eighteen months or so, and came chanting into this cabinet of a bathroom as Odhran was relieving himself. She was chattering in her manifold, mostly senseless baby way but suddenly pointed rather casually at his penis and said *goose*. The word was clear. She repeated it. A day he was bathing also, at the end of a week of sickness; laid in the wide shallow tub that had seduced them when they'd viewed the apartment years ago, looking opulent and modern in a hotel kind of way, the bath with a wall of steamed mirror over it. The white slack matter of his penis floated ghostily up. Sunny burst in again and did a turn in the room chattering and pointed, once more saying *goose!*

'Goose, she called it,' Odhran had told Lena afterwards. He was frowning.

'That's gas,' Lena had said, at first. Then reflected on it. Or felt the soundless gathering of goose-shaped thoughts, plague doctors, all around her – an old man with his wrist bent stiffly and his fingers like a beak: see the goose, the goose! Fingers that snapped like beaks on buttock cheeks. Where is the goose? A man's arm hidden in his jumper, poking up with antic actions like a cobra – see the goose, pet the goose! At once: an elderly dishevelled janitor in the rented Stoneybatter hall where baby massage class was held. Sliding open some door or rolling a low piece of furniture by, waving and winking at all of the fat babies.

She thought, in short, of paedophiles. She thought of that seedy or sickly register in which old men spoke to her when she was a child.

To Odhran she'd instructed, 'Be careful of who Sunny talks to.'

'She doesn't talk to anyone but us,' he reminded her.

At that time, when their daughter was eighteen months or so, this was true. Now it was less true. *Goose* had passed, and Lena's stroke of paranoia about outside influences, about predators, had receded into the storeroom of her mind.

Now, in the bath once more, on the night of death at Montessori, she felt the ever-dauntless throb of worry once again. Someone had to be impinging on Sunny in some unseemly or abnormal way, there had to be something she'd seen – about death, or being born again, or ghosts. This would be it. It would be an irresponsible influence.

Lena dried off, feeling feverish and purged and ready to pay attention.

In the morning Lena watched a news clip on her phone. A man in the Middle East sat with his infant daughter, who had been wrapped in her shroud. All that showed at the top was a scrap of hair with a fabric bobbin, the same sort of fabric bobbin Lena routinely found between cushions or suspended in dust bunnies by the skirting boards. The man was speaking blankly and the translation read *my daughter, my beloved*, and Lena, as she was wont to do in the face of these images, began to cry. She was sitting in bed, drinking coffee as Odhran escorted Sunny to the front room and cartoons. It was Saturday.

My daughter, she thought. My God.

'She cannot watch the news,' she told Odhran later.

'Right.' He seemed always caught by Lena's instructions, as if tugged abruptly out of deep thought. 'Yes. Give her ideas.'

'It must be coming from somewhere like that,' Lena said.

To Sunny, experimentally: 'There are sad things, very sad things, in the world.'

In her bedroom, on her white Ikea shelf, Sunny had a picture book entitled *When Sadness Comes to Call*. It was illustrated simply. Not all picture books for children were – some were stressfully psychedelic, others photorealist, and some sort of smugly hipster or of an international hipster imaginary. But *When Sadness Comes to Call* simply told the tale of a boy who found Sadness, a blue glowing spectre, at his door. Sadness carried a suitcase and sat glumly on the couch or walked around, pooling blurrily into itself, much like a human oppressed by sadness truly felt. Lena, the first few times she read it, had felt moved. Sadness could not be hidden; it could sit so close you couldn't breathe. It needed to be welcomed in and given tea. It needed to walk in a forest of luminous trees.

'You can try to hide sadness,' Lena read to Sunny that night. 'Do we try to hide sadness?'

'He hiding him in a press,' Sunny glossed the illustration.

'Do we have a press like that?'

'No.'

'We do! Mama has a cupboard with a mop in it, just like that.'

She asked: 'Do you feel sad, sometimes, Sunny?'

Sunny replied, 'Sometimes my body makes me sad.'

That Monday, armed with this new and opaque information, Lena put in a call to the public health nurse and summarised her situation cheerfully. It had to be by phone because only the most insane or litigious problems earned an actual meeting with the nurse. It had been two weeks or so, Lena explained, since Sunny had begun to make these remarks. And no that was not very long, but they were really quite persistent, several times a day.

'Is there some kind of,' Lena was delicate, 'psyche evaluation you can do?'

'No, no.' The nurse did not seem surprised by the question. 'She goes on the waiting list for the HSE psychiatrist. If you don't want to just wait and see if she grows out of it.' There was a beat. 'Are you concerned?' the nurse asked.

'I mean, no, probably not so much,' Lena reneged.

'They say all kinds of things.'

She sensed the nurse had sighted an ending to this conversation and was steering her that way. By the elbow, say. With warmth.

'How long is the waiting list?' Lena asked anyway.

When she brought the answer with anger to Odhran that night he shrugged and told her, 'In parts of the country it would be twice that. Three times that. You would literally die waiting for anything.'

Lena sat next to him, in front of the television, and began there and then to write an email to the local party representative. She would complain of the wait for any appointment and attempt to cut some kind of notional queue. She stopped when she realised she could not describe Sunny's condition – report, issue? – without saying *psychiatric help* and this term, freighted as it was with violence and shame, defeated her.

When she was little, the crazy people at Saint Dymphna's, where her father had worked as a porter and finally as manager of facilities, were there because, her father said, life seemed insane to them – marriage, children, eating, sleeping, having or wanting a job or a holiday, all of this was a record playing backwards. And at some point in childhood she'd watched the film *Eyes Wide Shut*, or at least the occult orgy scene, the backwards chant of Romanian Mass, and this cruelly numinous backwards chant became, for Lena, the unguent unearthliness of madness, at least for a time. She felt instinctively that her father's casual blandness as a person either resulted from or simply complemented a life spent marvelling at the insane.

He could not have said *record playing backwards*. She'd added that.

Lena thought firmly: this was not Sunny's world. The little girl was agile, funny, quick; had been in the seventy-fifth percentile of every developmental spectrum since birth; woke and carefully slid on one of a series of hairbands every day; held a foot out to model or marvel at a yellow sandal, a runner with soles that lit up on impact in a flickering strip, socks with faces or polka dots. She drew spirals, pulled, it looked like, by a constellation of gravity poles and called these *flower beds*. She said please and thank you and farted for comic effect and was frightened by the advertisement for Paramount with the chattering CGI goat. She could count to twenty, speak three lines in Irish, write the letter S. She noticed if any of her more confrontational or just unchic toys had been siphoned off by Lena covertly. She puzzled, Mama, where my bear, where Minnie Mouse, where *gun*?

3

At the end of November, Lena recorded an audio clip on her phone:

> This is Sunny. I am Sunny. My real name is Sunniva. Nickname; your nickname is Sunny. Your full name is Sunniva. I live in DUBLIN EIGHT.
>
> Tell Mama [*whispers*] About the chair.
>
> The chair! There was a photo of me, and I am standing beside a chair. It was a pink chair [...] the cushion was pink. No, I was not sitting on the chair. I was wearing my communion dress and I walked down the stairs. I had a baby brother. I received the [...] eucharist!
>
> I died in water. I was lying and crying in water at the side of the road.
>
> [*Crying.*]

There was a photograph of a chair. A chair with a tufted cushion and a tapering back. In the photograph, Lena herself, aged eight and dressed in a communion frock, sat smiling and holding her prayer book in a dainty, mannered manner on her lap. She was gap-toothed, with freckles and a satin headband. There hung a blue backcloth behind. This photograph was contained in an album in Lena's father's house and Sunny had seen it when visiting.

Lena asked Sunny, 'Are you thinking of the picture of Mama when she was a little girl?'

Sunny repeated, 'No, I was wearing a dress and I walked down the stairs.'

'Mama wore a white dress,' Lena insisted smilingly. 'It was a communion dress. Do you know what communion is?'

Sunny looked at her mother as if this was a crazy thing to say.

Sunny had not been baptised; nobody was baptised anymore. It was a sacrament Lena disdained, but walked about under the seal of nonetheless. Had it been wrong, withholding that? Sunny would never make her first communion. Lena did not think she'd ever discussed any rite, any spoke of the ecclesiastical wheel, with her child.

What she remembered of her own first communion was just that same breathless and long-coveted satin dress, ballet length with a bendable hoop; those crisp ribbons and clear plastic beads in a drip-drip-drip from the satin band twisted around with silver foil. It was fabric as avenue to another realm, a sacred realm, a supple realm of cloud and chandeliers; of heaven as cartoonish campus on which people stood in recesses of cloud with plaster garments frozen mid-ripple, people composed of starlight and papier mâché and plasticine.

This was not Sunny's world.

Lena asked, 'What is eucharist?'

Sunny answered, 'I don't know, Mama. Can you think?' She pinched her little chin. She went back to playing pony club again. This was also the response Sunny gave when asked what kind of snack she might like, or what treat: Mama, can you think?

They had last visited Lena's father months before. Lena did not go there often; she did not like visiting. Her father no longer lived in the semi-detached house of her childhood, but in a new house on the edge of town with his partner, Rosemary. Rosemary was ill in a way Lena and her brother Rex once found hilarious, or at least cruel quarry for jokes, but which now – in light of motherhood, Sunny standing by for bad examples – was only depressing. Lena's father and Rosemary had bought the house a decade ago; the house she'd grown up in, narrower and darker, somehow recurring to her in impressions that were shady and forest-like, had been sold. Her father was also retired now from his job at Saint Dymphna's. The gothic hospital, which stood close to the coast near Portrane and had roofless cement cells scattered in a field at the back, for the airing and isolation of violent inmates, was changed since his time. It took only day patients and was likely open, progressive, benign, franchise-like.

Out of duty, in September, Lena and Odhran drove to Balbriggan on a cool Sunday afternoon. Rosemary met them at the door in a state of excitement, blush-like teething heat in either cheek. She was small and made herself smaller by stooping a lot.

'You are early,' she accused.

Nothing was ready, she said, and your father is gone to Aldi.

She sat them in the front room. It was pristine, and held a large cabinet of wine and liquor bottles that remained unopened except at Christmastime.

Sunny made at once for the glass bowl of blue marbles, an ornament from the noughties, and dug her hands steeply into the marbles before lifting these and beaming at the sensation of density. A vast flat-screen television filled the window.

As Sunny plunged for marbles again, Rosemary twitched.

'That's not a toy,' she said.

Sunny looked at Lena beseechingly.

The front door popped to, then slipped shut rather feyly, as if by a breeze. It was shut again with intention. The bang carried all through the walls.

Lena's father entered. 'Well, hello,' he drilled. 'Hello, hello.'

Lunch was egg sandwiches with onion, chipped raw tips of onion, and Lena found her thoughts flowering wildly at the hostility and creativity of this; she longed to say to Odhran later, you see, the woman is actually a genius, but realised also the only person who'd find this as thrilling as she did was

Rex. And Rex lived in London now, with a girlfriend who answered his emails for him. OMG, so nice to hear from you Lena, she wrote.

Excluded and aggrieved, Rosemary's Maltese Shih Tzu pressed its face to the sliding door and watched them. Sunny could not get over the dog.

'Doggy come in,' she pleaded.

'After the food,' Lena said.

'But let the doggy in and I'll play with him,' Sunny said. 'Mama, look!'

'I know. He's lovely.'

'So cute doggy.'

Tsar was admitted at last. Sunny did not, it turned out, want to play with him; she backed against a couch with her hands curled up. In this, she was a city child and both her parents privately ashamed. Tsar had to have an operation soon, Rosemary scolded.

In despair, Lena hit on a distraction. 'I wonder,' she said, 'if those photo albums we used to have are still here. They were on the television shelf in the old house. Do you remember?'

'Anything from the old house is in the box room,' her father said.

Lena took Sunny upstairs. They passed the small bathroom and its cold, almost sacred scent of soap-on-a-rope-era soap. Into the boxroom, which had many boxes in it, and three old-fashioned leather-bound photograph albums on another deep shelf.

The first album was from the nineteen-eighties. Lena let out a sigh of fondness when she saw it – it was filled with weddings, the weddings of people she didn't know, weddings of her parents' friends and siblings and cousins and neighbours and work colleagues. The yellow tone made every tableau appear steeped in the light of a late-year afternoon. Everyone was young but looked gouged or harrowed by life already, the men so skinny they had Adam's apples all; the women giddier. Virgins, she thought, going into the night.

The next album was newer. These were pictures taken on Lena's communion day, a decade later at least than the weddings and young people: pictures of the long table in the function room of a pub and the children playing in sunlight outside the pub afterwards. She stood, freckled and squinting and with shoulders crunching forward in self-consciousness, an awkwardness troubling now to behold, in her dress. It was flattened by light and appeared as an outline of empty white. The final picture was a formal portrait of Lena with the blue backcloth and gap-tooth smile. She remembered the photographer and the treat of cocktail sausages for breakfast and the backcloth stretched between free-standing poles.

'This is Mama,' she said. 'When she was eight.'

'Mama.' Sunny savoured the word. 'Can I go back down to doggy?' she asked.

'Sure. We won't be staying much longer though.'

Downstairs, Lena's father was sour with Sunny too. 'Are you afraid of a little animal like that?' he asked. He offered Lena the photograph albums. She refused.

Neither Sunny nor Lena had mentioned the photograph since the last trip to Balbriggan, but now, in the apartment, after the voice note had been replayed, Lena was sugary again.

'When we were in Grandad's house, I showed you a photograph of Mama in a dress. When she was a little girl.'

'And a cake,' Sunny remembered suddenly.

'And a cake! Of course, a wedding cake. Yes. So you have been remembering those photographs.'

Sunny pondered and then asked, 'Am I in the photographs?'

'No.'

'Was I in your phone?'

'No, petal, and those weren't taken on a phone. Those were taken long ago.'

'I lived long ago,' Sunny offered. 'But then I died.'

Lena sat with Odhran that night, with dinner, after Sunny had fallen asleep. Night came in so early, she felt ornery, tetchy. Already sick of wintertime. She played the voice note and he raised his eyebrows and assumed an expression that was difficult to read.

'Are you worried about this, about Sunny?' she asked.

'No,' he said. He raised his hand and spread it, as if casting grass seed. They were sitting at the little disc of table under a light. 'She is so happy, so normal, so cute; I look at it that way. I am not worried about her.'

'You don't find it disturbing?'

'A little bit. But you're maybe, like, fixating on it.'

She had expected this quiet accusation. Welcomed it even. It was a version of the world he'd told her from the start, since the birth and afterwards – a reality in which she was always worrying needlessly; in which she was alone and too forensic in her parenting; in which she was the fretful, testy one. In which she stayed at home and became tepid in herself.

'That's what I think,' he said. In the pause, the low bulb glowed between them, freight bayed by somewhere – muffled – on the streets below.

'Sure,' Lena said. 'I just have to, you know, get to the bottom of it. Something is obviously influencing her. TV or another kid, something she heard – she is intelligent.'

She remembered the steeliness with which Sunny would sometimes look at her back in the toddler days – days of surly self-importance, before the little girl was socialised or learnt to be cute. The round face of an infant, like yoghurt but animate, regarding her mother with a curious ruthlessness. And this was certainly projection and neurosis and insecurity, guilt; and who would blame either of them, Lena or Sunny?

Life was lonely sometimes, the primary passion of umbilical connection had been severed, they were just like any couple getting to know each other after a honeymoon.

'Exactly, she is sensitive.' Odhran was sincere.

And then he amended this: 'Bright,' he agreed. Intelligent.

Lena was grateful for the emendation. She did not want a sensitive child; she did not want a gifted child; she did not want a special child. She did not want a rare child, an artistic child, a complicated child. She had not wanted a sensitive or gifted or special or tortured husband either and had succeeded in avoiding this superficially interesting, actually fatiguing, fate. She'd considered herself special all her life and it lead to nothing but suffering.

4

For Christmas they travelled as always to Odhran's family in Clare, driving to the great white farmless farmhouse at the foot of Glennagalliagh. It was a young tradition: leaving in weak sunlight and heading west, watching Dublin exsanguinate into its hinterlands of outlet malls and racecourses and turbines, clawlike strips of shelterbelt proceeding over the fields. Afternoon ebbed to evening and, after Tipperary, the roads lost streetlights, cat's eyes, hard shoulders. Even the throb of white lines in the headlights disappeared.

Closer to home, the hawthorns converged overhead. It got dark. In the valley below there were new white houses that tore from the darkness, lit from every angle, and then older houses glowing like candle stubs against slopes of black. The sky was clear and ice was forming.

When Lena was a teenager, she and her friends would sometimes blitz through backroads, passing eighteenth-century milestones and accident altars and sometimes towers or the torsos of old churches looking romantic in moonlight and streetlight, but that was in County Dublin, and it was never dark for long – towns, housing estates, manorial houses, airport runways intervened. There was the sea.

Here the remoteness was not quite enveloping, but intense.

'Slow down,' she said.

'Huh?' Odhran sat up.

'We're going really fast. It's getting icier.'

'I could drive this in my sleep,' he said. But he slowed down. He took the cattle grid and dressed stone entrance of his parents' house at a sensible speed.

A screened veranda had been set into the front of the house: they watched the headlights sweep over the backs of wicker chairs and flash for one arresting instant in a mirror on the wall. When Odhran killed the engine the upper windows of the house shone gold and blind. Lena could only yield to the house itself – to soft upholstery, deep-set squinting windows, and the yellow kitchen, dry and dim and warm from the range, in which a dishwasher would froth and mutter civilly as they sat at the table drinking tea.

Draughts chased through the house like water; beds were boggy with floral eiderdowns. Downstairs, Odhran's mother Sonia had begun stripping rooms and painting everything in earth colours. She had discovered in her seventies the neutral, unharried palette of affluence.

Into this beachy mood came adult children, in-laws, grandchildren. There were best bedrooms and lesser bedrooms, bath towels chapped from washing and bath towels that were new and compromising in their menopausal opulence, as large and luxurious as christening blankets. When the house was full you heard it slam and groan and tick in different places, hissing always as it rinsed the air with artificial heat.

Sunny had been born on Christmas Eve. Lena was sitting placidly in a cubicle of blue eating chocolate baubles, meant for a Christmas tree, when a nurse had poked cheerfully in and announced availability. They were going to induce her; she'd been lingering too long; she vomited all the chocolate up as soon as the drug hit and contractions came battering down like the wrath of God. Lena thought about it on every birthday, including this, Sunny's fourth, as they watched her open presents before the fireplace in the centre of the house.

Lena knew there would once have been a kettle over this fire, probably; later in history, a ladder for drying clothes you could fold out of the chimney breast. She had been trained from an early age into a sort of non-specific reverence for details such as this. Now it was caged by a wrought-iron fireguard and the mantelpiece decorated with bog oak figures.

It was festive in the house: there were children everywhere, interacting in trios or throwing tantrums, dressed it seemed in scaled interpretations of athleisure. Sunny, wearing her mermaid costume, bent over the task of twiddling with a toy coffee machine. It went *snap* and then *gush*.

'So make me a mocha latte,' Odhran was squatting at her level, holding a beer, 'with orange sauce.'

Small hands snapped and waited primly for the gush.

One of Lena's sisters-in-law, Elaine, her long hair freshly ombré and her hands, Lena noticed, as bony and veiny as Lena's own – they were all getting older now – stood next to her and said, 'So, is Sunny OK? I heard she's been saying things about— I don't know.'

'Death,' Lena conceded.

The woman laughed nervously.

'Mama.' Sunny looked up. She was excited but firmly so. 'Mama,' she repeated, 'will you pretend you don't know I have a coffee machine?'

'Sure.' Lena placed her glass down on the long loaded arm of the mantelpiece. She made to cross the room, picking around children and debris. 'Oh wow, a coffee machine.'

'It's mine!' Sunny's smugness turned to thrill. 'Mama,' she was standing up now, excited, 'will you pretend you don't know I have a mermaid dress?'

Lena said curtly to Odhran, that night, 'When did you tell them about Sunny?'

'Just Mam.' He rubbed the back of his neck bashfully. 'You never said to keep it secret.'

'She told Elaine.'

He laughed at this; she disdained Elaine. But Lena was uncomfortable.

'It looks like it's me,' she said.

'What do you mean?'

'I mean, they'll assume I'm letting her be influenced by something – or it's something strange about me. They'll think we're not taking proper care of her.'

'Nobody could ever think that,' he said.

On Saint Stephen's Day, Lena volunteered to travel with Sonia and two of Odhran's brothers to the graveyard at Templekelly. There was a ruined church building, rashed over with evergreen growth so completely the two standing gable ends looked like trees, and headstones dissolved into lumps by age. In the new section lay the grave of Odhran's father, on which they laid a Christmas wreath and observed Sonia crouch to pluck weeds from the crisp gravel. Across the silver grave the shadows of both brothers, of Lena, attenuated.

Lena had come along for the break from childcare and from women and had no particular feelings about her father-in-law. She often felt bratty when visiting this family, who took themselves seriously in the style, she felt, of all country families who possessed land.

In the early days of love, Odhran had detailed to her a childhood memory. He was seven or so, moving through a bungalow where some cousins lived, all of it empty and enchanted, sun through picture windows and a kitchen clock with a pendulum crooking to and fro; faded curtains emitting smells of detergent and horsehair; terracotta linoleum. Somewhere nearby there were scented haystacks and the sound of mowers.

And then, in this memory, he turned into a living room, the false chimney breast of brick spreading upwards like a mural or a tree, buttery brass pokers, and many men – countrymen, in suits, sitting and standing around to talk with his father, who sat in a chair.

This sudden gamut of maleness struck him, as a child, and attracted him, he said. One or two men were uncles and others were neighbours or strangers and they must, he knew now, have been readying to go door-to-door or to a meeting, on the campaign trail for Fine Gael. His father had been active in the party and his own father and uncles messengers, during the War, for the IRA. None of them fought in the civil war, but receded into alignment with the Treaty quietly. They were, Odhran said, candid, practical, agricultural people.

In the first telling, Lena had wondered at the humility implied by this – of the candid and practical and agricultural. She wondered if some ancient part of her identity would be wakened, with curative results, if she stayed with Odhran and had his babies and accepted a monocultural fate. She'd grown up in a town where land was rabbit-scarers cracking off at intervals all night until the bypass opened and grids of new houses surged forth, pushing back the grazing fields. Now she just looked out the window at Ireland like everyone else.

After the grave, Sonia, Lena and the sons crunched down the slope from the cemetery and went into a small old-fashioned bar. It was empty but for an elderly man with a newspaper. The barman was apple-cheeked and cheerful; the scene was Hollywood. Lena drank white wine with Sonia and asked her, on an impulse of generosity, for her opinion on Sunny. Sonia had been a GP; she'd retired just before Lena met Odhran.

'If it isn't stopping after two months,' Sonia said, 'and she's too young for psychiatry of any kind. Of any meaningful kind.'

She paused for thought.

'If it isn't stopping, you can only be curious. Ask her about it.'

'I don't want to encourage it.'

'Encourage what? It might be true.'

'You think it's true?' What relief to think of this. Lena almost laughed.

'It might be true,' Sonia offered. 'You cannot know.'

'True,' Lena kept pushing, 'that she has lived before?'

Sonia said, 'Look, most of this passes by five or six. I've known magical children in my time. They're all telepathic, for a while, you know. They talk to ghosts.' She seemed almost to be losing patience. 'Don't worry so much about it.'

In certain cultures, she reminded Lena, it is completely

normal for a child to speak about reincarnation. Whole cultures take it for granted.

'I've known a few magical children,' she insisted. 'They grow out of it.'

The brothers were uncomfortable. They turned the conversation to the recent anti-immigrant riots in Dublin. It had also been raised on Christmas Day.

'Were you worried?' they asked, again.

'We didn't know it was happening,' Lena told them wearily.

There was a further brother, the eldest, who lived with his family in Sandyford. Lena wished he was here. We don't go there, he would say; nobody goes to O'Connell Street. Only the scaldies go to O'Connell Street. Oh sorry, Lena! The salt of the earth!

They presumed Lena's cosmopolitanism coded her as woke. Which it kind of did.

But she did not, now, want to talk about riots, racists or O'Connell Street. She was having a break from childcare and now enjoying her wine. Back at the house, Odhran would probably not think to give Sunny lunch – if the other kids and mothers were around, pillaging chicken or handing out stollen and the brass section of gifted biscuit tins, she would get fed. It would be fine.

Lena gazed neutrally at a stained-glass window in berry colours and asked suddenly, 'Is this where we went for a drink after the – after Seán's burial?' She knew it was.

'Yes. The owner is a cousin of my own,' Sonia replied.

Lena had been pregnant with Sunny at Odhran's father's funeral. She had sat, beached and aching, on one of the banquet chairs flanking the coffin in the inner chamber of the funeral home, where friends and neighbours arrived mutedly and looked for somewhere to hang their jackets since it seemed a little off to approach the corpse with a jacket on. Odhran and his brothers buzzed about in diplomatic mode. 'Yes it's been a shock,' they said dully, although it had not. Sunny was there, close by, almost done really, with hair and mousey fur over her back and shoulders, waxy overlay, nestled in Lena's body, launching the occasional sickening kick. She'd been growing and fusing mere yards from the remains.

In those days, Lena was rather flippant with Odhran's family. She felt fundamentally other to them, sort of genuflecting and disappearing into kitchen tasks throughout the week of death observances. People who visited the farmhouse entered rooms with purpose and began at once whispering sympathies at Sonia or Odhran or Odhran's brothers or Maeve, his sister, and these people ignored Lena. It was easier to sit pregnant on a boggy eiderdown out of sight, the affront of her own inconsequentiality as an interloper balanced by the great and sinister luxury that came with incubating another Flynn – one of them, or so they believed.

One glass in, Lena relaxed a little into the family unit, which chattered quietly without her. After the pub, they returned to the farmhouse, driven by one of the brothers, as freezing fog smeared the mountains out and the light, lurid as alpenglühn, died.

Then they became trapped there, lazily for the most part, until New Year, because the roads were invisibly slick.

'I on holiday with my cousins,' Sunny said brightly every morning.

'I saw a dog in the garden,' she claimed on another day, although there was no dog.

On New Year's morning, as Lena and Odhran made coffee in the farmhouse kitchen alone, he turned to her. 'This year, we'll buy a house,' he said.

'I like your optimism.'

'Lots of things can happen in a year. She's starting school.'

And I can go back to work, Lena thought. He was going to tell her she could go back to work. Go where though, and do what?

'You have faith,' she said, coyly but not unkindly, cradling her cup.

'I have promise.' Odhran grinned. 'I am a catch.'

He put his arms around her, surprising her with this. Her frame was tensed against him with aversion and embarrassment. She held the cup at a safe remove.

'They're all asleep,' he said. He held her tighter. 'I'd like to have more babies with you.'

It was a whisper; fierce and close to her ear, but sibilantly so.

He broke away. He was not often literal or ardent in this way. Or not these days. He'd said it before of course: more children, a house, space and light and a plan rather than doing everything as it seemed by the seat of their pants, playing at adults in a buy-to-rent glass-walled tent.

They left his family, when the roads thawed, with a sense of expansiveness, and it dwindled out all the way home.

5

Now it was January – another January – and work resumed, and Montessori resumed, and Sunny continued to talk about dying and living before in precisely the same circle of terms; Sunny continued, sometimes, to ask: Mama, can you *think*? Lena paid increased attention to television, to library board books, to overheard conversation, to Montessori reports.

They had been living in the apartment for just over four years now. At first, the lease had been a source of serene excitement, as if they'd won something, the new-build finish that was cheap and depthless as a hotel or a hospital, easy to clean. Sunny was imminent. Life, having slowed down and billowed out rather boringly between twenty-seven and twenty-nine, now opened into thirty with a crystal rationale. None of their friends had children yet.

At thirty-five weeks Lena had landed at the maternity A&E swinging a candy-striped holdall and glowing with can-do attitude. Her waters had broken, barely. The barely was a thing it seemed. The doctor – young and male and gay of vibration – explained that, first off, the test stick had hardly coloured (What? she thought) and secondly she was extremely dehydrated.

'I am?'

'You'll need a drip and we will have to admit you.'

She found the prospect relaxing.

Drowsing in triage, having sent Odhran home for a thrilling

sleep, like the sleep of Christmas Eve – and it was almost, literally, Christmas Eve – she saw a woman whom she recognised from antenatal class curled in a wheelchair, vomiting, lifting her head to breathe with dragging vigour, telling a triage nurse: my husband is working abroad. He's in Zurich. She pitched forward and puked again. Lena thought it better not to salute or address this woman in her hour of desperation, or first hour of desperation, when they found themselves in cubicles adjacent to one other. The other woman moaned and gasped as Lena lay there, mortified.

Two days later, two days of stewing central heating, scratchy bedding, magazines, they interrupted her composed eating of chocolate baubles to say: there is a slot! And off she went.

The labour came in convulsions. It was like getting caught in the jaws of a subway car. She asked to use the bathroom and stood there, fitting head to foot, having an actual fit, teeth chattering bones rattling and she stared at the padded hospital toilet off a hallway and thought, how can I escape? She didn't want to do it now. She repented, she had been egregiously naïve, she would withdraw and find her coat and boots and walk into the night, against a slanting veil of rain, run down the littered lane of wing mirrors and windshield glass and past the blocks of pious corporation houses, Rosary Street Lourdes Street Ave Maria Street. Find someone who could advocate for her and tell the doctors, Mrs Marley Flynn has changed her mind.

Back on the gurney, it got worse. With laughing gas, an intact afternoon from adolescence descended in its full emotional and sensual and sentimental granularity, taking her breath away. She was fourteen and hiding out in the library. It was a dark room full of religious textbooks, war-on-drugs textbooks, morality manuals and guides to the European Computer Driving Licence. The window looked at the wall of the convent, flecked like pewter, behind which thin crucifixes paraded across a burial ground. One grave was new, it had earth heaped in the shape of a sarcophagus.

She was reading a book of poetry by Les Murray, which a teacher had given her because she wrote poetry and Les Murray was a convert to Catholicism.

In a poem: the literalist/the lateralist. She had no idea what that meant.

And then 'The Apologist', by REM, a song not listened to for fifteen, sixteen years, invaded nasally Lena's brain: I'm sorry so sorry so sorry so sorry so sorry so sorry. I get down on my knees and pray and now it was 'Bizarre Love Triangle'.

Visions cleaved like her body was cleaving and the drugs said: this is reality, a hallucination of options and layers you are only in a moment through delusion or collusion you could fall out of your body blow around the globe a ghost the stakes are low.

Then the pranging guitar and percussion of 'Bizarre Love Triangle' broke down into a sassy little synth and she felt breakfast cereal in her mouth, it was ninety-something kitchen radio hallucination now. Lena dry-heaved and dry-heaved and tasted Cointreau, Kahlúa, blood.

Do you want to die, it said, now or later we will leave it with you.

Stop it.

This is reality. You should know that. This is all reality is.

Stop it.

Life is a mystery; everyone must stand alone.

'I don't want to die,' she told Odhran.

He smiled, confused. 'You won't.'

In a moment of quiet, it might have been hours later, she felt a clear and compromising desire to void her bowels and told the midwife, who was the only other person in the room, 'I need to push – I think I'm going to poop.'

'I will get a pan,' the midwife said. She was jocular. 'Good to get it out of the way.'

It was not that; it was not that. It was the baby.

The midwife flew to the door and the door banged, a great jarring terrible smack, and she called levelly, Helena is in the maternal. Quick, please. Who is here? Out of the skies. And out came Sunniva, tearing her mother to the power of four inches and shitting, straight off the bat, into her mother's open hand. No end and no beginning you're here with me it's like a dream heaven help me.

The baby was born with her eyes open and uncannily alert and pretty much everyone said this, perhaps even the midwives in their satisfaction and relief, perhaps even there and then in the delivery room with toast and tea, now there is one who was here before.

It was a turn of phrase. They meant to say she looked bright; intelligent.

And that was that. Two days later, Lena brought her home, in shock. All the windows of her first world like a cold panopticon. The weather washed and foggy and expressionless.

And then: Sunny was three months old when the pandemic lockdown hit, when the government command was issued in its unlikely and faintly facile way, that spring.

Odhran liked to recall his final meeting at work, the paper cups stained by pastry grease scattered on a conference table; excess printouts with their scraping staples slopping to the floor; the spring sun prim on the panes of the building opposite.

Lena in particular pictured the paper cups afterwards, desolate and incarnadined, and the frigid light returning and returning to the room for the weeks it was left empty. Everyone had travelled home expecting to go back the following day and so the many, many communal spaces of labour in Dublin were struck all at once by a spell of abandonment.

Yes, imagine the empty room, Lena encouraged, like a Raj palace after the cholera and stampeding evacuation and little Mary Lennox, forgotten, picking at cold food. Now Lena was alone all day with Sunny as Odhran worked from the box room and there was no traffic, no mother-and-baby group, no trips to her mother's or to Glennagalliagh.

But when it ended, the pandemic, sinking into oblivion, she returned to work. To the job that had been suspended by unpaid maternity leave and then pandemic pay. Sunny was one. Lena returned to work even though civic life was only semi-open and her job was not a career: her job was in arts-adjacent hospitality.

She returned, that is, to the Georgian house museum on Henrietta Street, with a brace of paper masks and arrows stickered on the floor to guide tourists around the exhibit. It baffled her that there were still tourists.

Going back to work made her feel wobbly – sometimes there descended louring spells of dread, a sense that something here was deeply unnatural, and she would look with despair into the combed, creamy ceiling that was ruched in the centre by cherubs, feel the air of the vast room like a scooped-out fruit, and want to cry. Sunny was with the childminder. Suddenly, vacant spaces where thought should reside opened inside Lena. She could not remember how to think, what she'd done with those spaces before.

One evening six months in, when Lena arrived to collect her from the childminder's, Sunny was sitting in a silver, embossed armchair, apart from the other children, stunned. Her cheeks were red and sticky with tears.

'Sunny had a slip-up,' the childminder told Lena. 'When we were putting on her coat.'

This was a padded floral jacket that kicked out at the waist. It was heavily lined and a struggle to get on.

Lena felt ready to understand. She only asked for what happened. The woman had jerked Sunny, had needed to jerk her or jerked her – more likely – in impatience, in reproval, by the arm when she was forcing the jacket on and now Sunny's shoulder was dislocated.

'That's dislocated.' Lena was pale.

'It's not. It's only a strain.'

'That is dislocated.' Lena was shaking once again.

Sunny, just eighteen months, began to cry; her cry was panicked and two of the other children fell silent and stared.

'Mama,' she shouted.

'I will need to call my husband.'

'You've upset her,' the woman said. 'She was fine before you arrived.'

Sunny's shoulder was reset without melodrama in the A&E of, this time, Temple Street.

That night, Lena had Odhran call the woman to let her know Sunny would not be coming back.

'She started crying.' Odhran looked disturbed when he returned from the balcony. 'She said she is really fond of Sunny and it was an accident.'

'I can't send her back there.'

'I get it. I understand.' But he was alarmed.

The cost of a creche was more than Lena's salary, and anyway every creche in the city had waiting lists. She stopped working, had not worked formally in over two years, forsook the computer and crumbling owl, left this particular corridor of life behind. She knew it now as another chilled interior space in her mind: shady, waiting, intact.

Each weekday morning, now, Odhran left for work and left her with the washing up. Lena delivered Sunny to Montessori and strode home, returning, these days, almost exclusively to clean. There were surfaces buffed in rotation to repel the ambient dust; there was laundry, always laundry, and projects that demanded more commitment, like the conscientious decanting of Sunny's newly outgrown clothes into piles – one for charity, one for storage, one for packaging up and delivering to a sister-in-law whose daughter was six months younger than Sunny. Twice-weekly Lena baked the family's bread, a soda loaf the size of a weight plate, tipping flour and oatmeal into a bowl without needing to think about it anymore.

Long ago she'd read the actual contents list of a sliced pan and quailed at the additives. It surprised her, the bread-making, but really it was satisfying to pulverise a wad of dough into a scorch-marked loaf tin – memories of Play-Doh and infant anal retention, possibly – and fill the whole floor of their building with folk aroma.

'You're the woman who bakes bread,' the sex worker downstairs said to Lena one day.

'Oh yes!'

'Good for you.' The woman's voice was clipped and rich.

Some daily jobs required the moving and clearing of furniture; others, her very favourite jobs, the obtaining of products from outside the house. The gargantuan Spar on the corner was expensive and depressing, reminding Lena of single-life dashes to buy cookies and cider or vacuous tomatoes, and the nearest Aldi was on Thomas Street. It was also a bad Aldi with excess stock laid out on pallets and Lena recoiled from that. Just last year, a luxe Tesco, air conditioning set to cruel, opened on Smithfield Square. It was possible to walk to the Luas at Heuston and travel there, but the walk was too substantial to permit of shopping bags. It was never worth driving in Dublin either. You had to weave, to thread between students and tourists and holy fools who halted suddenly, drunk or high, and began beckoning at the clouds or lowing in code to one another from all four kitty-corners of the street.

These were Lena's, automatic yet unreconciled, thoughts on most weekdays.

On other days, days of energy, of wilful if not vindictive self-care, she rode the Luas all the way to Jervis and shoved through the crowds to the Ilac library. She borrowed or returned literary novels of violently uneven quality and felt cast, by this praxis, back to the school holidays of her adolescence, when all she did was sing and read and swim.

In the wet days of winter, when it was not possible to go to the park or the playground or the gardens, Lena sometimes took Sunny for a treat to the hipster coffee shop on the corner of Emmett Road. It was quiet there, the walls blank but for sans serif printouts about coffee, the off-white politeness of open laptops making Lena think of a dentist's waiting room. They ate lemon and poppyseed muffins and played the rhyming game.

Coffee?

Oh – toffee!

Mouse.

House.

Louse.

Cows.

OK. Game?

A long pause.

'Nothing, Mama,' Sunny said.

'Lame,' Lena offered. 'Tame? Yeah, you know, that wasn't a good one at all. You think of one next for me.'

'Coffee,' Sunny said.

At home, rain loosely splattering against the many windows, Sunny played with her ice cream station peacefully. Each afternoon, then, the smell of fried oil and damp detritus of vegetables. Between three and four – the hour of fatigue, weak light, eternal return – memories of childhood, boredom bearing down with rain and the smell of boiling vegetables, brought her to a soft state of astonishment at the closed circle of life. Of its design. She had not, she saw, been extraordinary, or escaped anything.

To this, that winter, was added Sunny's strangeness: a rigid carousel of eucharist, dress and death at the side of the road. It became gradually folded in with every other ordinary thing. She was waiting it out, Lena thought. It would pass, like every phase – like making strange with Odhran, refusing coloured foods, crying at night, throwing spoons. Like the earlier and more mysterious habits of puking profusely after feeds, of howling from seven o'clock in the evening until nine as if timing it; of not passing a stool – remember that! – for days, so that Lena had to poke a Q-tip into the minuscule hole and swivel it tenderly. Feed Sunny brown sugar dissolved in cool boiled water. Accept, when Sunny began to teethe, sudden bites on the nipples and, once or twice, the throat. That time of life when she might call a helpline semi-regularly to have someone say, with patience, yes, and is this your first child?

6

In April, better weather began: thin days conceding to milder temperatures, pink light through the pollution haze over the basins and the Park. A tender energy of Easter registered. In better weather Lena and the other mothers of Montessori began to see more of one another.

They were not friends, these women, in the sense once understood. Neither comrades nor intimates but proximate and desperate, like sister wives.

Company, its promise, made Lena's morning, one morning in April, feel particularly witnessed and intentional. She passed it cleaning the kitchenette. She pushed the veneers of the presses into place, then mopped the lemony laminate and enjoyed, as ever, how contained a space it was. Lena sometimes liked living in the apartment. It was too small, bared by huge windows so their clothes in sunny weather seized crisply over the clotheshorse, but it was also, consequently, noncommittal in spirit, effervescent around her, in daylight.

When she'd finished the cleaning she lay on the couch she hadn't chosen, of terrible gizzard leather or whatever, the worst leather, with feet propped on the backrest, listening to a record by John Carroll Kirby. The music was simple formulae and trills and sounded like someone rehearsing. A door to the balcony hung open to a breeze, and from the street beneath she heard traffic and gulls and sometimes voices, laughter or the calls of children from the flats.

The music, she had explained to Odhran, was written on a residency in Italy. Lena herself had once travelled to a residency on Inishbofin; this was with Cian, her musical partner, and years ago. She didn't bring it up in the telling and anyway Inishbofin was a different proposition to Italy, much different, but the idea of suspension was the same – of being held in place, sustained or hosted or even fawned over. The idea of being contained by a location that was radically specific and unyielding in its energy attracted her.

The John Carroll Kirby album dawdled along with beautiful, fluting little essays in elegance. It had the ease and intelligence she associated with some of the women novelists she'd borrowed from the library: unseen or entirely diffuse money, simplicity, chapel candles and espresso cups and muslin moving in moonlight. Women travelling to Europe to have photogenic breakfasts.

The album was not like the album she herself had helped to write on Inishbofin, but it made her think of Inishbofin and that she had, at that grandly dramatic time of life, been happy for a time there, with Cian, hair snagging and woolly and abundant in salty wind.

Lena was older now, less beautiful than she had once been, but still erect and consciously posed. Her hair, once heavily long, was cut close to her head and brought the sharpness of her features into new repute. Today she wore a denim dress to the knees. She had huge bruises on her knees from repeatedly walking into the glass-topped coffee table scattered over with Sunny's drawings and plastic farm animals and vocabulary flash cards.

She had ten minutes of John Kirby Carroll left before it was time to pull on tights and fetch Sunny from Montessori, to meet Caoimhe and Orla: ten minutes of empty time. She felt somewhere in her the stirrings of old habits and memories, days when she might start tinkering with a song or smoke a cigarette and walk, distressed for no reason, into town. But instead she got up, found her shoes, tramped to the lift and rode the lift because, fuck it, why take the stairs. She pushed her sunglasses over her eyes and stepped out into what had, in the past, been the courtyard of a military barracks, then a wasteland, now a plaza of apartments integrating the alcoves of a livery stable. Beyond these flowed the slow river, the potted gardens and felted boardwalks of Islandbridge. Diesel dusted the air. She missed her bike and itched for it but couldn't take the bike because she had this date of sorts with the Montessori mothers and that was why she was wearing the denim dress.

Clap-clap, flat leather brogues, stupid to be wearing formal shoes. Dublin was simply filthy: grit, airborne grit, adhesing to the skin. Brief blast of air conditioning from the gargantuan Spar. Fretty rattle of the traffic lights, one-two-three traffic lights, to cross the junction from which lanes charged east into the city proper and its featureless expanse hung under a shimmer of chemicals. Lena felt grateful for the shade offered by the high perimeter wall of the Royal Hospital, and patted one or two stones out of habit as she passed.

Sunny liked this part; shadowed by fatherly slabs, she would ask about Bully's Acre, the burial ground, behind.

'Hundreds of dead people,' Lena told her. It was probably irresponsible to tell her this kind of thing, but after months of hypervigilance it had become tempting. The imp of perversity or sabotage or the absurd.

'Are they dead, Mama?' Sunny asked every time. Sometimes, 'Can you show me dead, Mama?'

'No.'

'On your phone.'

'No.'

The phase had not passed. For months, Sunny's past-life claims had continued to follow a limited script of side-of-the-road-in-water, eucharist. Occasionally communion dress. It was consistent and creepy but stayed within a certain cryptic horizon. And then, a week or so ago, some movement – 'Nobody know where I go. Everybody was looking for me.'

'Who was looking for you, sweetheart?' This was Odhran.

'My family.'

'We are your family.'

Sunny had blinked. 'My other family.'

She said *fam'ly*, pronouncing it always as *fam'ly*: Lena explained to people, Sunny was a Covid baby, her speech is still a little delayed. But she is of *above average intelligence*. This point had once been made by the public health nurse.

'You were like that,' Lena's own mother remarked.

'Yes.' Lena was intelligent and had wasted it heroically.

She did not like *my other family*, did not like this at all, but recalled also a story from her own childhood. In this story, four-year-old Lena refused to draw a picture of her parents at school because, she claimed, her parents had gone away, far far away, forever. Her mother laughed to remember it. She said, 'You probably just wanted to draw something else.'

She said, 'Every child wants their parents to go away.'

Sunny was a dazzling child, pale and peachy with golden-brown hair her mother curated so it dropped in a wave to her waist. Her eyes were blue. When Lena had dressed her that morning, twisting the hair into fat plaits, Sunny had smelt of the tomato tang of beans. Lena rapped her hands on Sunny's behind: bum-bum, pudding. Wibble-wobble, jelly-belly. Who is loveliest?

'Beautiful Mama,' Sunny had said, clamping her mother's mouth shut with her thumbs.

Where the South Circular began, Lena turned into a street of bay-windowed Victorian terraces. It was the eye in a storm of engines and jackhammers, with cats streaking out of bushes and the easeful tick of freewheeling courier bikes. Sunny's Montessori was a double-breasted house with colourful animals in the windows. Orla waited there already, and Lena was relieved. She felt like the more confident, less difficult woman around Orla, who was tall and solemn and dressed in a dandyish way, wearing shorts and a button-down shirt today.

'All set?' Orla held up a smart red Scuttlebug now.

'Oh I brought Sunny nothing.' Lena was dismayed.

Orla set the toy down. 'She can have a go on this.' Her long brown shins were bare and also bruised. Lena asked if Orla, too, walked into coffee tables; the other woman paused and then smiled distantly. 'I chase the dogs,' she said. 'And fall.'

Orla's husband was a surprisingly attractive man – conventionally attractive – who made documentaries and knelt to receive ecstatic slobber from their rescue lurchers when reunited with them.

'Caoimhe is coming too, yes?' Orla asked, staking the claim of Caoimhe between them early to prevent gossip or ambiguity.

Lena nodded. Caoimhe was petite, intense and musical-theatre loud. She worked in comedy. As in, for real. Lena had watched videos of Caoimhe's comedy on YouTube. She wrote for TV, or for TV production companies.

Orla, in her solemnity, worked for a publisher and sometimes did translations. She was working on one now, she said; a story in German. It came partially decoded by the writer but there were terms that Google Translate turned up crazy, she laughed, like one this morning: *meat lingerie*.

'Meat lingerie.' Lena widened her eyes.

'The closest I could get to it was meat lingerie.'

Caoimhe was crossing the street. She glanced left to right with a self-conscious look, then dashed to the gate and crunched the coffee cup she was holding flat. She looked around fruitlessly for a bin. Other mothers had gathered. The spheres of a frothy blue lilac bush were close by and eerily motionless, without bees, slightly wet.

Caoimhe landed with a brazen echo of the word *lingerie*. 'What's this, ladies?' she asked lazily. 'What's this about lingerie?'

Orla explained. But then she said, 'I figured it out. It was *flesh-coloured bra*.'

The door opened and out came the children, each pausing on the step, several being distracted by the chessboard tiles embedded in it.

Always and ever lay the prospect, prepared for them by films and fiction, that your child would not emerge – perhaps, even, that there would be no child, you had no child, a glitchy sweep across the surface of the cosmos wiped this life decision and its implications, its encumbrances, from the record. You might drift empty-handed off towards Rialto, eat a cream bun, tragic with stale beliefs and hang-ups from a childhood – your own childhood – which still tyrannised you. You might have all the time in the world.

'Ah, flesh-coloured!' Lena reprised. '*Fleisch*.'

Caoimhe's daughter, Imogen, appeared first. She wore a little handbag and was tan. Sunny came next, in ditsy jeans and a jumper that said LOVE. Orla's son was named Oscar. He trundled over finally. He was sturdiest; his eyes roved the horizon as he reached for his mother's hand.

Sunny had a paper plate painted like a ladybird. Someone had written *Sunny* on the back, to differentiate it from the twenty or so painted ladybirds of the day. Why was Sunny carrying hers? Lena would have to carry it now. She wore a banana-shaped crossbody bag that bisected the denim dress and jacket and kept her arms free. It would not fit into that.

'You look nice Lena,' said Caoimhe suspiciously.

'Rosie was not in today,' Sunny told her mother. 'Maybe she on her holidays.'

'Was Mandy in?' Lena asked, nominating the girl Sunny had seemed attached to earlier in the term.

Sunny thought for a moment and then answered, 'No.'

The women and children moved into the street, back onto the stressful South Circular. The dry snarl of a motorbike cut off talk and a man, shirtless, strode past, barking at a phone, tracked with wonder by Oscar, whom Orla summoned with a tug of the Scuttlebug. Imogen had no vehicle either. She looked darkly at the little boy, rattling forth and propelled by his feet.

'Did we say the Gardens?' Orla asked. Everything she said, Lena thought, sounded listless and depressed. She did not wish to be there; none of them did. It was simply their life.

They passed, saying little, the gargantuan Spar and the

many-laned junction and the gaol, an old-timey castle of a gaol, and the hotel and the high wall of the Royal Hospital and crossed the warm tarmac and entered the War Memorial Gardens. Sensing a lag in supervision, the children began to trot, then sprint, towards the slanted trees and the wooden stile they liked to linger on, challenging one another to jump off it. Sunny was slowest and least confident, Lena noticed with a pang. Oscar's toy lay on its side and Orla whipped it up. She carried it; Lena carried the paper ladybird, Caoimhe the increasingly farcical coffee garbage.

It was simply their life. Somewhere, in the midst of it, they'd had babies and shared, between them now, discrete commitments to remaining in the city and living in the shade of former lives that were utterly urban in their selfishness. Lena for one could admit to a recurrent feeling of disconnect at moments like this, when she stood in vain or baiting relation to other women but also had Sunny, the option of total existential immersion in motherhood, to hand; when she felt both armoured by but also guilty at her vanity and longing for attention.

She enjoyed Caoimhe, however.

Caoimhe sat on a picnic bench. From there, they could watch the children playing a chasing game beneath a sessile oak like a crinoline. In the air they smelt the sluggish river smell. They discussed the children. Oscar had lately stopped crying when dropped off at Montessori; Imogen, fixated on her father, had banned Caoimhe from the bedtime routine.

Orla uncapped a water flask.

'How is Sunny doing?' she asked.

'Very well,' Lena said. 'But she still talks about it, yes. The previous life.'

'You should go on a podcast,' Caoimhe said. She placed two long hands on the tarry wood of the picnic table; they popped with coloured rings. Caoimhe dipped her chin, looking up from under her eyelashes. She seemed to be channelling a character, out of habit perhaps, but it was unclear what character.

'Then they can do research and find out if the story really does match up to, like, your ancestors.'

'Do you think it's ancestors?'

They looked at Lena awkwardly. They did not think anything. They didn't take it seriously.

'The magical child,' Caoimhe said. 'Wasn't that a book, the magical child?'

'What do you think it is?' Orla asked Lena.

Lena said, 'I've given up wondering. She's always been healthy, there's no movement on the psychiatric thing, and anyway the nurse was kind of like – what is the problem?'

Orla was looking at her. She said, 'There's not much more you can do.'

'Exactly.' Lena felt irritated. Always, she thought, one shares *mothering intimacies*, and the rest of the mothers clam up. They shared her fear of a contaminating weird. All of this hysterical acceptance and empathy, vestigial online activist affect, was bullshit in the end. For understandable reasons: she did not want a gifted child, et cetera.

The river slid by. If they walked on, along the river path, they would get to Chapelizod and the darker gates of the Park. On the water, there might be rowers making for the boat club. Months back, Caoimhe had pointed her gloved hands at the boat club, sequestered on its little plateau opposite them, and told them about a party she'd attended there. As she spoke, Lena looked above it, into the shady incline of the Park, and thought of a pretty colonial cottage hidden there in which she'd spent a day, a night, and emerged barefoot in the twiggy dew to greet the sun. She'd been with Cian then. These days Cian occurred to her as an involuntary mugshot; she saw his face, his eyes; felt an imagined substantiality between her legs.

Where was that house? Who owned it? They'd used all kinds of houses; they were troubadours and welcome everywhere. Mikey O'Hara had sourced them or booked them or liked them or whatever; Mikey was their manager-cum-minder, and owned, at that time, all the spaces and places and even the session musicians they worked in and with.

'Maybe she's just a reincarnated person,' Caoimhe said. 'Like, for real.'

'Well, probably not.' Lena was distant. This was pushing it.

Caoimhe, really, was a bitch. Quite unrepentantly. There had been a night last winter when they, Orla and Lena and a few others from the group of people they knew in common in the city, went to a show – a comedy show, a good one, in which three girls sang an acapella 50 Cent song – and the trip had been organised by Caoimhe, but Caoimhe got drunk.

To Lena, she had said, 'I have a place I'm going back to, and it's not my house.'

She'd named a man. He worked in the music industry; Lena knew him by name. When she was still singing, he would have been starting out. Caoimhe didn't know about that. Did she? Caoimhe had never given any indication of familiarity with Lena's music career. The career that was.

'Not my house and not my boyfriend,' Caoimhe sneered.

Lena had thought it sad that a mother, aged thirty-five, would say *boyfriend*. It made her feel better or less resentful of being cornered by this burst of drunken triumph in the club. Caoimhe had continued, 'It's not enough for me, one man. Is it enough for you?'

When they'd sent her off in a cab Orla said, 'I can't do The Club anymore.'

'I never enjoyed The Club anyway,' Lena said. She asked, 'Has she really gone to knock on that guy's door?'

'They've been meeting for a while.'

Lena cocked her head to one side. 'Oh.'

'It's none of our business,' Orla said.

They cab-shared home. The subject never came up again.

Lena had married Odhran hastily, when she was pregnant. To the registry office, for lunch in a place made extinct in the pandemic, and home. At the time, she'd told herself it was romantic because authentic, but that night in the cab, held up against the wrathful glamour of Caoimhe, it seemed small. Plenty of things Lena considered beneath her also happened to be things, she knew, that might mean pleasure and homewrecking and debt. For this reason she liked – enjoyed – Caoimhe, even if she was a bitch.

'Imagine,' Caoimhe tried again now, at the picnic table with its odour of creosote, 'she's a specific, like, reincarnated ancestor?'

Lena was mirthless. 'I don't know. My ancestors are not the kind with records.'

'Have you looked?' Orla seemed interested.

'Nah.' Lena paused. She'd never looked into her family tree. Was this also beneath her?

For her wedding, she'd worn a simple white pinafore she regretted – her breasts, swollen with hormones on the day, crushed against it dowdily. But Lena had also ordered herself a treat: a veil that splashed forwards and backwards either side of a comb. And then, when she'd left the apartment in a taxi, she'd forgot it and was married without it. She was married bare-headed and basically, without any mystery, in flat shoes and a pinafore dress. It amazed her afterwards, at the time and now, how angry she felt when she thought of the forgotten veil.

Just then Oscar, still with the round face of babyhood even though he was three, approached them to ask if they could go to the flowers now. Imogen and Sunny, who had been sprinting between points under the tree, came when called, and the group moved uphill, through the lime avenue. They came to the walled garden. Springy joggers panted past. Light rinsed through the trees that stood around as grand as horses on parade. There were no flowers really, just the pale green insect limbs of wintering rosebushes.

In the sunken garden, there were huge pavilions and stone pergolas shaggy with greenery and stalks in dead discs of soil, and a pond that was brown and inert, and steps descending like seats in an amphitheatre. The children began at once to run around it, dodging walkers, Oscar's scuttlebug rattling as Imogen dragged it by a handlebar.

The mothers sat, this time, on a stone seat. They were quiet for some moments. They were tired and realised this whenever they sat quietly.

'So many dates here,' Orla reminisced at last. 'Back in the day.'

'Really?' Caoimhe seemed surprised. 'It's a weird place for a date.'

'It's lurid,' Lena said. It felt like a silent, frightening room in which Empire was ever Empire and the sun would not set and so on. She leant to pick at an itch on her foot, sliding a foot into the cooler air. She thought of Sunny and ancestors. Sunny had also asked, of the Memorial Gardens, are there dead people here? Lena perked up a toe. She might have walked barefoot through this place when high one time, when staying in the colonial cottage probably – she couldn't remember now. Or just couldn't place it in time.

Dublin was so boring sometimes. The events of life happened in the same locations, over and over again, until it felt no more monumental than a travelling theatre set.

'Do you see that?' Caoimhe asked. She shielded her eyes and nodded, rather than pointed, to the long grass of the meadow beyond the pavilions; in the shady dampness, in the shadow of a wall, some people lay in the grass on a rug together.

'See what?' Lena followed her gaze. And then, 'Oh.'

It was a couple, who had been entwined, and now something flickered into the distinctive, repetitive motion of bobbing, there, in the long grass. They were watching it, the three women, like the secret detail in a formal photograph – for it moved, twitching, tiny but unmistakable, when all around the classical architecture boomed emphatic distraction and the rattle of the toy carried on, and joggers drifted in and out of a field of vision framed by the pavilions, and nobody watched the blowjob happening except for Lena and Caoimhe and Orla.

'Now,' Caoimhe said finally. 'That's fantastic. Let's wait here and shame them. Let's all smile at them at the same time.'

Orla said, 'They really shouldn't, with children around.' She stared as if thinking hard. And then she was angry, standing up.

7

That evening Odhran arrived home morose.

'You know that I think we should move,' he said.

'Yes.' Lena knew. He made this declaration as if it were original.

It was not just the rented apartment that was a problem, being too small and too spackled with adhesive veneers and too expensive and never theirs. It was a slower grievance that had been working on Odhran for a long time. Things in the city were provisional and exposed. Something would have happened today – at work, or viewed from the Luas – to impress this upon him freshly. Lena, distracted, did not ask.

He lay on the couch and put his hand over his eyes.

'Silly dada,' he proclaimed.

'Oh you're all right.' Lena was sewing. She was putting subtle stitches in a large silk scarf to wear it as a top in summertime.

Sunny, pushing the last of her risotto around a plate at the table, said, with thoughtful poise, 'I want a biscuit please.'

'Not yet.' Lena glanced up, then back at her scarf. She was doing a job tonight; she was leaving, she alerted Odhran, in twenty minutes. He sprang up jaggedly and went into the bathroom to shower. Lena slid past him to store towels, dressed in a fresh white dress from her singing days, then grabbed her jacket and satchel and chanted, 'Bun, or two biscuits only; it's a bath night and don't leave it late.'

'Bye-bye, Mama,' Sunny called mournfully.

'*Ná bí dána*,' Lena said.

She left. There was spirit suddenly. She clattered, unpractised, down flights of stairs. She met nobody – not the battered couple next door, not the escort, not the young Brazilians at the end of the corridor. She emerged into the street feeling like she'd forgotten something.

When young, Lena was accustomed to being noticed. The gaze of others lit upon her in a casual, easy-to-handle way: they looked up on instinct when she walked into a café or a lobby or an auditorium or mildly, half-unconsciously, tracked her as she crossed a space and turned the space into theatre. Most women pass through this golden age of the gaze, its outer edges rougher with the prospect of stalking and assault – or just envy – and then pass out of the other side unawares, like the cartoon coyote running on air.

This moment, for Lena, had taken place four years ago, when she had disappeared behind a pram and then a buggy and then an easy-fold stroller and now the lustrous evolutionary gambit that was Sunny drifting brightly by her side. It was OK. It wasn't restful yet – that, she knew, would come – but just OK, sometimes a source of grief, and also quite often a health-and-safety hazard because, just as in her shining days, she travelled around Dublin on a bike.

This bike was cheap and small. Never in her life had Lena paid serious money for a bike.

She stood now on the pedals and trudged uphill to the junction over the bridge, quieter in the evening, and into the cycle lane running parallel to the Park. Above the walls of the Park, horse chestnuts baring stamens bloomed. The city looked stunned and drowsy in the evening gloom. She followed this route into traffic and helter-skelter, where cars and busses and trams and jaywalkers and other cyclists produced snarls of sudden irritated attention and her legs, exposed where she'd hitched up her dress and put two knots in the cotton, felt at risk to all manner of imagined snags and scratches and life-changing surgical grafts.

She came to Capel Street and slipped off the saddle at last. She was always trembling with fear and exertion as she locked the bike.

It was vanity, really, the bike. She would not take Sunny on it, this was dangerous, and yet she still shot herself into knots of trams and busses and tourists and drunks out of lingering whimsy; it was whimsy, it was one of those unforgivable indulgences. There were times when Lena fantasised about dying, being released from obligation, while still retaining the moral high ground a mother killed by misadventure simply couldn't retain – she thought about this every time she attended a cervical smear exam, for example.

Imagine cancer and cancellation. What kind of mother, as in love with her child as any other, also privately imagines such a thing?

Lena walked towards Essex Street, invisible to the tidal rush of young men making, in a demonstrative group, for Panti Bar.

Lena sometimes worked off the books for Rita Conway, who ran a company importing and upcycling vintage clothes and who also gave smart little sewing masterclasses to smart young women. These she marketed with a visual sensibility that crossed Rosie the Riveter with rockabilly and, lately, she'd branched out into hen-night packages. On these nights, she paid Lena or one of her other assistants to pitch in with cocktails and affixing bobbins to the several Singers set out on workbenches in a rented room above Essex Street. Lena had always sewn; her mother had taught her as a child.

To reach the room of Essex Street, you had to climb four flights of shallow stairs with landings as truncated as chicanes. Lena was breathless by the penultimate, where she also sensed a second human presence in the airless ancient vacuum of the stairs. Doors gave off into corridors rented by a solicitor and a counselling service.

The second presence on the stairs turned out to be a petite

woman with long, crisply styled blonde hair. She wore a puff-ball dress with striking – from behind at least – epaulettes of some kind. The back was creased in the distinct regrettable way of cheap fabric retaining the ass shape of a chair, and this was saddening somehow, because the silhouette was great. Good design and bad fabric, Lena thought.

The woman was walking slowly, each step dragged or forced, and beginning to tilt tiredly to the wall. She was not drunk: she sensed Lena's arrival and looked over her shoulder, revealing a face full of freckles and dark lipstick. The face looked momentarily utterly lost, utterly exhausted, until it cringed into a smile.

'Hi.' Lena beamed back, already in work mode. 'Are you heading up to the hen?'

'Oh.' The woman stopped and looked at her.

'Reap and Sew.' Lena pointed to the ceiling. 'One more flight.'

'Oh,' the woman said. 'Yes.'

Lena passed her and strode upstairs. She felt the burn of the woman's gaze and wondered faintly if she'd recognised her, and whether this was from music or media or just some kind of embarrassing interpersonal intensity years ago – who knew, this was Dublin, it happened all the time. The woman was both familiar to her and a type. Something in her listless, dragging fashion and actual fashion – the epaulettes had not been epaulettes but ribbons – gave off a tiresome vibe, and hen nights often hummed with tiresome vibes.

Lena swung into the room, an old workshop with sash windows that looked out on the boiling movement of Temple Bar, and found Rita setting up liquor bottles on a table, while the clients, laughing spectacularly and gesticulating, perched together on workbenches.

Rita gave Lena a nod. Lena began briskly slicing lemons. She felt herself watching, with something like a tincture of dread, the door, waiting for the woman on the stairs.

'How are things?' Rita asked, coming over. She was short

and curvy, wearing a polka-dot dress with a ruched, reinforced bust and black hair in victory rolls. Against this display of titillation, her expression was dour, however, and her manner that of an unyielding dinner lady or housekeeper or similarly archetypal tender of class grudges. Lena felt she had been raised by such women and chastised all her life for being soft by such women and that her, Lena's, soul knew only submission in response to such women.

'Grand,' she answered. 'Nice to be out.'

How was Sunny? Rita asked. Sunny was yummy: wants to choose her own outfit each day and it is always a dress with leggings, never matching, two neat plaits but twisted into a bird's nest if there is time; she has learnt the first verse of 'One Big Love' but keeps stopping to ask, Mama, what does that mean? She says she wants to be *an artist*. And how were Rita's sons? One gobshite for the Leaving Cert this summer, and doing no studying, only out wearing the arse of his trousers sitting on walls or playing video games; the youngest, soft Liam, wants to start taking creatine. Better than cocaine, Rita said. The things they eat are absolutely disgusting, she added, like one of them finished off an entire tub of cheesy coleslaw out of Dunnes with a fucking spoon the other day – just ate it with a spoon.

The woman from the stairs entered the room and approached the group, who squealed in greeting, with open arms.

'Ladies, ladies!' Rita cried out suddenly. 'To your machines, ladies. Lena here will be serving some gin-and-sin. And I mean the cocktail, though if youse want to sin, sin away, just remember these machines sew fingers too and you've all signed a waiver and any injuries are your fault I am afraid. And yes, I have alcohol-free orders here: pink lemonade? Let Lena know as she goes. Let me get the speakers.'

Even in this listing, sooty building, the room felt wide and expansive, as if it had always been a workroom or a storage space, had known machinery forever.

Rita dabbed at a large laptop until her Spotify playlist

erupted, losing its privacy, from two portable speakers. This was all the stranger for the mournful mode it happened to be in, playing 'Cold, Cold Heart', a song that stung Lena back to a night of radio and night feeding when Sunny was newborn. She'd felt the house in Clare, where they were visiting, was eerie and that something climbed the stairs to watch her in the dark. It peered over the spindle. Oh the smell of old coal also, when the heating came on. This memory was distracting her.

She felt safer when Rita changed the music up to something new – something rubbery. Pop music. She took the jug of cocktail and divided it into tumblers, then arranged these on a tray.

Rita tapped her on the shoulder as she passed and muttered, 'Bride and bride, both here.'

This made Lena soften. No men, she realised.

One bride was plain and stylish in her straight black sleeveless dress, a huge tattoo glimpsed partially through a cutout at the back. The other woman was a skinny and vivacious American, who began at once to make a speech thanking everyone for joining them.

'I am,' she insisted, 'just like – wow.'

Lena served inconspicuously, dipping around the group. The quiet bride turned with fright when offered a drink. The other had let her eyes fall shut for emphasis as she spoke, engaging with everybody else. She was hot, this American, and lots of work, Lena thought.

From a cupboard at the back of the room, Lena produced Kilner jars of buttons and sequins and beads, boxes of coloured thread, a wheel of pins.

The classes always proceeded in the same way. Rita delivered instructions in a vampy deadpan and participants became tipsy and giddy and teased each other and sometimes got up to dance and produced, usually, ragged sets of embellished underwear. Lena sewed quick eclectic headbands for Sunny or stitched the equivalent of a doodle and unpicked it at the end. Otherwise she checked work, made smiling adjustments to errors while leaning over the machines, close to the bodies and perfumes and breath and hair products of other women, hovering in this stage of fleeting intimacy, or mixing more drinks. Songs would be requested on Spotify. Quizzes and question-and-answer games based on the marriage itself – where a couple met, how well endowed, what favourite meals, trivia, in-jokes – were played out.

Lena always thought about sex when she watched all this, if distantly and from a place of detachment. When she got pregnant with Sunny, all notional attraction to other men disappeared, like a mental illness, leaving her in this fearfully self-regulating sexual cell. Did engaged couples know this? Probably.

She was standing at the window again now. The evening had completed itself. Temple Bar below teemed cheerfully – pubs filling, drinkers standing in the street. It was nice and fresh to stand here in the chill let in by the window. It was pleasant to be out of the house.

A song came on. Picking, hesitant, standalone guitar. The sound of strings being played in a damp room, on a grey island, the world without muzzled by rain, and then the incline of a voice, starting low and climbing with a catch, a note that would sound every time, and then her own voice – sugary, young – joining in, sealing the weaker voice, male, into harmony.

Lena had frozen in ready anger for several moments before she knew why. It was not Rita – Rita was at the opposite side of the room, rooting in a Tesco bag for gin; at the laptop was the woman from the stairs, her face ruddy now, the dress with the strange silhouette catapulting attitude across the room. Lena looked at her blankly and the woman looked blankly back.

And after a moment Rita, now reading the back of a bottle, said, as if to herself, 'Here's our Lena on the Spotify.'

'I knew I recognised you,' one of the other women said.

American bride spun around. 'Who?'

'Lena Marley, the singer.'

'Oh I'm sorry,' American bride smiled. 'I don't know her.'

Lena thought of saying *big in Germany* but that wasn't actually true, so she simply nodded and, in a minute, the room had reoriented its interest – all but the woman from the stairs, who approached her with a new, imploring aspect.

Lena raised her eyebrows in expectation. She was disturbed and furious – she knew the fury to be unreasonable, neurotic even, but the rush issued from some primordial place. It was the desire to fight. She remained, nonetheless, rigid by the window ledge.

'I remember you,' the woman said. 'You knew my sister.' The woman named her sister and Lena nodded guardedly at her.

'I didn't know her well, I'm afraid,' Lena said. 'And – well.'

The woman had locked eyes with her. Now she looked stony again.

'I was sorry to hear about her,' Lena said.

This sister, from way back, Lena remembered her. Lena reached.

'I'm Elva Fanning,' the woman said. 'My sister was Lydia.'

Lydia Fanning. A girl: white dreadlocks, posh accent, organised club nights – a runner? A hanger-on? Sang in some bands. This was the 2000s and Lena herself was terribly young and these kids from the city, or the suburbs south of the city, all knew one another already, they were in gangs and formations; it was exhausting, or had been at one time, to explain to people that she, Lena, was not intimate with any of Cian's friends.

The woman from the stairs was Lena's age and had probably been a younger sister. Yes, the sister, she remembered her, she saw Lydia before her once again – an abrasive person. The word came: *abrasive*.

God, those awful people.

When Lena was older, gone from Cian, hardly performing at all, right before she met Odhran, she had read about this sister walking into a lake somewhere to drown. She had been reported missing after posting a screed on Facebook – about her father, about in-patient services, about God. Lena had read about it because, yes, she remembered now, Cian sent her a link or an email, and underneath this screed a great many people posted tributes and capslocked professions of grief, and all of these sounded semi-literate and out of their heads, and she remembered now what Cian – being so abstentious, so severe – had said: *drugs, drugs, drugs*.

Father, hospital, God.

She, Lena, had answered: why are you sending me this?

It was a hideous memory.

She gazed back at this woman, who must carry the hideous memory everywhere, even though she looked chic and vehement and formidable.

Lena said slowly, 'I find it strange when people know me. It was all so long ago.'

'Oh you were very good,' the woman told her, as if she had been asked.

Rita signalled to Lena. Lena was relieved. 'I've got to get on with this,' she said, returning to a warmer tone but dipping away from Elva before the other woman could respond.

Rita was rearranging spirit bottles pointlessly; she gave Lena a look.

'Not easy being famous, is it,' she said.

'A nightmare. Can't go anywhere.' Lena was surprised at the assistance and the wisdom it seemed to suggest.

A faintly canine sense of being cornered made her think, unwantedly, of a column posted to an online magazine in the weeks after she'd left Cian's band. The column reported that she would not be finishing the European tour. It reprinted a photograph, one of dozens on Shutterstock, of Lena with her guitar gazing jadedly into space and wearing a short black cocktail dress, onstage: *maybe*, the caption read, *she's feeling lonely and vulnerable?* It was such bullshit there was not even a byline to pursue. She thought at the time: some little wanker, some little toerag, some little prick. But said nothing, because nothing ever came of saying anything.

She had been seventeen when she began – seventeen when she auditioned, and in her first year of college. After her audition, Cian walked Lena across the street to Kennedy's, and they sat together in a pew. There were rings of water on the tabletop. He asked her, are you old enough to drink? Yes, she said. Her age had never prevented anyone from serving her before. But then Cian returned with Britvic and asked, why are you studying history?

And Lena, without emotion, said simply: it is a story with weird things that don't make sense anymore, and I want to find the sense. She meant something particular then, and it was spandrels – she was reaching for metaphors and mystical signs and those elements in the environment that seemed to suggest people thinking differently, more delicately, once. She already knew this made her different from the other students because, in the first, they were almost all boys, and in the second they almost all intended to go into politics.

And later Cian told her, I wanted to eat you, I could have eaten you, you were so prim.

8

Lena and Odhran had met at an event in the backroom of a social space in Smithfield. She sang 'God Bless the Child' and provided a piping harmony for a man she knew who salvaged folk tunes. She was twenty-nine; the band had ended years before. At that point in Dublin's history social spaces – shop units repossessed or half-finished storage facilities – were cheap to rent and easier to squat and this gave rise to a brief, warming, deluded mood of improvisation and community among people who had not emigrated. Lena was still on this periphery, in the sense that she lived in a houseshare and was finishing her degree belatedly.

Anyway, on this night, she met Odhran, in his work suit with tie loose, drunk and for some reason attending this event and he came up to her afterwards and he was handsome, arrogant but feminine in that irresistible way, verbose and pretentious and hyperactive. He recognised her. 'We've met before,' he claimed. They exchanged numbers.

The next day she searched for him, and tapped through enough wide-open social media pictures of Odhran enjoying sunsets and many-peopled brunches and animal fosterage with his live-in girlfriend to make a decision.

I'm wondering if I have the right number, he messaged, because you're not answering.

Yes because you are married.

Married no, he wrote.

The lack of surprise or denial caught her off guard. For a moment she almost felt like the one in the wrong.

Weeks later – months perhaps – a direct message: I am single, he wrote, and I'm sorry for being so disrespectful to you.

And to her, Lena replied.

Trust me, she'll be fine, he said.

This woman had been cheating on him with a mutual friend. They'd had, he told her later – when she'd agreed to a date – a threesome with the mutual friend, who was a woman. All three had been cruel to one another. It was an ugly scene, he said. Her mind swelled, as he spoke, with sexual empathy.

'I just feel,' she said carefully, stirring her coffee, 'that this is a messy situation for me to come into now. Like, you need time alone.'

'You are sensible,' Odhran agreed. Then they went back and had sex in the apartment he'd been fixed up with *by work*, opposite the Bord Gáis Theatre. The space was as sterile and smooth as a laboratory. He'd been working in tech then; he found it, he told her, irritating. Also, he still worked with the ex-girlfriend and the friend they'd lapped up between them. Even now, Lena sometimes ventured to imagine Odhran with two women wrapped around him, pale limbs cluttered kinkily with Bold Will Hold tattoos, and the thought made her so excited she committed to hushed, hasty sex at the next opportunity.

'What will you do?'

'I'll leave,' he said, and he did. Odhran was good at following through.

They dated through the last yellow days of summer and into a mellow autumn. Odhran knew about new restaurants that served one thing and one thing only and were closed, the next time you passed on the tram, within weeks. Lena took Odhran to gigs. She brought him along to a show at the Sugar Club that was inexpensive but specialist because the performer, Mae Quinn, was niche. Lena had toured with her aeons ago.

'Literally never spoke to me, not once,' she chirped. 'It was aeons ago,' she repeated. It was, she meant, charming now, because historical.

There was a queue, but it was silvery still in the street, a blue moon filling up over the Green, and nothing of the experience felt inconvenient. Odhran wore his long wool coat and this, with the close-cropped curly hair and hawkish nose, made him glow with corporate energy, a quality rare to the point of exotic in Lena's life at that time. She was dressed in a see-through high-necked mesh top with a pair of trousers cinched in at the waist. Her neck looked long; her wrists were long, her fingers long and ringless and white.

He moved from foot to foot and looked over her head, modelling his tallness, nodding shortly at someone further down.

'Who's that?' she asked.

'Oh just a girl.' When Lena turned at speed, he laughed. 'It's a person from work.'

She was not interested in his work. He took her for a tour of the tech place before he departed from it, another glass-fronted bell of a building on the Silicon Docks. It was splashy and colourful as a new shopping mall. She could not say what people did in it except move data around or something, code. It seemed as aimless to her as unpicking rope.

Now, queuing on the long orange pavement as busses paused then blasted up Leeson Street, she felt returned to her element. She knew the score. She turned the tickets over in her hand. She'd played here many times. The green room was a weird little overflow bar.

Inside, he tilted towards the bar. 'Find a seat and I'll find you,' he said.

At one of the elevated tables, she folded her coat and stretched her bare arms before her. On each wrist a wooden bangle painted with flowers chipped against the table surface. She watched people beneath her prang out the cinema seats, swivel about, greet one another, or stare at the stage with tension and purpose – those people had come alone. She'd toured Europe – in a minor way – with Mae; now she thought for some reason of Gdansk, rising wintery and minty in her mind, of the soaring civic centre in the dockyards and the plate of smoked fish, smoked bread, smoked meat, smoked cheese, smoked pickles, thimbles of vodka consumed with a party of people that had included huge imperious broad-shouldered Mae, a woman of mannish, unbending attractiveness, holding court and speaking directly to some people while wholly omitting others, one of whom was Lena, and why not, after all, Lena was nobody. Small guitar-picking girl picked up by Cian as a garnish or arm candy.

They were already being managed then by Mikey O'Hara, who was insane. He'd sent them a chequebook. A note with it, or something conveyed by a lackey, said: the girls need new dresses.

'Who will choose them?' Frances, the cellist, had squeaked.

'Cian,' said Lena. 'He owns us. Let him choose our dresses.'

In the booth, she caught Odhran's eye as he wound between tables with their drinks. He said something about the crowd. It was not really crowded. Now they were sitting they felt monarchical, looking down at people, settling primly in.

'Tell me about this singer,' he said.

'She's difficult.'

But Mae had a sweet, soaring voice, ethereal, distinct from her square shape and severe face. She did not address the audience, but moved between synthesiser and guitar before a screen of plasma oscillating, orange and red, like a lava lamp. Her songs this time were about astronauts, though you would not know this by the lyrics and lilting. At the end, she took up a squeezebox and handled it sternly, looking like something from a genre painting.

'Thank you,' she said huskily to the microphone. There hadn't been an interval.

Back on the street, walking into step by the silent lighted mansions of the Green, Odhran was bemused.

'I see why you like it,' he told her, 'but yes, it was difficult.'

'It lingers. You'll see. I will lend you the album if you like.'

'I've seen you perform with Cian,' he told her then, suddenly. She wanted to go into the Shelbourne and this was the opportunity to skid to a halt and look at him daintily.

'You can tell me about it,' she said.

On barstools, with cocktails, he did. Lena saw herself or her décolletage upended in a tarnished silver mirror over the bar – upside down, decapitated. It was not an interesting story: at some festival, on Smithfield Square, makeshift and rigged up with Heineken banners, he'd seen Cian as part of a set or stage play four or five songs belligerently before turning to wink at the beautiful girl to his left, in a torn-up dress, very eye-candy girl-bassist kind of thing.

Lena sat stiffly, hurt. She did not speak.

'And we met at a party,' he reprised into the awkwardness, 'at Trinity. Long ago. I think I remember your brother,' he said.

After a pause, she began angrily rubbing an eye. 'My brother went to DCU. You never met him, that is someone else. He hardly socialised. He lived at home. It was some other woman too, probably,' she said.

'Are you annoyed at something?' he asked finally.

'I was not a girl bassist.'

'You know what I mean. I was young, that's all I remember.' He sipped his drink, looking around as if noticing the fluting baroque room for the very first time. It was filled with tourists drinking erectly and seeming oppressed by the formality.

The date became chaste. Lena took the bus home alone.

The next evening, Odhran appeared at the door with whiskey and two gurning monsteras, since he had not been able to choose between them. As they sat at the kitchen table, one of Lena's housemates appeared in her crushed pyjamas – she was the youngest, her hangovers were collaborative and socialised – and began to make tea in a mug reading DESPIERTA DE BUON ROLLITO! and when she left the room, Odhran said, 'That vibe is musty,' which was cruelly funny, so they moved upstairs. Later, lying under the sheets looking up at a Velux through which you could hear the boring broken roar of traffic, he asked, 'How are you thirty and living in a houseshare?'

'Bad investments,' she said. The inference stung. 'Before this, I lived with Gwynn.'

'Ah yes. The psychiatrist guy.'

Gwynn was a psychotherapist actually, but Lena answered: yes.

'What happened there?'

'It had to do with his son,' she said. 'He has a son who is unwell. He's a teenager.'

Living with Gwynn had been like living at a hotel. Crisp and clean and with each material need catered for. It had lasted just three months, but cost her a lease.

Odhran now was annoying her. Quickly and suddenly she had shifted.

I could burn it all down, she thought. What difference anyway.

In the first sweet weather of April, she had terrible, wonderful, stormy-weather elegant dreams of remorse and architecture. She'd been seeing Odhran less than six months when she found out, peeing blithely on a brush-tip without expectation of anything but another cycle delayed, made late aimlessly, it happened all the time, but what a shock she got when that was not the case at all. The line was pale.

'I have been here before,' she told Odhran. 'They can be wrong.'

They bought two more, and it was not wrong, and she began to shake from head to foot.

Odhran said, 'Don't panic, we were never very careful; and what else were we planning to do with the next decade anyway? We've probably peaked, professionally.'

At this, she shrieked with empty laughter. 'Peaked!'

‘We have demonstrably peaked.’

‘You can be unhappy about it,’ Lena said.

‘I’m not unhappy about it.’

She was sick with it; that began early. Rushing to the toilet with its strained nineteenth-century plumbing in the ever-wet basement of the Georgian house museum, driving up purple chutes of blackcurrant juice and chocolate, little fronds of undigested matter sticking to the porcelain like moss.

On and on it went, a journey of months over churning seas. It was impossible in this state to feel anything less than sacred, chosen, full of excitement, and soon – really soon, after the twelve-week scan – she was looking forward to it.

At two months, Lena travelled to see her mother in the Naul. Her mother had moved into her own deceased parents’ house and redecorated it. Their deaths had been slow and logistically unremitting, involving homes and debt guarantees attached to the house, but because her mother had no siblings, the place was left to her. It was a simple rendered bungalow stressed, within, by woodchip and browning macramé and a lot of thick terracotta crockery. On that day, Lena had driven Odhran’s car out of the city and through the hayseed and sea-salt haze of Fingal to arrive on a breezy afternoon. It was June. The front door was open, and when she stepped in, she smelt fresh paint and bleach.

‘Mam?’ Wind chimes chittered minorly. Her mother had painted the hall pure white, the kitchen pure white, and had the homely yellow plastic kitchen replaced with chrome and cream. Her mother sat on the ledge of concrete at the back. It jutted from the house and then stopped short of a drop to the unmannered green flow of a small garden. A washing line was stretched across the grass and held up, in the centre, by a spar of spongy wood.

‘Hello.’ Her mother had heard her, but remained in her chair. The clothes on the line were her mother’s things – linen slacks and a collection of simple white T-shirts from Dunnes.

She wore a necklace of shells from her holiday to Portugal. She extended a cool hand and clasped Lena's for a moment before letting go. They drank coffee in the open air, which was bright but raked with little breezes and not so comfortable, and Lena told her about the baby.

'Congratulations,' her mother said. 'And is this man someone you are sure of?'

'Yes.'

'Because children are difficult. And men are different when they get used to you.'

'Odhran is very decent. He's the most decent man I've ever been with.'

'When a child comes,' her mother continued, 'bang go the treats, the holidays, those road trips – no privacy, no time. Love is over. Now, don't get me wrong, people can go on loving one another, in a way, yes, but it needs to be a very different kind of love, and in my life I've very rarely seen any couple really capable of that love.'

'Right.'

'So make sure to keep your money separate.'

'I have no money.' Lena smiled.

Her mother looked irritated.

'Let's hope he's generous then,' she said.

Lena's mother had hated her life as a wife and mother and worked, as soon as she legally could, to get out of it. She had moved for years between her parents' house and various substandard rented flats, always remaking every place she lived in beautifully. Or at least Lena had once found these cooling places beautiful; looking back, they were probably kitsch, reflecting her mother's provincial grasp of urbanity and ergonomics and minimalism. Yes, she'd hated life as anyone's wife and anyone's mother but never, before now, given her daughter any explicit advice on whether or not she, Lena, should marry and have children or cohabit or travel or work or study or do anything. She never seemed to have strong opinions on Lena's life.

'I think I'm lucky,' Lena told her now.

'Oh, you've had it easy, yes. But keep your money,' she repeated, 'separate.'

And she had. Money, and other things.

9

At the playground that weekend, Lena stood with Caoimhe watching their children rattle around the bright equipment. There were many other children, clashing sounds of complaint and enthusiasm, and sometimes – they thought – carrying whoops from the monkeys in the zoo. When this happened, the mothers cocked their heads or held their hands behind their ears and cried after their children, Listen! Monkeys in the zoo!

Lena wore a wide-brimmed hat and Caoimhe a boxy peaked cap. Caoimhe's body was as slight and tight as a child's in her soft T-shirt and jeans; Lena, feeling lugubrious in broderie anglaise, sweated quite a bit.

She began boldly. 'You are from Ranelagh, right?'

'It's Renelagh,' Caoimhe joked in a dull way, as if obligated. She'd been muted and testy all morning, rubbing her eyes. She was *parenting solo* because her partner was visiting family in Westmeath. 'No, I never go,' she'd said, 'if I can avoid it.' Her partner worked for an advertising firm and had been the brains behind a Gas Networks Ireland awareness campaign involving a cute woman dressed like a Little Trees car freshener: Caoimhe. The Little Trees lady drifted to and fro, then began to dance in a jagged, demonic fashion, eyes wide, like the dance scene in *Metropolis*, and this gave the advertisement cult appeal. It had many complaints, apparently, but nobody could articulate why they disliked it so much. Lena knew this because Caoimhe had told her.

'I met someone the other day,' Lena continued, 'you might know.'

'Oh dear.'

'Someone from my past life, so to speak. When I was singing.'

'Oh?' Caoimhe turned back to face the playground. She was tracing Imogen, struggling chimp-like to stim on a wire bridge, as Sunny swung – leading from the core – on one of the soft leather swings. Other people's children, limbs and co-ords and those distracting tinselly Alice bands, flashed like schools of fish between. Caoimhe said, 'I still have your albums somewhere. Or album.'

'Not *my* albums,' Lena corrected. 'Cian Mulvaney. Singer-songwriter and heartbreaker.'

'Ha, yes.' Caoimhe smiled at her now. Caoimhe was dimpled and tan.

'*I'm wounded and soulful*,' Lena said in a singsong voice. 'Come closer.'

Cian was wolf-eyed, short-tempered and magnetic. He'd phoned her after the audition and drink, but waited for over a week, like a cruel suitor.

'Wasn't he your boyfriend?' Caoimhe asked.

'He was for a time. He fired me. It was years ago. Fired me from the band.'

'Bit of an arsehole thing to do.'

'Yeah well.' Lena felt compelled to look about for somewhere to sit. The benches were packed with parents in primary colours and older kids. The grass was possible, but to initiate this would be intimate: she imagined the corkscrew into lotus position, the invitation it implied to confession or girlishness.

Her career as a singer, as a songwriter, had been more substantial than Caoimhe's tone would suggest – she, Lena, had been pretty almost famous. It was a moment in music when CDs were cheap and touring cheaper still. She'd been twenty-five when it ended for good. She didn't write songs anymore. It was not the real, or final, or intentional subject of her conversation with Caoimhe.

'This woman I met,' she said. 'Her sister was on that scene. Back in the day.'

When Lena named Lydia, Caoimhe said, 'Oh yeah. Killed herself. That was weird.'

A lot of people might have said *sad*.

'Her sister,' Lena specified.

Elva was this person's name: Elva was the living sister. When the woman had told her, I'm Elva Fanning, my sister was Lydia, Lena had nodded silently.

'She's an art person,' Caoimhe said of Elva now. 'Or she owns a gallery. No – she manages a gallery. Something like that.'

'Do you know her well?'

'No.' Caoimhe looked bored. 'I just know people. There was a gang,' she gestured, 'I used to be in with. Some of them successful, actually. Actors and so on. *Hooker-waitress*,' she sang suddenly. She dropped some names Lena knew. She was still watching Imogen. 'That family.' Her eyes were on the child. 'They lived in a house with.' Caoimhe drew something in the air with her fingers. 'You know. Castanets.'

'Crenelations?'

'Like a castle. What did I say?' The laugh was a single bark. 'Castanets.'

'Anyway, this woman crossed my path,' Lena continued, 'and kind of – confronted me. She got straight into it. She said lots of people on the scene knew her sister had all these problems or did nothing or just encouraged it – drugs, I presume.'

Oh, you were very good, the woman had told her, before leaning vehemently into this. Lena was cornered by the window, forgotten by the rest of the hens. Elva's eyes were wide, not eccentric but in warning, like an animal, and her voice given to over-enunciation.

'People exploited Lydia,' Elva had claimed. Lena repeated this to Caoimhe.

Caoimhe looked sceptical now. 'Why did she say this to you?'

‘Cian maybe.’ Lena’s boldness failed her. ‘He had,’ she said, ‘other girlfriends.’

‘I see.’

‘She used to hang around with bands, this sister. Elva’s sister.’ Lena named some names now herself – there were a few she couldn’t fully recall. ‘That gang,’ Lena said. She pictured, unbidden, blurry people climbing in and out of cabs. ‘Elva seems to think her sister was involved with Cian.’

‘I am confused. Weren’t you there too?’ Caoimhe asked.

‘That’s what I mean. I didn’t really know him, or those people. I was really just. I mean, I was incredibly naïve when I was younger.’

Something happened, then, which was strange. Caoimhe appeared to mute herself, to smoothen her expression and detach. In the moment Lena felt she was accorded a kind of privacy or space. It made her feel ashamed.

‘That girl,’ Caoimhe said at last, meaning Lydia Fanning. ‘Like. She used to go missing a lot. I do remember that.’

‘Yes. I know.’ This, Lena realised, was what she wanted: consensus.

‘She was troubled. I mean, some people just took a lot of drugs. Once I think they found her in a hedge. Yes. It was a hedge.’ Caoimhe’s laugh was bubbly and deep, like the laugh of a toddler. Her vocal range was wide. Usually she spoke in a nasal squeak.

‘I mean obviously she must have been quite a vulnerable person,’ said Lena, watchfully.

‘Indeed,’ Caoimhe said. ‘There are people about, though,’ she continued. ‘I mean, you really wouldn’t know what goes through their heads.’ For the next part she assumed a plummy accent. ‘Consider those gents in the Gardens last week. Public fellatio, in daylight.’

‘I thought that was a woman and a man.’

‘Doesn’t matter. Perverts. Have you ever seen the like? I have. In this Park, I’ve seen all kinds of things.’

This digression seemed deliberate. Caoimhe did not, Lena

thought, want to talk about the drowned girl; there was something to the story even she found discomforting. Sunny, she noticed, had moved away from the swings.

Lena felt a need to persist.

'I think, basically,' she said, 'I think bad things just happened on that scene.'

Caoimhe looked at her for a moment.

'Well, sure,' she said.

'It got me-tooed in the pandemic.'

'It did?' Caoimhe was amused.

'On Twitter. Then that was shut down after a day. Libel laws.'

'No safe quarter,' Caoimhe said. 'Comedy just had Dave Dunne. He took the condom off one day in the middle of sex with somebody. Great lamentation. Searing bravery,' she raised a hand, 'of the girl who keeps going, and then cries Swedish rape.'

Imogen broke towards her mother suddenly.

'We have to go now,' Caoimhe said, dancing her around. She added, somewhat spitefully, 'I must give your album a spin.'

Lena waved them off and waited, even though she also had to go. She felt unburdened of something and also, lingeringly, necessarily, embarrassed.

Caoimhe, she understood, was a risky person to confide in. She might gossip or just, as she had done, mock. And yet it was better than telling Odhran, to whom Lena confided little, these days, that did not concern Sunny. It wasn't that she mistrusted him; only that she found him faintly, hintingly hostile towards tales of her past now that they were older, and settled, and done provoking one another into erotic action or emotional violence.

'Sunny,' she called now. 'Snack.'

Sunny ducked out from the crowd obediently. As Lena was separating sticky crackers her phone spasmed, showing a rare WhatsApp message from Caoimhe. It was a link to the website of the art gallery on Arran Quay. The woman from the stairs at Reap and Sew was resident curator, or one of them.

Sunny whined at the distraction and Lena tapped the message, causing a heart emoji to bubble up.

In the first months of Sunny's life, when Lena was alone all day, she often strapped the baby into her sling and set off with a Silvercross bag on her back to visit galleries and shops in the city centre. She could recall, at this point, essentially none of it, but knew she'd passed through the provisional-seeming structure on Arran Quay; it had an earth floor, or the exhibition had. Blunt white pigs carved from wood. Or ferns, huge, washed ferns, in plates of glass.

Elva, the curator of crenelated origins, had played her song to get her attention and then approached her and begun – rudely, she felt now; bullyingly – to talk about her sister. It had been awkward for Lena. 'We can talk more,' Elva had said before she left.

'Would you like a lolly from the kiosk, love?' Lena asked Sunny now.

Sunny nodded, perking up.

When they'd bought it, she led the little girl under a tree to sit in the shade. Lena swept off her hat and let it fall into Sunny's head. Sunny giggled obligingly.

'Mama?' she asked. 'Am I going to school?'

'You're starting big school in September.' It was a conversation they rehearsed frequently.

'And what will I bring in my lunchbox?'

'Oh, wraps, pasta, fruit and some chocolate.'

'And they will heat my pasta up.'

'If you ask.'

'And I might ask and I might not ask. Oscar,' she said, looking around the crowd, 'he have his *wrap* heated up in Montessori.' She looked at her mother with a soliciting grin.

'Heated up!'

'Yes, he have his wrap heated up in the microwave.' She regarded her rocket lolly, still so deeply frozen it looked like metal. 'My lolly,' she said, 'is too cold.'

'And what will you wear to school?'

'A uniform.' Sunny licked again. 'Will they heat my wrap up?'

'If you ask, I'm sure they will.'

'Oscar has only one mama.'

'You have only one mama. Everyone has one mama.' Lena thought. 'Except children who have two mamas because the mamas are married.'

Sunny looked puzzled. Lena found herself leaping up.

'Let's walk!' she said. 'Your lolly will melt in the heat.'

She replaced the hat on her head and fished in her bag for the crushed white sunhat that was Sunny's.

That morning, the kid had drawn a picture of two mamas, mama of before and mama now, showing the freakishly figurative shape of Lena and another, larger, hovering figure with black, scrambled lashes of hair. She had cried when Odhran, before Lena could stop him, had told her she was hurting Mama's feelings and then, unhelpfully, qualified: the mama of now. It was a matter of twenty minutes and forgotten fast, but Lena looked at Sunny now and wondered if she should make another voice recording. She did not want to think about it.

It was not a short walk back, down Chesterfield Avenue, to Islandbridge – or not for a four-year-old. Lena repented of leaving the pushchair behind, or the scooter, and allowed Sunny to dawdle in preoccupation. Were she alone, she might hit out for Chapelizod or ride her bike into the countryside that lay close by, finding tumbled mansions and laneways like the winding lanes of Clare. She'd been bored a lot, in life. She was a person who tended to bored.

After Sunny was born this boredom had moved from background to foreground and became tangible, almost kinaesthetic, because it went from being an imposition to *the point*; the point of childcare was hovering, hollow, to the side of the central character, which was now the baby, like a cipher or a character in a video game: moving frantically and mindlessly through sterilising tasks or running on the spot, vacuous but magnanimous, for the purpose of witnessing enrichment.

Dragging up Chesterfield Avenue in the heat, for example, watching a sundress splotched with daisy heads be stained by a lolly, watching Sunny lift her face to squint against the sun across the street. This was boring and yet freighted with such meaning. It was meaning Lena could only partake of by proxy unless she gave in to the egoistic image of herself *as* hovering.

Again she realised, with clarity, how many things, seemingly small or petty revelations, about herself and about human nature had revealed themselves to her. So many events in her life folded out of the darkness; so many things were lit by new light. Projections fell away. The city was only a salad of parallel lives. Her body was a vehicle of decay sustaining, through nourishment and effort, a relative beauty; she had not, for all her reading, truly understood literature and she'd been too lazy to understand music as anything other than mimicry. She was not particularly talented and more given to reproducing the plainer, ungainly attributes of her parents than ever transcending them. She felt agitated and wanted to look at her phone.

She sometimes imagined herself, standing on a stage with her hair Mary Magdalene straight to her waist, a guitar in her arms and her mouth captured in that photographic O, the siren lasso, of a certain image somewhere – online or in print – and thought of the normal moral vanity of that and wondered, then, if she'd gone too far in the other direction. But it had become clear, even in those early days of staring at art in galleries, that Lena's mind had become a surface off which impressions slid. This intensity of exhaustion and solitude hadn't lasted, but when she had quit work and stayed at home – 'for the time being' – this sense of being blank or surplus needed a mythology. For Lena, it became one of sacrifice.

Not sacrifice to Odhran and Sunny, but to that almost kinaesthetic force of boredom. Boredom became a network of sensations to which she would attach her attention. Just now it was heat, the sun weighing on the wide-brimmed hat, and an ache in her feet.

'No,' Sunny complained.

'I know, honey. I'm sorry.'

'I want to be carried.'

'I can't.' Now Sunny had stopped completely, on a dusty piece of broken wall where a car had clipped the pavement at the junction. It had happened recently. Lena looked at it more closely. Steel girders were exposed through the crumbling cement.

It was her own fault, she thought, for bringing the girl this far. Lena bent down and let Sunny climb onto her back, clamping her legs and sandals at Lena's waist. She was heavy, but Lena was able to balance her weight. Sun splashed the windshield of a Dublin Bus bouncing stiffly over a speed ramp on the bridge. There were old trees, gnarled and surprisingly massive at the canopies, shading the pavements. When walking up this street, it looked expansive and interesting, like a different city. When driving it, however, you saw that the street trees teetered and convened to form a kind of tunnel, and close it off.

10

When Odhran first brought up the prospect of buying a house, Lena said, well sure, everybody would love that, everybody can dream. For most of her adult life, she'd believed such a thing was not her burden to carry nor aspire to, since it would require a personal history so radically retrofitted with sensible decisions as to become unrecognisable. She imagined home ownership like she imagined being blonde, or blind, or a man.

Odhran had been withering. 'You are such a girl,' he said.

'Exactly,' Lena smiled.

This was in the pandemic. He'd done sums. He was tremendously sexy with the sums. There was a spreadsheet printed in the empty office at work and he explained; there was a flowchart of processes and a strategic plan. He tossed it towards her with a gesture of fatigue. When she resisted, he told her that some of the flowchart decisions and so on had been tendered, originally and tentatively, by the ex – tattooed, bisexual ex – way back when *they* had considered house hunting and this had the intended effect of summoning forth Lena's competitive side.

Though at first the response was a body blow in return.

'Yeah I've stalked her Instagram,' she teased. 'She owns an apartment herself now.'

'So I heard.'

'Didn't need your salary in the end.'

'Oh but you do.'

'Ha!' Lena was breathless. 'Ha!'

Two years since these first projections were made, they looked for houses. Sometimes in a scattered, browsing style; sometimes in a targeted and narrow way. It meant, since they'd begun the process, long drives. Sunny was younger then and they attached themselves to an agent on the southside, who sent them to tramp through sixties family homes with floral carpets and disability handrails and avocado toilet suites. But when this agent realised they were not serious, she stopped calling.

'She's on to us,' Lena remarked on a trip through town. It was autumn or winter; there was papery rain.

'On to us how?' Odhran replied, annoyed by traffic, listening to the agent's phone ring out on the booming Bluetooth connection.

'She sees we won't get a big enough mortgage.'

'She doesn't know that.'

'She asked me what I did and I said *homemaker*.' She should not have said this; it was a ridiculous thing to say. The imp of mockery.

'You'll go back to work.' Testily, he slowed down to the ticking indicator. He looked around and yanked the steering wheel as if he were a helmsman in a storm. They rocked into a new confusing street in the Liberties that looked pedestrianised but was not pedestrianised; the brickwork of the road and path were just similar.

'She's on to us.'

'We can get a mortgage for that amount.'

She looked at him. 'No,' she said. 'We can't.'

He was angry with her, but she couldn't stop. 'It is impossible.'

'Would you,' he hissed at her in fury one night, 'would you just lie down and die or whatever if nobody came to fucking – *do* your life for you?'

'I'm doing my life, asshole.' She was wounded.

'Don't call me an asshole.'

It was a language of love. They had sex more frequently

in weeks flavoured like this. The problem was failing to get mortgage approval in Dublin city or its first rind of down-at-heel suburbs meant widening the loop to encompass towns and townlands and zoning proposals abutting other counties – Wicklow, Meath, Kildare – or just in other counties, like Meath and Kildare. They could not afford actual Wicklow. Wicklow was worse than Dublin. Lena came to see her aloofness was futile and immature; she came to realise that, if Odhran lost faith, she herself would be devastated. The steel of entitlement at his core was useful and attractive to her even if it meant watching him grasp, sometimes shamefully, at phantoms.

It was in this spirit of capitulation and, indeed, domestication, that Lena began at last to collaborate.

Now she agreed to drive, on odd Saturdays, for the most part, to Meath and Louth and, today, to Rush, close to where Lena grew up, to look at open-view housing estates.

'That estate in Rush,' Odhran clarified now, standing in the kitchenette.

Lena had returned with Sunny, from Caoimhe and the Park, and was drinking a tumbler of water between mostly rhetorical gasps of relief.

'Do you think,' he asked, 'we should go have a look?'

'I do. It's nice out there, anyway.'

'I don't think we'll buy one.' He was looking at her.

'We would need,' she answered patiently, 'to get a mortgage first anyway.'

Together, they finished putting away groceries. Lena changed Sunny, stuffed a tote bag with snacks and clothes, and took her downstairs to wait for the car. When Odhran drew up, they climbed in and took off. He had shaken off the city after twenty minutes of inching through dollish streets and crossing the bridge at Phibsborough. As green suburbs came on, Lena proposed they play her new download, a book called *Pleasure Activism*, over the Bluetooth connection.

'You only picked it because it says activism,' Odhran teased. 'Imagine if it was called Pleasure Fuck Everyone Else.'

'Yes.' Lena was sanguine. 'It was Orla's recommendation.'

'For pure pleasure,' he persisted sharply, 'what would you really listen to?'

Lena answered 'Enya' without needing to think about it. She sang along to 'Orinoco Flow' as the energy baited by Saturday traffic gave way to the blasted palms of the coast.

Other people's Saturdays, crowded cars and plodding joggers and café terraces, passed with infectious aspiration. This was pleasure here – neighbourliness, retirement. A mist that seemed to suggest reticence laid restfully over the sea.

Sunny said, 'Oh no,' and vomited her ice lolly. Lena changed her T-shirt in the car park of a carvery pub. They passed the marshy flatlands of the bird sanctuary and were swallowed by the blossom tunnels of the countryside. This was not committed countryside, but a land of greenhouses shining in the afternoon sun. The air tasted of hot soil and sea salt through open windows.

'Where are we going?' Sunny, back in her bumper seat, asked.

'To see houses,' Lena trilled.

'I don't want to.'

'Not for long. Just a look, OK?'

A short row of narrow reddish houses stood on a flattened site, with bunting and gravel demarcated for parking. Lena's attention fell on a crop of giant hogweed looming at the edge of a ditch like sea monsters.

'Have we seen this one before?' Odhran asked.

'No.' Lena was unpopping Sunny from her seat.

'Can I have treats?' Sunny asked at once. She scrambled down, forgetting the request, making for the showhouse. There were balloons.

Odhran asked Lena too quickly if she could imagine herself here: yes, she said, she could imagine herself anywhere.

Cian and Lena had, at one time, a conversation. They were talking with friends – with some of Cian's friends, a couple who lived in a housing estate that was an earlier iteration of this current, brand-new, housing estate – about an interview in the press with a French writer who'd been living in Ireland for a while but was now leaving for Spain. In the interview, the writer remarked that, while the Spanish and Irish were both Catholic and repressed, Spanish people had broken with the Church because they were interested in sex. The Irish had broken with the Church because they were interested in money.

This was a shaming indictment. Even Lena, young and awestruck by disposition, understood that. The men, Cian and his friend, agreed. Irish people were only interested in money. This made them boring, venal, culturally basic and emotionally immature. It also kept everyone busy and provided a principle around which to organise life when religion was gone. At the same time, for people like Cian and his friend, and like, by extension, Lena, poverty and indifference to money made them not un-Irish but somehow more Irish, in a sincere and original way. She'd believed this, she realised later, for a really long time.

'In every one of these houses,' Cian told her later – meaning, she deduced, the house they'd visited – 'there are wire CD racks and kitchen tables and, like, laminate flooring. The sound quality is the same. I mean, your voice sounds like it's ringing in an empty space.'

He'd been driving, not looking at her. She often felt deeply melancholy for him, even then, because he seemed never to allow himself to enjoy anything.

Sunny was now in the backyard of the showhouse, which was a rectangle of plush new turf without any plants. She had unplaited one plait and was stroking it in distraction.

'Do you feel sick?' Lena asked her, putting a hand to her forehead.

Each time she did this she recalled, with a sting of alarm, the last visit to A&E and the child in resuscitation. Had the child died? Who had it been?

Mostly, Lena avoided this path of thought, but it could

disturb her in lonely moments, like this moment, which felt like a small flake of known loneliness in a new location: the loneliness of days spent in a house or apartment, caring for a child. If they moved here, her life would be close to how it was now, but with two floors. Maybe other mothers, suburban mothers, to replace the urbane and bitchy and basically enjoyable Caoimhe and Orla. Long dresses, she thought suddenly, with splashy patterns. Dressing like a wedding guest at weekends.

Each room of the showhouse was different and each painted in provoking colours – deep navy, yellow orange, pond green. Furniture was unmatched and surprising and tiny. It smelt richly of vanilla pods. Each light fixture was startling, bulbous, like couture. Self-conscious couples with bored children and older people – people with money – crushed through it, cringing apologetically at one another. The two young estate agents were busy flirting together. In this last long patch of garden, Sunny reached the end of her tolerance.

They set off on their journey back to the city. It was evening now.

'It's nowhere near the station,' Lena remarked, using her local knowledge for the first time. The only other relevant thought had been a realisation that one of her schoolmates once lived close by; she'd spent the night at a sleepover in the family's bungalow, running through the field at night with knobs of burning sage for some reason.

She could imagine, yes, life in a house out here. She could see raincoats heaped on the bulb of a banister and smell a lingering dinner as it wandered through the rooms like a child on a rainy day. She could feel the coolness of rain suspended in the air above yielding turf when she opened a back door to call a cat or deposit a binbag. She was not angry at this vision, nor especially stimulated by it. Precisely what boundaries she might use to define herself, what taste might represent to her, were weak categories of knowledge now. But probably she did not want to live in a housing estate; probably she needed the city around her.

'It wasn't for me,' Odhran said. He was thinking.

That evening, he said, 'Here is what I'm thinking. Something we should think about. Maybe we should move away from Dublin altogether.'

'To Clare,' Lena said, anticipating.

'Yeah.'

She allowed for a pause before saying, 'No work.'

'I could apply for remote and drive in, say, once a week only.'

'Me.'

'Not necessarily. Not necessarily at all – you think there's nothing down there because you come from Dublin. But there's lots. And Galway and Cork as well, they are drivable.'

'Odhran,' she laughed. 'They are not.'

'In Clare we could afford something on my salary.'

'Would it be one of your mother's houses?'

'It doesn't have to be,' he said.

'Can I think about it?' she asked.

He looked happy. 'Of course,' he said.

They were sitting on the balcony, in the last of the blue-pink evening, because the forecast was for warm grey rain soon. They'd been drinking from bottles of light beer. Across the street, in the flats, somebody was playing dance music from a balcony and the children – who always seemed to move as a group – were whooping and rallying. Dogs were walked below. Each owner paused to check their smartphone whenever the dog stopped to pee. The trees of the Park looked like static explosions.

During the pandemic lockdown, when Sunny was tiny and Lena's sense of shrinkage, of her needs and routes and ambitions withering in real time, truly took root, you could stand on this balcony and hear such country silence, like the birds discoursing in the trees of the Park carried in a low mesh of sound, which, once tapped into, filled the mind like hallucination.

Then, the smell of fertiliser and of new growth on the

riverbanks travelled to the balcony too. Sunny, the monkey-bundle, could rest in Odhran's arms and look sagely over a world that seemed a century younger than it was.

Lena stepped inside now, and met the contained heat of the apartment. She felt attached to it, she moved inside it like familiar clothes. She used the bathroom, then peered into Sunny's boxroom, which was dim and smelt of menthol. Always she wanted to get into Sunny's bed, to spoon or cradle her, but knew that this would wake her and that would be a disaster. She could write a song about the great romance and luxury of those hours when a child slept. Maybe she would write songs if she lived in Clare and didn't have to think of work ever again.

She had worked, enjoyed her work, in the Georgian house museum. She led people through tight, miniaturised, ornate rooms, and into the big central reception room with its bouquet of music and fruits in plaster on the ceiling, its gold leaf, its fireplace; she imagined, herself, some drunken squire lately returned from church-burning, calling for raspberry port, drying himself by this fire – some great ghoulish mound of a person. Pox.

'Georgian society in Dublin was always kind of proximate to Satan.' She'd said this to Odhran early in their acquaintance, for some reason. Proximate to Satan.

She crossed back to the balcony. The air was so heavy around her. Would she lie down and die if someone did not do life for her? She was so often so tired, you see.

'Next weekend,' she said to Odhran, 'when we go to Clare? Don't say anything about thinking of moving there. I don't want Sonia, you know.' She wished to be tactful. 'I don't want Sonia getting ideas about it.'

'No, of course not.' He was grateful.

II

There were five more days of Montessori left. The weather, after May Day, changed: rain tore through the dead heat and then relaxed. It was still warm, but the air tingled with imminent, stormy energy, and the dirt of the city became a live odour, the odour of earth.

At ten o'clock on Wednesday, one hour after she'd left Sunny at Montessori, Lena received a phone call from one of the staff.

'Sunny is upset,' the woman said plainly. 'Very upset here now.'

'Is she sick?' Lena was confused.

'No, she is very upset, and we think we need Mammy to come.'

Lena was halfway to the junction on her bike, pushing the heaviest gear as if walking through a peat bog, when she realised the bike was a bad idea. She felt disorganised and spun into the world half awake.

Sunny was sobbing a little still when her mother arrived. 'Baby hen,' Lena hurried to her. 'What happened?'

The children had seen an airplane in the sky, inching over the small concrete garden they played in. One little girl had insisted that the chemtrail was a rainbow; Sunny, infuriated, had told her it was *a chemtrail*. Lena had not realised Sunny knew this word.

Is a rainbow, said the girl.

It's not a rainbow.

It is if I say.

It is a chemtrail, Sunny had shrieked, and then she climbed over the flowerbeds and clung to a greasy, rainy railing and refused to move even when the rain came back. The other children had watched her, delighted, from a window. Nobody could manhandle Sunny and she could only be compelled to get off the railing, they said, when Lena was called.

'We told her Mammy was coming,' they explained.

'Well first of all,' Lena said, 'it sounds like it was a chemtrail.'

They did not find this funny.

Lena brought Sunny home, by the hand, leading the bike like a pony beside her.

In the lift, she spoke. 'Sunny, why did you get so annoyed?'

'I can't remember,' Sunny said. But in the apartment she lay on the sofa and cried. She had a slight temperature, Lena told Odhran later, but it went down easily. It was wholly emotional. The outburst – it was all emotional.

Odhran said, 'I don't get it.'

Lena said, 'Don't look at me like I should.'

She went to bed and could not forget about it. It was at this point that the guilt began.

Should something awful be wrong, should something be pathologically wrong with Sunny, surely she needed to know?

By *pathological* she realised she meant something like mental disturbance; like mental decay. Like mental health. Did a four-year-old have mental health? Emotional health? You cannot just decide anything is a rainbow *because you say* and maybe Sunny, vehement and certain as she was, felt only irritated at the self-indulgence, which was understandable. But the intensity seemed problematic.

Words like *comorbid*, *disordered*, *polarity* – these words sprang up like dull objects in Lena's mind. She thought of those children who walked around in furious circles or could not be reached, could not be spoken to. The gluey backwards chant of Mass. A little girl she knew in childhood who came around the back of the house to poke Lena in the belly button and say, ladies bleed out of their belly buttons. And afterwards Lena's mother banned her from playing with that girl again.

Her mother had also asked her, when she was pregnant and visiting Naul, 'And what will you do if the child has a disability?'

'Deal with it,' Lena had turned back firmly.

'And how?'

'Well I wouldn't know how until it happened.'

'You would still have it,' her mother had said. Lena realised she was referring to the private screening test she and Odhran had waved off casually, setting the brochure tactfully aside. It had once been illegal and now cost five hundred euros and was not, they felt, necessary, with their being so fascistically healthy, or imagining themselves to be fascistically fortunate.

'I would still have it.' Lena had frowned and held her mother's gaze as she replied.

'Well good,' her mother said flintily.

In the morning, Lena had Odhran drive them, before work, to the GP clinic off the Navan Road. Lena was still registered with a GP here, because it was impossible to find a new GP willing to take patients in Greater Dublin.

She disliked him. He was a thin man with glasses, her own age, who'd once refused to remove a skin-tag from the side of her left breast on the grounds that he did not have staff to supervise *and ensure no allegations of misconduct* should she bare for him her breasts. This was not something Lena would ever forget, but clearly the doctor had forgotten and greeted Sunny, now, directly, like rapping on a drum: 'How are you today, miss?'

'I'm fine, thank you,' Sunny said.

'This will sound strange,' Lena began, heart sinking with self-consciousness, 'but I'd like to ask about checking Sunniva out. With – like, an MRI scan,' she said.

He stared at her with a tiny curl of the lip. It was the breasts all over again. He asked questions and, as he did, he cuffed

Sunny to the blood-pressure machine and continued to speak to Sunny instead. 'This will squeeze-squeeze-squeeze!' he said.

'The nurse could take bloods, another day this week,' he suggested.

'What do you think?' Lena assumed a look of concern. The man was so young-looking – small and poorly developed, as if he'd been ill or was still ill.

'What,' he asked, 'does Sunniva think?'

'Mama,' Sunny told him seriously, 'doesn't remember when I died.'

Lena could have snatched her up into a hug. Instead she nodded seriously.

'Yes,' she said. 'Yes, that is exactly what I mean.'

'Let me call Ava,' the doctor decided. He called her then and there; she was the nurse, and took Sunny and Lena into a slight little sterile room. Lena did not know why bloods were being taken in any capacity and, when she asked, Ava smiled grimly through rabbit teeth.

'Iron and white blood cells and so on,' she said. 'We'll see if this girl is a healthy girl.' To Sunny, she explained, 'This will pinch.'

'You can have treats after, sweetheart,' Lena said.

The little girl cried and cried afterwards and was sobbing still in the Insomnia Coffee, huff-huffing before her fruit muffin.

'I OK,' she sighed eventually.

Lena had not, she saw, got far. Delicate as she had been, they did not take her seriously. Probably there was some coded note on her own file now, some variant of 'MOTHER CONCERN'.

She reached across and stroked the little girl's cheek. Sunny flinched.

'Am I sick?' she asked.

'You're not sick,' Lena said, 'but the things you say about dying before, about the mama of before, we are wondering why you say these things.'

'Should I not say that?'

Lena sighed. She felt tired again.

'You should say whatever you want,' she said. 'Like, for instance – if you are sad.'

'Sometimes body makes me sad,' Sunny said again. She was dragging a fingernail, like a paper pearl, back and forth through a scatter of water droplets on the surface of the table. Above her head, the two tongues of a plastic plant extended from a shelf. A woman at the till announced suddenly, strangely and much too loudly, 'And do you know what else? He cannot taste a thing at all.' The barista nodded blankly through a plume of steam. It did not have the desired effect and the woman said, more vigorously, 'Not a fucken thing.'

'Can you explain,' Lena asked, 'what you mean – how does your body make you sad?'

Sunny's eyes were downcast. She answered, 'It just makes me sad.' She glanced up abruptly then, tossing back a wad of hair. 'I can't live like this,' she pledged. It was a line from *Frozen*, the Disney film. Lena smiled broadly.

'I can't live like this!' She echoed back.

Her phone, just then, began to whine. Expecting Odhran, Lena was surprised to see the doctor's number flashing up.

'I just have some more questions,' he said, 'and a gap in my schedule. Does she talk about being alive in, say, a specific time?'

It was such an odd question Lena frowned and looked beyond Sunny to the car park, the window now smattered by a shower of rain. The pellets of rain looked thrown, like a handful of stones.

'No,' she said.

'I suppose I wonder if she's been watching or reading something.'

'Yes. But she's four.'

'And then what I should have said in your consultation, really, is that we need to think of you, of what is going on for you, mentally.'

'Uh-huh.' Lena was unyielding.

'And I don't see any diagnosis here of PND, but you might have seen another doctor for that.'

'I was never diagnosed with postnatal depression.' Lena nodded thanks as the barista, freed from the loud woman, dropped a piece of paper and a plastic cup of chewed-looking colouring pencils onto the table. Sunny plucked one of these dutifully up.

'You can make an appointment through the secretary to come back and talk about that.'

She would not. They would grasp at it and write her off as malingering. They would blame her for Munchausen's by proxy. Something stealthy and insidious like this. She rehearsed her excuses to Odhran, who would ask. It was a *them* thing, she would say.

They had form. At thirty-five weeks, presenting to the midwife clinic on Thomas Street, Lena had been told the baby was shaping up to be nine pounds at full term and began to panic. 'I can't do that,' she said. It was too big, she meant. She would die of a nine-pound vaginal delivery. She could imagine vein-webbed membranes swelling and splitting apart, the pain hot and particular even as the machine pain of labour mowed on.

The midwife had assumed a look of incredible insincerity and asked, in a honey voice, 'Whyever not? Why are you so upset?'

'I'm too small.'

'The body can do amazing things,' the midwife said. Still, her eyes were artificially wide and her lie like a nursery rhyme. These people were simply never on your side.

'How would I go,' Lena asked the GP now, 'about getting a referral for an MRI?'

His pause was false, rhetorical and cruel. 'Why?' he asked.

'In case there is something going on. With.' She looked at Sunny. 'With the brain.'

'To be honest, you may have to go into A&E for something like that.'

Oh my God what bullshit, she would say to Odhran later: what a prick.

'I'll do that so.' She set her jaw.

'I'm dialling you through to reception,' he said.

Lena hung up when he did. It was raining, truly wetly, now. She would order a cab. She would not be walking anywhere.

Sunny was born deliciously robust, fat and pink as a Renaissance Christ child, and eight pounds ten. Her face was round as a large piece of fruit. They'd never seen so round a face. In the ward every other mother had undergone an emergency caesarean and only Lena could walk; she abused the shower, using it twice a day, sending jets of water from the peribottle up between her legs, emptying her bowels like a good patient, eating chicken dinners at midday.

One woman lay, post-haemorrhage and croaking into a phone, by her silent baby, who was swollen out with diabetes; the other woman turned her face away when the consultant came to speak to her. Turned her face clean away and stared at the wall.

Lena had watched them closely, these luckless women, from the side of her eye. She felt spared and springy and relieved to have only a tear.

If she did it again, she might not be so fortunate, she thought. The bottom might fall fully out of her. This was one of the reasons she was frightened about doing it again.

Sunny's good health, her resilience, had continued through each infant illness and weaning and receiving positive reports from Montessori, where she enjoyed tidying the bean-shakers, wooden pegs, flowerheads. Where she once flushed an overfull toilet, causing the water to crest and cascade over the rim, then belted silently – sensibly – out the door to the yard behind the building, only halting when she knew she was clear and safe.

Odhran was right to observe that she was happy, and healthy, and intelligent, and there was no reason why her mother – equally robust – could not give her siblings. It had been easy to fall pregnant the first time, as easy as a sleight of hand, a forgotten ritual, a stroke of deep ancestral competence.

But there was a time, when Sunny was younger, in which Lena was unhappy. Late autumn in that year had a feral palette so that, in the afternoons especially, things appeared singed by – seriously – hellfire; desolate but menacing.

At such times in her life, when she was unhappy or macabre, Lena was reminded rhythmically, in the sense of a plainly circadian reflex native to her nervous system, of certain minor but formative traumas from childhood. Quite a few were descriptions of madness. Her father often told his children things he should never have told them. This is how she knew there was a priest who liked to chew on grass and mutter to himself, compulsively, the word *psychiatric*, pronouncing it *seeky-atric, seeky-atric*. She also knew of a schizophrenic who rose at dawn, when ill, to see the three crosses of Golgotha – Christ and the thieves – emerge from a torment of storm clouds and pour light into the sea.

In that feral and igneous autumn, when Sunny was almost two, Lena imagined these crosses crowning from the reddish dawns she watched from the balcony. She felt like this was perhaps an album cover she'd seen or something but also the testament of the schizophrenic, which disturbed her enough to take lustre and remain in her mind for the rest of her life. She was not going mad but giving image to a feeling of contagion and dread that persisted all day, peaking in the small hours of the morning, when the baby woke up and screamed.

Like an iron spike, the sound of the baby's cry. Lena's body bolting upright into instinct and sprinting to the baby's room. Sunny bellowed from her cot and reached for her mother, shouting, 'Up!' She began each session with this searing and immediate, dialled-up cry, not gathering strength incrementally or building to anything – just straight in, planar, with the rage of an illogical god. It was the worst sound in the world. Lena would never get used to it.

'No,' she would say, 'no, lie down, baby, lie back down.'

The baby would not. It could really go on. Ten minutes, twenty, stretching without losing intensity – peril, the world was ending, the baby would die of not being lifted up. When Lena relented and lifted her, Sunny would sob and swing her head back, crashing her forehead against Lena's collarbone; if the cries subsided, it was only for as long as she was held. Placing her back in the cot was like lowering a cat into a bath: Sunny clung to the edges animally, commenced her death shriek once again, kept this up for – oh, forty minutes, an hour, two hours even; often Lena was still up, warming a bottle of milk or letting Sunny pace warily around the dark apartment, three hours later. Night after night.

Midnight to 6 a.m. became contaminated. It was impossible to reclaim the sleep. Lena felt foggy and depressed. It seemed it would never relent.

She began in these sunken hours to experience a numbness towards Sunny, and then sometimes to feel hatred for her child; for her life, for the decision she had made so stupidly; she'd want to smash objects or jump clean off the satanic balcony.

'I should never have had you,' she said to the baby, who screamed.

'I should fucking kill myself,' she said.

And then, during the day, Sunny would often clasp Lena's leg silently while Lena was cooking or cleaning or pausing, fatigued, to stare into space, and Lena knew this was because the baby felt uncertain if her mother loved her; felt remote, unloved, and this was Lena's fault, because, after all, Sunny could not help her toddler need for sovereignty and broken sleep and cubbish panic at being, theoretically, sleep trained. It pained her to experience and to look back on now, flushing with shame: I wish I'd never had you, how I want to die.

Everything that happened around a baby would be absorbed. Goose penis, for example. Like, what the hell was that. But no – she had also been told an alarming amount of it, of personality and disposition, was genetic, and somehow that felt qualitatively worse.

There was a cab here now. The light had flattened completely. It was raining in a large way, cold and loose, falling straight, like thin old copper money long ago.

12

Lena had, in her teens and twenties, written songs for the band. She wrote one, for example, about a day in her childhood: she was nine or ten years old, and her mother handed her and Rex a crisp, unforgettable tenner to buy lunch in Macari's. Such profligacy was so rare it should have aroused suspicion, but it didn't, because Lena and Rex – who was seven or eight years old – were distracted by the plan.

They sat in a plastic booth in Macari's. They shared a tray of chicken and chips and two cardboard cups of milkshake, liquid stiff enough to stand in the straw, and watched people pass by in the sunshine. The place was empty but for Lena and Rex and the man behind the counter. Talk radio was playing very loud. After the news bugle, a voice declared that the death of a woman in Balbriggan had been upgraded to murder by the gardaí and then named the woman concerned. She was an elder sister of Lena's schoolfriend, and she had fallen down the stairs. But actually she hadn't fallen down the stairs: she'd been murdered by her boyfriend, whom she lived with on Harbour Street. She'd been beaten and thrown down the stairs.

It was a huge deal. Murders were even rarer than largesse. The pure gust of the newsreader's voice remained with Lena all her life, its confidence, the transformative stroke of local naming, the lust for gossip and distinction that still affected her if she heard the word *Balbriggan*. Evermore were the salt of the chicken nuggets, the milkshake standing in the straw, spritzed and mythological in her mind.

She had many beautiful memories of childhood: of the beach and the library and the cold prompt properness of school, of singing *take me back to the black hills, the black hills of Dakota* from the stage of the convent auditorium, of the blessing of boats and graves and the opening of a nightclub and dancing to 'Komodo' and the student days she spent taking orders in a little brown café. Of waiting on the rain-black platform for a train to town and singing lessons at the Academy. But this lurid punch of bloodlust, an event in which she had less than a peripheral part, was the one she wrote a song about. The song was called 'Draft' and although it was only a B-side, it was something people still mentioned to her.

'Of all the songs you've written,' Sonia asked, 'what is your favourite?'

'It's a song called "Draft",' Lena said.

They were in Clare, and outdoors, in the late evening. Lena looked around the garden table, a wooden circle in need of staining, and at the hacienda archway a few yards away. Citronella candles like yellow cakes burnt on the outdoor shelves of the archway, which led to a covered alcove and the back door of the house. It had been added to the farmhouse in the seventies and resembled a pontoon dock. Sunny liked to jump off it and shout: splash!

The early-May night was warm, and Sunny rather recently asleep in Odhran's old bedroom upstairs, wearing her new pyjamas. Sonia had opened a bottle of wine and led them to the garden table, the patio of mulch, to celebrate. Ceremony was something she did. She was a gregarious person. It was a word Lena had, in the early days of life as a daughter-in-law, struggled to hit upon; the word of Odhran's world.

'Gregarious,' he'd said, a little leadenly. 'It's a Munster thing.'

It was, though it could be warmer than Sonia's edgy incarnation. She was socially gracious but sort of steely and remembered every single thing you said, was liable to bring up even minor things – concessions, fine details, admissions, dismissals.

She was smoking a cigarette now, a quirk she described as a treat. She held it up freshly, with poise, like a film character. It made her look young. You saw the beauty she had been.

Odhran pulled his phone out and found 'Draft' on Spotify. To him this sort of thing was an act of love, but Lena cringed as her voice wavered in a tease and then steadied, and sang about clouds looming like Christmas toys and ordinary death.

It was not a murder ballad – it sounded like a love song.

'You have a beautiful voice,' said Sonia, 'and it's a shame you don't do it anymore. Was there a lot of glamour to it, music?' she asked.

'No, there was a lot of budget touring,' Lena laughed. 'We used to go to Berlin to have recordings mixed because there was a guy who did it cheaper there, until – I guess with the main album, the one we released when we were signed and so on, the one you can, you know, *buy* – that was a producer in Kells; we lived with him for a few weeks. Camp beds in the barn. We were managed by Mikey O'Hara for a while.'

'He's a property guy now,' supplied Odhran. 'And he owns bars and things.'

'An impresario.' Lena reined it in. She was liable to become effusive in the light of their attention; always she regretted loosening into effusion around Sonia.

'You were really very good,' Sonia repeated. She glanced at Odhran, who was scrolling on his phone. He put it down. 'Still working, are you, sir?'

'That's it now.' He blushed.

'It amazes me, the bad manners,' Sonia said. 'The first time someone picked up their phone and started texting or whatever in the middle of a conversation with me – well.' She drifted the cigarette into the citronella dimness around them, expressively. 'I thought some terrible news had come in.' She looked at Lena.

'He was better about it when we first started dating.' Lena

smiled coldly. 'He would always say *sorry, I just have to check this*, and be quick. It pained him to be rude.'

'Yes, they behave well at the start.'

Odhran said, 'Lena does it too.'

'I do not.' Lena continued to smile. 'I read something that said looking at your phone, or a screen, when you're with children makes them feel empty, and I knew what it meant. My mother was a very preoccupied person,' she said. 'We never got on.'

Sonia's enthusiasm, which could seem like warmth, often tempted Lena into reflecting ungenerously on her own mother. This was in spite of the fact that Odhran told her that Sonia, a GP for all of her adult life, would leave them with the housekeeper during the long many-brothered summers of childhood. His father worked as an accountant. Together they owned properties dotted about Lough Derg, in Mountshannon and Scariff and Killaloe.

Odhran's first memory was of being dragged, by the ankles, from under a couch by the housekeeper.

'It wasn't enlightened,' he said. But Sonia was, Lena felt, enlightened now – wreathed by grandchildren, holiday tan.

'I try to stay off the phone around Sunny,' Lena concluded, looping back.

'God only knows what these phones are doing,' Sonia said.

The song had completed and another, from the album, began to play. Lena did not need to ask Odhran to change it; he switched up, setting off the Mary Latimer playlist they liked to listen to in the car. Certain hooks, the wistful efflorescence of harp, put Lena in mind at once of billboards and specific windfarms on the road from Dublin to Clare.

'Draft' was an OK song, melodically, but the way in which she'd seeded the story into the lyrics, the way in which she'd tried to obscure her egoistic impulse to dramatise, seemed so juvenile and obvious to her at this distance it made her fatigued. Not ashamed but bored. It was an exercise she did: to raise these past versions of herself like cards, to turn them over and contemplate, allowing life and blood to drain right out of them and dying to herself, in miniature, repeatedly. Since the encounter with the GP on the Navan Road last week she had also been trying to do this, in quiet moments, with the grainy memories of what he – the GP – might have called *PND* in his lightly scathing, practised tone.

Much of it was a secret, you see. Odhran had not seen her threatening to kill herself. Nobody knew of her recurring dream about walking through the blasted archway holding the severed foot of a child; never had she sketched for anyone the smouldering crosses at Golgotha. She did not describe to anyone the days she had spent not eating in pregnancy because her throat would close – those blurry days of muffled ears and pearly light and a sense that maybe life could stop or just suspend itself for long enough that she might get some objectivity – nor the cool, quiet sensation of pure detachment she could still achieve sometimes, like a comfort break. It was unpleasant to wonder if these tendencies could contaminate Sunny.

But just now she felt happy. It was pleasant already to sit in the smoky, pinkish dusk of citronella and look at the mountains shouldering into one another overhead; to see the distant pylons of the aerial tower and lonesome porchlights glowing on the mountainside. It was pleasant to think about Maeve, Odhran's sister, arriving tomorrow.

'You will drive to the airport,' Sonia rehearsed again. 'Will Sunny want to go?'

'I will dissuade her,' said Lena, lifting her glass. 'She won't enjoy it. She might get sick as well. And Shannon is not as exciting as Dublin airport – she thinks she's getting Burger King if she goes.' Pleasant also to share this fondness with another interested woman. Dear examples of Sunny's cuteness often seemed to slide off Odhran's automatic smile.

'You're staying the whole week to see Maeve?'

'Part of the week. Odhran can work from upstairs if he has to.'

‘It’s a quiet time.’ Odhran yawned. At home, in this house, he became lazy. Lena found his behaviours privately childish, how he waited to be waited on, and never washed up. Most of the holidays they took were to this place, barring one or two breathless jags to London. This struck her now as tragic. She looked at Sonia, who holidayed all the time, in the manner of her generation, flying places to sit in the sun with widowed friends from her doctoring days.

It was another casualty of early ego-devotion to *authenticity* that Lena had neither holiday habits nor old – in the sense of established and disinterested – friends.

‘Before it’s too dark,’ she found herself proposing, ‘can I take a little walk?’

‘I’ll come with you.’ Odhran stood up.

They felt like kids out of earshot of the adults, with Sunny gone. They moved in the dusk beneath a slant of outdoor lights and into the vegetable garden, where a pretty little greenhouse sat in outline, like an ornamental lantern. Three romaine lettuces Lena had toured earlier seemed to be the only things still open and green. A hedge that was simply too thick – distractingly, haggishly thick – had an arch cut into it which echoed the hacienda arch of the farmhouse. It was not unlike a dream or like the setting of her nightmare of the severed foot of a child.

The house was half an acre away by now. Through the arch, empty arable fields opened in total silence and dissolved into greenish gloam.

This land no longer belonged to the family but to an amalgamated neighbouring farm. It was sold before Odhran was born. A spare, aged uncle had managed it, apparently, when his parents had died, but soon hit out for England and left the gun dogs locked in a shed. Literally. They were half starved by the time someone called Odhran’s father. He sold it all happily.

‘Farming is a bust,’ Odhran said. ‘Or farming on that scale.’

The uncle died in London when Odhran was a child. This

was how they found out where he'd disappeared to after locking up the dogs.

The arch of foamy hedge made it look as though the fields were a wonderland, a zone beyond the threshold of culture, when really they were only silent and brown. Here there were paving stones set in a circle around the large vegetable patch.

Lena walked. She said, breaking the silence, 'It's just lovely tonight.'

'I'm relaxing,' Odhran said. 'Feeling the work-head loosen up.'

'That's good.'

'It's just these mad things people send,' he continued, 'criticising things. Random things.' There were stars above – layers of them.

Lena knew all about what was going on. She knew Odhran was organising a symposium at which delegates would discuss what to do with the large, redacted archive of patient records collected from three Dublin asylums that had operated into the noughties but dated back, more or less, to the Free State. Specialists and academics from Europe would come and give examples of how similar data in Norway or Portugal or regional Britain had been analysed and used. There was a chance, he explained, to do something ethical or helpful or maybe influence future policy, though ultimately it would all be outrage and condemnation and editorials and other things people liked to do in the Humanities. Lena was ambiently interested in this project because of her father; she'd been less interested in the digital archiving projects, the artificial intelligence projects, the three-dimensional online resource for mapping projects.

She smiled now. 'First it's fun and then it's tedious,' she said.

She'd borrowed this: she paraphrased him. She was, she thought drily, such a diligent wife.

He ignored her.

He asked, after a silence, 'Does Sunny like it here?'

'Yes,' Lena said blankly.

'She went to sleep so easily.'

'We are on holidays.' Her voice was sharp.

'Of course.' He reached out and caught Lena's swinging hand, surprising her.

Sunny was abundant in Clare. She left Lena alone for hours at a time, amused by somebody or something else. It left her mother with new craters of headspace in which earworms and grudges circulated vaguely; in which she could not think of where to put her energy.

'The pressure is off here,' she said, airily, exploring.

'Totally. You seem calm.'

'Am I not generally calm?'

He looked at her with something like a smirk and she laughed and said, 'Am I the problem? Am I neurotic? Is our kid weird because of me?'

He smiled ahead, shaking his head. 'Not weird. Just a little intense.'

'I am intense,' she said. 'Yes. I have always been told I'm intense. You know, the doctor wanted me to come in and talk to him separately.'

Odhran raised an eyebrow.

'About being intense.'

'I don't understand.'

'About being *depressed* and, I don't know – influencing Sunny, exaggerating.'

'You're not depressed.' He seemed affronted on her behalf. She was grateful and then distantly insulted by the tone of authority. His eldest brother, Cathal, had been depressed at some point, to such an extent it created a family problem and everyone else seemed to maintain a kind of winnowed but persistent animus against him for this reason. She would not like to think Odhran would judge her, howsoever dully, for being depressed.

'Well I mean,' she said, 'I'm just intense.'

Lena wished she were alone in this landscape suddenly, with

the hills and the dimness functioning as a purely aesthetic event. It might rain tomorrow, or just remain grey.

They turned back to the house and saw a slip of moon shining over the roof. Sonia had gathered in the glasses and blown out most of the candles and disappeared inside. Seeing this, Odhran said, 'Let's hang on a bit.'

In the darkness, at the table, he took her hands. 'I'd like to fuck.'

'Where, though?' Lena sat up. She had not expected that.

'Greenhouse,' he answered, unsmiling.

'You are terrible,' she said.

But she followed him impishly, back over the path to the greenhouse and the gloating romaine lettuce and the disenchanted arch. When they re-emerged a half-hour later the house itself was as still and quiet as the fields.

13

Asleep in the attic room, neither Lena nor Odhran heard Sunny whimpering, weakly, after two. But Sonia did, and Sonia climbed the stairs.

'What's this?' she asked softly, coming through the door.

The child sat up in bed, her little face severe and beautiful in the moonlight. The room had been one of the boys', long ago – there was still a strip of football stickers level with Sunny's elbows on the wall. Sonia lit upon this at once.

'Desperate,' she said. She sat on the bed and inclined to the task of picking at the corner of a sticker with her fingernail.

'I'm sad,' Sunny said.

'Did you have a bad dream?'

The plaits walloped softly to and fro as Sunny shook her head.

'Look now,' said Sonia, peeling a sticker away. It left grey adhesive like a stain.

'You ripped the wall.' Sunny was amazed.

'Oh it's all to be painted. All of it. Looks appalling. And now,' she turned with a smile to the child, 'if you say nothing to Mammy and Daddy, do you want to come downstairs and keep me company?'

Sunny had a way of communicating thrill, and agreement: she flared her nostrils and nodded her head, looking scandalised. She climbed out of the bed in a thin knee-length nightie with a character on it, something indistinct.

'Who is this?' Sonia asked. Sunny glanced down.

'Is Igglepiggle,' Sunny said.

'And who is he when he's at home?'

Sunny giggled woodenly.

Sonia said, 'Let's find you a cardigan.'

The steep, shallow stairs of the farmhouse were lit by the light of a white lamp on the phone table and bare but for three holy pictures that had been hanging there for all eternity and were, at this point, invisible to Sonia.

Sonia was also awake on account of a dream. She could not remember the content, only waking with a jerk at midnight – which was not long after she had gone to bed – and thinking clearly of a girl she'd studied medicine with decades before, feeling the full name of this woman in her mouth, since of course this girl grew into a woman and married and had children and left medicine and died just recently. They'd got a round-robin email from the alumni organisation at University College Cork. There were many; death notices of known and unknown fellow students, but Sonia had paused at this one, maybe mentioned it to other people.

Oh, I studied with her long ago, she said. But she never practised medicine. Something about her father dying young, I think.

There were things Sonia could remember from that time. She still saw, for example, the empty face of her first dissection subject, but on reflection it sometimes twitched into the palsied face of a poor lady she had as a patient later, a diabetic, silver-eyed and rheumy, poorly dressed. Impossible the cadaver looked like that. And yet the face of her old friend, this woman whose life came back to her in sleep only as the elegant arc of a name, was beyond recall. They shared a room on a group holiday to Greece. Or was it Mallorca?

Sonia's own mother had died during one such holiday. She died when Sonia was away. Sonia was on the beach in her bikini when somebody from the resort reception came down to fetch her. She was twenty-three; her mother had suffered a stroke.

Sonia was narrating this to herself now, as she descended the stairs, in her head. I was twenty-three, so this was nineteen-seventy-seven. We were married in seventy-six and had Cathal right away. My mother never met my children. Can you imagine that?

She had said this aloud, this kind of thing – she said these things all the time. She looked back on her life and narrated it in a tone of folksy wonder that was regionally specific and also unique to her; uniquely disassembling. She took a long time saying certain things so she could buy time and read people's expressions. That was a doctoring trick: watching people betray themselves gently, subtly, sometimes not so subtly, in a straight-backed chair.

So here she was awake with the past around her, and she never minded that, and here was Sunny also – not her youngest grandchild, but close. The elder ones had iPads and cystic acne and would not listen to her advice, not even when she sourced and sent a box to Dublin, to take chasteberry supplements.

'I'm down in the back room and I'm having a cup of tea,' she told the child.

'I want some water,' Sunny said.

Sonia filled a tumbler in her cold kitchen, then crossed to the cavelike parlour behind the stairs.

'I not know this was here,' Sunny said, looking around.

'You didn't know,' corrected Sonia. 'Well, this is Nana's special room.'

It was a women's parlour from the farm days; small but inviolate in its privacy, with a dresser of Delft and a shy fire set into a square of green tiles.

'You were in here too, when you were very small,' Sonia said, 'because your mother used to feed you in here – I remember her taking you in here to feed.'

'From her boobs,' Sunny specified.

'Yes.'

'Is there a ghost in this house?' Sunny sat on the couch, which was shallow and silver-grey. She seemed to be making herself comfortable, arranging a woollen antimacassar around her as if it were a blanket.

Sonia rested back in the armchair, resuming her tea. The grate was cold; her eyes fell on it, then shifted to Sunny.

'Well now, madam,' she said. 'You need to tell me if there are any ghosts in this house, because I don't see ghosts, I am an old lady.'

Sunny picked at her toenail. 'Why,' she asked, looking down, 'are you old?'

'People get old, everybody will. You won't be old for a long time, though. You have a long, long time left before you are old.'

'And I die.'

Sonia waited.

'Nobody remembers,' Sunny said now – sullenly, with purpose – 'when I died.'

'Well,' said Sonia, 'you don't seem to remember either.' Sunny cocked her head. 'You don't remember the details,' Sonia explained.

Sunny echoed *details* and screwed up her face in a faintly hammy way – it was one of her things. She had picked up these gestures from adults around her, or from television.

'Water at the side of the road is not details,' Sonia said.

'What's details?' Sunny asked.

It was possible to get bored and irritated quickly, but Sonia was willing to wait.

She had a patient, years ago: a permed woman with anorexia borne of family scarcity and a habit of going without, or of fixing myopically on what she could and couldn't eat, not because of vanity but because eating too much of something might leave siblings and elderly relatives and ultimately children – children and a husband who worked as a farm labourer – with insufficient food. Her philosophy, its scarcity and near sterility, was actually highly sensible. She was managing it so she could have more children. She became pregnant with twins, lost one, and came in of occasion for blood pressure checks.

The woman would bring, as Sonia narrated frankly in her head, the little girl, the surviving twin, and this twin became famous locally for not only remembering her twin – her brother, stillborn – but seeing him, pointing out where he was perching or sitting close to her, what he was thinking; she became famous locally for remembering, then, members of her family long dead before she was born, remembering for example the circumstances of an accidental death way back in the 1940s. She remembered somebody lost to appendicitis during the War. She remembered personalities from her townland. When a man went missing from Ballina, the little girl said *he is in dark water* and the man was later pulled out of the lake.

That child, Sonia reflected, would be in her thirties now. The family, everyone, had taken it in their stride – had not been perturbed, nor had Sonia. There were easy beliefs then, in folk remedies and a tame robin appearing in the garden after a death, about covering mirrors and stopping clocks and praying to Saint Anthony to find lost things, although personally Sonia found that habit a rankling, townie thing – Saint Anthony help me, Saint Anthony help me, people forever losing their keys and hats and throwing their hands up. That was childish. Find your own things. Somehow it was petty and polytheistic and primitive. And yet this surviving twin, the little girl, could see and know things and it seemed at the time mildly spooky but never perturbing – no, Sonia monologued privately again, protectively.

When Sonia monologued in her mind in this way, with an ardency that implied social stakes, she knew it was driven by loneliness, by a need for an interlocutor, by the need for her husband – dead – or her sisters, who lived abroad. It happened more and more lately and perhaps it had begun with an encounter, two or so years earlier, with a local psychic or medium or *woo woman* or whatever Aude was; a lady who'd spoken to her about her dead husband. She thought of Aude now. She was a young woman with a child and lived somewhere outside Feakle.

Sonia carried in her mind many lives and diagnoses and old friends who were, increasingly, searchable on RIP.ie. For most of life, you are striking forward and then suddenly, like an airplane finding its level after a tilt, things become planar and contained. You feel you are still, in space, occupying one room of many in – what? The kingdom of the lord? A life with more absences than presences, or at least more absences than before. It was perhaps this evolution that had released her from some of the suppositions and beliefs of her conservative career. She had always been open to letting people be ill in the way that they wanted to, and kept her religious beliefs – such as they were, mostly a matter of anniversary Masses and praying the rosary in trying times – separate. As she got older and sat through funerals, she couldn't help but wonder if the barriers between this world and the next were in fact more permeable, even malleable, than they had seemed. In many ways, such suspicions tallied perfectly with the folk beliefs of her parents and grandparents, all of whom were in the next world, or else still in this world, who knew, taking on some other form.

She did not know what she believed anymore. But it was not a stressful thought.

'Granny,' said Sunny. 'I think there is a dog in the front room.'

'Oh yes?'

'I see him. Is a brown dog.'

'You might well be right.'

Sunny looked at her, seeming to concentrate. Fuzz of new hair in halo at her forehead, each plait anchored with a patterned band.

'Is he a ghost?'

'He must be, there are no dogs here anymore.'

'He is a dog for finding birds,' Sunny said. 'But birds that are dead.'

Sonia was quiet.

At last she said, still quietly, 'A gun dog. That's what you call those dogs: gun dogs. They find birds that have been shot.'

And, of course, it was wholly possible the child had overheard some version of the story about Jackie, her husband's uncle, the man who locked up the gun dogs and vanished emphatically into London. Before Sonia's time here. It brought her to the place; this man she'd never met nor heard anything much about.

But then a night in the nineties, watching *Coronation Street*. The trill of the phone in the frigid hallway and the shock of being addressed by an officer of the Metropolitan Police. They had a box of ashes, a pauper's cremation, and last known address the now farmless farmhouse with its new family – Sonia's family. She felt protective of it. Did they wish to collect these ashes? Jackie had been hit by a train. He was living in a hostel. She had thought with horror of street drinking, stinking rags, red biddy. Good grief. Her husband would be wounded to hear about it. She'd need to ask him and call back. Could she have a number, a contact?

Sonia did not fancy flying to London for ashes, no. But Seán was swift: he flew out the next day, and interred the box of ashes himself in the family grave at Templekelly. She recalled him leaving at nightfall with a gardening trowel, since it was against regulations to stealth-bury ashes in paid-up graves. An image now more comical than macabre.

None of the children knew about this. She'd never told them about the call, the overground train, the plastic box of ashes like a schoolchild's sewing box.

Of course, they knew about the dogs. Her daughter, Maeve, lived in London now, and Sonia found herself saying to Maeve in silence, not for the first time, how you can stand that callous place, I do not know. People would walk over you in the street.

It was the right thing, of course, to bring the ashes back – who knew what restlessness a soul might feel if placed in a pauper's grave somewhere in Dagenham or whatever. Sonia felt a slight pernicious flush at having ever wanted to leave Jackie there. Forgive me, please, she thought.

'Gun dogs,' she repeated. 'They can be beautiful dogs, very sweet little things.'

'You should not shoot birds,' Sunny insisted suddenly. She looked astonished, tossing back her scratchy antimacassar. 'Nobody should hurt *birds*.' She seemed to find it funny and preposterous, much like the way children reacted, Sonia thought, when they found out where sausages came from.

'In the countryside, you see,' Sonia said, 'you can't have too many of certain birds. Pheasants, for example – let me tell you there is no stupider bird.'

Sunny was shrieking now, incredulous.

'Never mind birds anyway.' Sonia set aside the teacup, sitting forward. 'Tell me about the other things you see.'

14

Odhran woke first, early, when mist still clung to fields and hills and smudged the far horizon out. It burnt off as he travelled winding minor roads and onto the motorway, driving wide of Limerick City and past the eerie gridded town of Shannon to the airport.

Before and after the motorway he met tractors and trailers and slowed to a drag. It got hotter, like something willed. Overnight, they'd tilted into June.

In childhood the airport terminal at Shannon seemed to soar above Odhran, lavish and glassy, promising foreignness. These days, it looked squat, apologetic in design. The car parks were crammed, but everything seemed gloomy and sleepy inside, and as he arrived at the gate he saw his sister emerge at once, after a consignment of American military staff. The latter walked in two straight lines: they were not being drilled, they just walked that way.

Maeve was narrow and tall, with hair that was dark and narrow on her back. She looked like Sunny. She pulled a huge matte gold suitcase. Odhran, who had not had time to prepare himself or acclimatise to the dimness of the terminal, so immediate was her appearance, felt disoriented, and pointed to the suitcase.

'Staying all summer or what?'

'Presents,' she smiled. 'For the girls. Not for you.'

'I barely made it here on time,' he told her, taking the case by the handle. 'There was a lot of farm traffic.'

'Oh farm traffic,' she said. It was the start of hay saving time. It had been dry. Trailers clanking on axles like tentpoles took sudden corners without warning; wisps of straw caught in his windshield wipers. It didn't change, or not much, but felt, each time he came home, starker and more remarkable to see industry made visible in this way.

Over the years of living in Dublin home had first become reified, melancholically – as a reservoir of affections that felt static, Clare congealed, like something heavy Odhran was carrying around. This remained the case until, entering his late thirties, he began to shake it off and see it anew. Mostly because schoolfriends had commenced the drift back from Dublin and London and bought newbuilds, used their parents for childcare, popped up on LinkedIn working for multinationals in the Shannon Free Zone. They were clipped and cheerful and defensive about it. His brother Aidan knew two to three retired or just abdicated Irish-American compradors, men with reputations in the Kingdom of Saudi Arabia, who liked it here and so built passive mansions on the Shannon. These houses could be glimpsed brittlely, glinting between screens of copper beech, if driven by on certain roads.

You would not look at farm traffic and suspect any of this. He liked pointing it out to Lena when they drove around. Money simmering like wickedness in Arcadia – this was sexy, was it not? Also banal actually: the schoolfriends and their newbuilds, everything.

Maeve had been in London for four years. If she carried any congealed Clare with her, it didn't show. She had a boyfriend now, his mother had informed him the night before, but she wouldn't bring this boyfriend back; the boyfriend was a mystery.

Odhran relayed this to her now, as banter. She'd left when she finished college and he found it difficult, with the passage of time, to relate to her intimately or easily. There was more than a decade between them: he'd been thirteen when she was born, both averse to and distracted by the idea of his parents having sex. Because she was tall and striking and took care with her appearance in a simple way, unstyled but also streamlined, he found her intimidating.

'I will bring him back,' she said now, of the boyfriend. 'I'll show him the hay.' She looked around.

'Are you hungry or anything?'

'No, let's get on the road.'

In the car, he pestered. 'Why won't you take this guy home?'

'You know yourself.'

'I don't.'

She was grinning, but seemed tested by the question. 'You know. I'm not completely sure about him yet.'

'Heartless woman.'

'Yes.' She pushed off her trainers and pulled her knees to her chest. 'Now tell me,' she changed, 'about my Sunny-bun.'

He explained to her about starting school. She was technically registered to begin at a Catholic school – a large one, hundreds of children warehoused in what was admittedly a beautiful modernist building that looked like a monastery, like a Vatican Two monastery. This would be fine, but she wasn't baptised, obviously, and they didn't believe and so she remained on the waiting list for an Educate Together in Broombridge – longer commute but communist values, et cetera, and randomly it's considered a deprived area so they get hot meals.

'That sounds incredible,' said Maeve.

'It does, but she'll most likely be in the Catholic one.'

Lena was profoundly excited about Sunny starting school. She, Lena, had adored school, and sighed even over the Catholic uniform, which was basically just a tracksuit with piping and a crest. Lena knew Maeve would agree it was a shame the pleated pinafores of yore had been done away with in Catholic schools.

Maeve said, 'I *do* agree.'

She asked, 'And how is Lena?'

'I mean she's great,' Odhran replied.

'Is she going back to work?'

It was an unexpected question; planned. They were coming through Montpellier and soon the simple Soviet majesty of the hydroelectric dam would rise into their horizon. Lena loved the power station and the kitschy paintings of its construction by Seán Keating. She hadn't been brought there on school tours innumerable growing up.

'We'd love to see her go back to work,' Odhran said cautiously. 'But it's complicated. Although Sunny is starting school, so.' The river reappeared. Slanting banks of sheep wool wadded in the grass.

'I'd say she'd love to go back to work.'

He wondered if Maeve believed he was preventing Lena from doing this. It was almost purely the opposite. Without an outlet beyond sewing and Sunny and baking bread for some hysterical reason the tenser side of her personality came to the fore. Sometimes he came home to be greeted by her stiltedly, like a stranger; he would have then an uncanny sense that she'd been doing something underhanded or taboo before he came through the door. And oh the dread of returning in the early months of Sunny's life – she would have speeches prepared, how he'd led her on and let her down and now she was nothing but a skivvy, and all the time the apartment impossibly spotless; unnecessarily clean. The greedy engine of her attention. Things were so much better when she had a job.

'She's lost her confidence,' he decided. Someone, he realised, would tell Maeve about Sunny's past life pronouncements. If Sunny didn't say it herself. 'Sunny says funny things recently.'

'Oh my goodness, tell me.'

'She says she's been born before. She says she can remember her past life.'

'What?' Maeve turned to him now.

'Yeah.' He smiled weakly. 'It's kind of funny. See if she says it to you.'

'Wow.' He was relieved when she sat back. She said, 'Celestial child.' She did not seem to take it seriously; this was also a source of relief. Odhran felt embarrassed to talk about it, only able to bring it – thinly – to his mother, mostly out of helplessness. Sonia had done precisely what he'd wanted her to do, which was to claim it was no big deal. He loved when things were no big deal to Sonia. Things like failed love and work errors and public humiliation. Were his father alive, these things would be big deals; Odhran might sit shotgun by his father on this winding, frowsy road and feel the pained, expansive silence of concern or of his father's mind working its machinations, lining up solutions expensive, serious or humbling.

'Your turn,' he said. 'What's been going on with you?'

'The ladies,' she began. The ladies, her housemates in the dainty Dulwich houseshare, were at odds again. It related to the fact that one of them was having an affair with a married man. This was everybody's business after Tuesday Vermouth now. They'd been to see *À bout de souffle* in the BFI and now she realised it was actually very tedious, that film, and that NewYorkHeraldTribune! was responsible for a lot of bullshit, and now she'd been promoted in the buying department of the branch of Barbour where she worked, it felt harder to get out of there, and yes, she was trying to get out of there. They only needed her part-time.

'There is not,' she drawled, 'a lot of textile innovation going on at Barbour.'

She'd sold all of her graduate collection and there was more, there was the online shop, but if she wanted to set up an atelier it would need investment.

'Your fellow,' he said. She was quiet for a moment and he frowned. 'You're not the one having the affair, are you?'

'No, I am not the one having the affair. He's a guy from head office. He's divorced. He innovated a marketing plan for Gucci in the 1990s – designed a newsletter that looked like an art magazine. No, seriously, that was his ticket to ride.' She said, 'I don't even remember the nineties.'

'Sure you do. Clare won the all-Ireland twice.'

After the bend for home she rolled down the window, and a warm breeze vented the car with the smell of chemical fertiliser.

'Must you,' he said.

'Manna from heaven,' she laughed.

Odhran dragged the matte gold suitcase up the drive and Maeve went ahead, slightly shy as she ducked into the house and was embraced. Lena was there, with Sunny standing solemnly between her legs, and Aidan, and Niall, who was married with four children but had arrived that morning with two. They were boys and nobody looked forward to seeing them. Aidan and Niall, in their forties now, still lived in the region; Odhran and Cathal, the eldest brother whom nobody ever saw, in Dublin.

Sonia waited in the deep heart of the house, laying out food on the kitchen table. When Maeve came in, she put out her arms and said, crooning, 'How I wish you'd eat. You know in the end it is ageing for a woman to stay so thin.'

'I'm fit.' Maeve went at once to the kettle and lifted it from the range. 'It isn't the same thing. Sunny!' she cried. 'Where is that sunshine girl?'

Sunny pushed through the house and sat herself on a kitchen chair, wriggling into position, with shining eyes.

'Wait until you see what I've brought you,' said Maeve. 'And Mama too.'

'I want it now,' piped the child.

'Breakfast first,' Sonia said.

Odhran felt the house pivot into its active, more performative, identity as a *destination*, as the place that brought them together again.

The kitchen table in the farmhouse was as long and wide as a church door, supported by claw-footed legs that had been gouged at by dogs and children for a hundred years. From the range, there rose a constant and oppressive heat, which was why Sonia left the French doors on the new side, the extension, open in summertime. Large copper pots that had once been in circulation, once tinkered regularly, now hung on the walls as decoration. There was still a miserly little Sacred Heart and a few mildewed scraps of Palm Sunday palms on the wall above the range. They were there because it was difficult and perilous to access the wall above the range. It was the kitchen of many comingling and riotous adolescences – the kitchen in which his father, working late, might wait under the ceramic lampshade to trap a son who'd driven drunk from McKeogh's and was attempting, now, to pass like vapour through the house. Their father's Mass card, or one of them, was still there too, pinned to the fridge.

On this table, now, there were many plates of fried food and bread, none of which Sonia would eat. She sat slicing a pear with pointed indifference.

'OK, everybody, sit,' said Maeve.

The two little boys began complaining about presents. Niall, their father, was frowning at his phone. As he sat, Odhran looked covertly at Lena, who sometimes did an impression of Niall, gazing tragically at sports results, then wheeling around and waving his hands and saying good fuck but will ye only fucken tell me what ye want for the dinner, where's that woman got to, and flailing for Elaine. Niall was lazy and, they agreed, had married a shrew.

Aidan, by contrast, was gay. Nobody knew what he got up to romantically. There was literally no data at all.

'I'm not staying long now,' Aidan warned, also sitting down.

'Is it busy you are?' asked Maeve musically. She was pouring tea. She had taken an aggressive approach to her own return, wielding the teapot and parodying the accent.

Aidan did not seem to notice, but lit up to discuss the two cafés he co-owned with a friend in Limerick. They ran coffee-tasting classes and masterclasses. Offstage Odhran liked to make venomous fun of this, but Lena – in Dublin, or just in private – said, 'You may laugh, but think of all the ass at that.' He looked again for her eyes and she looked back. She was sitting opposite him, cutting up sausages on Sunny's plate. She smiled scrupulously and he thought *ass* and remembered their sex in the greenhouse, the air metallic with geraniums, the night before, and he felt safer in the midst of this dangerous family. For they were certainly dangerous, emotionally speaking, or could be. Sonia especially.

He loved, he realised suddenly, having Lena here, bringing her here to be his companion and play-adversary; to mock him with fondness and slot in with the other women, peeling vegetables or administering treats to children, her sharper side concealed and the stately city sleekness of her mannerisms on the surface instead. She made him proud at times like this. She would, he dared to think, be good out here. She would never melt into a scene or community; she would not disappear, like Niall's wife, under angry shrewish childrearing – she would not be like Keelin, the singsong CEO-style wife of Cathal, nor would she get homely and crooning and local like the girls he'd known at school, hotties now standardised by kids, seen leaping sometimes in and out of SUVs on country high streets, bearing breakfast rolls.

Lena would remain herself, he thought, but softer. Aloof and polite and well brought up, which was kind of a mystery to him, something to do with her mother's old-fashioned moral code, with her father's complacency.

Maybe she would like a newbuild. Probably she would love something easy to clean. White walls to put pictures on; a square lawn for a playhouse and chaise longue.

'What I think,' Sonia, holding her hands up and seeming to direct her speech at Lena, was saying, 'when I see you all is: I think of the mess. You know? I think that I'm going to need lots of help to clean up.'

'Of course we will,' Lena said.

'Because when I was young, I was able for guests and breakfasts and dinners and all the rest of it, but when you get older, I'm afraid to say you think of one thing: mess. And sheets and beds to be turned around, and so on.'

Maeve had this effect on her. It seemed worse every time. Maeve's difference was a betrayal – all the rest had tried to leave but failed to stay away or outside of her remit; all but Cathal, whom they hardly ever saw, and in whom Sonia had always been the least interested.

Lena was nodding at Sonia's complaint and the long dilation of listening to this complaint began to feel like work. She was also nervous of sausages, having heard terrible stories of children choking on sausages and grapes and marbles and being strangled by curtain cords and swallowing detergent and waiting in the long grass of agricultural prairies to be hacked apart like corncrakes when the combine harvester reared up, satanically, from the long grass.

She watched one of Niall's boys slip blank-eyed under the table suddenly and root around, causing a great scraping-back of chairs and exclamation, and making for the hallway.

'He's looking for presents,' the other boy explained.

'I'll bate the arse of him,' said Niall wearily. He did not get up.

'Here's a plan.' Maeve pointed a fork at Lena. The fork held only a robust slice of beef tomato. 'Let's go out for a drink.'

Later, she meant. Later, they went out for a drink.

15

Lena volunteered to stay sober and drive. This made her keeper of the evening, or scribe, and she responded by walking behind the siblings, falling out of conversation, across the crunching car park and into a roadside pub. Niall had blessedly left; despite his warnings, Aidan remained, and Odhran and Maeve. Lena felt surprised at Aidan's endurance and how watchfully happy he seemed, keeping close to his younger sister like a dog.

The sky was pink and the landscape, in its evening sweetness, sublime; it was easy to forget when you got used to it, to be surprised again.

She remembered with pathos that the Irish for dusk was *clapsholas* and felt the effort of *holas*, pronounced *hullus*, in her mouth as the silenced *s* flashed in her mind and this was a poem at school – it was taken from a poem at school. It was also a word Cian liked, even though he was not sentimental about the language the way so many musicians were.

She was tipping into the past a little now. Walking through a pub door is always the same experience. You could make an end-of-life supercut of yourself walking into bars, all over Europe, wincing at the whiplash of attention or caught up in nervous conversation with a friend. It was something like a line in the novel she was reading, in which a character observed that the smell of cigarette smoke brought her back to every moment, every time of life, in which she'd been around cigarettes – in the company of people smoking cigarettes – and compressed these into a single archetypical sensation. Something like that.

Lena longed just then to be back at the farmhouse, Sunny asleep, reading her novel on top of a made bed. With the window open and the smell of mown hay and silage.

But she was here, walking into her hundredth pub, instead.

She looked about for the Flynns. They'd passed out of a side door and into the beer garden, also crunching with gravel and fenced around with Heineken barriers. As they sat at a picnic table and Lena stood above rooting for her wallet, she saw spines of silver, like silver thread, in the parting of Maeve's hair, and this relaxed her for some reason. No, no, no, they said, she would not be the one to pay for a round. She sat down. Odhran went in, and people in the dreamy light of the beer garden glanced over at Maeve.

'You are a local beauty returned,' Lena said.

'There is a girl over there,' Maeve said, 'and I swear.' She named a name; Aidan nodded urgently and Maeve said, '*Do not* turn around.'

Someone was smoking close by. Lena felt a sense of acquiescence that was languid and lucid at once and which she associated with Foreground Boredom, the mindful mode she drily accessed day-to-day. It filled her like warm water. She could commit to the moment in all of its banality brilliantly: feel the grain of the tabletop, absorb the festive outline of a hairstyle in her eyeline yards away, and know the almost seething peace of the hills in her body.

This was happiness, she realised with dulled surprise. The conviction would pass. It was too absolute. Nothing of Foreground Boredom could remain absolute.

When Odhran returned with drinks and a teenaged barmaid bearing further drinks, Lena held up a message on her phone. Sonia had sent a photograph of Sunny, bathed and wearing pyjamas, sitting on the backyard pontoon dock.

'What is that in her mouth?' he asked.

'It's a soother. I know. Where did she get that. One of the boys probably.'

Aidan inclined his head to see the image now. 'Did you let her have one?'

'When she was tiny,' Lena said stiffly. 'I mean, only at night.'

'She used to have it hanging out of her mouth,' Odhran laughed, 'like a cigar.'

Lena tried not to be provoked. 'She gave it up years ago.'

Maeve asked if it harmed their teeth, the teeth of children that is, and Lena explained that no, they were designed, like, orthodontically now. Also, this photo was obviously a joke because Sunny was four and no longer needed one. What they *do* say, however, she continued to explain, conceding and feeling interested in the theory, is that sucking on a soother creates *oral fixation* or produces orally fixated adults and probably that was true: everybody she knew had soothers and everybody, pretty much, in her generation was almost certainly orally fixated.

'I'm not,' declared Aidan.

Lena observed Odhran's astonishment, and then every long beat of mute despair at being unable to make the joke he wished to make.

Maeve said, 'You're right. I'm only happy when I have something in my mouth.'

'Do you still smoke?'

'Oh.' She smiled at Lena. 'Now you've put the idea in my head.' She looked again at the photo of Sunny. 'My mam is good with her?'

'She's great; they're like peas in a pod so far.'

The siblings, Lena had learnt, considered their mother antic, maybe insane. They all also went to her for counsel and even financial bailouts regularly.

'Has she told you all about the ghost dog?' Odhran asked. He was stroking his sweating pint glass, relaxing.

Lena said impatiently that this was certainly something Sunny had overheard. She'd heard about dogs at the farmhouse and extrapolated. No, she explained – Sunny wasn't *lying*, Sunny was simply four. The world to a toddler is a sensorium, she explained. But gun dogs were for certain something adults talked about. She had almost been pleased to hear of the gun-dog thing because this was far removed from backwards chants and Golgotha and this was credibly a fact about the house Sunny may well have overheard and in its telling, in its shrugging revelation, it suggested something that wasn't about Lena's own influence after all. She did not say this part out loud; she simply said, 'The world to a toddler is a sensorium.'

She also said, 'I would like if your mother didn't encourage it. I mean, just because, you know, Sunny will go on and on about it, potentially. She might like the attention.'

This was the kind of slightly sleazy sleight you could perform with a little child: pretending they were annoying, socialising the notion of child *as annoying*, to ward off dissent.

'It's cute,' said Maeve uncertainly.

Lena had seen Maeve in action in London, where she worked like a machine. She rose at five and combed her hair, Chinese-seeming in its straightness, and pushed it into an austere sculptural bun. She did yoga while playing voice notes or went to the gym. She worked, on the days she worked, long hours, moving lightly in Scandinavian trainers, and when she was on her own time, she sewed or undertook stressful communications with the company she used to run up cheaper versions of her clothes – some place in India. The thought made Lena and Odhran uncomfortable. It was difficult for them to square the apparent geopolitical callousness with the tepid but omnipresent progressivism of their own generation.

When Maeve went out, it was to art movies and new mid-range restaurants or to gallery openings and she had no money but looked expensive all the time. Consequently, she could seem a joyless person – underweight and strained. She was kind but she was serious. She moved through the world with an industry Lena had never known, never desired nor aspired to, and could not really understand. What Lena did understand, however, was the kind of woman Maeve wished to dress. This woman was rich but looked sensationally plain; her hair, like Maeve's, was frictionless as fabric, always long, and her complexion bare; she wore trench coats in shades of taupe, mushroom and rice paper.

Lena had once outlined the terms of this woman to Maeve. It was a look only a life of poised nutrition can obtain, she said, for, just like trauma, the conditions that allowed this kind of woman to occur were set in place and then erased themselves before the age of two. You could not become this woman after the fact – there was no growing, grifting, hustling, starving or drugging. No surgery. She simply existed, with the purity of an indigenous shrub. Maeve had laughed with offended surprise and said, never mind PR, you can write the copy for me.

Odhran asked Maeve, now, 'Have you ever seen ghosts in the house?'

'I have,' Aidan claimed quietly.

Lena did an outsized, vampy turn. 'You what, Aidan?'

'I've seen the ghost of Dad in the house.'

There followed a pause of perplexment and awkwardness. Odhran was frowning at Aidan a little too hard. Maeve sipped her gin and looked away.

'Well. You have to tell us now,' Lena said.

'Do you want to hear about it, really?' Aidan asked.

Aidan, like Odhran, was slender and tall, but less acerbic of personality. It was easy for Odhran to deride him because he was so vain of his cafés but also because he was the child that came after Odhran, the baby boy who stole Odhran's crown at one time, and a buffer against any ire that might otherwise be directed at Maeve.

'It was just after the funeral,' he said.

'You saw a ghost,' Odhran prompted sharply.

'OK. So, I was staying over, and it was just me – just me and Mam, that is. I was by myself in that little room beside the stairs at night. I think I'd been taking a call or something.

We were in the middle of acquiring the unit in Castleconnell at the time; there were a lot of calls.'

He waited, but nobody asked about the unit in Castleconnell.

Aidan continued. 'I heard someone come through the hallway, like come down the stairs and through the hallway, you know? I thought it was Mam.'

He paused again. Lena said, 'It wasn't your mam?'

'No.' Aidan took a breath. He was, it seemed, enjoying the attention, but also anxious about something – proceeding anxiously. 'I got up and I went out and I think I said, like, Mam?, or something, and I saw a man. It was Dad. I mean, it was absolutely his – you know, shape. His height and his walk and stuff. He had his back to me. He went into the kitchen, sat down by the door there, and started putting on his welly boots – you know the way he always used to sit there and put on the boots.' Aidan mimed his father's pose; stooping over, pulling on boots. 'He did that literally every day before he went out the back or down to the greenhouse or for a walk. It was his shape. And I felt like I had gone mad or something.'

'Aidan.' Odhran sounded horrified.

Maeve said nothing.

'But it also wasn't him. I had this strong sense that it also wasn't him, because he was dead. I didn't say it out loud but I remember thinking, *Dad you are dead, you should go*. And he was gone then. It was over in a second.'

The silence that followed this story was profound. Lena's boredom evaporated, replaced by an extreme unease.

'That's completely crazy,' Odhran said at last.

'Why didn't you ever say anything?' asked Lena.

'Because it's crazy!' Aidan laughed. He looked at them one by one, smiling. 'It's crazy. It was like a hallucination. You think: I'm tired, I'm upset, my father is dead, I might be seeing things.'

After a moment in which he sipped from his pint and avoided their eyes, Aidan looked up again urgently. 'Don't tell Sonia,' he said.

'God no.' Odhran had recovered. 'We'd never hear the fucking end of it.'

'Aidan that is the creepiest story ever,' Lena said.

He closed his eyes modestly. Maeve did a strange thing – she reached out and patted his hand.

'Oh, I'm OK,' Aidan jumped.

Odhran said, 'It's your round.'

As Aidan stood he smiled at them, smugly, and joked. 'You'd better not all start talking about me now.'

When he'd left Maeve spoke at last, saying, 'Look, maybe it happened.'

'My mother,' Lena remembered, 'used to dream of the ghost of an old neighbour standing in the doorway of her room. Just a few times. I think she said, *You're dead, Mary, go away*, and it went away or whatever.'

It was a much darker story actually, but Lena stopped at that.

'Amazing to appear to Aidan though,' Odhran said. 'Of all of us.'

'When he gets back, we should move in.' Lena shivered. 'You've all got your beer jackets on, your gin jackets. Poor me I have no jacket at all.'

Odhran had turned slightly sour. 'Let's just go in and find him,' he said. And then another stroke, another beat, another tableau like a snapshot: Lena, entering a bar.

16

The bar was busy, though many people pushed outside in busy, chatting gangs. Lena gave one last look to the countryside around. Dusk had come on suddenly and brought with it the frontier chill of vacant landscapes, an immensity that needed to be vacated for safety reasons overnight – the large emptiness of an emptied space, or a space populated by something malevolent. It was the weight of depopulation. The fields and hills had not always been so deserted. People believed they still heard sounds, and laughter, and shouts, and the crackle of fires at night; people believed, or some people believed, that this eerie ectoplasmic silence was made up of spirit presences.

Which was why, Odhran had told her casually once, you didn't walk the fields in the dark.

There was the story of the last witch to be burnt, in Ballyvadlea, in the next county, and the rhyme: are you a witch or are you a fairy or are you the wife of Michael Cleary? Down here they sometimes pronounced the name *Clary*.

Inside the bar, the sound of the crowd was a canal lock sheering open in cataract and, even though she was sober, there came also an unstoppable comorbid surge of associations and effulgent thoughts: glaring, half-forgotten known unknowns. Years ago, for example, when she was still a young teenager, Lena visited a psychic who worked from a little shiplap grotto at the bottom of a yard in Killester. It was a summer evening and there carried the sound of footballs blasting on gable ends. The man told Lena: you will have one child, a girl, you will go to England and your husband will be English; you'll give this man a hard time, my God, such a difficult time; thirty-six will be your best year – no, I'm strict on this, thirty-six – and: funerals in the next nine months. I don't know. He frowned. Maybe you won't go to the funerals. As she rose to go, he added, you've been here a long time. Over and over again. Sumer.

'Yes,' he agreed with himself. 'Sumerian.'

She'd had to look this up and it was flattering all right, she'd give him that. Her mother and aunt, a schoolfriend, had all received readings from the Killester clairvoyant, and took it for granted that at least some of these seeds sprouted – funerals really were attended, houses built, husbands met or parted with, college places offered, requests for forgiveness made by an unknown ancestor standing in hip-high grass and twisting a flat cap around and around in his sweaty hands – that was somebody's weird reading one day. They all believed it easily. Nothing they were told was unreasonable. *Sumerian* had slid into her head a handful of times over the years, in the many years since, which must mean she believed it, a little bit?

You could believe such a thing and live easily without dwelling on it. Like the time, she thought now – almost saying it, preparing to tell Odhran, say – she got the AstraZeneca vaccination and came down with a reeking fever and dreamt of the Heart Sutra. No seriously, she would say, the Heart Sutra. *Form is only emptiness / Emptiness only form.* This really happened. She'd found it enchanting for five minutes and then moved on.

After the GP, a week ago, Lena had watched a lecture on YouTube. The professor, whose style of delivery was tripped up by catches of breath, spoke about the unseen worlds of children, of angels and dreams, in a spellbound style that made her seem affected and irritating. The research content came from interviews with children, but Lena wondered cynically: yes but, who is talking to these children? Adults spoke about God and angels and dead relatives and monsters and ghosts. Adults contaminated. It seemed silly to her that they might take these children's testimonies without correcting for influences.

There was another video, one she'd seen years ago and sifted through the offal of the internet to retrieve, which came to mind. In this, a succession of children in Limerick in the nineteen-nineties described paranormal happenings and ghosts they were familiar with to the Folklore Commission. A big black dog, one said, come down the alley at Tanner's and bite off your head if you look at it. A big banshee, another said, live in the Daly's field where the football pitches is and she scream in your ear and your family, they will die.

Against this backdrop, Lena was coming to realise that she had, at least until now, believed, in an unexamined and practical sort of way, that Sunny was not capable of true imaginative originality. That Sunny's behaviour and patterns of belief could only ever reflect Lena and Odhran's own – reflect their conscious world, the assumptions they had and the rules they reproduced. It was true: children came into the world with a set of genetic mechanisms, Lena further thought, less confidently, but the rest was environmental. She also saw that this belief in her and Odhran's influence was corroborative: it was a theory she'd acquired and sustained in conversation with Odhran. It existed only inasmuch as they believed in it.

Her thoughts circled back to Aidan's story. She was reminded of a cringing country tendency to embrace all things folksy in this way, to lay out ghost stories as gossip. In her childhood there had been this tendency in the town also, but it was urban. Mostly poltergeists.

And in fact the dream her mother reported concerned a neighbour who had, it was known, been abused as a child.

She'd discussed this for some fraught reason with Lena's mother. In response, her mother put distance between them and said later, Mary was troubled.

But after Mary died, after Lena's mother attended the grimly unadorned funeral, she dreamt of Mary holding clawed hands out in the darkness, claws like trees. *I have been a waif for twenty years!* Or was it wraith? *I have been a wraith for twenty years.*

'I said, go away, Mary, you are dead,' Lena's mother recalled. She was ill-looking.

'Why do you think,' Lena had asked, 'she ever confided in you?' It was truly mysterious, considering how mirthless and forbidding Lena's mother was.

The question had seemed to rankle with her. 'How in God's name would I know?' she asked. 'I hardly knew the woman. She would only glom onto me is all.'

Weariness spread through her now like a drug. She was not afraid of the ghost story, but felt unnerved and looked glassily at a wall of framed pictures, photographs as slight as tiles, which showed eighties and nineties darts heroes and session musicians captured candidly in washed-out camera light – in each case, they were ranged before or around the huge hoop-shaped fireplace in the dark centre of the bar. The pictures documented a camaraderie she felt herself condescending to without being able to prevent it. A simple-minded past, a time when woolly-headed farmer-bachelors looked openly, vacantly, into the camera lens, veins crisp and pink in their cheeks, each face as round and unkempt as the face of an infant. One man, his arm drawn back to launch a dart, had a body like a stained, ungainly sail dragging beneath him.

They were all dead now, every subject in these photographs, undoubtedly.

On Inisbofin, long ago, she and Cian and the singer Cas Cronin had taken singing lessons – so to speak – with an old-style singer. Cas contracted it for them. It was just for an afternoon at first, but the session cantered into the night. The old man was lean, with a defined skull and feathery lemony hair at the top of his head, like the bachelor dart-players. 'When we sing this,' he explained of a *sean nós* song, 'we hold hands like so' – he took her finger up, and held her arm in the air at an awkward angle, suspended – 'and turn it round and round like so.' It was a kind of cranking action, like winding a machine.

'I've seen this,' Lena said.

'It is to hold us both in this world. It is to stop either of us falling into the otherworld.'

Sean nós was delivered through the nose. The contours of the lantern skull came into renewed focus as he sang and stared right at her, transfixing in his vigour, and then afterwards said, 'Fierce harsh on the aul adenoids, you know.'

'I can't do that.' She meant that she could not sing that way; it would feel artificial, even condescending or exploitative. She felt so far from having ancestors.

'Just croon it to begin with, all the songs,' the singer advised. 'Just do that privately because they need to be sung that way to begin with, just to get proper sense of them. But don't record that way if you'd prefer. Only you mustn't sing any of them, in *sean nós*, alone.'

'I need a minder.'

'You must have someone to hold you, to keep you in this world. You promise that?'

'I do.' She'd laughed. It was long ago.

She felt a shiver like a fever run through her now, in the pub, all these years later. Emptiness.

'Anything to be said,' she asked Odhran, 'for heading home?'

'Ye have to come with us or ye get no lift!' Odhran was shouting over the noise to Maeve and Aidan, both tipping coffee-coloured shots from a circular tray. Odhran was flush and his accent had come skidding back and it was unwarrantedly erotic; Lena thought about him pushing into her broadly underneath the beams of the attic bedroom.

'It's OK.' Aidan splashed his hands up. 'We'll get a cab.' Maeve's eyes were glinting. It was unlike her, Lena thought, to drink heavily. But she was relieved, and in the cool of the car park there was sudden silence and a sky of densely serried stars. Some stars seemed to slide idly forward – these were, she realised, satellites. In the country darkness, they could see it all.

She drove carefully down the narrow angular roads and felt glad of the need to remain distracted and alert. At the farmhouse, they slipped in swiftly, shushing one another, passing the door to the women's parlour, which was ajar. Odhran nodded into it.

'There you go. There's the ghost,' he said.

'It was in the kitchen,' she corrected. 'Now come and fuck me. But don't wake Sonia.'

'No.' He was solemn. 'Important not to do that.'

Odhran had long legs, long shoulders, an indifferent almost insolent manner of turning her onto her front and pinning her arms behind her back and coming with a heavy gasp. It was this faintly brutal side of him that came out in the dark and which she found compelling, like a thrum of violence, or just wickedness, and made her wonder about how he was with other people – cowed or grateful or greedy or commanding. Sometimes she would ask for stories, for his arsenal of images: the girl fingered under a bouquet of shopping bags on the top floor of a bus; the girl who lay in wait with her ass in the air on the floor; the threesome that ended his cohabitation lease with its lazy tangle of tongues and limbs.

And yet she never met these, ever, with her own mythologies. Men she'd been with in her luminous, musical years held no further interest to her.

She thought of Odhran with interns, babysitters, mutual friends. He demurred from these fantasies. 'You would not like it,' he told her firmly. 'You just want to pretend.'

They lay in the gluey aftermath glutted with satisfaction. Sleep came like a stone drifting slowly but surely to the shadowy floor of a liquid chasm. At some point, late, no phone or clockface, Lena listened to Maeve arrive back and move tidily about below. It struck her that sound carried and perhaps Sonia heard them, but then they were married after all.

17

That was not the end of it. Things got weird again at the beach.

A further day of Maeve had passed; the weather stayed steady, and the family travelled to Fanore. Aidan was absent. Odhran drove Lena, Sunny, Sonia and Maeve. Niall and Elaine, all four children, followed in their broad-snouted estate car. It took two hours to cross the county and enter the pale prehistoric pavement landscape of the Burren, dry-stone walls and Winnebagos slowing traffic on the tiny roads, and arrive at the coast, where it was windy and the waves were high.

Odhran flipped off a brother's surfboard several times. He then abandoned it, peeling the wetsuit away as he crossed the black and golden sand. Maeve, in a straw hat, was building sandcastles with the kids.

Lena sat on a picnic rug and Sonia in a deckchair. The children wore wetsuits too.

As he approached, Odhran heard them calling him.

'Listen to this,' Lena said. He couldn't read her tone.

'Something Sunny said yesterday evening.' Despite being practised and sitting upright, Sonia seemed confused about the details. 'Yesterday evening,' she repeated, 'when you were all out at the pub, before bed. We were having a chat. She started talking about *a woman I know* – I mean saying this, a woman I know. This woman that I know.'

Lena was staring beyond him now, with a frown. A man

from a neighbouring group was stripping to swim and he was solid-looking, and tan. Odhran felt conscious of his relative thinness and seized a sandy towel to scrub his hair.

'Was this an actual person you know?' he asked.

'No. I can't remember the description exactly. Sunny, what was it?'

The kid was levelling off a bucket. She scraped her spade across the top. Her hair, damp from splashing, was also the colour of wet sand. She said, looking down, 'A woman you know with three holes in her head.'

'What?' Odhran dropped to his hunkers before her. 'Holes in the head?'

'Bangs on the head.' Sunny shrugged. She was lining up shells. She looked ashamed at his reaction, which made him feel bad about it.

'Just that,' Lena reported quietly. 'Holes or bangs in the head.'

'Do you want to paddle again, Sunny?' Maeve asked.

Sunny nodded.

'Another ghost story,' Maeve said to Odhran, standing up. She was smiling in a hard way, almost a smirk. She and Sunny wandered towards the crashing water, lost at once in the crowd. The tide was not out, but the space was still a wide expanse of dark and veiny sand.

When they had left Sonia explained once again. 'She said: Granny, you know a woman with three holes in her head. She had three bangs on her head. You know her from when you were little, like me. Little,' she repeated, 'like me. She says just that. And I ask, but Sunny, how do I know a woman like that? She lives near the road, she said. Near a road.'

'The side of the road,' Lena said.

'Strange.' Odhran sat next to Lena. He saw goosepimples on her bare thighs. She wore large sunglasses and a hoody long enough to cover her swimsuit and she was being frosty with him, in the way of couples in a crowd. It was odd, since they'd made love the previous night, meaning sex had been achieved twice in one forty-eight-hour cycle and even within the confines of Sonia's domain. But that morning Lena had told him off for sleeping in.

'I might have wanted,' she'd hissed, 'for once in my life, to sleep in.'

'So do it tomorrow.'

'Why wouldn't it occur to you, though? Why wouldn't it even occur to you, say, to dress her when I'm showering or feed her or something and not wait for your mother to do it. You're on holidays. When is my holiday?'

'What difference,' he'd asked, 'does it make if my mother does it?'

Now Lena turned away and looked blandly at the surf, and drew the hoody around her. 'It gets worse,' she remarked, still not looking at him.

'You see,' Sonia continued, 'when she says *road*, I remember something, and this is something extremely specific and from long ago and it jumped right into my head.' She paused. 'Well, years ago, they widened a road out by Bridgetown, very near where your uncle Edmund lived. I think they almost doubled the size of the road.'

'I have to say,' Odhran intervened, 'that I think describing a woman with *holes in her head* is extremely weird and something she has never said before.' He looked up at Sonia from the rug. 'You didn't say anything to her like that?'

'No. She came out with it by herself. I mean, I wouldn't know what kinds of things she says or hears about.'

'When they widened the road,' Lena took up, 'they were hitting a burial ground.'

Odhran realised they had been talking about this for some time, when he was surfing or toppling repeatedly off the tacky narrow platform of the board; they'd been through it, through the details, a number of times, and now it was being rehearsed again.

'It was a cilín,' said Sonia. 'A burial ground for unbaptised babies. You know they used to have those in every parish;

every place had a cilín for babies who died before they could be baptised. But it had been an abbey or something older than that, I think.'

'I remember this,' Odhran said. 'Did Dad know the guys in the council?'

'Yes. The council archaeologists had to excavate the cilín before they could widen the road, and they reburied what they could find in the cemetery in – oh, I don't remember. Might have been Bridgetown. Probably. It was Dermot McGowan in the council whom your father knew. He used to call out to us.'

Sonia had raised her hands to organise this data in front of her.

'He was married to a McKeogh from Ballina.'

'Right,' Odhran said, allowing impatience to show.

'In the cilín,' Lena was looking at him at last, 'there were mostly children but also some adults.'

'This was a very sad kind of council project,' his mother said. 'There was a Mass said, a reburial. There is a monument somewhere to them.'

A gull sheered over them and made for the dunes. There was a line of people slanting down the dunes, holding ice creams. The beach was wild and bare, used mostly for surfing, overlooked by hills of white and silver-blue limestone. Despite their stony soil, the hills were gridded out by ancient walls all the way to the top. Odhran loved it better, loved all these Atlantic beaches like bared teeth better, than anything on the continent.

The first time he'd brought Lena, she'd said first, 'Oh I was here before, for a wedding,' and then, 'Jesus, it's phenomenal.'

'Dermot McGowan who knew your father overlooked or managed it,' Sonia continued. 'So they had a write-up of what they found in the place, all the burials they found and the bones that were left. Some of them were very old and some were only from the nineteen-fifties, but I would say it was mostly the nineteenth century or so. And as I said almost all babies. I can well remember reading this report and I remember because those hills all around there – my brother, your uncle Edmund, still lived out there at the time, and I had family from around it. My family came from Clonboy. So I remember asking your father for the report.'

'Oh,' Odhran said leadenly. 'Was there some woman with holes in her head?'

'Well yes.' Sonia was sharp. 'It was almost all babies but for a few adults and one of these was a pregnant woman. With holes in her head. She had been hit at the back of the head three times, with something sharp, and buried in the cilín.'

'Sometimes,' Lena said into the silence that followed, 'people buried strangers or murders or suicides or, you know, undesirables, in the cilíní.'

Lena had studied history, but Odhran knew this too. He also felt *cilíní* was a bit of an indulgence when she might have anglicised it to *killeens*. He thought this so swiftly and subtly it was basically unconscious, manifest as more impatience with her.

'So, a pregnant woman,' she continued, 'might be there because she hadn't been churched. Or else nobody ever knew she was there.'

It was still difficult to read her tone; the sunglasses reflected flying foam and other people. Someone – a child, not Sunny – thumped past on the sand.

After a long moment, Odhran said, 'It's a bit of a reach.'

'It came back to me, immediately,' Sonia said. She sat forward, looking flushed. 'I remember it very keenly because of the detail. A skeleton, you see, with evidence of pregnancy – that would need to be quite far along to leave any evidence at all. So this woman was murdered, who knows when, but probably the nineteenth century. It may have been a cilín, but before that it was an abbey or a monastery – it was something holy, and there was a pattern rock.'

'Everybody knew it was there. But I've never heard stories, not even folk stories, about a murder.'

'You might,' Lena suggested, 'look up coroner records.'

'So what are we saying exactly?' Odhran was irritated. 'Are we saying she's – what, she's a reincarnated woman with holes in her head?'

'Look.' This was Lena. 'At this point, I am just getting really confused.'

Odhran looked to her coolly. 'Confused,' he repeated.

'Like.' She opened a hand towards him in appeal. 'What if she does know things? What if she can see things or somehow know things? What if that is a possibility?' She seemed pained to say it.

His irritation flashed to rage and then recoiled, like a fire extinguishing, into something like protectiveness; Lena was not gullible but she was, he understood, something of a vulnerable person sometimes. Sensitive. He felt a certain mannish urge to insulate her from Sonia, who was his mother after all, but this was why he was – in adulthood, with affectionate firmness – inoculated against Sonia.

'I don't believe it is.' He said it clearly and remedially. He wanted his mother to put these loose and kitsch ideas right out of Lena's head. He wanted to cut Sonia out of the moment entirely: Sonia, pulsing like a beacon with her grasping new-agey late-life leanings. Mostly it was harmless, but this would not be harmless if she got into Lena's head.

Something came to him – Montessori, the book about Montessori teaching they had browsed on enrolling Sunny. At Montessori, they were opposed to fantasy; they focused on wooden toys in hands, implements and miniaturised versions of adulthood; they favoured white walls, low hooks, woven baskets of maracas and blocks. At the time of reading it, Odhran had experienced a sense of calm identification – he, too, disliked fantasy, or whimsy, and anything from the Marvel Universe, for example; he saw in this dissent an enduring and moral and almost fatherly concern with truthfulness. And Lena, who bought woven baskets for maracas and the wooden nuts and plugs of Sunny's ice cream station, who did not use euphemisms for genitals and declined all suggestions of having Sunny baptised, who was plainly atheist and millennial in her minimalist taste, he thought, complemented this. She was sensible.

Also, however, she'd been difficult when Sunny was small. Also she'd been fretful, macabre, even threatening. Once she drove all the way to Naul, to her mother, leaving Sunny with him in the night. Then she wouldn't speak to the GP because the GP was, apparently, a dick. Sonia wrote a prescription they had to renew, shamefacedly, at the pharmacy in Nenagh – nowhere else would take a script from Sonia. Lena took a week of sertraline and desisted.

'I've got a handle on it,' she declared.

'Please don't tell me you think she is telepathic,' he addressed her now.

'How else do you explain it?' In her sunglasses, his own face, made convex.

'Well, I mean like, *many* ways.'

Sonia, keen to have attention pivot back, returned to the woman with holes in her head.

'It came right into my mind,' she insisted grandly. 'When Sunny said it. I felt very sure it was the thing she was referring to.'

Odhran felt an urgent, unexamined desire for motion, and stood up rudely, and walked into the beach crowd. The sky was a full and generous blue, reflected as blazing pockets of surface water on the dimpling, compact sand. It was easy to find Maeve in her straw hat. She and Sunny were inching into the waves, holding hands. Odhran began to sprint flat-footedly towards them, refastening the half-peeled wetsuit and waving as he went.

'Do you want to go right in with Daddy?' he asked.

When a wave rolled in, lardy but ardent, he jumped, and Sunny at his waist raised her chin above the spray to squeal. There was sand in her hairline, like shadow, and her pot belly sat snugly under the palm of his hand. If they lived here, he thought, he would take her to the islands in the ferry off

Doolin to camp at weekends; she could learn, when she was older, to surf. If they had more children, there would be less intensity, less brittleness, between him and Lena: energy could be spread out and met with the energy of the landscape, but also of a social scene he could still interpret and navigate with status. It needn't include his brothers – he reached out, in his imagination, to friends. He could stay working in Dublin. They could keep that as an option, back to Dublin again, if it didn't work out.

It was not a pipe dream. It was not a fantasy.

When Sunny was born he had not felt the shock or claustrophobia people predicted – though she was unexpected, and although he was young by city standards then and living in the city, not like his friends who'd married out of college and put up dormer bungalows or bought off plans from narrow, cheaply improvisational housing estates; even though he was inexperienced with children and in his prime, really, he did not feel shock or claustrophobia at all. The adrenaline of her emergence and her tenderness. Her stoutness. How she fixed her gaze on him finally, at about six weeks, and looked amazed. How easy it was, in the end, to clear space for woven baskets and wooden pegs, to keep his head during tantrums and open out his arms to her afterwards. To zip into A&E and talk importantly to doctors, impress upon them an inborn authority – how easy, in the end, to grow fully into himself.

'Daddy, should I pee?' Sunny shrieked now, still on his hip.

'Not all over me. I'll put you down in the shallower part.'

'I don't know if I peeing,' she shouted, 'because it's cold.'

Maeve caught her, running, in a large towel, like a bat. Sunny took off ahead of them then, stepping around jellyfish, winding back to her mother again.

'What did you think of that story?' Maeve asked.

'It's Mam,' he said with anger. 'Lena has no defences against that. But she shouldn't indulge it. What if Sunny hears, like? It will scare her.'

Maeve said, 'I mean, Sunny is the one scaring people, to be fair.'

At this, both siblings laughed. Relief spared Odhran something – panic, probably. He only needed to take things in hand, he thought.

18

Odhran sat next to Lena on the bed and pulled off his socks and began to flex his long feet and toes. They were back at the farmhouse and it was beautiful outside, the evening time. Odhran sighed very slightly with a pleasure that was tangentially sexual.

'I have a proposal for you,' he said. It was seven o'clock; Sunny was out, with Maeve and Sonia, calling in on neighbours or looking at horses in the pinkening stillness. From the back of the house, from the attic, Lena gazed at a long lathery shelterbelt that was stark as a drill in winter but soft, in summer, with growth. It arched across the whole horizon.

She knew what the proposal would be and, punkishly, wished to obstruct.

'I might call the doctor again,' she said. 'About a brain scan.'

Since the beach, things had softened between them – it was necessary to soften eventually, like putting on a brake – even though they hadn't discussed it yet. She felt a little bad. And yet, she was also trying to shock: brain scan sounded more graphic than MRI.

'Why?' he asked, as she'd expected.

'In case it's hallucinations. And – something is wrong, organically.'

'I see.'

A pause fell between them. He lay back. She waited for him to take the bait.

'It's not—' he began.

She knew what he was going to say – she turned to him, receptively.

'It's not helpful to let my mother get carried away.' His voice was gentle.

'I know. I always do that.'

'It's not your fault. You're soft.' He smiled. 'But don't be minding, like, ghost stories.'

'So what if Sunny is ill? Or – disturbed?' She no longer felt this. Now that she no longer felt it, she could say it openly. She felt something stranger, something like a seduction, now that she was out of her life and drifting uncertainly in the cloudy idle kind of rhizodic zone of suggestion represented by Clare, and the farmhouse, and Sonia's stories.

'Sunny isn't disturbed.' Odhran said this mildly. He was staring softly at the ceiling, scratching a toe. 'She's susceptible. To your stress.'

Grief, or shame, like a hot spring. Lena turned her face away in surprise.

'I have a proposal,' Odhran said. He hadn't noticed her face.

'Is it to go and view a house?'

He grinned and sat up, heavily dimpling the bed. 'You want to, don't you?'

'Yeah, go on. I'd like to see.'

After he had risen and left the room, she lay still for a moment, staring. She could not say which was worse, her neurosis or the influence of malign or benign paranormal presences; though, actually, it was obvious which was worse. Mother concern.

In the car, she caught his arm. 'Tell me I'm not messing up our child.'

'No, no, that's not what I mean.' He took off. 'No. I only mean Sunny always responds to you and you don't need to like,' he thought, 'give it oxygen. She's imaginative. That's all.'

'You really think so?'

'I think it's unhealthy to fixate on things. I think we should focus on the future.'

'Ah. More children.'

'And a house.'

'A big McMansion,' she droned. 'Mass-going children. Bouncy castles. SUVs.'

'I was literally,' Odhran said, 'about to say SUVs.' Under the deadpan there was earnest, open, excitable energy: he was, she saw, serious about this.

It was thrilling, enlivening, now, to set out on the winding blue-black road alone, just the two of them. Golden haystacks stood about in the shocked, shaved meadows and a spangle of insects shone over every hedge. The lake came in and out of view as a bar of depthless, hovering blue. They passed homesteads heralded only by high wooden gates, gateposts with decorative granite balls like bowling balls and topiary. They passed wide-open barnyards in which dogs and toys were strewn around and pristine trampolines stood vacantly. They passed a strange little rectory pushed so close to the road Lena could see shampoo bottles bleaching on an upstairs windowsill. The long, elegant wall of a demesne.

A village came on; a market square, chippers, the busy glass of a new Spar.

'Even further?' she asked.

'Not much more.'

Outside the village, a gravel yard of freight lorries lay suspended by the eerie, regular poles of a pine plantation. Further on, up a soft hill, stood a bungalow with two big crescent arches on which plaster had been scalloped campily. A deep picture window in the gable reached, almost, the floor, and was sliced into featherlight squares.

No, thought Lena neatly, at once.

They parked before it, in the yard.

'This guy's not here.' Odhran began dialling on his phone. 'Oh great, no bother,' he said, and a car erupted from the frowsy gateway to the road and came to a tight stop next to them. The estate agent was elderly, dapper, and snapped out of the car like an umbrella.

'Mister Flynn, what a pleasure. How you've grown,' he joked.

'Good to see you, Martin.' Odhran adapted his slow paternal mode. 'This is my wife, Lena.' It always sounded a little improbable.

'If we've met before, and I forgot, I apologise,' Martin said, shaking her hand. 'You meet so many people and more and more young people too.'

'Will we look?' Odhran was nervous.

'Ye go.' Martin held up the key. Its fob was a leather loop. Lena rather coveted the fob. 'I'll wait in the car a bit; I have some telephone calls I must make. Even on a lovely evening, Lena,' he smiled, 'you have people anxious and ringing you. It's a time we have so few places going up, they are practically queuing round the road.'

She was about to say something about Dublin, that they knew all too well about queues trailing around blocks, but stopped herself and remembered the context and nodded instead. When young, Lena had been wont to launch into monologues of warmth and amity that seemed agreeable but were in fact tedious; in womanhood, properly speaking – properly occupying it – she realised everybody wanted her to shut up. It was restful and chic to shut up.

They entered: the door was of dark and heavy vinyl, two gold chains hanging loose and swinging as they pushed it to. Lena thought: safety feature. Fear? Roving gangs on the hunt for power tools and powerlines skulking up from the pine plantation, scary moonlit shadows, shotguns, gun dogs, guard dogs, farmer-bachelors hunched over oilcloth tables eating tinned soup watching *Nationwide* and pricking up their ears to the panic of dogs? Though this had clearly been a family home and its interior, flowering before them now, was gravid with feminine energy, potent as potpourri. Dark flock carpet and two-tone wallpaper stripes, an umbrella stand, a peach kitchen with a teapot shaped like a red hen forlorn and funny on the countertop, alone. In the living room, the navy rugs were embossed with old furniture coasters. They moved to a bedroom with paperback books in piles against the wall, empty otherwise, and to the cold grey bathroom with its several suction grabrails cluttering.

Someone, she thought, had once been deeply proud of this house.

'It's in probate of course,' Odhran told her. 'But all of these old houses are.'

'What do you think?' she asked.

'Like stepping back in time.'

'Where did you find out about it?'

Sonia, he explained, had travelled out here regularly to see the old woman who wouldn't leave. Sonia was retired, but knew this woman for so long, she went anyway and had an old colleague sign off on scripts. She'd taken blood pressure and prescribed pills and persuaded the woman, eventually, into a home. All her kids, she tsked, are in New Zealand. At the wake last month, she'd enquired about a sale. It wasn't listed yet. This was a little grizzly to hear but Odhran anticipated her, and laughed.

'Scouring the death notices for a house.'

'Well, you know, somebody's got to live in them.' Lena wished there was something to sit on, to contemplate, but it seemed people had pillaged the rooms. The yard behind was a sawn-off square of grass and had been cut recently. There were no flowers, just the screen of plantation trees an acre down. 'I could not,' she thought aloud, 'tolerate those trees.'

'It's an example,' Odhran said. He put his arm around her awkwardly and she froze, discouraging him. 'They want three hundred.'

'Lol.'

'They might get it.'

'Not from me.' It was harsh. She softened her tone. 'It's worth knowing,' she said, 'getting an idea of it all. But do you really want to be this remote? It's just.' She stepped away. 'I grew up in a town and I live in a city and I don't even know how to live like this. Are their burglars? Do you do like a ceilí or something? Do you have to drive everywhere?'

'Well obviously you have to drive everywhere.'

'I'd be afraid of going mad.'

'There are houses in the towns.'

'I would like to see houses in towns.'

Martin, the estate agent, had dipped through the huge brown door. Preoccupied, he pushed the stand of umbrellas back with a foot.

'A grand lady,' he began speaking before looking at them, 'but you know how it is. People let houses fall out of fashion. They don't see fashions changing.'

'Did they build it themselves?' Odhran asked.

'They did. In nineteen-seventy-two, I believe.' Martin raised a file to his face. 'So the septic tank is new, from two-thousand-and-seventeen, because the old one was illegal or whatever. Also they have that whole acre out the back. No internet ever unfortunately. You'd need to get a line in. One thing I advise is get that request in quick. But planning permission would be easy out the back there. You might not need it at all.'

He was giving them this honest and amenable overview. Lena felt it happen; felt a family fan out into the rooms and gradually scrape and paint the walls, clutter the yard with plastic junk, erect a trampoline like the taut palette of a huge open-mouthed animal, have twinkling Christmases and drunken arguments and at one point the woman, yes, the wife and mother, would capitulate and go out to buy double-lined crushed-velvet curtains that stormed to the floor because no matter what else she did that picture window was draughty and cold.

The ghost of the earlier woman, waked in the proscenium space of her own velvet curtains, might smile, hovering wispily to the side, at this capitulation, dreaming still of a dresser of Delft she once loved and locked which had long ago been dismembered for firewood.

'Thank you,' said Odhran, 'we'll be in touch.'

On the drive, he was calm. 'Thanks for being open to this.'

'Something to think about,' Lena said. 'I would,' she repeated, 'be honestly afraid of going mad.'

'That's because you're imagining yourself stuck with Sunny all day in some kind of death house,' Odhran told her. It was incredibly candid and precise.

She said, with wonderment, 'Why yes.'

'And it wouldn't be like that. You're too Dublin. You just don't understand what kind of life we could have out here – afford out here, where we can have space. There are schools, doctors, everything. This part of the county is affluent. It's not like those boarded-up towns you see in the midlands and it's not economically depressed; it's just underdeveloped. In terms of housing stock, I mean. That makes it cheap. I've been thinking about it.'

'Oh I can tell.' She was not put out but impressed. She liked being told what to do. In such situations, with madness and the maudlin tendencies within herself close to the surface or just held up like options, like *tableaux vivant*, it was better to take advice.

'Obviously,' he deferred, 'the choice will always be yours.'

I have never made choices, she thought. So few things were ever my decision at all. Leaving the band, for example, the event that made possible the rest of her life, was not her decision but foisted upon her as an act of romantic aggression mid-tour, when they were in Glasgow. She was twenty-five. Cian took her out for coffee by herself.

'You understand you are not needed,' he said, 'and we need to get leaner as a unit.' They were in Glasgow to start the tour, moving down; a string of regional British cities, London. They were touring with others. It had been planned and stage-managed and portioned out.

Outside a café in Glasgow, she'd stared at him, uncomprehending. It was wet – it had been raining recently. The street was whipped with wind and it led to some great municipal park; there were fruit-and-veg shops, ethnic shops, small fashionable cafés. Everywhere, elegant tenements massed in autumn colours at the sky. The sky in Glasgow was as wide and deep and pitiless and persistent as a Dublin sky.

'Will I see out the tour?' Lena held her poker face.

'No, no. You can go home whenever.' He didn't look at her.

'What does Mikey say?'

He laughed. 'Do you like Mikey?' he asked. 'I've heard he likes you.'

'You can't just tell me to leave.'

'You really want to stick around?' He laughed again.

Still he couldn't look at her – he'd put on sunglasses, was chewing anxiously on nothing. She glanced down at the lipstick print in coral on the rim of her coffee cup. She felt she had interpreted the world, her tea-leaf reading of reality, violently wrong.

She did not stay; of course she could not. She demanded three months' salary to leave at once. She got one month. She packed her guitar, packed the dresses, sobbed in anger all the way to the airport. But after that she never cried about it again. Nor did she feel vindicated, particularly, when she heard of him holding a phone up to a small crowd in a venue somewhere, months later, asking the audience to chant in unison: *Lena, Lena, Lena!*

She only said coolly, to a friend who asked about it, well, I didn't get that call. Maybe he is leaving crowd-sourced stalker messages on someone else's phone.

And in retrospect that was incredibly fucking weird.

How quickly years shrank down to size and became the same planar ever-now. What relief to be in this different place. It felt like grace; it was a sober, adult thought.

19

They were halfway back to Dublin when Maeve messaged Odhran. I'll come and see you later in the week, she said. And then: How soon can I come? Can I come and stay?

We could have driven you, he replied. We left an hour ago.

Last-minute panic, she answered. Mam.

She would take the train. Sonia had proved too much.

Lena felt a faint and delicate dismay at the thought of hosting on the hop and began to think about bedlinen, much of which was stippled with stains explainable and unexplained. Maeve landed into Heuston the following day and bowled the rose-gold suitcase all the way to Islandbridge herself.

That afternoon, Caoimhe phoned Lena – actually phoned – and Lena almost dropped the phone with fright.

'So are you free tonight?' Caoimhe asked. 'Because I have two pieces of gossip and one pertains to you. The other is about Orla.'

'Oh my God.' Lena sat on the arm of the terrible leather couch. 'I am, I think. But I need to bring my sister-in-law, she's visiting. She's very nice. She's very young.'

'Well, grand. Just don't tell Orla.'

They met at Café en Seine, which had been Lena's idea. Caoimhe said, 'What', and Lena pleaded, 'I don't know where anybody goes, literally, anymore.' It was a weekday and still the great tinselly hall was packed and echoing, but they sat on the terrace outside, where buddleia spiked smokily from vines draped over walls on either side. The summer sky was pale blue, chasms high above them, skated over by airplanes. Maeve wore a high-collared shirtdress and looked like a nun but ordered a glossy chalice of beer.

Caoimhe looked at her for a long time before saying, 'Your skin is like cheesecake.'

'Thank you.' Maeve blushed.

'Tell me my gossip,' Lena commanded.

'Your girl Elva,' Caoimhe pivoted immediately. 'She is getting divorced. And guess who from?'

Lena was frowning, greatly underwhelmed by this revelation. Caoimhe paused and plunged.

'Mikey O'Hara,' she said.

'No.'

'Somebody had to marry him, I suppose,' said Caoimhe. 'Then get divorced.'

'No. You can't be serious.'

'I am.'

'Dublin.' Lena was genuinely let down by the coincidence. 'Dublin,' she explained, 'is so small, I am like literally fucking embarrassed for it.'

Caoimhe looked at her strangely when she said this, seeming not to understand.

'Isn't he?' Lena began now.

'Yes.' Caoimhe met her levelly this time. 'He's completely insane.'

'No, I mean didn't he – beat up some girlfriend or other?'

'Oh. No.' Caoimhe sipped her cocktail, consternated. 'No, that was exaggerated.'

'I'm sorry,' Maeve was sitting erectly. 'But who is this person?'

'He was a property speculator. And an artist, actually.' Lena flipped out her phone and began scrolling Google, looking out for a coherent result to present to Maeve. 'Here's Wikipedia.' She passed it over. 'Oh my.' She laughed, sinking inward, feeling warm. 'I knew of him kind of back in the day. He managed us. Oh, let me tell you something,' laughing again, 'my

God, we were at this party once in some hotel in the Docklands – I can't remember which one – after a show in the O2, or the 3, or whatever it's called; we were at this kind of suite party and a runner comes over to me says, Mikey O'Hara has a car outside for you. I had to ask a few times what he meant and what he meant was: Mikey has sent a car to pick you up and take you to *an intimate gathering*.'

'And you didn't go?' Caoimhe looked angry.

'Not at all. It sounded like he was going to kill me. I was twenty.' She said, 'To be fair, he was probably twenty as well.'

'You should have gone, you virgin.' Caoimhe was joking, but there was edge.

'Not my style. When I think, though.' Lena felt fond. 'An intimate gathering.'

'He's owned a lot of companies.' Maeve was reading from the phone.

'In a manner of speaking. It was always his father's money or some REIT or share in this and that. Thing is, he also made stupid big sculptures and owned a lot of art.' Lena took her phone back. 'It was the Boom,' she told Maeve. 'It was a different time.'

'He lost a lot of money, but I think he's OK now; he still owns quite a bit. He has an art collection and you see the odd article about it. He's involved in films.'

'In a way, it was all impressive,' Lena said. 'But I did think he was abusive.'

'Nothing I've heard.' Caoimhe was firm and, it seemed, proximally offended by the idea. 'I mean, it's a fairly broad church these days.'

They had fallen into three reveries. Lena said at length, 'So, divorced?'

'Messy, allegedly. She is back in the castanet house.'

'How do you know these things?'

'I just know.' Caoimhe was restored.

Her knowledge and reach was so parochial, Lena, aloof and protected from it, felt condescension: these gathering waves of influence and importance, which swelled so much of a certain kind of Dublin, only ended up breaking into petty little hisses on the bulwark of Lena's remoteness. Part of this remoteness was her social otherness, her lack of connections, and part of it the greater edifice of Odhran and Sunny and boredom and detachment and indifference.

It had not always been like this. Once, she felt, she had been part of it, and it had seemed vital. She'd been singing for a living and even dropped out of her degree; she was busy, needed, rarely alone. Always in company. She remembered, for instance, sitting here, in Café en Seine, some ten years ago with the band. They were discussing Sony, who, at that time, proposed to take them to America and record. She remembered that even then she distrusted the scene itself, though, or distrusted the waves of influence and importance it produced.

'We shouldn't do it,' she'd said. The table became animated. Everybody looked at her. She named two bands they knew. 'They tested with Sony, they signed over the copyright, they had to do this. And then' – this they knew, but she explained again – 'the label decided to hold onto the albums and not release.' She sipped her drink. 'They will do it to us,' she concluded. 'It's like they are collecting souls.'

Cian stared at her. His arms were folded. He had a beautiful face, lean and expressive and intelligent. They were sleeping together.

'She is right,' he said suddenly.

'So that's just it?' The others were shocked. But for Frances, the cellist, who never cared.

'We can talk about it more,' Cian said, 'but Lena is right.'

Her heart might have burst, that moment, for pleasure. They were sleeping together and nobody knew and now he listened to her, almost crazily; listened to everything she said. She never repented of the decision in the years afterwards either. It had not been real: not Sony, not America, not fame, not youth, not boom.

Oh but the seduction, she thought now: well, in a manner of speaking, it was real. A memory that was never other than raw of a cottage in the mountains and a rainstorm ranting down; of a girl standing braless in a vest, gooseflesh, moving to place her guitar against a chair, moving to the pane of glass that looked towards the gate and a light on the gatepost.

Wicklow was not like Clare. Wicklow was peopled and glamorous. But it was just the two of them in this remoteness; she was on fire; he stood behind and pushed one cold hand without asking through an armhole of the vest and stroked her breast, the globe of it, making her jump slightly and gasp and he said, 'Don't be frightened of me.'

He said, 'Your heart is going so fast.' He tried to laugh. But his breath was heavy. 'I want so much to touch you,' he said.

'You're already touching me.'

'If you say so.' He was entirely still. 'I will touch you all over. I'll touch you everywhere.'

'OK. I say so.' She smiled. She was terrified.

In the bedroom they undressed separately and she delivered herself in a blaze of embarrassment, unaware – she would think later, with rue – of how delicious and young was her body at twenty-two, how plump and full of blood, how elastic and worthy of his gasp and his groan and insistence, over and over, of I've wanted this, I needed it. He would – she had to think about it and count – have been thirty-five, thereabouts. It seemed really old at the time. It was not so old to her now; not so intimidating.

There was something exposing and vindicating in a man putting his tongue between your legs, then pulling on your nipples with his teeth, exposing himself, vindicating you; it was not your fault, none of this desire had been invited, you could not help it, you were blameless, you could only lie back and feel him enter with friction, almost losing control of himself, hissing, you're so tight, a silly thing to say but true, and finally the power came: she wrapped her legs around him, came easily with a scream of triumph. She was blameless.

He fucked her with preposterous tenderness, almost reverence. He could not be normal about anything.

She must, in the afterglow, have had wifely thoughts. She must have thought: now he has harmed me and owes me and also he could hurt me terribly.

The most famous song Cian released with Lena as singer was a cover of 'Something's Gotten Hold of My Heart' and you could still listen to that: it was on Spotify.

You touch me and my mind goes astray!

Amazing to think of her bravery: it turned the band against her, this favouritism. They did know, on some level, about the relationship, of course, because she was too young to conceal her cravings and because he had unpicked every objection carefully, showing delicacy and even devotion, for several years, and they could see. She would never love someone like that, with the hungry bluntness of her body and such arrogant trust, again.

And this was restful really, who could be doing with living that way. It was lonely. But here was a bar full of men, for example. Would she ever love again. Love another. Would this life now be a past life – imagine that. Prompts from nowhere, prompts from absent friends, fell about her inconsequentially. Passion had devolved to maintenance between she and Odhran, yes; it could not be otherwise. The price of passion was pain.

'You might have been Missus O'Hara,' Caoimhe teased acidly now.

'It was nothing like that.' Lena was honest. 'He hardly interacted with me.'

'There's still time.' But Caoimhe looked sour, then preoccupied.

Caoimhe, Lena thought, was one of those people whose brilliant insensitivity led to a loud, eventful life. It was a kind of entitlement you needed to inhabit at an early age. Lena did not begrudge her this but would never, in her shyness and shamefacedness, mimic it.

Even if you would of course miss crusading sex; who wouldn't miss such a thing. She wondered if Caoimhe would be knocking on doors tonight.

It never paid to think in this direction and Lena felt wary of it.

She had been quiet for a time and now Caoimhe and Maeve were discussing London.

'You must know Róisín Regan and all that gang.'

'By reputation.' Maeve's face was a mask. Lena felt compromised by the idea that Maeve was regarding them, regarding Lena and Caoimhe, their lives, as either future versions of her own life or cautionary tales. The latter felt somehow more likely.

'She has written a few articles for *New York Magazine* now.'

'Her novel was mediocre.' Lena re-entered the chat.

'It was?'

'No style. Just like – words.'

Maeve laughed, seeming less reserved. 'I mean, it was a book, right? They tend to have words.'

'I mean words with no music to them. And extreme situations, all this gritty urban bad-sex shit, sort of juvenile. I don't see why you'd bother writing a novel if you can't write. You could just do a photo montage or, like, an essay for *New York Magazine*.'

'Do you have good sex in London?' Caoimhe asked.

Maeve was getting used to Caoimhe, but still, once again, blushed. 'I was seeing a man who worked at Burberry. He had a very swish apartment. It was not gritty.'

Lena, swingingly proud of Maeve in this moment, also echoed to herself, *I was*.

Caoimhe wanted to know his name and where the apartment had been located and sat up, triggered into longing, leaving Lena to watch and contemplate and recall Maeve landing up, early, to Heuston with her little golden suitcase, spending hours playing with Sunny voluntarily. Avoiding the adults; saying oh my, show me more, whenever the kid pulled a trick.

'Aunty Maeve,' Sunny called. 'Can you pretend you don't know I have a horse?'

'My goodness,' cried Maeve. 'A horse.'

Odhran had wanted to know about the boyfriend, and Lena knew why, even if Odhran did not: he wanted, always, to see people coupled off. As he aged, Odhran felt impatient with those who did not follow his example. She disliked this trickle of insecurity; she wanted to tell Maeve, have as much fun as you can. I should have had fun and not drifted around this dusty city in the aftermath of Cian, which, she knew now, was precisely what she'd done. Because she was ashamed and the shame dredged up the shame of her childhood – its smallness and meanness and her parents' inattention – and ran and ran. A waste.

She thought of the party from which Mikey had tried to summon her that time, so long ago, but realised she could not actually remember it. It was simply a thing she happened to know had occurred. Visuals, sensual content proving anything, were lost to time, since although life once seemed continuous, whole years had by now been compressed into facts and totems. Would she have found it exciting to answer the summons and get in the car? Probably not. When she was twenty she was frightened by men as opposed to excited by the idea of frightening men. By twenty-two, by the time she and Cian became a couple, it was different – she had grown more confident, reckless, curious.

Lena was a little bored now in Café en Seine. But so rarely *out*.

'I think I'll have another,' she said. 'Ladies?'

'I'm good,' said Maeve.

Caoimhe squinted. 'I had them mix this drink for me. I'll go up in a moment to explain it again.'

At the bar, Lena gripped the gold rail to cool her palms and looked at a greenish reflection of herself in a wall mirror.

As she paid, she remembered something and hurried back to the terrace table with her wine purposefully.

'Tell me about Orla,' she said.

'Ah.' Caoimhe ceased rooting in her bag and placed her elbows on the table. 'So, she's in an open marriage now.'

Again Lena felt queer pricks of shock and redundancy at once. The claim was both remarkable and banal: juicy in its intimacy yet simultaneously devoid of edge, as if any expectation of drama or implication or even a plot was gouged in advance by a kind of lukewarm, overfamiliar, even egregious kind of topicality.

'How do you know?' she asked.

'Her husband is seeing someone who works with Chris' – this was Caoimhe's partner – 'and she had to explain. She took him to a work party.' Caoimhe said, 'Advertising is pretty much nothing but work parties.'

'That doesn't mean—'

'Oh, I believe it.' Caoimhe stood now, preparing to go to the bar. 'It explains her vibe. Don't you think it explains her vibe? I think it's crusty polyamory. Not sexy. Earnest.'

'They have a kid,' Lena told Maeve.

'So do plenty of people. Here, be back.' Caoimhe melted into the crowd.

'You seem surprised.' Maeve was, finally, enjoying herself.

'I shouldn't be. People are all at this now. I quail,' she reclaimed herself, 'I *quail* at the thought of all the admin and also most women I know are working through, like, attachment issues. Isn't that messy when it's spread around the place?'

Maeve shrugged.

'Oh, I don't approve.' Lena huffed playfully. 'I very much don't approve.'

'Odhran is my brother,' Maeve said, oddly, then. 'Well, one of my brothers.'

This hung in the air a moment and seemed beside the point but also darkly freighted. Maeve was preoccupied for a beat, and then asked, 'Why did you get married?'

This was a different thing. A ruder topic, actually.

'I was in love,' Lena replied.

'Do you have to get married if you are in love?'

Lena took a mouthful of wine and thought. 'With a child.' she began. She sighed. 'With a child, everything is less important; you, I mean, are less important. Your quest for fulfilment or whatever.'

'It's a sacrifice.'

Lena looked at her steadily. 'Yes. You want them to have, I mean, a stable home life. My parents, for instance, were chaos. And it followed me a lot when I got older. For Sunny I want the absolute opposite. I want her world to be extremely safe.'

She felt anguished and fell silent for a moment. She said, 'Safe, that is, from me.'

Maeve stared back.

'Safe from my worst emotions. Safe from any chaos I might bring. And Odhran is the same. So you have to shelve all thoughts of, like, soap opera. You have to be a proper communist. I mean it.' They were both laughing now, thinly. 'To each according to his need.'

'Not loving everyone, loving the world?'

'That's Christianity. And no.'

Caoimhe returned with a cocktail in a glass like a meat-eating plant. 'I believe it,' she reiterated, sounding drunker. 'It explains the crusty vibe.'

'Oh I'd like one of them.' Lena sprang from her chair. 'How do they mix it again?'

She tried to imagine what kind of person Orla, in her plain and inexplicably Teutonic way, might pursue sexually, beyond the strangely handsome man she was married to. Strange because his looks were so inordinately normative they didn't make sense for Orla. Women, Lena thought abruptly – Orla would pursue women. Of course.

They left, a little later, and the warm night met Lena and made her tired.

She thought of the open fields of Clare. They were mutinous and silent to the point of ecstasy, standing all about like walls. Here the city's cliffs, greenish and fluttering with modesty tarpaulin high above the churn of Nassau Street, were without mystery. Nobody knows me in Clare, she reflected. Why didn't I think of that before? And I know nobody. It should have been fun to go out and visit some vision of singleness but had not been; the sameness, the sour little snatches of triumph over other people, had left her depressed.

She anticipated the bright tram home, the second tram, the long walk down the *tabula rasa* of Old Kilmainham Road with the prison and the museum looming like grain silos.

Maeve pulled on a light leather jacket and said, 'Some friends are all in the Ginger Man and I might join them, is that OK?'

'Of course.' Lena was embarrassed. She thought the younger woman might have been dying to get away. Her night held more potential than theirs. 'But you'll need – a key?'

'Odhran says he'll stay up.' Maeve held up her phone.

'Oh he does, does he. Well, enjoy yourself.'

She left Lena with an empty feeling and Caoimhe, gurgling with mirth, by her side.

'Your girl Elva may be on the warpath,' Caoimhe advised. 'You know in lockdown Mikey disappeared and started tweeting from this conspiracy theory account.'

'I'm less and less surprised by your revelations.'

'He was sectioned. It really blew her cover. Turned out they'd been living on some kind of farm.' She paused to re-sink a foot into a blue pump. She held onto the fluting top of a wrought-iron area rail. 'Living on a farm in Wicklow, not drinking fluoride or whatever.'

Lena said, 'I don't think I can hear any more of this.'

Caoimhe was surprised.

'Isn't anyone normal?' Lena asked.

'This is normal. You just live a sheltered life.'

Cian used to tell me that, she almost replied.

20

When Maeve left, Sonia changed the bedding on every bed in the farmhouse and hung this out to dry in an incredible dry and close heat which had descended across the countryside. In the mornings there was heavy mist on the mountains and in the afternoons it felt as if the ozone layer, that imperilled film they were hearing about so often in the eighties and nineties, was definitely burnt away. She sat in patio shade and watched the bedsheets dry. It was greatly satisfying to think they would hold onto that heady outdoor atmosphere. But later that day, as the heat intensified, the smell of some dead thing in a hedge or barnyard filled the air, having nowhere to go and no wind to thin it out. It turned shrilly metallic by late afternoon, as if someone had attempted to dose it with disinfectant. She knew better than to worry about bedsheets taking on the smell, but it ruined the effect.

She polished the large wall-length vanity table, its fitted frameless mirrors, in the attic room that had been Maeve's. Seán had built this table for Maeve when the girl was twelve or so. One might suggest, Sonia thought, that her vanity stemmed from that single devoted decision to cover an entire wall in mirrors and create excessive amounts of space for make-up and creams. Maeve would do her homework here, where she could look up and see herself.

Sonia had anticipated the visit but did not mind Maeve

leaving, really, when she did. Always you were basically disappointed by anything you looked forward to.

She decided, abruptly annoyed, that the cleaner could sort out the rest of the house when she came next week. Sonia had evening plans but drifted into the kitchen for tea in the interim, filling a glass with tap water to cool down. It was then that she glanced at and fixed on a little white card embossed with print that was fastened to the fridge. She had magnets from everywhere – Corfu, Jersey, Tenerife – holding up papers and cards and notices and photographs and bills. The little white card had not even yellowed with time.

She'd picked it up years ago. It was a mild day in winter and Sonia had travelled with Noeleen Reddan, whose daughters were then in Australia, along the crisp yellow coast of the lake. They looked into the green plains and huddled spinneys of the Whitegate estate, with its Victorian mansion like a hotel hidden somewhere near the private cove and harbour on the lake. It had been sold for two million to a property consortium in twenty-twelve. They discussed this gossip, the estate lying mostly empty ever since, as Noeleen's Land Rover purred like a little spaceship into the wilder woodier richer uplands towards Scariff and Cregg Woods.

They were driving to Raheen Wood. Today was the day of the advent fair at the Steiner School. Noeleen Reddan's son was married to a German woman who taught at the Steiner School; they had several children and all of these dressed in undyed fabric, copying texts like little monks – *I look into the world in which the sun is shining in which the stars are sparkling in which the stones repose* – by the light of beeswax candles, presumably. The advent fair was very nice, Noeleen said, because you could get all kinds of Christmas crafts.

Sonia, at that time lately widowed, was conveyed about by friends often. She was taken to Galway, Cork, the Burren, to Dublin by one of her daughters-in-law, and to visit indigent families by Imelda, who worked with the Vincent de Paul charity. She enjoyed this and it wouldn't last. It was like getting married and doing a tour of family branches, but in reverse.

'She's that bit humourless,' Noeleen said of the German daughter-in-law. 'But God love him, I don't know what else Derek could do. That boy was always quiet as a mouse.'

'I remember,' said Sonia. Sonia had prescribed Derek sertraline at sixteen. Noeleen looked at her sideways, now, aware of having disclosed something without any return.

'How are yours doing?' she demanded.

'I have a lovely new grandchild in Dublin,' Sonia said.

Where the road was exposed, wind whipped pertly from the lake. There was no parking to be had opposite the tree-tumbled gateposts of the school, and no parking in either of the waste yards set aside on the road ahead. Cars lined the scrap of path, nose-to-tail dolphins. The sun was low and clear but the landscape hibernating, hostile, dun. Where they parked at last, in Mackey's yard, the ground was saturated; like dough beneath their feet.

'Foolish me,' Sonia said. She was wearing loafers with patterned inserts and the earth would cling to them.

'I'm afraid it's mud the whole way,' Noeleen told her.

They picked along the pathway into wind. Beyond the gateposts of the school the mud steepened, but there were trees ahead, the ground now packed and rolling with irregular rocks and stones as artificial and exotic as a zoo enclosure. From the trees hung rope ladders and tyre swings and, through the trees, grouped distantly, they saw wooden chalets. People and children milled all about. Sonia, dressed for the town for no sensible reason, moved cautiously over the stones.

'It's nice, isn't it?' Noeleen asked.

It was nice. It looked like an illustration of a ringfort from a children's textbook, and the chalets with their wooden hooks and simple wooden benches made her think of her own schoolhouse in the mountains, where she had to speak Irish and carry peat donations for the fire. But then she was sent to boarding school near Limerick, with the nuns, and it was parlours and starch and sanitary pads like bath sponges and scholarships from then on.

Noeleen's daughter-in-law was bare-faced, bright-eyed, with capillaries broken prettily across her cheeks and a sack-like dress. She was baking biscuits in a room teeming with children, low tables dusted with flour and mittens on strings, and her expression remained harried as they approached her. Noeleen's florid introduction was met with a harried unshakeable face.

'Yes the children and Derek are somewhere,' the woman said. 'We are very overrun.'

Back outside, Sonia watched an attractive young couple with elaborate knapsacks separate two squabbling toddlers. There was a happy energy now, and a gauze of rain so soft it seemed commissioned by the canopy; it seemed to exist only here, and not in the greater atmosphere. They moved towards a larger chalet and a display of home baking Sonia queued for, wearily. Both women sat with cake and coffee in a classroom. On the board, fluting, timeless, slightly gothic script had been half-swiped away, but Sonia could see the words LIGHT OF THE BEASTS and nodded at it and said, 'God above, look at that.' She laughed.

'Oh, but it's no worse than a normal school,' Noeleen, going native, protested. 'With crucifixes everywhere.'

'The light of the beasts,' Sonia read out loudly. And then, unbidden, into her brain it came:

> Christmas Eve, and twelve of the clock.
> 'Now they are all on their knees,'
> An elder said as we sat in a flock
> By the embers in hearthside ease.

And a rush of emotion pushed behind her eyes, and made her hot.

She felt chastened as they found a bin for their paper plates and walked into the charm of the rain again, the space itself strangely windless. They followed signs to a steamed geodome at the other side of a basketball court which was, underfoot, entirely muck. A man was whittling. They passed the whittling man and into the geodome, where stalls had been set up.

'I'll find you,' Noeleen told her, drifting off.

It was here Sonia stood before a table of blue felt, browsing little stickered bottles of ointment and oil, aware pleasantly of the din of people filling the geodome, her mind fixing in idleness on the Hardy poem, when the woman at the stall frowned and caught her eye.

'Your husband,' the woman said.

Sonia started. The woman was aged in her thirties, with a wind-chaffed complexion that was soft and blooming youthfully. Her hair fell in unstyled kinks to her shoulders. Her eyes were brown. Sonia did not know her or many people like her. Sonia stared back.

'Do you want to hear it?' the woman asked. The tinny din around had subsided, it seemed, or would so in the memory and vignette that would come.

'Go on then,' Sonia said.

'Your husband has not left you, he's actually following you. A tall man, lean, good-looking. When did he pass?'

'June,' Sonia said, unruffled. 'And it was not a shock, he was well prepared and aware he was going to die. He died of cancer of the pancreas. It was never in doubt.'

'Did he follow you much, when he was alive?'

'Not at all. He was his own man.'

'Do you mind me saying this?'

'I suppose.' Sonia found herself breathing in heavily. She was alarmed; she was also oddly consoled. 'I forgive you because I assume you are away with the fairies or whatever.'

The woman laughed, although softly. Her accent was mildly foreign. 'He is following you,' she repeated, 'and I would be happy to talk to him for you.'

Sonia bristled. 'And what would you say?'

'To leave you now. If that's what you wanted.'

His clothes were at home, they were still in the lovely old

cherrywood wardrobe, creaky and freakish, that lived – had always lived, since the time of Methuselah – in the back bedroom. Sonia could not clear them because to see them hanging there, bereft and shrunken, was to imagine his body as a baby and a young man. It was to imagine him as the tender helpless thing he'd once been, when he was small, before they met. It broke her heart that he was only a child who grew into a man and then died and she could not protect him from that. To cope with this, she needed strictly to remember him as a man, which is to say a symbol, not a human thing with thin contingent shrunken bereft suits and hats and slacks. She would go home and call her sons. Or at least call Aidan and Niall, and instruct them to sort through and pack up their father's things. Niall would probably send his wife. She would do this today.

'Well, you've surprised me this day,' Sonia said to the woman, at last.

'My name is Aude.' On the jars and bottles it said *Aude Renggli Reegan, Herbalist.*

What a name, Sonia thought. Beautiful. Like ark, or aubade, or *bád*.

'Here is my card,' said Aude.

Sonia left the stall after that and, distracted, ran into Noeleen. 'I offered to take the children,' the other woman was complaining of her daughter-in-law, 'but she said no, they have to stay and keep helping, apparently.'

'You know Cathal, my eldest, had an Austrian girl that time.'

'That was in Brussels?'

'Yes. Very plain she was. But you know, she had this great self-possession. Anyway, he was in pieces afterwards. I never knew why it was such a big deal, but they're terribly – candid people, or something.'

'It's arrogance.' Noeleen's mood had soured. The veil of rain was thickening. They left for home, finding banners and signposts felled and flapping in the wind that had been oddly absent on the grounds of the school.

Sonia popped Aude's card onto the fridge, with photographs and prayer cards and the Serenity Prayer, and a day later telephoned her from the hall.

'Now you said something about asking him to leave.'

'Yes.'

'Would you come to me for that, or would I go to you?'

'Whichever you prefer.'

Aude lived near Feakle, which was a drive around winding minor roads by the wet despairing light of the late afternoon. Her house was a clapped-out bungalow, ill suited to Aude, it seemed, but inside she had decorated the shelves and ceilings with dried sticks and moss and flowers. Her four-year-old child was sent to the front room to watch television.

'Is he at the Steiner place?' Sonia, nervous and needing conversation, sat at the table. Before her was placed a huge painted bowl of fruit and on the hob a large pot simmered, smelling of garlic. The bare window looked onto a plateau of stunted grass. Aude seemed almost embarrassed as she lit a white candle and took Sonia's hands in her own long, cool hands.

'Seán,' she said. 'Sonia, your wife, loves you very much but wishes you to go.'

There was a pause.

'There is no use following her around; unless you have something to say, and if so, you can tell her through me.'

Another pause. Sonia thought: Seán would be mortally embarrassed to do something like that. She thought of his shame at being exposed by this young woman. She felt tempted to tell Aude it was OK if he wanted to stay, he was always welcome, but this was not in fact the case; in fact, ever since the geodome, Sonia had felt incrementally terrified by a creeping, moreish, perverse sense of being observed and appealed to, and she wanted it to stop.

'Is he – has it worked?' she asked.

'Maybe wait a few days.' Aude looked strained. 'Then let me know if the symptoms have passed.'

Sonia became upset then, or, at least, Aude responded to her as if she was upset, gripping her hands and looking further strained and saying, 'It's OK, grief is unpredictable.'

'He was a lovely man,' Sonia insisted. 'He was the loveliest of men and a good father. I never had a day of trouble from him.'

'And in the next place,' Aude said softly, 'he will be happy.'

'Will I see him again?'

'In a manner of speaking,' said Aude.

No, she did not want money, or at least claimed she did not want money. Sonia left her fifty euros in an envelope anyway.

On the drive home, Sonia was suddenly angry, then humiliated, and then, watching television with her feet up in the darkness of advent, relaxed. She could never tell anyone about this, not even her sisters; they would believe she'd been fleeced, or even that she should call a priest. Sonia literally did not know any priests personally anymore.

This thought struck her as singular and a pity and served as a distraction, sending her in search of her address book to double-check.

Thoughts of Aude, meanwhile, remained obscure. Like objects in cold storage for four subsequent years, by which time Aidan and Odhran had long emptied the rosewood wardrobe and donated clothes. In this time the little card reading *Aude Renggli Reegan, Herbalist* remained clipped to the fridge with prayer cards and postcards and vitamin lists and a dismaying roll of photobooth images showing two of her teenage grandchildren crushed together on a stool wearing glittery boas and two strips of ultrasound photographs indistinguishable; remained pristine as a print in snow.

Sonia parted two magnets now and picked it off and frowned at it. Maybe the number had changed, or Aude had moved. Hippy types were forever coming and going from East Clare. This was something, she thought with a lift of ambition, that the internet would know.

21

After the night at Café en Seine, Lena's head became filled with the possibility of moving to Clare. It was so abstract she could meet it like a manifestation board – pretty, elliptical, aspirant – and so bowdlerise the very idea of home ownership, of acquisition, itself. Like the time she watched a landlord wrench a washer tight to a water pipe and say, a screw between his teeth, 'Houses are nothing but trouble, girl. You own a house, you are never done doing work on that house.' She had thought, how rude. Every tenant in this place is a failed probation away from *the side of the road*.

But now if she contemplated fixing her own water pipes and bleeding radiators and so on, it really did seem intimidating. Who did you call when you lost your keys?

When she conjured Clare, then, she imagined open roads and not the dusty little death-bungalow with its crop circles from coasters in the floor. She did not talk about it with Odhran in detail yet. It paid to be careful. His enthusiasm, that element of hyperactivity that might have been kind of glandular and took hold of him and related, she always felt, in some way to his physical skinniness, could be irritating if he thought he could get his way. Breaking a lease in Dublin was also at least as fraught a decision as having another child.

In this atmosphere of private giddy imagining, Lena felt lighter of mood than she had in a while. When Sunny asked, on Thursday afternoon, 'Mama, did you go to a place with heads?' Lena did not hesitate, but followed her first synaptic snap.

'Yes, honey,' she said, 'it was called Inisbofin. Did I tell you about it?'

Sunny looked doubtful in Disney style, scrunching up her face. 'I don't know.'

'Come here.' Lena beckoned from the couch and took Sunny on her lap, tilting her back antically until she was cradling her. Sunny laughed.

'Now you are like my teeny-tiny baby,' Lena said. 'I'll tell you about the place with heads: there were lots of skulls, which are skeleton heads, lots of skeleton heads and they were stolen and put in a museum. For heads. Then the people who lived in Inisbofin got them back.'

'Can you show me,' Sunny asked, 'on your phone?'

Lena did: she showed Sunny photographs of the skulls in their polythene bags, chinless and tapered at the front so that they looked like novelty candles.

She remember the island. In particular a long evening after the singing lesson ended, in the lighted bar over a drop to dark water on the pier side; the stacked and singsong architecture of nineties and noughties tourism initiatives, the smell of salt and rot. Cas Cronin, who was a quiet and sinister person missing some quality – missing it on a pathological level, like a key neurological pathway – that might have made him seem remotely normal, returning to a bollard on the pier to smoke in the gloaming. It returned to her as an image.

'Somewhere I will take you before school starts' – Lena let Sunny wriggle to her feet again – 'is the national museum. We'll see the Egyptian mummy, and the bog bodies. Those are dead people who were left underground for so long they are squashed.'

'I'll be afraid,' Sunny said.

'Are you afraid when you think about dying?'

Sunny thought. She said, 'Sometimes I am afraid.'

A letter had come, about school. Lena had put it aside and

out of her mind. When Sunny scampered to her room, she turned to Maeve. Maeve was sitting at the kitchen island, watching, the whole time. She was leaving for London the following day.

'That was good,' Maeve said. 'Like, being open with her like that.'

'You saw that right? She asked me about the heads?'

'And you knew what she meant.' Maeve smiled vaguely, inwardly. 'Or like, made that conjecture.'

Lena nodded stiffly.

'Maybe she didn't – mean those heads?'

'Maybe.' Lena sat on the couch and chewed on a nail. 'Maybe I mentioned it before – around her, maybe, and she remembers. She has an appointment,' she said, 'with a play therapist. I used to know this guy years ago. I looked him up when we got back from your mother's.'

'What does that involve?' asked Maeve. 'Play therapy?'

'I don't really know, but I guess you can tell things about a child from the way they play. Also the parents – watching the interactions and so on.'

'Interesting,' said Maeve.

They were going out tonight, Lena and Odhran; Maeve had offered to babysit. Neither could think of anywhere to go and so, at nine, when the night was still purplish and sliding into the storm season of July, they walked to the stile that accessed the Park and climbed the steep stairway of packed earth and sleepers. The magazine fort, square and high and slit with apertures, like a suit of armour, stood before them, and there were joggers and straggling parties of drinkers on benches and in the meadow around the Wellington Monument.

'Will we just walk?' Odhran asked.

'We could cross all the way to Park Gate Street and go into a pub,' Lena shrugged. She spritzed open a little can of gin. 'I've got one for you.'

'Indeed.' He regarded it plainly. 'This is kind of a girlie drink.'

'It's discreet.' They dandered up the pathway that was picturesque, between high cooling pines, not making for Park Gate but wandering without particularity. It was a route they'd taken regularly with Sunny in her sling in the first flowery months of the pandemic. Death was happening somewhere, they were told, but not close at hand. At the Royal Hospital, the government set up a field morgue, long white wedding tents, that never needed to be used, but at one point the prospect of a morgue a half-mile up the road was sobering.

Lena had been able at that time to blame lockdown for her deranging isolation, for the days drawn out opaque as coloured slime, for the nights of radio documentaries and the drill of the bottle-maker when breastfeeding was given up. They were online all the time and talked about life online as if it were real life. Discourse flinched, then plunged towards certain storylines and impulses, mostly negative. Everybody, for example, was scoffing at the UK and its softer lockdown policy; then certain edges of the Left were scoffing at Ireland for being so infantilised and there would often be people bleating in terror about Covid and long Covid and lying awake worrying about marginalised communities and also solidarity signs and gestures and Lena sat outside of this, unmoved, feeling like a snob. Until something happened to bring her into it, briefly and painfully – something to do with Cas, who was always a bad omen.

'Remember we used to walk here so much in the pandemic,' she said now. It was a trite attempt at connection and boring to utter in itself.

'I don't think I remember anything from that time,' Odhran said, shutting it down.

The letter that had come, welcoming Sunny to Saint Michael's National School, was something they had to talk about. Lena had phoned the Educate Together at Broombridge to learn that Sunny was sixteenth on the waiting list.

'That's fifteen evictions or absorptions into the Gaelscoil before she has a chance of getting in,' she told Odhran now.

‘Yes.’ His face was hard to read. He sipped from the can of gin by raising his whole hand artificially high and bringing it to his lips self-consciously.

Would it matter, they wondered together, where she went?

Both Lena and Odhran had been given the standard school experience of their generation, in a time before coding and multiculturalism and ASD: a strict curriculum, frequent speeches about hell, May altars, unlimited Irish, analogue bullying. In the time since they’d been ambiently encouraged to overstate its mistakes and predations and imagine themselves oppressed by the state in this additional, retrofitted way. How bad could it be for Sunny to receive the updated version? Lena did not, as she explained to Odhran now, necessarily wish to withhold, say, Jesus.

‘Jesus,’ Odhran echoed. ‘Imagine what she would do with the idea of Jesus, nailed to a cross.’

‘It’s no weirder than death in water at the side of the road.’

‘Exactly.’ They laughed.

What the hell were they going to do about this. What were they talking about. What was this death with heads and holes in heads and eucharist. For months, they’d pushed through versions of this conversation, rehearsing the same bafflement or diminishing it or becoming heated about it or disagreeing or agreeing on some plan to tolerate it, dismiss it, remain curious about it – every possible response, unto what had, now, become a state of apathy. It was as if they’d discussed something for so long the syntax had crumbled into nothing and become nonsense, sound and fury, *seeky-atric, seeky-atric.*

In the pandemic Lena’s ex-boyfriend, Gwynn, had messaged her, to her surprise. I wondered if you were doing all right, he said. Oh yes! I am married with a new baby. You are! He did not send emojis; he seemed genuinely thrown. He did not follow her on Instagram anymore apparently. My goodness, congratulations, he said. He sounded English even in his dispatches. Gwynn was a psychotherapist. He met her on an app. Sitting into a booth of Metro Café on their first date, he – stocky, dark-eyed, handsomely substantial – said, 'Maybe you get asked a lot, but were you a singer?'

'Yes,' she said.

'I didn't recognise you,' Gwynn smiled with small white teeth, 'but my son did.'

'Oh?' She put on her most polite face.

'He's fifteen. I was twenty when he was born; it's why I stayed over here. He lives with his mother but comes to me every weekend.'

'You showed me – to your son?'

'Well, the dating thing was his idea.' Gwynn beamed as if enchanted by the fact.

She did not expect to see Gwynn again, except she did, for he was intensely polite and interested. He was a Lacanian. He disagreed with CBT and also the creep of that denuded Buddhism you saw in mindfulness and so on, though he felt uncomfortable about this and a friend named Eleanor he referred to more than once, a colleague, was deeply convinced about mindfulness and so on, so. They sometimes argued about it and also Eleanor, it turned out, had been his girlfriend, they'd lived together; now he lived alone in a white cottage near Laytown in Meath. This was not far from where Lena grew up.

She said, 'Oh yes, I know that area well.'

'If you ever visit,' Gwynn told her, 'we can walk the whole length of the beach.'

She did visit. She found a warm house filled with the dark furniture he liked to collect and with whole walls given over to shelving for books. You sat at the kitchen table on pews from a church. He moved with the adorable nervousness of a man trying to impress and they walked on the beach, spring wind swelling back at them like an unseen bellying sail, passing some horseback riders and the hoofprints of the horses, all the way to the navigation stacks at Drogheda harbour, and back to the house. Back at the house, Lena thought of the woman Eleanor rather a lot, suspecting every single indication of femininity – a patterned duvet set, William Morris crockery, a Bridget's Cross above the door – and felt brattily inclined to persevere.

There was a reticence between her and Gwynn that never quite abated but felt also like a form of mutual privacy; his desire to impress extended to a sexual tenderness and, when her lease was renewed and the rent set at a higher rate that June, she moved into the cottage for three disastrous months. The son, Jamie, was unwell with some nonspecific consuming anxiety. She hardly saw him and when she did, those hours he spent out of his room on weekends, she saw a keenly underweight young person with large wet eyes and a habit of crunching his wrists together, pushing his arms out stiffly ahead of him, as if handcuffed. It was such a radical and unnatural physical pose, she almost longed to mimic it. She was studying and working part-time. She was often at the kitchen table, on the pew, with books and notebooks. Jamie opened the fridge and then left the room without taking anything out of it and, one night, wakeful with contagious anguish, Gwynn said, 'I think he is feeling tense about the house not being his anymore.'

'Wasn't it Eleanor's?'

He blinked at her, wounded. 'I suppose. But that was different.'

She found a room and moved back out. It was a room in Phibsborough; it had a moulded plaster fireplace and seven other tenants in lesser rooms off a steep stair carpeted in the colour of liver. The houses had been built for senior prison officers in the 1890s and, walking down the high street and turning at Doyle's Corner, the red barrels of the prison complex came into view. Its windows, like those of the magazine fort, were medieval slits. She did not want to meet Gwynn in the house, but directed him to a café on the next block instead.

'I don't think we should see each other anymore.' He looked relieved, but also upset. She wanted him to blame the kid, Jamie; she wanted him to blame himself, his preciousness, his tenderness, his need to be liked and respected, the inadequacy of such things in a Lacanian of all people – that thought climate, she figured, would need balls. Afterwards she would feel ashamed of her haste and high-handedness but Lena in her twenties could be nothing but hasty and high-handed and self-interested because Cian, the aborted outline of her first original professional life, was so embarrassing a precedent, no further risk was permitted. She felt still like her small, sealed self and that this man would regret it and maybe he did, who knows, she didn't hear from Gwynn again until that day in the pandemic.

Congratulations, he messaged, that must have happened fast.

How is Jamie? she asked. A long answer followed: eighteen and starting college, his mother and I worry but he's improved though there are relapses and this lockdown is affecting him badly and so on. She felt warmth towards the boy only then, since now she had a child of her own and could imagine the strain but also suspicion that you – your errors and caprices, bringing women in to live with you randomly, for example – might have weakened your child's resilience somehow, made them insecure or predisposed or just too watchful to relax.

Would you think about that? She thought this now, about Sunny. She wondered once again about Sunny. It was a drab thought. Lena wished to move away from it.

She would do it, she decided. She would bring it up. 'Tell me,' she held up her hands to Odhran, 'about the school possibilities in Clare.'

He brightened. 'There's an Educate Together in Limerick,' he said.

Odhran loathed Limerick. It made him actively distressed to walk through it.

'And the Steiner School,' he continued, 'and smaller parish schools with no waiting lists.'

'Steiner.' Lena, open always to any hope of characterological change, raised her eyebrows.

'We should start her in Saint Michael's,' he said, 'and we could take her out.'

'I suppose. It's harsh.'

'She's very small. The only other option would be keeping her out for another year of Montessori, and she's too intelligent. She would be bored.'

'Also,' Lena noted dully, 'we won't get a grant this time.'

They sat outside Ryan's, on a picnic bench. Because it was warm, because the sunset looked volcanic and air hung static, like fabric, in the streets, people sat on kerbs and gulls stripped a chip packet in the middle of the road. A man was asleep or passed out on the pavement before the hostel and a group gathered around him waiting, it seemed, for the slow ambulance that sloped upwards towards them now.

'Oh dear,' Lena said. Odhran, unperturbed, took her hand and kneaded it absently.

She looked at him. His confidence was a condition of this kind of surface attention, an essential willingness to believe in a single succinct reality that did not differ much from the value system of his childhood, and she'd always valued it because it was different from her. Gwynn had been too weak a limit. He left no emotional trace.

If she left Dublin and moved to Clare, her world would be engulfed by Odhran's, and what was hers within it would need to find substance through Sunny, and this seemed absurd and yet obvious because it was what many people did.

What many women did, that is: surrender power in the world.

'Change of subject,' she said. 'How do you feel about open marriages?'

'Well obviously' – he raised his pint glass to his lips – 'easier in Dublin than Clare.'

'Oh I'm not asking for one.'

He grinned. 'I didn't think so.'

If she moved to Clare, she would have no way out and perhaps this would be a warm and numbing kind of happiness. Not engulfment, but embrace.

He switched subjects, and began to speak about his eldest

brother, Cathal, who lived in Sandyford, and who Odhran proposed to call in on after work some evening during the week. It was not something he did often. Or ever. There was a reason, and Odhran fronted with this: 'Cathal, technically, owns the best house we have.'

It was a house in Killaloe, in the town, and it was rented out. Their father had left it to Cathal because Cathal was the eldest. None of the rest of them had been left houses.

'I see.' Lena sipped, carefully.

It grew dark, or just powdery. Now the Park was quieter, traversed only by ninja-like runners in Lycra and some tourists, the crowds thinning out. A morbid magic took presence in the darkening sky and in the shadows of the orderly alien pines. They walked, against a sudden steepness explained by humus banked and driven back by one of the thick external walls, to a margin of trees that was denser than the rest and where one fallen laurel like an octopod extended tentacles. They looked up at the magazine fort, which was brutally archetypal in darkness, like a piece of doleful furniture; like an obelisk or a catafalque.

They were remote, emotionally, for no reason other than the perennial sorrow occurring to and confining adults – cyclically, as metabolism – to the world of the lonely child inside themselves once in a while.

22

Cathal was a holdout. He came rarely to Clare. His house in Sandyford stood on a spartan block of large family homes that loomed like freight ships moored amid a preponderance of cobble lock. The streets were mystifyingly deserted on a summer evening. Cathal's wife and children were out of the country, holidaying in a grandparents' villa in Spain, and Odhran found Cathal taking in the air from a wicker chair on the back patio. He was rubbing the head of a sleepy setter with the ball of his bare foot, wearing a work shirt with the collar open. Cathal, at forty-four, was a senior civil servant in the Department of Foreign Affairs.

He offered Odhran a beer and directed him to the vast American kitchen, in which several appliances hummed simultaneously, before they sat on the patio.

In two years' time, Odhran would turn forty. He did not own a refrigerator. His refrigerator belonged to the landlord and he, Odhran, had no relationship with it, thinking of it only when something smelt inside, which was never, because Lena was so thriftily vigilant. His home was an apartment with slithering veneers and lemony laminate and he did not feel moral discussing more children with his wife because there was no room for more children. He could not open with this plaintive, pouting position; it would never be stated.

'I was sorry you didn't bring the girls,' Cathal said. 'I think I know what you're here about.'

Odhran smiled. Sonia of course.

'I'd like to start by saying' – Cathal raised his foot to rub the dozing dog again – 'that you might not want it at all, and be careful what you wish for, and I guess you've thought about it.'

In these gardens, in the evenings, the sweetness of lilac and laburnum filled the air of its own volition. Chemtrails crossed the sky and fritted, dousing, out. When Cathal was thirty and Odhran twenty-four, when the former was living in Brussels, something happened to bring his eldest brother into Odhran's ambit suddenly and with so much texture, it had seized in his mind and seemed now slightly unbelievable. Odhran was at Trinity, completing his master's, and Cathal working for the Election Observation Roster in a posting in Brussels. Sonia had landed up in Dublin one day, driving, with his father and the egregious Niall in the back seat.

'Why have you brought Niall?' Odhran asked in the Mona Lisa restaurant, where he agreed to meet them. At least he thought that was what it was called. It was next to Doyle's. Doyle's had a function room with flowered carpet and an anaglypta ceiling and a club night, or an indie disco night, or something everyone at Trinity attended on Friday nights. He never forgot the image of anaglypta shooting towards him and back again with every leap and whoop.

'We need you to go to Belgium,' his father explained that afternoon, in the Mona Lisa restaurant. Cathal had gone AWOL and his girlfriend, a bespectacled bare-faced Austrian girl they all found serious, had telephoned Sonia to announce they had broken up and he'd taken it very badly. A colleague in the EOR had put a call in too: they were greatly fond of Cathal, who was decent and craic, but hadn't seen him for two weeks and he was not taking calls.

Sonia managed two minutes on the phone with him and Cathal told her, 'And I quote,' she said drearily, '*not to darken his door.*'

'That's such a weird thing to say,' offered twenty-four-year-old Odhran, and it was, not only in content but in manner of expression; it was neither a family nor a topical phrase.

'So we have plane tickets for both of ye,' his father completed, 'tonight.'

It was exciting. Odhran was still coming down from molly from two days ago and getting, sometimes, sick, as he did in the bathroom of the Mona Lisa restaurant. After this he let his parents drive him to the damp houseshare in North Strand long enough to use the tilted, moulded shower and pack a small bag. He put a razor and cologne in a sandwich bag with toothpaste and two condoms, even though he had a girlfriend at the time. Riled up and slick with product and soberly dressed, he then travelled to the airport.

'Keep in touch the whole time,' ordered Sonia. She pressed a blister pack into his hands. 'This is only if he absolutely needs it and not, under any circumstances, for you.' It was Xanax: he and Niall took some together, instantly, in the departures lounge. This blunted the busy neediness of Niall, who was uncomfortable with Dublin and airports and baffled in Brussels, where they became shrinkingly shy of the prospect of confronting Cathal at all.

The apartment was in Laeken. At the first knock, Cathal shot his head around the door and looked at them blankly. A neighbour, a woman with a brassy dye-job and a Day-Glo shopping bag, pushed past them in the hall and smiled excessively into their faces, drawing the moment out.

'Ana called us,' Odhran said, in a condemnatory tone, after this. 'Everyone is looking for you.'

Cathal continued to stare. He looked sweaty and wild. He shut the door without a word. In the silence Niall rocked from foot to foot and said, 'What, we get out of here?'

'Let's call Ana,' Odhran hissed.

They did; they met her in a square, kitschly festive, and she was carrying flowers in a paper cone. She seemed impressed and interested that they had travelled. She did some food shopping as they trailed her, Odhran conscious of and embarrassed by Niall's bootleg jeans, his nervous tendency to scratch at dandruff and guffaw.

Ana stood on a corner with them, ready to descend to the metro, and said, 'Frankly, he is not accepting that I left and he has not been sleeping for a long time, he has been staying awake. I hope you can talk to him.' And that was that.

They returned to the apartment.

'Mam's called Interpol,' Odhran threatened through the door.

Cathal let them in at last. The place was a chaos of clothes and takeaway plates. It looked as if he'd been packing a suitcase; at least, there was a suitcase open on the coffee table.

'Why would she call?' Cathal said from the couch, red-eyed, and clawing at himself. 'They are watching me, I have to close all the curtains because they're watching me across the street. They know my route from work, they have people all the way, people everywhere.'

'We have pills,' Niall offered.

'We can get you out of here,' tried Odhran with inventiveness. 'We have clearance.'

But Cathal only glared at him and snapped, 'Don't be thick.'

'Do the cops have guns here or what?' asked Niall. It was a sensible question.

Cathal pleaded for Ana, but Ana, when they phoned her again, refused.

'He smokes cannabis,' she said sadly. 'He needs to sober.'

'I haven't smoked,' Cathal swore. 'I haven't left this apartment.' He could not leave because they were watching him, it had to do with numbers and dates; but who was watching him? He was dry on this point: you don't want to know, he said.

Niall asked, 'Do they rig elections, these people who are watching you?' which gave Cathal pause. It seemed he hadn't thought of that.

Looking back, it was unclear at this distance what exactly

worked to dislodge Cathal from the Laeken apartment. Niall and Odhran did not sleep at a hostel, but on the floor and sofa, spending much of the night cleaning the place and running with bags of rubbish to the underground garbage chute with the diligence and flow of their childhood chore sheet. Cathal lay awake and Odhran lay awake, thinking perversely of his girlfriend in Dublin – she was a business and economics undergraduate, she did not enjoy sex but he often woke to see her sitting in the deep dishevelled window of his room before dawn, having pushed back the curtain gauze, applying layers of make-up in her reflection by lamplight; there was no mirror in the houseshare. Years on when he would sketch this for Lena she replied that boys were despicable and she, Lena, was glad to have been spared such gruesome formative experiences.

In the end, he must have been persuaded – Cathal, that is – by their mother, once more on the phone. He flew home between Niall and Odhran with an IRELAND beanie pulled over his eyes, fingers trembling on the stem of a plastic wineglass and with the last of the Xanax. Their father delivered him straight to the Ennis inpatient facility and Cathal, realising where he was too late, protested only weakly, 'But I'm in these dirty clothes.'

And that was that.

At Christmas, when the brothers were again together, Cathal was contrite and gentle and spent several hours washing up with careful, reverential focus at the big cold dripping window above the sink. He went running every night after this, around the fields, wearing a reflective vest they could observe streaking through darkness like a comet.

He returned to the EOR and brought home an Italian girl who ate with relish and was watched with still more relish by Cathal as she ate and then Keelin, an Irish translator from Kerry, whom he wound up marrying. Odhran could not remember the Italian's name but remembered her relish and feeling horny, stoned and horny, at whatever Christmas dinner that had been.

Years passed: their ordinary lives. Cathal came infrequently to Clare but went, once a year, to the Camino, and logged ten days of silent Vipassana meditation in some mega meditation campus in Hertfordshire and posted photos to Instagram of him and Keelin and their adolescent children on cycling expeditions to the Wild Atlantic Way. When geopolitical volatility left the rest of them suspecting he had more compelling insights into Foreign Affairs, he answered messages and questions with banally passive or recursive leitmotifs: what do you think, these things are never simple, the Minister has many hats. He was, in short, so boring it seemed lapidary, conscious, chosen, provoking.

He was the first family member to manifest madness since the uncle with the gun dogs. Odhran had a lurking, unpleasant worry about Sunny – Sunny funnelling Lena, that is – and this tendency, which was clear: sometimes children acted as lightning rods.

Cathal owned the house in Killaloe because he was the eldest and also, Odhran felt, because their father had felt guilty at depositing Cathal so bloodlessly at the inpatient facility.

'I've been thinking about it,' Odhran said to him now.

'You work in Dublin,' Cathal said. 'Tell me how that works.'

As he explained, Odhran felt a nagging vanity and irritation at what seemed, he thought, like a petition; Cathal's serene expression and still garden of pale weedless slabs and short, bright grass and the deathly pyrotechnics of bushes and shrubs in frozen bloat behind communicated little to no empathy or even ordinary condescension. Odhran proposed to investigate buying the house at market value, no bidding, but this would take some time, and they might live there first and pay the rent. This would mean evicting the tenant, and was illegal.

Odhran nodded. 'Well, OK. To buy it then.'

'Market value.' Cathal sighed. In the silence, an evening wood pigeon cooed and then again. It seemed, also, to be seeking a response.

The house in Killaloe was old; one hundred years old. It was built by the Church when they were renovating the church building across the street: this church was bulky, unlovely, with a fey Italianate belltower too small for the building's size. It was a cottage with two fireplaces and a galley kitchen appended to the back, and it didn't have central heating. Their father had not willed anything that would invoke actual jealousy towards Cathal in the end.

'The tenants would have to leave voluntarily,' Cathal said.

'Do they ever complain about not having central heating?'

Cathal widened his eyes. 'Oh it has it now,' he said. 'We fitted that. We did a lot of work on it in the lockdown, when it was empty.'

'I didn't know that.'

'They would need to go voluntarily. It's illegal otherwise and anyway it wouldn't be fair.'

'Yes.' Odhran was flush. He wanted to leave.

'You don't need it anyway,' Cathal said. 'You don't want to live down there, with the dark winters and the long nights and nothing going on. How would Lena cope with that? She's from Dublin. Keelin wouldn't cope with it.'

'We can't stay here.'

'You'd get a bigger mortgage if Lena could work.'

'There is no childcare.'

'Well then.' Cathal held up his arms, a motion of surrender, and smiled. Odhran raised the bottle of beer to his lip to distract himself.

'So give up,' Cathal laughed. 'No solutions at all.'

The pigeon had not been answered, but it continued croaking cutely in some unseen immaculate tree. Sadness, or just fatigue, passed through Odhran like mournful music. It made him feel dignified: dignified in disappointment and defeat; dignified by honesty.

'I want to go back.' He said it quietly.

'Well, that's different.' Cathal was firm.

'I'd like space,' Odhran was bolder, 'and something that belonged to me. I think we could have more children.'

'If the tenants leave,' Cathal said. It was final, but kind. They wouldn't leave; nobody could leave. Nobody could go anywhere. They were jammed in place, time wasn't moving, time was elsewhere, time was no longer linear in any sense beyond the body, which would age.

'Nonsense,' replied Sonia when he called, driving home, in a state of rare but lyrically anguished loss and boyishness he remembered entering last when he found out about Lena's pregnancy. Her stoutness of tone bolstered him. 'There is plenty to look at down here. Never mind old Martin Fagan and his estate agency; there are interesting people and your brother knows them. Aidan I mean. Yes Aidan. Aidan is quite involved in things.'

'It feels hopeless sometimes,' Odhran milked it.

'Sure we all had recessions and disasters,' Sonia told him. 'Nothing is ever easy on anyone. Your father was terrified to take this house. Oh yes, them dogs in the shed, it was madness. You find a way.' She paused. She said, 'You focus on family.'

23

By the end of June, a leaden heatwave had set in, early in the year for heat, and when Lena biked to Reap and Sew sessions, her clothes clung to her tackily with heat. It was high hen season and she was taking many shifts and saving to pay the play therapist. This was an idea conceived of shortly after the holiday to Clare and, once committed to, it obtained the substantiality of a fact or something inevitable. She hadn't really dwelt on it.

'Are you having a holiday this year?' Rita asked shortly.

'Nah.' Lena fanned herself with the envelope of notes. 'I think we will be moving soon.'

'Oh really? Where?'

'Possibly Clare.' She bit her lip, oddly pleased to say it out loud.

Rita looked confused. 'Why?' she asked. 'Is something happening down there?'

'It's where my husband is from.' Lena described, as best she could, the coordinates and constellation of minor towns.

'Back in the day.' Rita shifted a large mason jar of beads. She paused to jack the sash window further. 'All around there was popular with hippies. New Age types.'

'Beautiful scenery.'

And with that, Rita's interest evaporated. She moved on to the subject of further work, at later dates in the year. Rita also did sessions in her own house, evenings, sewing and cocktails and Tarot readings, with her hair in a kerchief, like Zoltar.

'Would that interest you?' she asked. 'I could use some help.'

'Oh sure,' said Lena, unsure.

Just then the bride of the night arrived, bulking out at the front with a third-trimester pregnancy. She was heavy-lidded and lacking in excitement and spun one toe to and fro in a strange Orphan-Annie sort of movement on the dented rubber tip of her platform heel. 'Obviously I'm not drinking,' she said. The bump was at the sour stage, high up and sparking with heartburn, heavy in heat, a deformity.

'Is this your first?' Lena asked.

'No but we couldn't change the date,' the bride said flatly, answering a different question.

Lena recalled the rounded, juicy, lurid feeling of pregnancy and thought with abrupt recklessness of getting herself into that condition again. Of seeing the lip of the void but this time feeling ready for it. Of a whole new human swaddled stiffly in her arms.

At the end of the night, Rita said, oh jay, I meant to tell you – you have a fan who left an email with me, to give to you.

For one flaring moment, Lena thought of Cian with alarm and then said, 'Wait: Elva something, by any chance?'

'Yes.' Rita twitched it up on her phone.

Lena rode home, uphill and stiffly trudging this time. It was hardly dark – on the horizon, there was always a bleed of light, as if a battle were raging at a distance. She could not bring the thought of Elva to the forefront of her mind because it was too dangerous. It held out the threat of knowledge, that was why. Elva wanted to *talk to her* and tell her more and get her on side the way all scorned women do after a bad break-up. Lena tasted something of the embarrassment she herself would feel if forced to discuss Mikey O'Hara and all that content once again, to discuss the past, because since meeting Odhran it had been packed up as anecdotes deployed occasionally, shallowly; described sedately, unremarkable.

The thought that anyone else might have *their own version* made her uncomfortable.

Odhran was awake and reading in bed. 'I've been asked to go to the London symposium,' he told her at once. 'It's in about a month.' He spoke importantly. The room was dim but the big shaggy bedside lamp, like a lamp in a hotel, lit his book and bare chest too brightly.

It yanked her right out of Elva. 'Oh, amazing,' she said.

She felt he'd been waiting with excitement to tell her this. Both because it was fun to travel for work and he never got to anymore, or not so often, and also because it carried the risk of hysterical pushback from Lena. She had – at earlier stages in Sunny's childhood, when she was feeling more volatile – been nervous at the idea of parenting alone. But now, in the moment he said it, the prospect of a night or two alone in bed was nice. Something of it implied the glacial aloneness of her singlehood, a condition she missed.

'That will be fun for you,' she said.

'Yes but you might struggle,' he accused.

'I won't struggle. It's grand.'

'I mean, soon I might be, like, asking for a work-from-home situation.' He rose from the bed and wove around her, heading for the bathroom. He looked back at her coyly. 'I might be asking to work from Clare. Or somewhere.'

'You might be. You might be that guy.'

'So it's good to be present and visible and so on when I can.'

'Indeed.' She grinned back in provocation and slid into bed. 'Oh wow.'

'I know.'

'I have to enrol Sunny at the school tomorrow,' she said.

Odhran did not answer until he had peed, uncouthly and with the door open, but when he did, he said at once, 'I don't like the look of that school.'

'No. But we have no absolute plan.'

'Can you give me until – like, say, next month? By London? I'll make a plan. I have some ideas.'

'If it's one of your mother's houses—'

'It won't be that.'

'And not her house either.'

'You are welcome,' he said, 'to solve this problem yourself. If the many houses of bourgeois Clare are not good enough for you.'

Lena put her hands behind her head and said with false solemnity, 'I would never emasculate you like that.'

She felt, abstractly, that she should be defending something: her life in Dublin as she knew it, all their friends. But she did not. Elva's email was stored in her phone now and Elva expected some contact and that occurred to her, uncomfortably, as she rolled over to sleep.

In the morning, Lena met Orla on Emmett Road.

'So how do you feel about this?' she asked.

Orla looked cagey. 'Feel about it?'

'This school. And not the Educate Together at Broombridge.'

'Oh.' Orla was unwrapping something for Oscar. She paused; her hand was in the air. Oscar began to whine and reach for it, breaking the spell.

'I suppose, if I am honest,' she exhaled, 'I am not happy about it.'

They walked in dusty sunlight down a street of rubbish bags heaped up at intervals for the bin collection. Sunny and Oscar trotted in parallel, sneaking looks at one another.

'The thing is,' Orla resumed, after a long and thoughtful silence through which Lena too had been watchful, 'is it not kind of snobby to feel – a bit averse to, like, the local school?'

'Well, sure. But no parent *isn't* a snob.'

'You don't think so?'

'I think it's evolutionary. I wanted Sunny in the best school I could find, and that's not this.'

'Probably,' Orla corrected, 'it's totally fine.'

'I've so looked forward to her starting school. I've thought about this moment since she was born. Because, I suppose, like – I loved school.'

'Me too,' Orla said, unsmiling.

The school building reared back from the road and pavement, accessible through a series of boxy cement siphons painted white but splashed and grubby with wear. These were designed to shunt the children out gradually and safely into traffic, but served largely to make the women think of traffic: of busses, lorries, transit vans; the air a cakey cram of sun-dried, lingering fuel. The roof was pointed, with a long central window, like a seventies church.

Inside it was also as hushed as a church. By the doors, a life-sized Virgin with poppy lips and a look of perseverance. The air was warm with dust and coffee as they advanced, slowly and awkwardly, down a corridor. A hatch was marked by a jaunty, swinging wooden finger: here!

'Hello there. Birth certs, is it?' An avid little secretary pulled out spectacles and put them on. She dashed through both sets of paperwork, lingering on things for no real reason, poking out her tongue. There was something stagey and dated and familiar about the interaction. It made Lena think of being a child, of being at school, and of the stagey ways adults seemed to move. She and Orla, silent with respect and some perplexment, stood alert. From outside, the sound of the city carried with the muffled roughness of a tide.

After a moment, Sunny said ponderously, 'I never come in here before.'

'This will be your new school,' Lena tried. She felt chastened by the weight of institutional suspense; the silence, circulating monumentally.

The small group emerged into the sunlight soon after, blinking with relief. Moving back down the street, holding their children by the hands, was a quiet exercise – both absorbed in thought.

'If you want to come down to Stoneybatter and hang out,' Orla offered, 'we can jump on the bus.' The traffic seemed ravenous now: unceasing and loud. Her house was down one of the quiet blocks on which artisan cottages stood like dainty doctor's bags. There would be, Orla explained, a street party here at the weekend; did Lena get a flier about that?

'Yes!' Lena said. 'Oh yes. Thanks for reminding me.'

In the house, Orla pressed ahead of them and locked the thumping, whelping dogs into a yard at the very back.

'Doggies.' Sunny pointed, blankly.

They sat at the table and let Oscar and Sunny play in an adjoining, tiny, room. The place was homely and pastel. A large bowl like an opening flowerhead held fruit with leaves still browning, crisply, on the stalks. Orla leant her long body on the table, propped up by her elbows, and seemed troubled by something.

'Time is passing,' she said at last.

The silence between them had become companionable. Lena was not uncomfortable with it. She said, 'Odhran and I are thinking of moving to Clare.'

'Aha,' said Orla. She smiled weakly. She was still leaning on the table, reluctant to sit. She said, 'I thought you might.'

'You did?'

'How much longer can you look for a house in Dublin?'

It was rhetorical. How long indeed.

There was something imperious yet apologetic about Orla's personality, the noble self-absorption of the intellectual, that Lena found appealing. Now she sat in her kitchen for the first time and asked with boldness, 'Do you own this house?

Orla's response came simply. 'Yes.'

There was a sadness to it somehow. She felt sorry for Lena. Lena did not, in this instance, find being pitied offensive. It was a cute house; anyone would want this house.

'We'd like more space.' Lena was practising it. This *we*.

'And to have more children,' she added carefully. The hen of the night before returned; popping at the belly, rising from her chair with a wince to move to the bathroom. A momentous volcano of consequence brewing within her body; you cannot, Lena thought, have a pregnancy without there being changes. Cellularly, physically, spiritually. If she, Lena, had another child, it would open her life like a battering ram – in some form. Any form. You chooseth not the form.

She felt like saying this, spurred suddenly by excitement. She did not.

'I am having more children,' Orla said. As she did, she looked away, seeming to scrutinise the surface of her fridge, which was cluttered over with magnets and postcards, like everyone's fridge.

'Though actually,' she continued, 'Oscar was IVF.'

'I didn't know that.' Lena assumed an expression of friendly interest.

'It wasn't easy. It makes me think.' Orla straightened up suddenly. 'I have to act carefully; I mean, I feel as though I went through quite a lot to have Oscar. I cannot be flippant about decisions. That's why it bothers me, you know – the school.' She was speaking distractedly, absorbedly, to herself. Lena felt she did not belong in this moment really; the moment seemed private and intense. She had not belonged last night, at Reap and Sew. She did not belong on the Emmett Road. How long had this discomfort been part of her existence in the city?

Thus abstracted from the moment, Lena wondered if Orla felt people who did not have children via IVF were somehow less concerned or more flippant. But then again, she knew her accidental catapult to motherhood had made her, at times since Sunny was born, somewhat complacent. Seem complacent in context. She had at points over the years ranted at Odhran. Been ungrateful and flippant. That was true.

Another child would be intentional.

She heard Sunny, next door, say, 'My hair is longer than yours.'

'Kowabunga!' Oscar cried.

They were at their parallel play: side by side, but separate. A little like her and Orla. She wondered if Sunny would bring up her death.

Orla placed a coffee before her; milky. Earthenware.

‘I could go again,’ Orla said. ‘I could try for another. But it’s a tough process.’

‘Do you want to stay in Dublin?’

‘Yes.’

Lena thought about Orla’s open marriage. Specifically that this could not possibly be true – it seemed outlandish a proposal in the abstract, and ridiculous enkitchened, now, like this. Orla’s slow and almost spacey tendency to contemplation had the gathered, moneyed, settled confidence of an earlier era. Caoimhe was just feverish or something, running wild with bad gossip. Bored. Yes. Caoimhe was electric in her dissatisfaction.

She knew, Lena realised, little about these women’s lives, beyond their performance as mothers and the system of manners mothering obliged of them. She would not miss them if she left. They’d slide right off her, become memory quickly. They would not miss her. In Clare, nobody would know her, which was ironic or inverted really – to go to the countryside for anonymity, and not this tired sense of being known and watched and compromised.

‘It’s hard to stay in Dublin,’ she said. ‘If you don’t have a house.’

‘Once,’ she continued, ‘it meant very much to me to stay. I couldn’t imagine myself anywhere else. But the truth is – there is not a lot to keep me here, if you think about it.’

‘I thought once that I would have lots of children,’ Orla said.

This hung in the air as a melancholy non-sequitur. Lena sipped her coffee with detachment in response. She’d never thought about children before Sunny. What a strange way to have gone through the world as a woman for almost thirty years; not as a woman, really. Just a girl.

‘How’s Sunny’s past life?’

‘Still there. Same thing. We are taking her to see a therapist.’

‘She’s sweet.’ Orla sat at last, dragging out a chair. ‘Sunny is a lovely little thing. In your family.’ She hesitated then. She looked to the window.

A dog, clearly practised in this protest, leapt up at the glass – its thin head, humanoid and desperate, appeared, then sank away. Lena began to laugh at it. She disliked dogs.

'I wonder, like, if there were deaths in the family, around Sunny.' This was Orla.

'Odhran's father,' Lena said. 'When I was pregnant. That was all.'

'Oh, so her dad was grieving then,' Orla nodded. 'Perhaps that makes sense.'

Lena frowned into the middle distance placidly.

'Grieving,' she repeated. 'Yes. I guess.' She sipped. 'But since I was pregnant when that happened, I remember there was this sense of, like, the future, of continuity. I remember Odhran saying *thank God we're having a child*.'

And he had: in bed on the morning of the funeral, staring at the ceiling, he'd said, thank God we are having a child. He meant: thank God life is happening.

24

It was dark. Aidan woke with a sensation of preparedness, of wakefulness, but the ornate architrave of the bedroom door was still moving and ripening in the gloom: this was a dream, melting out like seafoam or steam, and in a moment it was gone, to his relief.

He'd woken because of knocking. The clock read 6.05. It was Saturday. He knew already who it was, who it would be, and so moved slowly. The knocking was contrite.

Mark Ryan stood on the doorstep of the ground-floor flat, hands pinned out of sight under his armpits, looking jumpy and glancing around. Behind him, the sun had long risen but it was buttery, sleepy. A barrage of ivy on the old wall opposite bloomed darkly and caught Aidan's eye. It reminded him of the dream. Mark cowered as if someone would hit him.

'I'm sorry, I'm sorry,' he said. Mark was considerably older than Aidan: ten years maybe, and Aidan was thirty-four. Mark managed a lab at the hospital. They had never been lovers, not even once, not even years ago. And yet this ground-floor flat had lately become outsized in Mark's mind and he had washed up at it early on a Saturday several times. Aidan felt a first wave of pity and then, under this, the swirl of rage.

'What have you taken?' he asked. Mark flinched.

'Nothing for hours; it's my head. It's my mind. I only want to be not alone, you know what I mean, Aidan, you know yourself.'

This was the cruellest angle of it. Years ago, at some party or other, Mark may have witnessed Aidan panicked or high or something else exposing, something which brought him to Mark's level – his affect tended to suggest this, even if Aidan couldn't remember – and the speed with which he slid the inference in made Aidan want to slam the door. Instead, he stepped back to allow Mark, smelling of drink, to enter. Mark walked fluently into the front room and lay on the couch. Aidan felt bested but regarded the other man with disdain.

'I'm going back to bed,' he claimed, but actually he walked into the kitchen and flicked on the coffee machine and the branch of weak spotlights. He had a short strip of garden outside, paved over prettily, and decorated it with potted shrubs. His ground-floor flat had the covert, shadowed aspect of an earlier age of design, but the wall of raw, faintly curving glass he'd installed at the rear made the garden pop like a hallucination.

He adored the flat. Irma, who came to clean it once a week, said every time, 'So nice and perfect for you.' She said it with fondness and nodded at him, inviting agreement. The first few times it made him blush like a compliment.

He'd bought it when he was still with Rory. Rory was annoyed at the time actually.

'Just like that?'

'Not like that. I've been saving for years.'

'In the city? You want to live in the city?'

'It is,' Aidan had reminded him calmly, 'the Ennis Road.' Which was a nice old rosy road.

By the time Aidan's father, ailing towards the hospice at this point, summoned him to his bedside one night, he and Rory had broken up. Unaware of this, his father spoke to him.

'I have seen, and people have seen, you around with your friend.'

'Rory.' Aidan's face was raw.

'I want you to know that I want you to be happy. Your

mother and I only want you to be happy, all of you. And if you want to live with this man you don't need to sneak around.'

'I'm not.' The tears had come. He couldn't fight. 'I'm not. He finished with me.'

His father looked alarmed. He turned shamefully, quickly, to the wall. At last he said, with strength, 'Well he's a fucking eejit then.'

Rory had never moved in; Aidan was alone here, and happily so, always. He sat in the kitchen now and tried to organise his thoughts about Mark, who could sleep on the couch for hours. He, Aidan, could not let this happen again. He would message people – their friends – to explain that either Mark must go into rehab or simply promise to stop washing up at doors.

'Mark is a vulnerable person,' someone – Rory – would say. They continued to own units and houses and to invest and work together even though they were no longer together. Rory was in fact shortly getting married to someone else. That person was less attractive than Aidan and so it felt gently OK; still, however, the mug-tree remained in place, and each time Rory came by, he said, 'Don't put these in the dishwasher. Promise me.' He held up a cup and made a joke of it. Aidan felt the intended intimacy every time.

And yet, on the subject of Mark, Rory and the others could be worthy. They didn't have to deal with this chipper harassment you see.

Sometimes several of them gathered to hike one or other hill at the weekend, flasks and keep-cups and several red setters, though Mark did not come along to these. Their group was partly composed from various aspects of the Chamber of Commerce, some financial and business boards, and an ambient queerness that was mutedly provincial. They formed a crew of different ages and stages but banded together, largely, on the basis of tribal affiliation, maintaining a more conservative or just local outlook than might have been expected from what his brother Odhran referred to as the *pink gilet gang*. Odhran, like Cathal, had sped off to do Business Economica Social Science at Trinity, then pivoted to tech, then tried to convert this supervillain's CV into a working life of civic patrimony. He oversaw grants that funded think tanks and postdoctoral projects with bizarre acronyms that sounded like fashion labels.

Aidan's sister ran an actual fashion label. She and Aidan were the capitalists; Odhran and Cathal the mandarins.

This was how Sonia saw it. 'I am proud of all my children,' she said.

Aidan made coffee and returned to the table, planning his move. He would need to appeal to the group. He disliked the idea that Mark, slanting towards his flat with regularity like this, illustrated a more widespread disrespect. It made Aidan look implicated.

The first time, Mark had claimed to be searching for another house. A guy from an app.

'But I can't find it,' he'd complained. 'And I think I'm too out of it anyway.' Then stretched onto the sofa and passed out. The drink and the encroach of middle age was making him bloated, unattractive; Aidan hated him, he thought now. I just fucking hate that guy.

By seven, it was daytime, rigid and beautiful, with traffic bristling purposefully outside. Limerick was so scaldy on Saturdays Aidan did not hang around; he drove out to Castleconnell, to his first café, and sometimes on to Birdhill, breaching the county border, to visit the other. He might find Rory there and complain once again that Mark needed an intervention, something that would not involve Aidan, something that would remove this problem from Aidan's life.

By seven-thirty, Aidan was showered, dressed, and rolling his Golf out of the garage sequestered behind the block. He'd left a note for Mark saying only: pull the door shut FIRM.

Before him opened a dreamy greenscape of picnics and bathing spots and customers motoring free of sunny hamlets purely for coffee and cake; a day of beaches and lakes and the abrupt icy breezes that might lift off beaches and lakes. It was in this mood of hot but lessening contempt that Aidan decided to get around to what his mother would call *a jobeen* and phone Odhran through the Bluetooth.

'Do you get up this early?' Odhran asked. Aidan heard a twanging laugh in the background – cartoons, kids' breakfast TV.

'Oh busy, busy,' Aidan said. 'You wanted to talk.'

'It's Uncle Aidan,' Odhran was saying. Sunny, her voice squeakier somehow on the line, greeted him and paused and there was silence. Odhran asking, do you have a message for Aidan? He was avoiding something; it was threatening to become pathetic.

'Mam has been on to me,' he offered.

Odhran cleared his throat.

'Excellent. Well, you know what I am asking then.' It was business time. 'I've been speaking to Cathal about the house in Killaloe – acquiring it, but he can't put the tenants out and anyway he isn't sure. I think he felt like he should offer an alternative. He mentioned you.'

'Yes.' Aidan was noncommittal.

'We want to buy a house in Clare.'

'I just wanted,' Aidan said, 'to hear you say that.'

Odhran laughed shortly. The cartoons had been switched off, or he'd moved to a different room. Aidan tried to recall their apartment, which he'd only visited once. It was to see the fleshy, fretful baby when one of the lockdowns lifted; Sunny, goggle-eyed and drooling, he recalled. The warm parcel of her body in his arms. He'd found her more delightful than his other nieces, his four nephews; something, possibly, to do with Lena's reticence. She was unlike his brothers' wives generally. He found it hard to imagine her living in Clare. There was, for instance, a ghostship fan website dedicated to her online, and she seemed to have no idea about it. It was made up of photographs snatched from the internet, of Lena at gigs and posing with Cian Mulvaney coyly, her wrists busy with woven bands, her long hair like an oil slick down her back. A forum in scratchy serif font still held strange little reservoirs of gentle gossip from the earlier 2000s: she was beloved, there. People wrote about meeting her. Well – like, one or two faceless avatars spoke about meeting her.

He had never mentioned it to Lena or to Odhran, who mostly acted as if Lena didn't have a past.

'You are right,' Aidan told Odhran now. 'It's all happening down here. You can do a lot from here. Particularly with the housing crisis; more and more people are coming down.'

'That's what I think.'

'Took you long enough.'

'You get used to a place,' Odhran defended. 'But Dublin has become difficult. There is a time of life for these things.' He paused painfully. Aidan wanted to laugh. 'I mean for me, like, I am at a time of life.'

'I get it.'

Aidan took a corner, spinning the wheel with playfulness, as though someone was watching. He felt hungry. He thought of eating; what to eat. He waited. Odhran seemed to be sighing or exhaling into revelation. Odhran said: 'I want to ask about your contacts or, like, what you know about any developments happening now.'

'Not a lot. That's the first thing I can say.'

'I would prefer to avoid involving Mam.'

'You don't want a newbuild though. You want something interesting.'

'Well.' Odhran's tone lightened slightly. 'I think we're open-minded actually.'

'Will you search from Dublin?'

'That would be more difficult.'

'Because you can come down any time. You can stay in one of the chalets.' It surprised Aidan that his mother had not suggested this; he wondered if she knew about it. Rory and Aidan had bought a block of fading holiday chalets because they were cheap five years or so ago and capitalised on the pandemic. People wanted to live in second homes or to send their adult children down to the chalets. He began to explain this to Odhran.

'Before, the council were pretty quick to notice if people lived in them full-time,' he said. 'That's technically not allowed. Since the lockdown, with the housing crisis, they don't bother; there are families living there, or couples at least. To be honest,' Aidan said, 'it's got so dingy we will sell, but it takes a while. What I mean,' Aidan continued, 'is you are welcome to jump into my one. It's empty – I left it unlisted this year because there was a big water leak.'

He paused and then said, 'So there is, like, a bit of water damage to be painted over.'

He would not, he realised calmly, be painting over it.

Odhran had fallen silent for so long, Aidan stopped speaking himself. He was coming into Castleconnell, in sight of the girlish spire of the church. It was sleepy here, architecturally Protestant, with a broad sweep of nineties semi-detached houses. These were the domain of children's bikes and spin-lines and made Aidan shudder to think of. His café was housed in what had been a barracks. For a long while, they'd spent lots of time and money sourcing lime to render the great gable end that faced the road; the use of lime, its production, had fallen out of style for far too long. Rory even gave a series of evening coffee talks on the local production of lime, on the many open kilns you saw about, like church arcades.

Odhran spoke at last. 'Are you serious?' he said. He sounded hoarse.

'Obviously if that sounds, like, horrible, you can ignore it.'

'It sounds helpful. Very helpful. I would like that. I think Lena would like that.' After a moment: 'And would you charge some rent?'

'I make about eight hundred a week off Airbnb when it's occupied.' He could not help this; he needed Odhran, quite simply, to know. 'But no,' he said. 'It's empty over winter anyway. We'd be heading into autumn and winter. Hold on.'

Aidan drew up at the café. It was a cube of glass punched through the building; still, the barracks' four stiff chimney stacks stood erect like candles. In the morning light, the lime wall was a wonder, glowing like snow.

'Hold on,' he repeated. 'What about Sunny? Doesn't she go to school yet or whatever?'

'Not technically,' Odhran answered. 'We could work something out.' He moved on quickly: 'I appreciate this, Aidan, and we'd pay you something; obviously we pay rent in Dublin.'

'I'm at work now, I'm afraid,' Aidan interrupted. 'Busy, all of that.'

'I want you to know we are really grateful.'

'It will be nice to see more of you,' Aidan said.

'I'm going to London next week,' Odhran told him. This added nothing to the conversation but signalled something, like a parting shot – importance, work abroad, diversity.

'Lovely spot,' said Aidan acidly.

Through the glass, he saw Rory's new barista, a lean and slightly circus-looking young man with a moustache waxed into kinks at either end. Something in Aidan was saddened by the moustache. The man stared ahead, boring into the wall of glass with a look of restless intensity; he could not see Aidan yet, emerging from the shade.

Aidan's heart rate had quickened in the closing moments of his conversation with Odhran. At first there seemed no reason for this, but then it became softly apparent what the resonance was. Last year, when one of the chalets had been filled for a week, the occupier – a single man – contacted Aidan over the website to ask if he could extend his stay. There was another booking incoming. 'I'm sorry,' Aidan said when he phoned the man back. 'But we're booked. I can help you find somewhere else?' he offered. He was not sure why he offered this.

'Oh, that's kind. It's complicated,' the man said.

Aidan's next instinct brought him to the chalet himself,

with a basin of cleaning products to act as a decoy. Actually they had a regular cleaning lady here too. The man was blond and stubbled and Dutch-looking, tall and expensively dressed, and all around the chalet there were suitcases in shrink-wrap, unopened.

'I promise I am not a drug dealer,' the man smiled. His name was Alex and he was from Capetown. He was here to move into the gatehouse at Whitegate House. He was a distant member of the aristocratic original family that had owned the house. They retained some kind of legal interest in it, a right of access, a partial lease. It was unclear.

'I'm going to be a kind of caretaker,' Alex said. Except the cottage wasn't ready; there was a literal hole in the roof, and nobody local had come forth to fix it yet.

'The place is under suspicion,' Aidan explained, almost ecstatic to be of use. 'The last owners of the big house defaulted on a lot of debts.'

'That explains it,' Alex said.

Aidan made calls. The roof was fixed. Alex camped in a single, sealed-off room until it was. The cottage was smoky and filled with heavy furniture that seemed to grope up the walls; with long-backed chairs and mouldering wall hangings like something from an ashram. An aunt, a spiritual quester, Alex claimed, had lived in it for a couple of years.

'It's lonely and kind of creepy up here,' he laughed.

Aidan felt so vertiginously drawn to the man, from the off, it was not unlike being on drugs, and deeply upsetting. A clasp and tug at the lower stomach, at the entrails – something dangerous, like the man would kill him or hurt him terribly in some physical way. Alex had icy eyes and a warm, highly practised manner, which made his company uncanny. He had tribal tattoos on both thighs. He kept sending Aidan photographs of various improvements around the cottage, or details of the grounds, by WhatsApp attachment. It was unclear what this insistent connection indicated.

One day, driving through Scariff with his mother, Aidan

spotted Alex stepping out of a shop on the broad market main street and this apparition looked so zingingly fake, like a cartoon or a timeslip, like a gargoyle: something animated but somehow deranged. This experience was so disturbing Aidan jumped and broke a sweat and accelerated for no reason.

Seeing him in the wild made Aidan realise, he felt, that Alex was real and could be seen by other people and was not a strange untranslatable secret belonging solely to Aidan and, in the wake of this, he began to distance himself. With time, the heat of humiliation that lit within him whenever he thought about Alex began to fade. What was this instant and irrational shame? It was a feeling he had not felt since secondary school, since the locker room or the GAA pitch or the shrieking mockery of certain coarser girls. It was as though he had known and been literally murdered by Alex in a past life and, on examination, this began to seem sincerely like an actual, possible, rational or at least intuitively accurate explanation.

After the booking that followed Alex's booking there had been no further bookings of the chalet. Aidan had taken it offline. He told Rory he had taken it down because of the water stain, but really it was a strange protective impulse of his own; he worried, neurotically, that Alex would try to book it again, that Aidan would need to face into a demonic bonfire of desire and fear again. He did not tell anyone because to do so would, he knew, make him sound insane.

When Aidan arrived at the café at Castleconnell now, the barista with the moustache nodded quickly to him, in military style. He looked irritated.

'All right.' Aidan opened and closed his hands.

He was about to make a point about stocktaking. He saw himself suddenly, opening and closing his hands like his father looking for something to do – like a watchful little countryman, avid and old. Alarmed, he whipped these hands into the pockets of his jeans.

'All right,' he repeated, and this time began to give orders. Through this second slab of lurid, hallucinatory glass, he basked in the snowy glow of the lime and the mirroring sterility of the café space, and came back to himself.

Shortly after they got married – after Lena and Odhran got married – he'd hosted them here on an evening, closed the café, brought out tapas and baskets of dried flowers and a fixture made from twigs and flowers, stony dead roses and lolling fronds, which was suspended from the ceiling. Lena was pregnant and trucking around with her obscene bump. She pointed up to the skylight, a chalk-white socket in the roof, and at the tossing of a cherry laurel outside. The tree had its vaguely yellow-looking blossoms, stalks like froth of scum, on display.

She told him it was a perfect, perfect room. She turned and told him this, with a sigh. She continued to waltz about, bearing the bump. He watched her and worried she'd seen the same design in places around Dublin and didn't understand that truly it was a perfect room, a perfect space, the whites and greens like heaven or like a dreamy palatial house, like a garden or a green maze; it was quite simply a beautiful place, that you could gather these separate elements together into artificial symphony, that this counted for something, that it was taste.

25

Sunny's dream: walking with her mother down an alleyway, internal alleyway, something like the farmless farmhouse and its alley to the side – walking this with her mother, seeing a sign for something high above a door. The sign looked like a shop sign but did not cohere into a symbol yet. It was only colour. Her mother left her there; it was a bathroom; there, she had to wait for Mama. From the toilet grew two blonde girls with their feet crushed in the toilet, sharing the tiny space, and on the side of the bath sat a dark-haired girl with angry almond eyes. Sunny felt so nervous of the girl, she moved off to the opposite side of the bathroom, a white light-filled bathroom, and felt the angry hatred of the dark-haired girl burn against her. A hand floated, a hand with no arm and no body, floated in, the hand floated around the room and hovered bodiless above the heads of the twin girls in the toilet and then above the head of the angry girl with narrow eyes on the side of the bath and then above the head of Sunny, where, in a flash of intentionality, it dropped and gripped her scalp like a woman might, an old woman, in the supermarket, unbidden, to say lovely child, are you good for Mammy?

Sunny woke and was not upset. It was a bright day, another open day, and she wanted to swim.

There was a stretchy swimming suit like Smarties, patterned with Smarties, in Sunny's drawer. She took it into her mother.

'I want to swim,' she said.

'Swim where?' Mama was folding clothes. 'We're going to the party soon.' Mama pulled out the unyielding jelly sandals Sunny had wished for but regretted because they were pinching her feet after a while. Sunny looked at them with a lump in her throat. 'You can do it,' Mama claimed. 'Just take your time with the buckles.'

She did not want to walk the long street. She'd seen a lorry bellow over the bridge last week, its dragon-snout smoking, the slam of spinning yellow metal and the smell of dirt, so easily a lorry like this could tip over and crush her, or Mama, who walked errantly ahead – who never seemed to pay attention where she walked. Sunny wanted the bus or the car.

'We need the exercise,' Mama said.

When Sunny regarded the swimsuit, she also tasted smoothness, crunch and smoothness, in her mouth – she tasted Smarties, felt immediate happiness. But once she wore it in the sea and Daddy said, look up! But when she did, she saw the clouds were chasing one way, out to sea, and then the tide was chasing a different way – moving towards her in frills. The disconnect, the drift in two directions, made her dizzy and she fell. She fell into the water, hitting a hard-packed bank of sand and sending sand up through the waves like smoke. She saw her father's face frowning and floating above her like the face of a bird.

'She can't walk all that,' Daddy told Mama now. 'It's too far. Think. You have Islandbridge and then the Park.'

'That's true.'

Sunny was relieved. Daddy would drive.

In the car, it was hot and sickening, but quick. They blasted up the steep street that was like a mountainside. Sunny was wearing shorts and a T-shirt and her big denim sunhat with the flower on it; she adored the hat.

Sunny could remember a huge straw hat that smelt of turf smoke; that hung on a hook over a fire. It was not a hat for wearing. It was not her hat. But someone's hat, above the turf fire. This was not from her life this time, but a different time.

She understood the difference serenely, but if she tried to hold it in her mind, it became wobbly and impossible to explain.

There was, for instance, a Mama before. She looked much like Mama now, but with long hair to her elbows and usually she wore a white nightgown. A different Daddy met this Mama, who was plump and white and smiling, in a street somewhere, a street of low red houses. He said: marry me. Sunny looked forward to getting married someday too. She went to a wedding once and that day they all watched a satellite, like an engine in the sky, tip by. The day of hitting sudden icy water at the side of the road.

'Moon landing,' she said aloud.

'One small step for man,' said Daddy, making a sound like a raspberry. This didn't make sense to Sunny. They often answered her with nonsense. It was mocking.

She wondered if her swimsuit was in the beach bag Mama carried with her for summer outings. This was plush and green like a football pitch. Mama rummaged in it to find tubs of olives, little oranges, the tube of suncream that always got in Sunny's eyes. Sunny was excited. She thought a street party involved garden hoses because she'd seen that on *Sesame Street*. Maybe they would put her in the Smarties suit and she could jump through arcs of water, be a horse.

'There is Sunny's school!' trilled Mama as she passed. But it would not be her school; she understood that. She was frightened of being there without her parents because how would she know where to go? And anyway the school had a *head* and this head was a skeleton, Imogen said. The head was a skeleton man hiding somewhere in the fearsome building of the school. In her mind she saw the hanging finger pointing, here! and it made her think of the floating hand in her terrible dream – of the hand closing over her head. Prickles all over her scalp like a spider had landed on it. They were parking forever.

'I feel sick,' Sunny said.

'Oh no.' Mama snapped out the door and snapped Sunny's

own door wide, then lifted Sunny to the street. Sunny paused for a moment, burped and retched, then cried.

'That'll do anyway, won't it?' Daddy asked.

'Sure. Where's the meter though?' Mama stood up straight. There was a little blob of spit like cuckoo spit on the pavement where Sunny had burped. By meter, Mama meant parking meter and not the metres of a swimming pool.

'This is going to be so much fun, Sunny,' she said.

Sunny's name was *Sunniva*, but Sunniva was not Sunny. Sunniva was a princess on the back of a schoolbag, an angry-looking princess with a crown, scarily self-assured, and this was Sunniva – it hung in Sunny's wardrobe. If Sunniva ever came out of the wardrobe and moved in the world, she would be naughty all the time. Sometimes Sunny did not like having a name in common with angry Sunniva.

'Oh look, baby,' said Mama romantically. They were, Sunny saw, on Oscar's street. She was amazed to see a bouncy castle, one of the dinosaur ones, fat and full of air, but empty. She felt sure its emptiness meant you were not allowed to bounce on it yet. There were people everywhere, and music, and the music was too loud.

'What is it?' Daddy dropped to her level when she beckoned.

'Too loud,' Sunny said.

'You can be loud too,' Daddy suggested. 'You be loud.'

Sunny frowned. She didn't feel like being loud. 'I want a lift,' she said.

'You've got too heavy. Come on, we'll find your friends.' He offered, instead, his hand. His hands were always browner and drier than Mama, who had cold and soft hands. They were coldest of all at her rings, the little diamond and the golden ring, which represented the fact that she was in love with Daddy, and could not have new boyfriends.

'I have a boyfriend,' Sunny said.

'Sure, you have Oscar,' Mama said.

This wasn't right: Sunny had Arjun, who was completely silent, but sat beside her and poured dried peas into her favourite cup. Most mornings he would approach her and hold out the brown basket of dried peas. Or had. Not anymore. Montessori was over, she was starting school, or just staying at home with Mama every day. Staying home meant Sunny always knew how many ice lollies remained in the packet and could recheck this every day. She was allowed an ice lolly after her dinner and, on nights when Mama worked, she and Daddy sat with their lollies on the balcony. The cars below passed like pigs. Daddy made the snorting sounds and sometimes called, hey man, your exhaust pipe! Your exhaust!

'The arse,' he said, 'is going to fall off that man's car.'

Sunny shrieked. 'You can't say arse!'

Sunny held Daddy's hands now, and moved through the crowd. This was the kind of situation that might result in her getting a nut ball, or a brownie. There were no hoses though.

A door was open and suddenly this was Oscar's house, the dark food-smelling forest hollow of the front room where the toys were kept. Oscar stood in the centre of it, naked but for his underpants. His daddy, laughing all the time, was dressing Oscar, saying, oh, we'll start again! It was confusing.

Mama put Sunny on the toilet seat in the bathroom. There was a drip-drip-drip somewhere, like something waiting, salivating. You must pee, Mama instructed. It was confusing. Sunny couldn't pee. Oscar, in the front room, acted as though he didn't know her – he stamped his feet and screwed his face up, shouting, no, no, no.

Outside there was dancing; Sunny was supposed to dance. She threw her arms out, her legs, and wobbled woodenly from side to side; she was a rocking horse, she was stuck in a box, she felt the rigid wood all around her; she was wood. She enjoyed this. She felt her body sloshing to and fro contentedly. Imogen had something in her mouth; she couldn't speak. Her eyes flashed darkly after Sunny like the eyes, sometimes, of Sunniva, or like the girl with angry almond eyes in Sunny's dream.

Nuts could be poisonous. You could die from nuts.

A child howled close to Sunny and Sunny clamped her

hands over her ears. She could not see Mama. Oh no. She shouted out, 'Mama!' Mama was talking, there she was – Mama was sitting on the window of a house, with a cup, speaking to somebody.

Daddy was nowhere. Sunny shouted. No one heard.

Imogen watched her glassily.

But then, behind Imogen was a woman. This woman's eyes seemed to steepen as she glared. She glared at Sunny; she was angry also, all these angry eyes. This woman knew something about Sunny, about the skeleton, about the mama of before. She belonged to that class of people Sunny sometimes encountered who looked at her with steep and rageful hating eyes.

'Go away!' Sunny said.

Sunny moved towards the side of the street where Mama was, but, when she got there, it was not the street. Mama was nowhere to be seen. The crowd had closed over the road. Sunny was standing at a large gate, also closed, over a yard, and it had been painted the same shade of brown as the houses around – it was huge, broad as the entire face of a house, but without windows. There was also something behind the gate. It was a dog. Or two dogs; Sunny heard it snuffling, terribly close to her ear. She had pressed her ear to the cold metal, which smelt creamy and cold, and she could hear the ticklish scratching of a dog or else two dogs. A partial whine; the swipe of a spindly paw. Sunny felt the cool grain of the surface against her bare arm and one bare leg. And then, in sudden explosion, came a bark so loud it caused her ear to pop; a bark like a smack and a rattling and it felt the gate would not hold, the dog would gouge her ear out, and in terror she looked down and saw no paws but something like the trotter of a pig. Sunny covered her eyes and backed off. She could pee now and here it came. A voice was saying, now don't be annoying them dogs.

But Mama came. Mama swept across the street and through the crowd with a worried expression, dropping to her hunkers, wiping Sunny's face.

'It's a monster,' Sunny said.

'It's a horrible, horrible dog.' Mama was angry, but not with Sunny. 'It's a horrible dog and we'll stay well away from him.'

'It's not a dog.'

I have changing clothes, Mama was saying to Daddy, just as Oscar's Mama said also, we have lots of clothes. It seemed incredible to Sunny that they could be calm. She felt the panic banging through her like the banging of the gate. The thing with hooves went stalking up and down, snorting and whining hoarsely. It would eat them, all of them, and yet they stood there in their adult apathy all yawns and nods and smiles and waving at their friends.

26

Lena did not often bring her daughter to the city centre, but here she was, on a morning in August, dismounting from the tram at Jervis with Sunny's hand in her own. The monotony of a reverse alarm ricocheted, like the flat word *Dublin-Dublin-Dublin* itself, throughout the street. The streets and light were cooler, as if things had been dialled down, as if patrons were soon expected to exit summer without being told explicitly to leave; as if the season in its sensuality was to be disavowed. Coats collected, journeys home.

'Mama can I have—' Sunny began, forgetting what she wanted instantly.

At the tram stop, a couple exploded into view, arguing.

'That's how you got lifted yesterday,' the man was roaring at the woman. The woman was tiny and antic in her movements as a little girl; she had tarry hair tightened into a ponytail.

'That's how you got fucken lifted, bawling like that,' the man roared.

The woman raised her fists and began to beat back at him ineffectually. He caught her wrists and yanked her towards him.

'If you get lifted again, I'm fucken leaving you to it,' he said.

'Don't be frightened, sweetheart.' Lena crouched at Sunny's level as another tram lolled in. It sprang to a halt with a glassy sound like beads on a breeze.

They had crossed town, but not by much: four stops.

Sunny finished crying and looked up at the narrow channel of Benburb Street, streaked by tinselly shopfronts and demolition sites like tundras in between the tall buildings on either side.

The therapists' rooms were at the top of several flights of stairs. Sunny struggled with the stairs. At the top a young woman was laughing fulsomely at something someone in an annexe behind her had said. She turned to Lena still beaming and gave Lena's suffering – the pricks of sweat and shortness of breath, the nervous child – a happy landing.

'Hi there,' the woman said.

Lena was strangely shy. She determined not to be shy in front of Sunny.

'Sunniva Marley Flynn,' she said at once, brittlely, 'for Mr Riley.'

The young woman's glee flexed into obligation. 'Take a seat.'

Lena led Sunny to a deep-backed couch and let the child climb into a perching position, her slim neck extended. Grey light fell through a small window, infusing motes that thickened in the orbit of a vase of false flowers. There were magazines but no children's toys, no crayons or block colours, only a peachy sensibility that put Lena, not unpleasantly, in mind of other people's guest bathrooms. She felt tired now that she was still. After a moment the child looked up and said, 'Mama, there are no toys.'

'I know. We should have brought a book.'

The place was so silent, the corridor and stairwell oppressive; the cheerful woman from reception gone; the din of traffic, hollers, from the street muffled and homogenised. Mother and daughter were uncomfortable, and could think.

Sunny asked, 'Mama, can I look out the window?'

'Of course.' Lena checked it wasn't open, even slightly, then returned to her seat.

Sunny peered down, full fathoms down, to the street, making small cooing noises of recognition and curiosity. What could she see? A tumult of unconnected, non-sequential human and machine movements; windowpanes parrying the blank unstructured sky.

In this moment of tired idleness, Lena began to think, randomly, of clothes. More specifically, of items of clothing she might obtain and combine with other clothing to look less dreadful. Sunny was four, but Lena had never recovered from the shock of losing her youth overnight – literally overnight – and losing, also, some sort of insulating veil, a sense of herself as punchily agile and attractive and acceptable in mirrors, smooth of brow and with surging curls like Sunny had now, handsome rather than beautiful but always slight-boned and essentially sexual in an austere but ultimately obvious way.

The day after she brought Sunny home from the maternity hospital, she tugged on the light in the tiny toilet and saw herself yellowed and sunken-eyed, as if all fatty deposits and liquid had been strained out of her; narrow, deflated, ghastly of hand and feet. Her hair lost its shape over the subsequent months, falling out all over the furniture, growing back neither curly nor straight but directionless. In the wild annihilating months of early motherhood, she forgot how to dress in anything but a series of dun-coloured shirts and jeans and then, on formal occasions, in the dresses she had saved from Mikey O'Hara's cheque; dresses more expensive than the rest of her wardrobe and, consequently, impossible to throw out.

Crazy to think she was still wearing those.

At first, she had embraced this annihilation – it annihilated everything, not only style but every vestige of a stable self – with masochism, but years had passed and it was ongoing, her affect dull and blurry, nonspecific: invisibility.

Now, in this stray moment, waiting in a waiting room with no need for action, with repose, Lena would wonder if clothes could solve this. But now the child was peeling away from the window and moving through the room in bored, exaggerated strides. She got a fright when a door opened suddenly and a long, thin man with a grey goatee leant out.

'Well hello,' he said.

Sunny turned tail and fled back to her mother's legs.

'I'm Declan Riley.' He shook Lena's hand.

'So nice to see you,' she said. 'This is Sunny. Not to worry, honey. Come on.'

In the little office room, there was a long loveseat, an Eames chair, a painted vase of further fake flowers wadded together dustily, a wall of degree and diploma certificates. Another window, small but deep-set, like a socket or something you might crawl into.

'All right.' Declan Riley began to scan his clipboard. 'You have filled out everything. Thank you. And Sunny, what a lovely name; Sunny is just lovely, aren't you?'

He did not look up while saying this. He continued, instead, to examine or feign to examine the clipboard. Sunny, intrigued by the oddness of an otherwise conventional, anticipated burst of praise, tucked herself back on the loveseat next to Lena and watched.

'My name is Sunniva,' she said.

'Do you want me to call you Sunniva?'

Sunny thought for a moment, then said, 'No.'

'Well then. Your mother has brought you in to visit me.'

The man was sitting in the Eames chair now. He set aside the clipboard with a sweeping motion to sit forward, long shins jutting upwards in velvet slacks, and leant his elbows on his knees. His fingers tented together. He had an alert look, an almost teasing look, and he was gazing animatedly at Lena as if about to burst out laughing, or provoke.

'Do you remember me?' Lena asked.

This had the impact she intended. Declan's fingers flew apart. One hand closed around an arm of the Eames chair, which was modular and had two rests instead of one. The other reached for the clipboard again and held it up defensively.

'No,' he said. 'No, I don't think I do. Helena Marley Flynn. No. How long ago?'

'You weren't doing children then; it was well before the

pandemic,' Lena explained. She began to feel bad for Declan, who had flung his power off so hastily.

'It was about twenty-seventeen,' she said. 'I was going out with Gwynn.'

'Oh Gwynn. Of course.' He looked at her softly now.

'We met at a dinner party. You made an impression on me.'

Sunny said, 'Mama, stop talking.'

'Yes!' Lena twisted to her. 'We are here to talk about Sunny.'

'You're a girl with lots of imagination,' Declan said.

Sunny seemed lost for words at this.

Lena found herself parroting the public health nurse: 'Above average intelligence.'

She was smiling as she said it but turning a certain spike of irony against herself, undermining the implication with drollery, and she wondered with a shaming flash why she needed to undermine Sunny like that. Because it was true. The nurse had described her as *of above average intelligence* and written this on the elliptical printout they received.

'So I see.' Declan had read the printout too.

Sunny looked at her mother. 'Will I have to do a test?'

'No tests,' Declan said. 'Only games.'

Sunny blinked up at Lena, growing anxious. Sunny who, days earlier, had pointed to a lone bird on a wire and cried, 'Oh no! That bird has no family.' Sunny who, on first seeing a wheelchair, shouted, 'Oh no! That man is tired.' Who liked to sit straight-backed on the couch and fold her hands in her lap and say, *like mama*.

Lena put her hand on Sunny's head. 'It's all good, love,' she said. 'Declan is going to ask me questions, and maybe a few questions for you, and you can play some games, OK?'

Declan leant forward to enquire of Sunny, 'And what is your favourite game?'

'Recycling,' the child said severely.

'There is a great toy here.' Declan stood up. He was so tall, it felt like legs alone were traversing the little room, blocking the window like a brain-zap, fleetingly. He drew out the large bucket drawer of a filing cabinet and produced an exceptional dollhouse, handmade and one-storey and salmon pink, a little SoCal hacienda. Sunny looked up at her with wonder, one of the emotions Sunny had lately started to ham up or perform.

'You can play with this while I talk to Mummy,' Declan said, the *Mummy* so serenely queeny it felt practised and almost edgy.

Sunny acquiesced. While she was kneeling on the floor between them, sorting out a few wire dolls with wooden limbs and plaited wool for hair, Declan picked up his clipboard briskly again and addressed Lena.

'Talk me through it,' he directed. 'You will have done this with the nurse or whoever you spoke to, the GP, but I'll need to hear it again.'

Lena looked at his interested, if somewhat closed, expression and wondered if he could really remember her. It was a party, close to the end, at a crushingly small but eccentrically stylish little terrace in Fairview; burgundy and ironic Mexicana, many bottles of red wine. Lena had got too drunk and been ill and had to sit alone in a small dark bedroom with the spins. She squeezed her eyes shut and thought, I do not love anyone, anyone. The realisation was anguished and weird. It was an afterglow of humiliation – something, then, in her short life with Gwynn was already latently humiliating. Declan came upstairs and smiled before her, kneeling down, and said with kindness, 'You came for a different kind of party, I fear.'

'I'm an idiot,' she'd tried to laugh.

'Not at all. You were charming and delectably young for an hour or so, and then you were drunk. We have all been there. We have all, at one time, been delectably young.'

She remembered this well but perhaps she did not want him to remember it. In the morning, Gwynn had told her quickly that she needn't worry about anything and Lena had stared at him blankly because she was yet to mention feeling worried about anything.

'Sunny is four,' Lena began now, looking into Declan's eyes.

'She was born in the Coombe and delivered normally. I was thirty. She's been in the seventy-fifth percentile of pretty much everything since the start. Her father and I have been married for almost four years.'

'Do you work?'

'I used to do different things. I worked in cultural heritage and stuff.'

'And Sunny's father?'

Lena was proud of Odhran's work. She explained it in detail.

'So no more Gwynn,' Declan grinned.

'A flash in the pan. Long ago now.'

'Well then.' He was stagey again. 'I'll have to ask you, I am afraid, to leave me with Sunny now. Sunny and I have serious fun to begin.'

He had not brought up the past life claims she'd reported to him in an email. Perhaps he was saving that for later, or would let Sunny bring it up.

Lena descended the stairs and chose a café just across the river, with a view of the crowds massing and flowing from a set of traffic lights. Outside the large window, bikes whipped by, tourists dove into a river breeze, a man with sagging trousers dipped over his phone and wove slowly, slightly aggressively, around a school of lawyers with binders and peacoats. Dublin looked good here. You would want to stay living in it. Though perhaps not with children rattling behind you, like cups on string after a wedding car; perhaps only single and sleek.

She felt immensely nervous as she sat. Sunny could be crying, hysterical; perhaps she would get a call from the receptionist. Declan was a strange choice and one which Odhran had pulled a face at, but something in Lena – when she found him online, remembering the hyperactively handsome man of a long-ago candlelit Mexicana enchantment, the fatherly friendship he'd seemed to extend as she sat in her miserable spinning loveless room – had longed for that same spark of recognition: had wanted to be seen, along with Sunny, tenderly.

Tenderly even in strangeness and isolation.

Sitting, sipping, the memory seemed embarrassing to her now.

It led to other things. It made her mind drift to Elva Fanning, whose email she had not used; whose gallery on Arran Quay she had, this morning, zipped by in the tram.

With these thoughts, there came the feeling like a dragnet. Curiosity and dread. She called to mind the people who did not look upon her with tenderness or recognition, beginning with Elva and proceeding to Gwynn and then certainly Caoimhe, the hostility even of Rita the last time she'd worked at Reap and Sew; the indifference of her father, who'd messaged to say they'd found more photo albums if she wanted, adding 'will be thrown out otherwise maybe' unnecessarily, another injection of that surprise belated venom which, it seemed, had come over her father as he aged. What did he expect of her? She was decently remote from both her parents. Everything they'd ever done suggested this was how they'd wanted it.

Cian. Cian had once looked upon her with tenderness. And then not.

I have run all around this city, she thought with callous grandeur then, in search of tenderness. All around this country; this *continent*, if you want to exaggerate slightly.

When she thought of Odhran's tenderness towards her, she felt hot and that she didn't deserve it and that he didn't know the half of it. This came with the painful voltage of an old unhappy feeling. He had found for them a chalet in Clare and Lena had said, 'Holiday chalet?'

'What do you think?'

Like an open road, blasting through a trompe l'oeil.

'I like it,' she'd said. 'I think I do. But what if we're stuck there? Or have to leave when the summer begins and have nowhere to go – and end up at your mother's?'

Would that be so bad, he asked; would that, he asked, be really so bad?

She'd been hurt by his tone, which was hostile. She had not meant to undermine the chalet idea.

When Lena collected Sunny, the little girl was smirking and Declan was smirking, as if both had been laughing together before she arrived.

'How was that?' Lena asked in the air. 'Will you go back next week?'

'I played with the mushroom playhouse,' Sunny said.

It was early August; there were three more sessions, but Declan sent a first report the following week. This was after Lena had delivered Sunny to him for a second hour. He sent it by email, and so her parents waited until she was asleep.

They opened it, on the balcony, on their phones.

Sunny is an articulate, intelligent, imaginative child, it began.

As they read in silence, the evening, balmy and reddish and generous, relaxed around. Gulls skied overhead, then landed on the flat roof of the flats and threw their heads back, bellowing. The sound was sucked into the street below, by engines and conversation. In the alternate city, the place they no longer lived in, people were getting started, there was calamari frying, alcohol and sex, but here they read and remembered occasionally to draw deep, sustaining breaths. It took twenty minutes or so for both of them to reach the end, begin again, then set the phones down before them on the little table. Odhran reached for his beer.

'Nothing,' Lena said. She was furious.

'There's two more sessions.'

'She has said absolutely nothing about death.'

'Isn't this a good thing?'

'She's been playing with toys and telling stories about skeleton headmasters and being delightful. For two hundred and fifty euro a pop.'

'It's a good thing, Lena. We shouldn't be upset.'

Lena felt the need to stand up. She held the cool bar of the balcony against her wrists. It had praised her, the report – *Sunny's confidence and happiness*, it said, *is a credit to her mother, the main caregiver. Mother Lena spends time playing with Sunny every day.* She was rattled by this. She felt undeserving again. She wanted to cry. She did not know why. Surely it was a good thing, surely they were being somehow released from something and Lena especially, most especially Lena, released from the grievous possibility that she was polluting her child with pure unreconciled weirdness; with postpartum insidiousness, with hereditary oddness, with the mulish rudeness of her father and the frightened frigid energy of her mother and the backwards chant, the desire to die, the regret she'd felt at having a child.

Why did it bother her? Like a funhouse, she thought abruptly, from nowhere. Like she had been in a funhouse of past lives and ghoulies and ghosties and chronic mental imbalance and shame – so much shame – but it was a funhouse, they were emerging and blinking into sunlight now. Which meant she had invented it all. Invented something. The misery of early motherhood; the murk of Cian and her embarrassment, the vindictiveness of her attitude towards Gwynn, her sense of superiority over Elva Fanning; her perennial sense of her marriage as a pose or piece of irony; her poise itself, her belief in herself as special.

All of this thundered around Lena as humiliation.

'What's the problem?' Odhran was light about it, but looked perturbed.

'We have not been exaggerating, right? We have not been imagining things.'

'No. But possibly she's just growing out of it.'

'Or the sessions,' Lena wondered aloud, 'just scared her straight. If *she* was exaggerating.'

After the final session, Declan addressed her, seriously.

'Bright children,' he said, 'are imaginative. You have done well sending her to Montessori, but I think she needs school now – to be occupied.'

'We enrolled her,' Lena felt a little desolate. 'But our life is kind of in upheaval. We are probably moving to Clare.'

'Probably?'

'I haven't decided yet.'

'Seems close to the line. School begins soon.'

'I will try to get her,' Lena promised, 'into a school in Clare. She's only four.'

'It becomes lonely,' Declan said. 'For a woman to be alone all day with a child.'

And that was it; rather damning.

Not damning, Odhran said.

'He called you a good mother. Things are moving now. She's getting much bigger. I think you're going to be stressed. You're doing brilliant,' he said. He had stepped back into that anodyne state of being, of married identity, the man who managed her and consoled her blandly.

However: 'We have to decide,' he said,

He was flying to London for four days. She would make her mind up in the meantime. It seemed clear what she would say. She had been offered the option of becoming somebody else entirely. Her sense of anguish was only a form of delayed euphoria. This was difficult to articulate and she felt grateful Odhran was not one of those men who expect to know you ultimately, or even very well; was a man who would not need to discuss these things.

I am free, she thought ambivalently. Turns out there is nothing crazy about me.

27

The next day, Elva followed Lena on Instagram, unfollowed, refollowed, unfollowed and refollowed several times. Lena emailed the address at last.

All right, she said. Whatever.

I want to warn you mostly, Elva wrote. I am writing something and people might appear in it. I don't name names, but it may be clear. We should meet to discuss.

With respect, Lena tapped, I doubt anybody cares much about me. I don't see why you need to speak to me.

I would appreciate it just so much, Elva said. She used emojis, which was disconcerting.

Something Sunny used to do – pretend, from morning to mid-morning, or at times of stress or shyness, to be a cat: miaow, miaow, in answer to everything. Can I talk to Sunny, and not the cat now? Miaow, miaow! Lena and Odhran used the emoji to explain it to one another: she's a cat today, cat now, the cat is out. It was shyness and theatre too. It was sometimes uncanny. Elva's streak of emojis was pure manipulation – a grin that curls – and Lena resented it.

Odhran was packing for London importantly. 'I need hardly anything,' he claimed. He would regret it, she thought; in London, in August, it was hot.

He left early in a cab and she saw him off, sitting in the grey suspension of a pre-storm stillness, the watery dawn. Soon it would cool again into a splintering little storm, nothing dramatic, only the crackle of ropes cracking apart, eaten by mice, say – why this image? Remembering something – all at once and, oh yes, she remembered it now. Ropes eaten by mice and snapping apart from the body of Aslan the slain lion in a cartoon rendition of *The Lion, The Witch and the Wardrobe* she had seen as a child: that was the thunder. Things withering and snapping around the huge heavy corpse of a great animal. An image of slackening and release when the slack and release has already happened. This was also, of course, an image of crucifixion, of the aftermath of crucifixion, the silent shock and dismay taken to a level of sublimity. Changes in life, for Lena at least, had this monumental quality and often brought the weather into it. Her life was changing, she thought with satisfaction, because this business with Elva and so with Cian would be put to bed at last.

There was more to it than she'd ever let on, and this was something she could accept now. She could sit on the leatherette couch and accept it in the private light of solitude: Odhran gone, Sunny asleep, staring down the city stoically, pre-storm.

In the meantime, Odhran rode his silent cab to the airport, air conditioned and brimming with delight. To be free of the hot apartment, its greenhouse-panopticon of panes, was delightful, and the oppressive pre-storm heat gave to everything an unearned aura of profundity.

The concourse of the terminal was ashen, but the terminal itself churning with holidaymakers and tourists, like the belly of a beast. It had none of the provincial desolation of Shannon either: this was Dublin, roaring with life.

Flying had never lost its sheen to Odhran, no matter how many times he had a shit time flying anywhere – it would never be other than glamorous. It made him think of a life in which holidays used to happen, cheap sun holidays with grappa and never-ending jokes about chlamydia, his twenties work life spent twitching over to London at short notice, dry and hyper from syrupy espressos. He found a place to sit and think and watch the snouts of airplanes trundle into the distance: he contemplated.

He was being sent to London to attend a large interdisciplinary conference at a time in history when the concept of interdisciplinarity had so run out of road it seemed anachronistic, basically embarrassing, as getting the ferry or attending a wedding breakfast or developing photographs in the chemist or any other originally wholesome and default cultural phenomenon which had slid out of relevance with unnerving finality. The great waste of energy that was webbing disciplines together within the university, to spread funding or just come up with new ideas, was only really practised under the auspices of government funding bloat. This was an unfortunate fact and it reflected the conservatism of government funding. He, Odhran, could see things like this because he was innately impatient and started out in tech.

But what matter. He stared into his scummed coffee cup.

Rain began. It did not hit the glass so much as manifest upon it as spores. It was the faint noncommittal rain of a pre-storm tension; it was home. He felt cosy in his life when he thought about home and the chalet, and the nibble of rain on the roof of a holiday chalet, which was a sound from his own childhood, and returning to him quietly. Since Aidan had called, a brittle scrim had closed in around Odhran, muffling and softening. He felt excused from life in Dublin and from the strange, strained year it had been in respect of Sunny and from, above all, the tiring indignity of still being here – in this place where houses were too expensive, the streets were more and more casually violent, his daughter was expressing vague unhealthy tensions and he, Odhran, had become truly bored.

Lena had asked him if he had a country snobbery about the city that was now coming out, and it was likely true, he thought: I am sick, he admitted, of watching people wake up in fucking doorways.

'As they do in Limerick,' Lena said.

'Yeah, but we aren't going to live in Limerick,' Odhran replied.

We are going to live somewhere with a big sky open over us and mountains in a slouch on the horizon. There are so many broad bodies of water. There are little schoolhouses with Virgins in small stilettoed shrines. I will be affluent instead of embarrassed.

And as he thought these things, looking humbly on the taxiing of planes, Lena sat in their apartment remembering the grey mornings of the pandemic and the earliest months of motherhood. At six months, they could sit Sunny up between them in the mornings, snug as a Buddha. Lena began to feed her watery porridge with a plastic spoon. The baby's eyes popped with amazement at the flavour, lips unpractised but smacking with appreciation.

It was a soft period, almost impossibly so, looking back – only the country silence of the summertime lockdown outside, the queue for a coffee concession ambling happily around the block. Lena's soul settled into a routine that felt simple but so protected she could be thankful for it. Her first great wave of anger and panic at Odhran subsided when he was forced to work from home for weeks at a time and could emerge to flirt with Sunny the monkey-bundle, swinging in her animatronic swing or rolling like a doughball on the rug. This was an easy phase, but it got difficult later, when the baby became more alert. She remembered this first instalment of bonding as sweet, though, almost like paradise.

Breastfeeding was over. Sleep was possible sometimes. But all the same, even in the fond fronds of the Park and with the birds returning, foxes even scanting sometimes from the grass verges of the motorway, there was a sense of low-tuned ever-peril, a kind of tension headache. Lena felt it when she walked Sunny in her buggy and baulked at excitable dogs, the odd motorbike accelerating, people with unwell energy veering actively up the street – the man who strode, muttering, and tried to walk into people's paths. Sometimes she padded about at night like an alert animal even when Sunny was sleeping, starfish, in the crib.

'I am a mother,' she found herself saying prosaically, privately. It was astonishing.

That must have happened fast, wrote Gwynn.

And then, soon after that, from Gwynn again: I have seen some troubling things online and I hope you are OK.

Her first thought was, with instant irritation, what is wrong with this man. But then he added *about Cian* and her pulse quickened – equally animally – in response. She was on Twitter a lot; they were all on Twitter a lot. It was at the height of its mulish, earnest, girlboss era; everyone was masking vehemently and scolding one another.

One day an eruption of pain at the death of George Floyd took its quaking, arboreal universe by storm. Lena watched it all, rocking her baby, feeling blessedly excused and clean, and then another wave of sexual assault disclosures followed, or perhaps that wasn't the order of things; she could not remember clearly.

It didn't matter anyway. It was only a crazy bouquet of impressions to her now.

She saw rows of coffins laid out in Bologna. She saw people digging graves on Rikers Island. She saw long decision-tree shaped sagas about coercive control; half-glimpsed polycules gone sour and girls insisting they'd believed such-and-such a minor celebrity, a public figure or folk hero, when he threatened to kill himself if they left. It was all pretty miserable and amusing and then it came one day for music, for a particular scene. This was what Gwynn had managed to spot and ensure she found out about.

No Eleanor then, she felt like mocking him.

Why are you sending me this?

Before she opened the thread, she knew what she would see. It was not about Cian initially, but Cas Cronin, the lanky chain-smoking hectoring orbiting sidebar character of her shining days. Cas who was always more famous also. More so than Cian.

Cas would come and pick me up from school, the scrambled avatar wrote, and give me alcohol. There was a whole group of us, we used to meet to go to gigs. We thought we all were his girlfriends. He used to make me do these things. The details were sketchy but vexing – also highly litigious. You could not publish allegations like this in Ireland. The libel laws were especially taut.

Solicitor's letter! Avatars flashed. Solicitor's letter again!

Like this could keep us quiet.

But it did, and they were washed off, all these posts. An accusation, incoherent or elliptical, would appear and be taken down and sometimes, rarely, shared in its screen-grabbed and desiccated state by accounts based in America. You could not be sued for repeating allegations in America. One woman described Cas's apartment, a place trashed, in disarray, a man off his face and pleading on the floor to be pegged or pissed on – crazy, banal things.

Lena never liked Cas. Cian kept him away from her – she'd only ever had to cope with him, really, in strong doses on Inishbofin. She knew he was something sleazy, somebody with a lingering smile and a tendency to whistle suddenly, straight out of nowhere, like he was insane. How any girl could be into that, could ever be into that, she didn't know. He was too tall and morosely dishevelled. He had a deep voice and a song that was used on an advertisement for Vodafone. She imagined herself explaining it to Odhran: it was kind of a moment. But she never spoke to Odhran about any of this. It lived on her phone.

He would do something crazy, an avatar wrote, then something normal, so you thought it was a joke.

Cas Cronin likes them young.

There were others. All of them. Cian Mulvaney, they wrote.

Slowly, a cloud of knowing crept over Lena, and the noughties – money, raunch, but also her own life of wearing cheesecloth, walking beaches, writing songs – recast ungenerously. People began to share pictures of her online.

Little Lena Marley, they wrote. How old was she? Sixteen?

All those bands who were managed by Mikey O'Hara, someone wrote.

She had never been underage. Nobody had ever asked her to piss on them. She almost wrote a comment on something, then resisted. She did not post on her Twitter anyway. Only shared. The messages appeared. If you want to talk, if you want to talk, I am with the *Examiner.* I am with the *Herald*. I am with the *Independent*.

This was when she became frightened and deleted her account.

I wrote Cian a fan letter, one girl said, and he sent me a ticket and met me afterwards, and we had sex in this house in Wicklow he would rent a couple of times. I was fifteen then. I looked older, but I know he had to know.

Lena had seen this before deletion and felt sick.

Yes, she thought now, four years later. I felt sick. The sudden twist of self-disgust. The woman in the picture was masked, with short hair; there was no name and no further details on the account, no sense of who she might be and how reliable. Anyone could say anything. But Lena knew it was true, and with this truth a deathly calm came over her, and she deleted the account.

All of it was gone within a week.

I'd like to be left alone about it, she told Gwynn. It was a stupid thing to say. It made it seem like it mattered to her. He'd undoubtedly punished her fully, then, for leaving him so imperiously; for proving he could not function as a man. No less than that. She thought this splenetic and outsized thing of Gwynn for a while, then receded, and came to see him as a meek person who probably felt bad about the way things had ended. And affronted a little by how fast she'd moved on, fully, to somebody else.

'There is some minor bonfire online,' she told Odhran.

'About Cas and Cian and people like that.' The gruesome thought of him reading the posts that had been deleted worried her, but he did not have Twitter anyway, just access to the Research Council handle once a month. During that time, he would repost press releases for international grants.

'Did anything happen to you?' he asked her frankly.

'No,' she said.

She said, 'I want to stay out of it.'

This was easy in the end. After a month or so the internet pivoted and, after lockdown, everything changed anyway. The days of outrage ran aground. It was easy to turn inward with a small child and to feel blank, as if she had been reborn. After all, she had.

28

Lena was fully prepared to present this overview of events to Elva Fanning when she made the mildly excruciating decision to ask Caoimhe to watch Sunny for a few hours the following day.

'Oh wow, showdown,' Caoimhe said.

Lena was surprised at her mellowness, which turned out to be exhaustion, when Caoimhe showed up at the apartment.

'I'm going to take them to the cinema,' she declared.

'Oh, I mean, I didn't mean you had to do that.'

'No, we want to, don't we, Immy? It's been hot for so long, we want to sit in the dark and eat crap. We'll be on Parnell Street. I can meet you afterwards.'

Sunny was uncomfortable but brave. 'Imogen pinches,' she whispered.

'Daddy's in London,' Lena explained. 'Mama needs you to be brave.'

Lena left them at the tram and walked to Arran Quay. The storm that had been so present the previous day had not come to pass; tension, persistently, rang. It was not unlike tinnitus. The river was low and giving off its later-summer reek and this made her think of many summers compressed, summer moments reeking archetypically, and the song 'Summer in Dublin', which she'd always disliked. She'd also disliked 'Raglan Road', always and ever, such a wearisome cloying drunk's song, full of sentimentality and piety, and she thought unwantedly now of Cas crowing it at her on Inisbofin: with her own name there and her own dark hair like clouds in the month of May. How was dark hair ever like a cloud in the month of May? It was as abstract and hackneyed as a devotional phrase. Similes and metaphors laboured to close the gap between different things, but there was such a yawning gap between these things it was only the lazy alliance of images purportedly beautiful. Clouds, women, hair. She'd had, indeed, an abundance of hair; she would take her time kneading and pushing it into a bun, staring into the middle distance, to irritate Cas. She would stretch up her body and model for him her delicate shoulders and rounded breasts.

God, she recalled with a jolt, he got into homelessness for a while. He was an advocate against homelessness. Lots of stony-faced monologues and impromptu fundraising gigs. At a point in time before much of that discourse pivoted to being anti-immigrant: Irish homes for Irish people, etcetera. Cas had been a face of anti-homelessness and yet had never said a thing about immigrants and you could make that look pretty bad if you wanted to, you could extract some shady implication from never *diversifying* empathy publicly, if you needed a weapon such as that and if you were the kind of person who weaponised things like that.

Lucky I'm not, she thought. It was kind of funny.

Lena found the gallery where Elva worked hidden nimbly between two defunct, shuttered language schools. It was cool inside and smelt faintly of hops or horses. The second floor of the building had been removed, such that a high ceiling fluted up like a chimney flue.

It seemed empty; it was an art gallery. They were often empty. As if she'd been watching from a window somewhere, Elva emerged looking smaller than Lena remembered her. She was dressed in a long, sleeveless column of blue fabric, like a statue. Lena felt hurried and unkempt. Clothes, she thought. She needed new clothes.

Elva stood in the open space and, for a moment, didn't speak. She had the same cringing smile as before – the half-smile, crashing with pity or tolerance, that Lena witnessed at Reap and Sew. The soul of a middle manager. Lena surprised herself with the briskness and cruelty and accuracy of this observation. It was something Odhran said about other people and then, once, in a moment of sorrow, himself.

'Thank you for coming,' Elva said. 'I have an office upstairs, but it's empty inside, if you want to see the exhibition.'

'Oh.' Lena took it in. 'It looks interesting. I'll come back.'

'It's closing soon, but yes.' Elva shrugged. There was aggression now. She was feeling self-conscious. Lena watched her, pointedly, from the side of her face.

The exhibition was beautiful. From a looming false fireplace suspended by cords in one corner there played a tape – a looping monologue, muffled, or the drone of a sean nós song. The singing style obliged the singer to hold a strained note, the nasal *néa*, between phrases, like a didgeridoo. What coincidence that this was the theme. She thought of Sunny, who had asked about the heads on Inisbofin. She thought: this is a popular theme, folklore and ancestors and folk music, no reason to think it is weird.

But it was weird a bit, wasn't it? The coincidence.

The head, the skulls, were before her mind again, and then also the catacombs in Paris – the Paris catacombs. How could she have forgotten the catacombs? She'd seen them with Cian, when they were passing through; she'd hurtled through the catacombs in horror and sacrilege at twenty – these people are dead! It was wrong to look at them! But then she had also gone back at thirty, right before her pregnancy, on a dirty weekend, and felt unfazed. All the noseless, droning, empty heads of the dead taken from many cemeteries and arranged in confected formation, in honeycombs and squalid altars, to warn and shame the living. And afterwards she sat in an expensive café, with Odhran this time, eating tuna Niçoise.

'I've worked with Georgian buildings,' Lena said now, referring to the exhibition. It was about Dublin, its baroque housing stock, which was really no more magnificent, Odhran often said, than your average English heritage town; which was filled with flues and chimneys and booming vacancy and into this matrix of images the artist inserted deep droning voices and sean nós laments and the nasal, implacable *néa*, and in this way the work was a work of mourning or commemoration or something adjacent to the underworld.

'We looked in the archives,' Elva told her, 'and found out that a little boy had died here, in this building, in the 1840s – a chimney sweep who got stuck in the chimney. That is part of the commission, or it's in the exhibition material.'

'How upsetting,' Lena said.

After a pause, Elva pursed her lips. 'Maybe we should go upstairs after all.'

Her office was not what Lena's office had been in the Georgian house museum. It was pristine, pallid with weak light through a porthole, airy with openwork furniture, spare. There was only one chair and so Elva sat on the low windowsill.

Lena saw she had become barefoot somehow, and her toenails were painted blue.

'Thank you for coming,' Elva began.

'I haven't spoken to Cian since I left the band,' Lena said.

'Oh I know.' Elva was smiling a little. 'The way he used to hold up the phone to the crowd, and ask them to chant your name, remember that?'

'He did it once or twice, I believe.'

'You were the model of class,' Elva said. 'Never to answer that phone.'

Lena nodded. People thought this of her, she knew. It was a useful thing to have people imagine of you. Especially in this close room, which was hot, with her hair ratty with humidity and the smell of the river, the smell of the sea.

'The relationship was over, and the band was over,' she

explained. 'There is no point answering the phone to an ex, is there?'

'When he's asking an audience to chant your name?'

'There is some exaggeration about that.'

Elva looked away from her then, out the window.

'Since Lydia died,' she said, 'I have been drawing and writing about her and then certain things have come to light about the way she was treated by men. And I mean, it is only part of the story. It's a small part really.'

Lena waited.

'But there are things I don't understand and I'm on this quest, in a way, to get it straight. Have you ever,' she asked abruptly, 'lost somebody close to you?'

'No,' Lena answered.

'The worst part,' Elva said, 'is not knowing where they've gone.'

It was a surprising thing to say. It was also an especially wrenching thought.

Why have I come here? Lena thought. She'd hadn't answered the phone to Cian, ever; she hadn't needed to answer the email from Elva. But Elva had a magnetism as well as a social influence Lena felt instinctually inclined to manage or abate.

Elva would talk about her to other people. Still she wondered, exasperated and perturbed a little now, what this was *about* and how soon it could end and when she might find the time to contemplate and interpret it in retrospect. She pictured herself on the sofa later, cooled by leather, balcony open and trace breezes of diesel, suncream, sea salt, bins; she saw herself free to sit alone, when Sunny was asleep, without Odhran and all the context he brought, and turn these things over in her mind.

Her old life was robust before her now already, retaining the colour and substance it had once had – back when she was young and unencumbered and unmarried and travelled light. When the city itself was for the taking, all possibility, and not this weighty river-smelling obstacle to family life.

And then Elva asked, sliding some board from beneath them, 'Tell me, how do musicians get paid?'

Lena blinked. 'Oh, a few ways,' she said.

Her suspicion was pricked. If this was about money, it would be more convoluted than she'd thought. It could not be about money, surely. And yet Elva was silent, expectant, looking at her with expectant eyes.

'How were you, for instance, paid?'

This was taking a liberty. Lena hardened. 'Different ways. Can I ask why you need to know?'

'Oh!' Elva laughed, somewhat artificially, and slid down from the windowsill. She walked, still barefoot and drifting, to a shelf of books and catalogues. There was a small stone horse's head, like something severed from an architectural plinth, on the shelf. 'I don't mean to pry, or like, pry unduly.' She held up her hands. 'We found out that Lydia was getting some kind of payment, at some point, some kind of stipend.'

Lena was quiet. 'From whom?'

'From Mikey.' Elva was dry. 'Mikey had a record of this. He said she must have been associated with Cian, because it was from that account – as in, she had some job associated with Cian. Runner or musician or just a kind of management role.'

'Well.' Lena exhaled. 'You'd kind of get paid from advances, from the record label and the publisher, and the band would be run like a business and everything bought out of that – equipment, lawyers, everything. Then we'd get the rest as a stipend or salary. I was on a retainer with Sony or whatever briefly; I was getting paid by them. Not them precisely.'

'Mikey's company,' Elva said.

'Yes. I don't remember Lydia working with us. I thought Lydia was kind of.' Lena paused. 'Well, for want of a better word, a *hanger-on*.'

'She was.' Elva was flippant. 'But she was paid for something, and Mikey says he doesn't know what.'

'You'd have to ask Cian.'

'I can't get hold of him. He doesn't answer anything.'

Lena looked beyond her awkwardly, then at her hands. 'Where is he?' she asked.

'Copenhagen sometimes, where he has a child.'

Lena's ears burnt, then her face burnt.

'Mexico City for a bit apparently. And Galway, when he's home.'

She was looking at Lena now, at Lena's blush. 'He makes music but it doesn't seem to be released, apart from Spotify, and something on Sacred Bones for a bit. He had a singer.'

Lena had seen this. He had a woman singing with him. She appeared in some stills and a silent video, sitting on a stool and folding her hands as she sang. All the comments were predictable: looks like Lena Marley, Lena two. Except this girl was like –

'Twenty or something,' Elva laughed. She asked, 'Did you know he had a kid?'

'No. I've told you. We haven't spoken for years.'

'I can see,' Elva said, 'that you're not going to tell me anything.'

'I don't remember Lydia.' Lena tried to be patient. Power had been with her and then it was whipped away and she wanted it back. Who did he have a child with? Was this child a small doll or marionette child, or a teenager now? A prop or a confrontation? That would be important, she knew, for Cian: Cian would hate a teenager.

And the line made her want to bark with cruel performative laughter. Cas now, Cas would love a teenager.

She continued to speak. 'And if I did remember anything,' she said, 'I would tell you. But it is unpleasant for me to go back over this. You know, I was young as well – he was my first boyfriend, really. He was hard on me.'

It was the first time she'd put it like this. She paused.

'He let me go,' she said, 'and I lost my job and I hadn't even finished college then. I don't want to be thinking about it. I am sorry for your sister. I hope you get him, or sue him, or whatever it is you want to do.'

'Nothing like that.' Elva was surprised. 'I just want to have all the information,' she said. 'My sister was ill.' At this, she moved to a bare wall and pressed her hands against it. It was an unusual gesture and put Lena in mind of Gwynn's son, stretching out his arms and forcing his wrists together. Holding torture poses was, her father said, a schizophrenic thing. Torture poses: could he have said that? Abu Ghraib, IRA: man contorted in a prison yard. What was a torture pose? Gwynn's son had only looked volcanically anxious and annexed off, as if the energy circulated hotly round and round inside him.

'It started very young,' Elva was saying to the wall. 'She was seeing things as a kid, practically. But then again our parents were absent a lot and it was a bit of an open house.'

She had fixed her gaze on something, looking entranced, or just private.

'She was kind of in her head and then, when she got older, they said it was bipolar, but then I think they gave that diagnosis for everything.'

Elva looked up, at last. Looked drawn. 'I spent years really hating her. I wouldn't open my door to her. I had Mikey more or less tell people not to give her work.'

Lena was amazed. 'Why did you do that?'

'I never wanted her to have money for drugs. I wanted her to come home. And it worked actually, but she died anyway. And nobody,' she finished with bitterness, 'will speak to me, except for Mae Quinn and, well. Now you have talked to me too.'

'Frances the cellist,' Lena found herself offering. 'Frances Keenan.'

'Where is she?'

'She's a session musician. You will find her easily. Frances was very nice; she was nice to everyone. She left the band young and got married.'

'OK.' Elva wrote this down. 'OK.'

'How,' Lena asked, 'is Mikey these days?'

'Diagnosed, thankfully,' Elva said, still writing.

Afterwards, Lena could not return to Caoimhe at once, or find out where the little party was. She sat on a stone bench back from the quays, close to the funny sculpture of a teapot Sunny liked. She had come here for something, she had undertaken this arduous and awkward interaction to produce some meaning or effect, and whatever vague desire line drove her to it was crossed and thwarted now – she felt useless, aggrieved in the end at being so useless, and sad. She had wanted to ask Elva, what do you mean by *a bit of an open house*? She thought she knew: the house of castanets, crenelations, sociable parents, maybe drinking or just people they were exposed to, a traffic in people. There had, of course, been families, households, like this in Lena's childhood. She imagined the affluent version might be as bad. Children who were handed around too much. Was it about that? And because she could not remember Lydia, she saw only the Facebook profile photo of a scowling adolescent who was not an adolescent but a grown woman with Neapolitan ice cream hair; who was a grown woman filling her page with rants about dual diagnosis and venom, and Lena saw also Cian's email, drugs, drugs, drugs.

Imagine being so fucking uptight, she thought, less heavily. As if we never did drugs.

Then there was that indecency you used to see on Facebook before people moved on from Facebook – fly high angel, have the best bed in heaven, love you, mwah, mwah, mwah.

Lena took out her phone and pulled up Cian's Instagram profile. It had not been updated for months, but there were pictures – pictures of Menorca, it appeared; some quotes from Robert Graves. Elva wasn't doing much sleuthing if she didn't see that he lived in, or travelled often to, Menorca now.

No pictures of him.

Lena, unthinking but operating with vindictiveness, began popping her finger off photographs, scrolling to pop off more – like, like, like.

I am here, she thought. Come down and fight with me.

29

There came a knock on the door of Odhran's hotel room. In fact it was not a knock but a burst of ingress – the door, opening.

'I'm sorry,' he called.

The cleaner waved a hand and tugged the door shut.

'I'm sorry,' Odhran said to the screen. 'Cleaner is trying to get in.' He was sitting at the bureau, with its surface panel of chipped glass, before a mirror and a row of electrical sockets. The socket at eye level, its silver square, was gashed and scraped faintly in a layered way, as if many people had bashed pins against it drunk.

'We won't be long,' Colm, his director, replied, though they probably would. He was speaking from the group Zoom call currently manifest on Odhran's laptop, the screen of which was sectioned into camera sweeps of various lighting quality. It was eleven, and already the first morning of the conference had been eaten by this minor crisis meeting. Everyone else on the call, board members and management, were back in Ireland.

'Either way,' Colm commenced explaining, 'we will keep the details to ourselves and especially Odhran, who's in London with a few delegates and the interns and the press team, yes? We will not give details yet.'

Odhran nodded wordlessly. He wore a white shirt, hastily buttoned to the top, and exactly nothing other than this; from the leather and studs of his strange sadistic chair there emanated a deathly cool and on his inner thigh there dried a trail of semen. Before the call was proposed and trailered by a curt message to his phone, Odhran had been masturbating breathlessly into the full-length mirror at the bottom of the bed. This was simply something Odhran did every time he checked into a hotel above a certain standard by himself. The greatest of these was ten years ago, on Brick Lane: a boutique space work sent him to in which hung a bespoke towelling robe embroidered with the word *Orin*, which was somebody's name, if not quite his, and which he had taken home.

'I mean.' A man on one of the screens with a broad forehead, winching back and forth in his swivel chair, tapped a pen against the side of his chin. 'I mean,' he said. 'How bad is it?' He laughed, mirthlessly, forgiving himself.

'We have not been consulted on several things,' Colm said. 'And I think we can take this as a sign of how things are progressing. Of course, there have been apologies, but really we should not be sleeping now. In fact, we might start as we said thinking strategically.'

When the call ended, Odhran gazed with some composure at the screen. The transition from wanking to looking worried onscreen had not been a fraught one; with age, Odhran inhabited himself and his eccentricities, for the most part, with equanimity. He had in fact been early and sat there waiting to be admitted, calming his breath

He wished, now, for Lena, to talk to her. He was supposed to be on Stamford Street, in one of the campuses, but only for mingled and observational purposes; nobody expected him to speak. And yet, he needed to appear there at some point. He had to be seen.

Hotel rooms made Odhran think of benders and suicides, even though he had never partaken, seriously, of these things. Against the banks of papery bedlinen he felt inclined to the very worst excesses of self-abuse and at this point it kicked in like a dormant addiction, validated if not provoked by smooth, anonymous and sombre furniture – in this case, a vast coffered leatherette headboard with studs to match the chilling chair – and signs explaining plaintively just how destructive it could be, environmentally, to wash too many towels.

Now, however, he was ready to leave. He needed to shake off a terrible tension. Also he felt he'd rather like the cleaner to come in.

Since arriving, there had been a hollow panic about Odhran, nonspecific – stress, the open thrill and challenge of something at work that was all-encompassing and time-bound – but also a strange lapping of information, a neap tide. It came and went from his mind. Colm was a friendly and capable boss, young and spread-skilled, with panache and the beta presence of a junior politician. But he was worried and performing or templating this worry visibly.

Forlornly Odhran pictured his own desk in the office in Dublin, the plane trees waving at the window, the large luxury block being built slowly and loudly across the avenue, the hoarding with its hi-res images of corporate smiles. Home, Work, Lifestyle, this read, as if these three phenomena were planar – equal – in their value, like a rhapsody, and actually if you thought about it, they were. From a certain perspective.

In the hotel room, sunlight soaked through a wall of tulle. He could not be made redundant easily and as he thought this, he thought: now that's a fighting thought. But he couldn't. He was basically a state employee. They all were. They would be deployed, trimmed out; lesser vessels sent to Revenue. It was an opportunity really.

'And it'll never happen quickly,' he explained to Lena, when he phoned her on impulse.

'Good God.' She was shocked. 'How long has this been in the pipeline?'

'Being eaten by science, well – that's always the case. It is a deathmatch from the start.'

'But it won't happen fast,' he said. Pleading.

'You're being pessimistic,' she suggested.

'That's the thing,' he said. 'I don't think that I am.'

Now he would need to leave, he would need to go to Stamford Street. But it was lunchtime also – all those little speared-through sandwiches.

I wish I were at home with you, he told Lena.

No you don't, she typed. You're having fun.

Alcohol, he thought. It was midday. Odhran showered fast, spraying water inexpertly across the floor and sinking two towels into the effort of absorbing it. He picked up the dreary sheaf of conference materials and pushed the door to, looking about for the cleaner, who was gone. Halfway to the lift he felt his feet in socks and swivelled, mincing back, for shoes. On the second attempt, he met the Irish intern, who was walking slow and stabbing at her phone. She was oldish for an intern and wore an Alice band in her hair. She looked up in surprise.

'Oh no,' she said, 'you've caught me sneaking back.'

'I've been on a meeting all morning,' he said. 'I'm only heading over now.'

'Lunch and the artists' talk,' she said. 'Do we have to go to that?'

'You can skip. I guess.' He was not really her authority. He must have looked confused because she said, 'Well thanks!' and went back to stabbing her phone.

He found the two other interns in the bar. The Austrian had been extracted from a solo project, writing up a monograph on Irish-German relations during the first decades of the State. The girl was American, named Jeni, beautiful in the most hygienic way, all clean lines and dewy eyes and the pert, packed-away bosom of a gymnast or ballerina, and harder to read. When Odhran paused before them they seemed to splutter into their drinks.

'Lunch,' they said, alarmed.

'And the artists' talk. Yes. See you over there.' He had to go straight to the campus now, and use Google Maps to do it, being so rarely in London these days.

Once, Odhran believed that he would live here, that this was inevitable, because of his intelligence and appetite. If he had, by now, his professional life would be a pacey vibrational thing, leaping up levels or crashing back to earth, though probably an absence of any connections, of any brothers here – Maeve in her distracted youth was useless now – would have worked against him. Irish can only go so far, his mother would say loftily. It sounded stagey and embarrassing but was actually essentially true, unless you had stamina and self-denial on a level Odhran no longer had: at this point, the softly jobsworth atmosphere of work in Dublin was more manageable. And this made him, occasionally, hot with the insult and its implication, that he had not been a contender, when he had. London was something he'd ceded to an inner laziness.

That said, he'd always had a job. Even through the most egregious moments of the crash he'd had a job. Dublin alone had tired him out; how wrong, he thought, I was about several things. And now, more and more, a certain half-remembered sense of ease and acceptance, the fairer winds of adolescence, caught his attention. He thought of Sunny under open skies and living with the lake, its unconquerable substance, all the silence it contained, close by. He missed Sunny terribly in London too, and it had only been a day.

The building reared before him as he approached from a bend in traffic, realising there was no obvious crossing and feeling, confusedly, that there was no obvious door. Stepping in, it was a glass porch like a foetid little greenhouse on stepping in. The two rooms reserved for lectures were empty, with a din of conversation carrying from the open space at the end of a corridor. Odhran approached this with trepidation. It was filled with people, moving and talking. They had all the fresh vigour of people just released into this foyer; things had only just begun.

Anja, who surely knew about the merger, swooped on Odhran at suitable speed.

'You have been a ghost,' she accused.

'Colm called a meeting.'

'Oh that.' She looked at him with concern.

He glanced over her shoulder, waving weakly and flashing a smile. It was a fluorescent atrium space lined with catering tables.

'You cannot say.' Anja was his own age, but she had four kids and a nanny. She was tiny, ebullient, efficient. 'You cannot say, I know, but I suspect we will be tweaking our CVs.' She laughed. 'We will be tweaking,' she said, 'all the LinkedIns.'

'No, please.' Odhran did not want to panic. None of us can get fired, he thought.

Peter, who was older and duller, shouldered towards them now with a wink.

'First panel was excellent,' the other man insisted before he had reached them. 'Just terrific altogether.' It hung in the air without context or any soil in which to grow.

'Well.' Anja seemed morose. 'It is the lunch now.' She gestured. The air was filled with people speaking speedily; things did look positive.

'I should eat,' Odhran said. He was planning, he realised, to drink.

'Where are the young people?' Anja asked. She was referring to the interns.

'Watching training videos, I hope,' Peter said. He disliked how poor they all were at coding. They had been gathered from research projects in history and international relations and had never, until the Council required this skill for cheap, been asked to code.

'We needed assistance to set up a – you know, laptop presentation,' Peter complained, rather astonishingly miming the bend-and-snap of an actual laptop, 'and they were stumped.'

Anja said, 'It was a Mac.'

'Everyone loses it,' said Odhran, 'when someone shows up with a Mac.'

He had loaded a paper plate with miniature bagels. He wanted to speak to Colm again. Ideas – monumental, poor on detail, but compelling nonetheless – were forming in his mind. Among them was to contact an old housemate, an old startup companion, who worked now as a parliamentary aide; he imagined the release of speaking freely, speaking candidly, with intelligence, about power. For this was it – power. Command. It came to that. He thought of the little foldout tables on Leinster Street, outside the cubbyhole of a café, where people sat and plotted openly in suits across the street from Leinster House. At least Odhran had always assumed it was some kind of blatant boarding school manoeuvre; plotting there before the great palace that now housed the government. Missives sent from Dublin about policy tended, he knew, to die out mutely in the provinces. Quite often my own father would say, he thought, articulating this as if to Lena, as if speaking to someone – quite often he would say, we killed that, quite simply; we put a stop to that, we ended that. This was the kind of culture that had to change. And what would make it change? Odhran had many thoughts.

He believed, to begin with, in institutions. He was Left enough to disdain pharmaceutical companies, Right enough to think strategically. No merger would leave him managing halfwits in Revenue. This he could say to Lena also, boldly: no merger will leave me managing halfwits in Revenue or the Department of Social Protection or anywhere.

I could consult, he thought. He felt anxious.

'What will happen,' rehearsed Anja miserably, 'is that no project from the arts and humanities will ever win a bid for funding against science. All of this,' she said, 'will be gone.' She referred to delegates.

They looked, as a trio, out upon the delegates. One team were restoring and archiving and commissioning artistic responses to the detailed restoration of a rural Hellfire club; the other was translating bardic sagas from Irish and logging these online. Their most important current project involved intersecting interests and the proposed online archiving of records for mental asylums. Arts commissions came out of that too. And some of them were beautiful. Lena had gone along to one installation – fabric draped around a pumphouse, ghosts or ghostly laundry or unravelled shrouds. This was before Sunny said anything about being born again. If there were a project on reincarnation, say.

He missed her. He wanted to squeeze her chubby calves. He wanted to go home and tell them: I am going to consult, go into government, something firmer than this.

By means of presentations, fast and slow, the afternoon passed. Odhran remained in the same chair for the duration, looking out on a building site, the spires and mutant spears of City architecture smogged and faded out in many textures against an azure sky. He observed with mild interest that the websites and Prezi slides of continental European delegates seemed to suggest, in taste and affect, the train stations and municipal shopping centres of continental Europe – almost Soviet in spareness, tending to beige, old-fashioned in a classic kind of way; the cultural signs of countries that did not feel a need for gloss or veneers or expense, whose streetscapes and infrastructure were built solidly enough the first time around. It was only Ireland that felt compelled to level everything to build bubble-windowed campuses or civic amenities that looked, in almost every iteration, as though water slides were involved somehow. As though all architecture aspired to the energy of a leisure centre.

In the later afternoon, the three interns returned, demonstrably tipsy, and asked him openly, is the Council doomed?

'We hear the rumours,' the American, Jeni, said.

'I hope I get to finish my postdoc.' The Irish intern was afraid. 'Should I go straight back to it now?'

'Every active project would be wrapped up in the event of a merger,' Odhran said.

'No more hotels for us,' said the Austrian intern morosely.

Jeni took this up with enthusiasm, her eyes a little shinier than they had been earlier.

'I am so getting my hotel on,' she claimed, 'it is so, like, not luxe but nice; I thought we'd be put in a motel or something, but they've even given us bathrobes.'

'Bigger stipends would be better,' the Irish one muttered, 'than hotels.'

Odhran messaged Colm, which was cheeky. 'Troops are talking,' he said.

'We're going to the Coal Hole,' somebody said.

'It's too small in there.'

'But there are many bars along the Strand. Everyone can find somewhere.' There were twenty to thirty people in the atrium space; nobody at the Research Council had made a pub or evening plan for this second day, because of funds. There was one formal dinner, on the final day, but nothing in between. It meant delegates would need to branch off into groups or grab reduced-price sandwiches in that disordered and impoverished student way.

Among the delegates, the British delegates, there was a lissom blonde woman who presented on the pictorial and affective history of Carnation powdered milk; everyone followed her with jubilance and listened to her plans for pubs on the Strand.

Odhran, half remembering, messaged Maeve: Be at the Coal Hole shortly, if you're around?

Not in London, she replied.

Not telling you, she told his row of question and exclamation marks.

When Sunny was one, he and Lena had travelled with her to London. Maeve invited them to a chaotic curry house she liked, inviting her housemate, Dawn, and Lena took one look – smiling dopily in the doorway, eyes flashing up to the warehouse ceiling and down to the popped collars and hollers of a large consignment of City boys – then said, 'My goodness, no,' and swept out; it was not, she smiled, appropriate.

'I'm happy to go back,' she explained, 'to the Premier Inn.' Odhran stayed and ate with them. Afterwards, Maeve accused him playfully of disputing every second thing Dawn said, as if trying hard not to seem as though he was flirting. When he left, Dawn had apparently remarked, 'Well, I totally would. He seems like such a good daddy,' she said.

The evening outside now was balmy and decent, populated by workers in neutrals bending placidly or blankly towards tubes and train stations. Each time he visited, the centre of the city was whiter, neater, and more middle-class; perhaps, he thought, he was remembering it differently once. All of the women could have been dressed by his sister. He might tell her that. She could take it badly though. Or not. She could be sensitive.

He was obscurely hurt, he realised, by Maeve not being in London. But of course she had something more interesting to do. Or someone. When she was at art school in Dublin, she used to stay overnight sometimes at Odhran and Ali's apartment, back when Odhran lived with Ali and worked with her, in the late-twenties twilight of playing house and getting fractious along with it, experimenting or making feints towards experimentation; going to a BDSM munch one awkward time, for example. It was held above a bar and involved sitting horrified on wooden benches in a bright-lit room, having consent explained severely by a man with nineteenth-century sideburns. The attendees all looked like people who couldn't get laid any other way and afterwards Ali had scolded him for talking about people uncharitably.

Ali liked fun runs. She did pole dancing recreationally. She posted a lot of near-naked selfies hashtagged Body Positivity even though she was by all objective measures very slim. He could never tell if it was a subtle dysphoria or a form of trolling. She liked dogs and those cafés that left bowls of waters out for dogs. She lived with her girlfriend now and someone had once told him – Lena, Aidan, someone else? – that she'd posted her wine rack and it was worth in excess of twenty grand; not the rack itself but the variety of wines, but her girlfriend was from California and maybe it had something to do with that. Odhran wanted to drink.

At the pub, he began drinking quickly, growing light.

Longing for that feeling that brought him above company and loneliness and quieted the mind. The American Jeni sat near him quietly, seeming on edge about something, accepting vodka tonics from Peter repeatedly until Odhran levelled Peter with a long and falsely puzzled look to calm him down.

The phone pulsed; it was Colm, with a short apology, indisposed for the day, and Odhran felt humiliation begin as a physical sensation, as heat rising from the base of his skull.

He was weakened a little by this. He should not have emailed Colm with anything chummy. He would need to tread carefully.

And with this, in a matter of moments, irritation.

'What is next for you?' Anja asked.

'My wife and I are moving to Clare,' he said.

The table turned – elements of the table – and Peter looked approvingly at him. 'Getting out of the city then?'

'I pay rent to a vulture fund. I am done.'

Clap-clap: there was a pitter-patter of clap-clap.

'You are jumping ship.'

'I can commute.'

'You are jumping ship.'

But: 'How can you leave Dublin? It's so pretty,' Jeni asked.

She held up a narrow arm, tan and dusted with pale hairs, raising a glass to her lips. She was not normally so enthusiastic or loud, and he could see she was getting drunk. She'd told him, or told someone, that as a younger person she'd done ballet seriously and wanted to be a ballerina, but stopped because she was too big. 'They would say, I can smell what you ate for breakfast,' she'd said – she'd certainly said this to him, or within his hearing, and it was somehow coarse and kiddish in that candid, lardy way he associated with Americans, and the light ironic confidence with which she conjured these coarser things, eating and smelling and breath, had humanised her, taken some of the sting out of her physical attractiveness as it occupied a symbolic presence in his mind. The appeal of that which he would not have.

This was something of an unreconstructed thought. He felt bashful – then less so. Who's to say you could not have her, Odhran thought. Who is to say that at all.

'Actually, straight out of college,' he told her, 'I lived here. In London.'

'What was it like?' She smiled.

The way in which she asked him this, the innocent and direct intimacy combined with just how banal and wide-angled was the question, made something change. Odhran felt the table shift, almost imperceptibly; it shifted into a mood of awkwardness and suspension. And then it shifted immediately out, reshuffling everyone's attention like fractals of colour shifting in a kaleidoscope, so that smaller groups of talk sprang into being and everyone closed out Odhran and Jeni and changed the subject and ignored them. Odhran and the intern were subsequently and within tipsy seconds isolated in conversation, face-to-face. It was as if the conversation itself had its own architecture. She was looking at him with a friendly expression. It was the loosest, simplest but most universal opener to the kind of talk that concludes in romance or sex; he had been in the world long enough, known enough conversational infrastructure, to sense this instantly, to feel its risk.

It was coming from her. She was drunk.

'It was a long time ago,' he said honestly, stumbling, with surprise. 'I don't even remember much. I was working for a startup but mostly remotely; I used to work in programming.'

'Oh my God,' she said. 'Boo.'

'It wasn't always so evil or fascist.' Odhran grinned, then dipped to his pint. Guinness in London tasted better than in Dublin. But it was a stodgy drink; better to order vodka or something next time round. He thought of his reflection in the large mirror, the towelling robe, the deep carpet, the gloomy hours permitted to him to keep going into the night.

He tried to describe the flatshare, the thirties apartment block with asbestos that had been in fact a haven. Most other information was boorish: the drinking and clubbing and women and rapid-fire, orgy-adjacent *pow-wows* with other young men fresh from BESS at Trinity.

He remembered suddenly an event. It was something she might understand. He began to describe it without thinking, scooping up details as he went. 'I attended a political meeting, I can't remember why, but it was in Westminster, in one of the buildings – it must have been a London Irish confederacy. At the time, there were so many new immigrants, we saw ourselves as a kind of bloc, a generation, and we thought we were going to change things, politically. Anyway, at this meeting, I remember a guy getting up – this *sleveen*, little short guy, to make a speech about diasporic voting rights. About how Ireland should extend diasporic voting rights, like let everyone living abroad vote, and that's when I pretty much turned against the whole London Irish thing or the Irish abroad thing or whatever.'

Her eyebrows were raised, encouragingly.

'Because I don't ever want to see the diaspora vote. Look at the US. They think we're still the *old country*, you know, virtuous and all that; they think we're dense, I guess.' He had lost his point. At the time, all those years ago, it had seemed important.

'Right,' she smiled. He was losing her interest.

But then she surprised him. 'Do you mean like, if the diaspora could vote it would all be conservative stuff?'

'Yes exactly. They'd vote against abortion and things like that. They want it to stay the same. It's also just a stupid proposal generally.' The bitterness was not real – it was old, so painfully outdated Odhran himself felt discombobulated. Nothing of his political consciousness at twenty seemed relevant now. Then, the crash and the exodus of young people seemed like a moment that would be historicised, but now it looked fudged and indistinct and unheroic.

'But could you,' Jeni inclined her head, 'argue, like, that a diaspora is more radical? Like, say, you have this problem with housing, with all the government being landlords.'

'Yes.'

'If you brought in voters from other places you might get a more radical vote.'

'Maybe.' He drank. 'They're probably more interested in reunification. Getting rid of the border with Northern Ireland.'

'You're not?'

'No. I've never seen the point.'

'What needs to happen, then?' Jeni was asking. 'What would happen to make things better, to fix like the housing crisis?'

Odhran contemplated, assuming a look of contemplation, and said, finally, 'Either full libertarianism or, like, full communism.'

He laughed shortly then. 'Or more postdoctoral projects. More funding stakeholders.'

'Oh my God, yes,' Jeni said. She spoke with such synthetic conviction he wondered if she thought he was being serious. He felt old and that the arrogance or optimism of his twenties was not even over, not even concluded – that it was, instead, under threat of evaporation as a phenomenon in itself. He had not lived historically nor changed a thing. He had been borne along by trends and tides. He felt tired and wished to go back to the hotel room and masturbate and think about her small athletic breasts tipping back, her waist arching back beneath him, the kiddish bass of her voice smothered out by a devouring kiss.

'What was that word you used,' she asked then, 'sleevey?' The bar was heaving; the atmosphere had become tilted and particulate. He had known she would ask this and felt foolish about it now.

'*Sleveen*,' he said. 'Like – a weak or obsequious person.'

'Obsequious,' she repeated, mock-seriously.

He left shortly afterward; healthfully, walking fast. Could you or could you not hail a cab in London now? Was that still a thing? The fresh air, the civil whoops and symphony of traffic, carried him; above the Thames, trying to have a profound experience of Somerset House.

Me and my wife are moving to Clare, he thought, rehashed phatically: me and my wife, why am I worried? It had always sounded like the title and the life of someone else, as though they'd snatched this happiness and it could be taken back. That was why Lena worried about Sunny. About putting the machinery back into action by returning to work and resuming the life beforehand and seeming to turn away from the claustrophobic life they'd made together in the year of the pandemic. It was clearer to him now, spritzed a little by beer, and made him achingly tender; not a little afeared. He had to protect her. Her thought this blurrily, realising at the same time he was lost in the region of little catacombs off London Bridge – hump-shaped bars and bodegas inserted into railway arches, tables on which candles dwindled prettily. As everywhere, in all cities, belligerent food delivery boys on hybrid bicycles.

In his mind, Jeni was replaced with Lena, or Lena was restored to him, and he thought with a tug in the abdomen of coming inside her and of the rich assurance that another child would be created, that he could, that this throb between them which had been so hot and wild when they first met could continue to produce heat and life and obligation and legacy and all the primal, hungry virtues he associated with children, with having children and surrounding himself with people, with living on in this way that was reckless and beyond all his control. He felt braver than the callow prick he'd been when he was young, and this was comforting.

God, he thought, I will be good at it. He would like a son. Another little girl would be so gorgeous but a son would level with him; imagine it.

He pulled up the satnav on his phone and began to wind his way to the hotel beneath the orange-dusted, richly demented and sort of sexy city night. He messaged Lena in affection. It will be OK, he wrote. He meant: change of scene will not dissolve it. Their resolve. She acknowledged it with a heart and nothing more. In the moment, it felt like clairvoyant agreement, as though his drunken whim had crossed the sea, and in the morning he would realise there was something dry and mocking to the heart emoji.

Odhran was woken by his phone after midnight. It was not so late, but he had fallen asleep in the towelling robe. It was Anja, which was greatly surprising.

'One of the interns has lost a keycard,' she said. 'I am not at your hotel.'

'What's happening?'

'I stayed with my sister in Catford. Peter is unreachable. Basically,' she sighed with amplification, 'basically it is the case that they need you to go down and vouch for them.'

'What, at reception?'

'Yes.'

The corridor smelt of perfume, of a known ubiquitous perfume from the noughties, and this was surely contrived in some way – a controlled ambient smell. In the lobby, there were lots of people about and it took him a moment to notice Jeni the American sitting listlessly in an egg-shaped chair. The Irish intern was speaking to the staff.

'We need to get her to bed,' she said.

'Yes, it is a group booking,' Odhran added, feeling tense.

The receptionist relented eventually. They supported the girl into the lift and upstairs, Odhran at every moment hypersensitive to the proximity of bodies; to the inappropriate risk. He backed off too fast at the door to their shared room and almost let Jeni collapse into the wall.

'Can you take it from here?' he asked.

'What should I do?'

He paused. 'Recovery position?'

'I'm OK,' Jeni croaked. 'I'll go to bed. I'm sorry, really sorry, like, Odd-ran.'

She'd reverted, in confusion, to the mispronunciation of his name. She looked over her shoulder also, pupils loaded and black.

‘I’m sorry I’m so sorry.’ She began to cry.

‘They can’t drink, can they?’ asked the other girl. ‘Until they’re twenty-one?’

‘I can’t come in,’ Odhran said firmly now. The situation felt ablaze with awkwardness. He glimpsed their girls’ debris across a bed – the arms and legs and sweeping tease of clothes. The Irish intern was serious and prophylactic, which was a good thing, Odhran thought, because in his anger he would like to fetch water for Jeni or something to eat and have her come around slightly, shamefaced, apologising for herself, and he’d tell her to sleep it off, but in the morning she would move towards him gratefully and take his erect penis in her mouth immediately, would climb lithely onto him and orgasm like a cheerleader. He would please her. He was older. He knew how to dominate and how to make her compliant; how to make her comply.

All of this was so transparently within his reach, he thanked the universe, really, for sending the Irish intern and her Alice band and anxiety.

‘I can’t come in,’ he repeated, ‘can you take it from here?’

‘Oh yeah, I totally know.’

What a farcical thing to have to deal with in the morning, he thought. He shouldn’t have gone to the pub. He should not do anything unthinkingly anymore.

30

Cian messaged Lena on Instagram, with a video attached. He also went swiftly offline, leaving her to read it privately. What a joy to hear from you, it said, and nothing else. A camera panned: it was a beach, by nightfall, reeds or other pipelike plants, a dream construction, beating back and forth in a coastal breeze. The footage cut off just like that. Lena had been lying awake when the message pinged in. She sat, her face spotlit with blue, and watched the recording again, baffled and also disappointed for some reason.

What a joy to hear from you.

Each time she played it, the video peeled past her emptily, devoid of meaning. Beach and slow drumming of reeds. It might be Clontarf, California, or Cornwall. It must be where he was just then. There was something to it, a quality of spontaneous surface poetry, banalised by convention, by his incommensurability with the internet, that she found stark.

There stirred in her a lush, almost nauseating, wave of pure desire. It was remarkable in its substantiality, familiar to her but so old – so old – she felt she hadn't contained a surge of libido this romantic and intense in a decade; since him, since Cian, really. Like a chakra opening or waters breaking, realising that the membrane keeping it in had been thin as polythene all along, experiencing it as saturation or oleaginous. Lust. And at once there descended sentences, something like cherubs with scrolls streaming out of their mouths, these scrolls crammed with momentous sentences: they said, don't be stupid. You've done all of this before. Too much of life has happened since to give this ardour any lasting meaning beyond mental illness, she thought. And delusion. And immaturity.

It was feral but also, she told herself, fucking kitsch, which was worse. If she responded, it would rot into one of those humiliating back-and-forth exchanges between young women and fuckboys you saw posted on Reddit or paraphrased to agony aunts and prefaced by a pleading and delusional need to be reassured this is love – that to be humiliated or mystified was really love; the love of wounded and soulful dogs.

The scrolls said: he dumped and fired you in a literal café. They said: you are an adult now. The handle of his account read *Big Sur*. Perhaps he really was in California or had lately been. And so what, flickered scrolls. Anyone can travel to California.

It was dark and late and cool and Sunny was long asleep, and Odhran in London, and there was a WhatsApp from him – It will be OK, the move to Clare, thinking of you x. Odhran was formal about messaging and always meant what he said. He missed her always when they were apart, missed her counsel and softness as a landing-spot: missed her more than she missed him, not because she loved him less but because she rather liked being alone. She'd taken a long bath and masturbated with a hand-mirror tilted Rokeby Venus style.

And then suddenly, without warning, Cian came back online. When the word lit up, her thumb stabbed madly at the screen to close the app and she had to collect herself. A siren slid by outside, agreeing.

Earlier that evening, she'd glanced down from the balcony alone and straight, immediately, into the rectangular window of a hearse. She'd seen a wicker coffin underneath a kind of pall, a wreath of flowers reading *Ray*. Never in all her time in Islandbridge had Lena seen funeral cortèges coming past. It didn't happen here, there wasn't any church.

The deviant nature of this vision, hearse with thin trail of walkers following, a single silent police motorbike, unnerved her deeply. It felt profane.

The hearse and its party turned, in total silence, into the courtyard of the flats.

As she sat cross-legged now, alone, in bed, a deep emotional seam opened in Lena. All of her composure and calm was ruptured entirely by the message and by that hot little pop of *online*: by the word that seemed to be synonymous with *waiting*, or *baiting you*, or *watching you*, or just *aware you are also online*. It was as if he'd entered the room. She felt afraid, and this feeling seemed to presage other feelings, even threaten to overwhelm her with sensations of guilt and implication and desire and confusion and to throw a kind of spotlight onto her, to demand that she understand herself.

Within her, she saw, there were violent unreconciled emotions she did not allow herself to feel or identify. They included a colossal, inexpressible love for Sunny and also for Odhran – a near-unbearable tenderness and rush of terror at the thought of losing them, a prospect that was always close to hand and callously done and happened to other people all the time – as well as a flood of desire for something wholly different, for the painful thrill of being chosen by one who seemed then, as Cian had once seemed, to have so many options and to represent the world as a thing you might conquer and consume. And so the bad part of herself who had known, deep down, how awful and nasty was so much of that world, who understood bleakly how weak links like Lydia Fanning could be devoured by it, existed still.

This side of Lena was a winner at any cost. It was the side she had to power down when she became a mother and she could not let it govern a single decision ever again.

As she lay down on her side and tried to quell all this emotion, to sleep, as she sensibly should, she imagined noxious seeds of insecurity or sadness planted in Sunny; planted by her, Lena, a mother who'd threatened to jump off a balcony.

Who had wanted to be vital and dangerous and pioneering and adored instead of indentured.

How could she reach out through the darkness, penetrate the child's body somehow, suffuse her with a certainty of love – how could she imagine this and then not act on it? Because a lot of the time she still wanted direly to get away from Sunny and from her responsibilities.

Lena saw that this dark force of love also took into it the energies of every crazy thing she'd ever done, every broken heart and depressive panic; the wandering hunger after Cian, the older poison of her parents' chaos; death itself. Men had wanted to punish her for withholding strong feelings from them. But the rush of emotion would destroy everyone, even Sunny, if released. She imagined herself pleading for Sunny's understanding; that would be an act of cruelty. She had to let Sunny hate her sometimes, probably.

She wondered then if her parents felt pain at all the ways in which she had, on balance, actually hated them. And Rex had hated them. And she never thought about Rex.

She was in fact a highly dangerous candidate for motherhood: stunted, nervous, vain. This seemed like something she must always keep from Sunny and be vigilant about.

Now it was after midnight, and still warm. Lena sat up again in bed and found the composure to block Cian instantly; she asked the platform to advise of any other linked accounts and blocked a separate one – an old one, CianArchive3 – and then she opened up her email, searched the last address he'd used, and blocked it too.

The gathered emails, those that remained after all this time, in the deep trough of her inbox all had one title, repeated like a motif, RE: UNPAID SALARY. Somewhere in there, Lydia, her death and the now-defunct Facebook link with its chaos and calamity, must surely be hidden under the innocuously hostile headline UNPAID SALARY. With this rubric, Lena, back then, had been able to tell Cian he owed her something repeatedly, and in many different kinds of language, and he'd released five hundred euros to her eventually. It was the deposit for a room in a houseshare; the room she left to live with Gwynn. Her history seemed bitty and conditional when laid out in this way. No doubt, if she read the emails, she would see she'd remembered it wrong. She would be embarrassed by her turns of phrase and self-presentation. Lena lit every email up by hitting Select All and then Delete.

After a pause, she pulled up Elva's email, blocked it; blocked her Instagram, the number she had given Lena that afternoon.

If there were more, she could just block them all. Just whack-a-mole.

Do you feel safe? she asked herself, nervily thrilled.

Lena, little Lena, but an object in the world, do you feel safe?

31

There is no such thing as future, just present becoming past. Lena had this thought, weighty at first and then platitudinal, in the shower on her third night in the chalet, right behind a lighter thought. She was thinking about her complexion, made ruddy by the gassy blasting pressure of the chalet shower, and that her face would be red-raw for an hour or so after showering. Standing there beneath the jet. And then: there's no such thing as future, just present becoming past, and of these three, the past is most significant.

Of course this wasn't true and probably it was unhelpful, morally speaking.

Here, she thought, offering: let's say my future doesn't matter anymore. Only present becoming past. Only the past becoming compressed like an ikon in my hands.

When she had another baby that would be another person in the world, another step towards her own death and irrelevance: relief, she thought, if not quite felt, regarding her face in the mirror steam. Red-raw, thirty-five years of sun damage drummed to the surface.

That would fade. She began to apply her retinol serum. The overhead light in the windowless bathroom had a legal strength to it – a light for preventing falls and injuries. In her own house, there would be dimmer lights or just a row of soft candles. Who wants to enter middle age looking at their own face reacting to water pressure and retinol.

A child would not so much bring the future as enlarge the present, she thought, severely now. Guessing at the future would be dangerous. A child would bring some blueprint of its own. That's what they did, she knew; the future was theirs, like wealth. Within minutes, she could not remember what she'd ever meant by this bouquet of affirmations.

Odhran was reading to Sunny on the little throw-covered couch. Autumn was coming and it was cool now, but the cool of resort beaches when the night suddenly drops. They were living, uneasily, within the contours of other people's holidays. It had only been three days.

Lying later beneath a cast-off Sonia eiderdown. Things smelt, nonsensically, of ginger snaps. As if made self-conscious by the building, they had not been amorous.

'Verdict, so far?' he asked.

'I like the mountains. I still see them. I still notice them, I mean.'

They were not really mountains – more large hills, rolling liberally into one another with the thoughtless, shaggy grandeur of massive dogs. There was a map in the welcome pack and Lena tried to name the hills, to identify Glennagalliagh, hill of the witch. Sliabh Bernagh and Moylussa. From this angle, there were tricks of perspective. They were positioned at the edge of town; from there, the road ran past one of the three private marinas, a hotel, a rubble pier. A glossy Virgin from the 1950s Marian Year of Whatever, primly insufficient in her grotto with a single blistered bench. The river was wide and crossed by a coarse stone bridge. Eel traps and netting, a lock for passing underneath with larger boats, tented the legs of the bridge.

'Eels are big here, in terms of council funding,' Odhran said. 'Eel control. Eels are bigger than motorways. Bigger than civil rights. Eels are everything.'

They had to be caught and directed away from the dam. There was a chute somewhere, cannonballing eels into the Shannon at intervals. Picture it.

He sang to Sunny: I am an eelman for the *county*, and I drive the main boat.

And on the fourth day, Odhran had to go back to Dublin; it was Monday. Their apartment in Islandbridge was still leased for three further months, slightly stripped of belongings but containing boxes and winter clothes. Lena had left bedsheets on the bed. She imagined it in semidarkness; she imagined daylight filling it prodigally, finding it empty again. It was the pandemic, the sun searching empty spaces, all over again.

'You could stay up,' she offered.

'I'll come back down if I can,' he said.

The morning was brisk. She turned out a wash and had Sunny join her in the snub of yard outside to hang this on a relegation spin-line. Spin-lines to the near horizon: the other chalets were vacant, or lived in conspicuously – garbage, bent-up garden furniture – by people they hadn't yet seen. Lena understood there to be some kind of bylaw about living there full-time. Their yards looked up to a rim of road and then a new motorway bypass which came crashing into the town before reeling eelishly upwards to wrap around it, feeding traffic towards Limerick and Dublin. It was so new the tarmac was still marked by signs and tokens where the workers had buried electric cables and storm drains. If you followed it upwards, arcing right over the river and the town, the picturesque Church of Ireland cathedral and blockier Catholic church, the stiff steel wings of the covered tennis court, there were high walls of rocks caged by wire and bright new barriers. It softened her culture shock because the rocks and wire and motorway barriers made her think of a suburban ring-road.

'People in the town are worried,' Sonia had remarked, 'about doughnuts or whatever.'

'Doughnutification,' Odhran supplied. 'It's always a risk.'

Lena had declined Sunny's offer of a place at Saint Michael's by phone. The secretary was impassioned, barking at her.

'You have to show that she is enrolled in another school.'

'She's not yet five,' Lena countered patiently. 'She can stay out for another year if she has to. We hope to find a place for her in Clare.'

'A whole year without school in that case, potentially. You need to show you've enrolled her in another school. We answer to social services. How do we know where you've gone.'

'Why would you care?' Lena tried to make light of it.

'And you couldn't say anything sooner than this.'

Her mother told them they were being reckless but holidays were all fine and well. 'Only keep your lease in Dublin, don't lose another lease. And get a job, Lena. All of us had to work,' she said.

'You worked on a sewing machine and bought your own house at twenty-one,' Lena retorted. She was no longer in any mood for this. 'With Dad, what? Pushing pill trollies around Saint Dympna's. Neither of you even finished school.'

'Excuse me.'

'Odhran and I have three times your education and throw all our money at rent. And it's a vulture fund. It's owned by a load of shareholders in America. Did I never tell you that?'

'These vulture funds,' her mother said. 'What even are you talking about.'

That morning, alone without Odhran, she felt tailed by Sunny, who wriggled up to kneel at the breakfast bar and began pulling, bored, at a stack of oilcloth tablemats. She had crayons and her ice cream station, several dolls, but she was bored. There was no mention of death; Lena contemplated this with appreciation. Nothing yet. It was a holiday. In Dublin and most recently, since Declan, Sunny might refer to it – the water, the side of the road, the family of before – once or twice a week, rather than day, as she had at the very beginning; it had been on the wane. It was as though, blinking stunned in the underwhelming aftermath of play therapy, they were all moving on from it, forgetting about it. They had metabolised the pandemic in the very same way and, folded within it, Sunny's first fraught, forgettable early months – sleep deprivation meant Lena did not, she thought, make memories, literally – as well as the flash of controversy on Twitter, of *Cas Cronin likes them young*. Since blocking Cian and Elva, there had been no movement or mention from them. It really did feel like a holiday.

'Can we go swimming?' Sunny asked.

'Well, actually.' Lena paused. 'I don't think we have your swimming togs. How about I ask your dad to get them from the old apartment?'

Sunny nodded covetously.

They were preparing to head out with shopping bags when Sonia's car appeared outside.

'Now I can see you on a weekday, just like that.' She cupped Sunny's face in her hands and bent down to plant a kiss.

'I want to swim,' the child tried.

'We can go to the hotel.' When she heard of the togs problem, she clapped her hands. 'Niall's wife,' she said. 'Will have one spare.' This was how Lena wound up riding shotgun with Sonia for half an hour, and parking with an avid little fan of partial U-turn on the gravel outside a tall, new, grey mansion without render. It had a preposterous pendant on the front: 2014. Sonia left them in the car and dashed to the door, returning with a paper bag.

'A few options,' she said.

'Did Elaine want to – come, or anything?'

'Oh no. She doesn't like being dropped in on just like that.'

The hotel, on the lake, was shaded by a strip of cypresses. There was a railway station here, Sonia explained, before the state pulled all the tracks up in the fifties and sixties.

'Out of spite,' she said. 'Because they had been put down by the British. Now we're looking for them back. Will we leave Sunny to swim, and have some tea?'

'Jesus no.' Lena was horrified. 'I'll go with her.'

They hadn't thought this part through. Sonia took herself to the hotel bar and Lena, feeling thinly pressed by borrowed time, pulled on the polka-dot swimsuit Elaine had lent her and plonked Sunny down on the chilly toilet for ten minutes.

'Please pee,' she said. 'Because in pools you know they sometimes have a special dye in the water and, if you pee, it turns purple.' This was an urban myth she'd heard.

'What's dye?' Sunny asked. Her two plump pale little legs emerged beneath the pot belly. She was so snugly, plumply, sweetly put together. Lena stiffened a little at the word, the homonym, thinking *death* and *die*.

'A colour you put into things,' she tried. 'Like hair dye. Or a colour to put into – clothes.' It did not make sense relative to pee in a swimming pool, she knew.

Sunny regarded her tolerantly. Sunny did not, she repeated, need to pee.

They minced across the wet unpleasant tiles and into the subterranean drone of the pool itself, which was generous in proportion and tiled in the style of the nineteen-nineties, conjuring every delicious swimming experience of Lena's childhood, only heated – warm, balmy of atmosphere, unlike swimming pools of the nineteen-nineties. Some children were having a lesson in a separate section and a man reposed regally in the squat, frothy jacuzzi. Sunny looked guardedly at the children and then began to inch down the slant to the shallow end. Lena gazed at her reflection in the window and thought, my hips never went back in after birth. They are just that wide now. They would be forever, and her breasts like a shelf of flesh above the ribs. She was softer all over and had fine lines radiating from her eyes, and she would never be young again.

Sunny, wearing a kind of modest mini wetsuit that was quite removed from the scrap of Lycra back in Dublin she referred to as her *Smarties swimsuit*, splashed and tried to doggy-paddle breathlessly. She looked lonesome, but unthinkingly so. An only child. Surely she would soon have friends, Lena thought, and be like the children having their lesson, each one as unthinkingly integrated as Sunny was not; surely she would soon have a sibling.

Lena had stopped vetoing ejaculation inside. Veto had been her only birth control method for years. Amazing really that she'd never been pregnant before. By Cian for instance, or Gwynn. Imagine that. No child support from Cian anyway. Gwynn probably in a pained and incrementally manipulative way; Gwynn had plenty of money and a scalable career profile. Funny thoughts to have – she might have laughed. Sometimes she ran, like a fire drill, through the process of leaving Odhran; thought about maintenance, escape routes, ways in which the moral high ground might favour her. Wondered if she could ever love again and then thought, with acute distaste, Lord no, I'm finished with men.

And this had something to do with having a daughter. A baton of sorts would be passed, and there could only be one beauty. Maybe soon I'll have a son. This cynical cycle compensated for the sting to her vanity represented by widened hips and Lena dipped lazily into the water, drifting in a circle around Sunny, keeping her eye always on the kid. Sunny gave little surges, small advances, forth, then played with a chewed-looking pool noodle. At last Sunny wandered to the edge of the pool and rested her elbows on the tiles.

'Can you die in a pool?' she asked Lena suddenly.

'Yes.' Lena spoke quietly. She felt dismayed. 'You can drown. That is why we are so careful, why we stay in the shallow end. And why you have to learn how to swim.'

'And if you swim you don't die?'

'Most of the time.' Lena leant her head on the tiles. 'Oh, muffin,' she sighed. It was here again. *Et in arcadia*, or just a cheerful hotel swimming pool, at the start of their new life. She would have to broach it sensibly, she thought, and continue to do so as Sunny got older. The report from Declan Riley had taken much of the sting out of it; a professional, at least one professional, believed Sunny was doing just fine and was not insane.

Sunny laughed at the little nickname. 'Mama!'

'Do you remember,' Lena jerked suddenly up, '*The Teddy Bears' Picnic*?' It was a children's play she'd taken Sunny to when she was three.

'No.'

'You do. We went to the Ark theatre. There was a woman on the stage, she was playing with a big teddy bear and a tea set.' It had been steampunk, dreamy, incantatory; Sunny, at three, had been surprisingly transfixed. It was one of a number of children's events Lena had attempted with her before Montessori began, in the dark days of staying up all night and trying urgently to find something to do in the daytime. They'd done craft workshops, made paper birds, rhyme-and-clap, baby jamboree, toddler jamboree, matiness in the parent-and-baby cinema club. Of the *Teddy Bears' Picnic* play Lena recalled the white staring face of the protagonist, a woman moving with robotic movements, slowly and almost nostalgically; her movement suggested silent film, living picture, something superannuated but formalised; this aesthetic was an adult one, she thought, but the children found it mesmerising.

'You said, afterwards,' Lena told Sunny now, 'that it was in your dream.'

'I don't remember.' But Sunny looked interested.

'You saw a play, which is people pretending to do something – like a game that you watch. The woman was pretending to have tea with the teddy bear. And then you dreamt about it, and a dream is also pretend, or made up, by your own mind in the night. It isn't real but you still see it and it still is – well, I mean. Important. Dreams are interesting. Plays are like dreams,' she said. 'But they are not real.'

'Like ghosts,' Sunny suggested solemnly.

'Exactly like ghosts.'

At this moment, a boy tore by them, hammering at the water inexpertly. Sunny screwed her eyes up and squealed in response. 'Too loud!' she cried.

'Splash back,' Lena advised.

The pool put forty minutes around. In the changing room Lena towelled Sunny down and checked her phone and continued, intrepidly. 'So when you think about dying before it is like a dream or a play,' she explained. 'You can see and think about it, it has images, it is like pictures, but it isn't real – it's a dream, or your mind playing tricks.'

Why didn't I put it like this before, Lena thought. It felt so intuitively likely to be true. The pageant of imagination; the drama of the child, of being a child, whatever that book about bringing up gifted children – being a gifted child? Was it that? – was about.

Sunny looked either doubtful or confused. She said, eventually, 'OK.'

'Did you have any good dreams recently?'

A look, like a stroke of motion, passed over Sunny's face. 'I don't remember,' she said.

After this, they emerged wet-haired and hungry and went to the bar. Sonia was sitting in a banquette with an empty coffee mug and a copy of the *Irish Times*.

'Take a look,' she greeted them instantly, 'at the light on the water.'

On the river, she meant. It lay below them. The light was ancient light. Further out, beyond the marinas tucked into reeds, beyond the beached forgotten pleasure boats, the lake widened into a series of islands and sunlight ridged it stiffly. It looked like Scandinavia.

When Sonia dropped them home Lena embraced her, waved, then messaged Odhran asking, how do we stop your mother dropping in at total random without warning whenever she likes?

Sunny drew at the coffee table. She drew a character they knew, the mama of before. But when Lena asked, with wariness, about the picture Sunny said, 'It's Sunniva.'

'Oh wow,' Lena replied.

Odhran called in the evening. 'So I'm staying here,' he said, 'am I? I am getting this swimsuit and a few other things.'

'We are grand here, only girls.'

'It's strange without you.'

'You have all that space. You could have an affair.'

The next day, a prosaic Thursday, Lena and Sunny walked around the cold and hushed cathedral unaccompanied. There were war memorials and a plaque shaped like a masonic plinth, dedicated to a dispensary doctor who had died of dysentery. Like a storybook or an English village. When they returned to the chalet, watching a sailboat peek between some trees, they met a woman slightly older than Lena with a long ponytail.

'I've come to introduce myself,' the woman said. 'I am a childminder with ten years' experience and three of my own; I live out in Tountinna but I drive in here frequently. There's references if you like.'

'Did Sonia send you?'

'Yes.' The woman laughed.

'Pleased to meet you,' Lena said. She felt breathless at the sheer nerve but also impressed. The hills had eyes, she was being watched, she was being managed, and it was by Sonia – Sonia wanted her to know that she, Lena, could go back to work and have help all the same. That in this place there was a system of support to be tapped into. But only through Sonia. Nobody would dislocate her child's arm in this tribal, closed-circuit place.

Sunny played by herself again. Lena would need to think of a way of meeting people, of making friends. There were two schools in the town, but it seemed premature to ask around about this. She thought of Declan, of the warning about spending all this time alone. Her quietness, her mutedness, would come to muffle Sunny's spirit without a city or, who knows, a childminder to intervene. A mother who is *kept busy*. She was meditating on this, casting about for ideas, as she packed away the kitchen after dinner.

When the phone buzzed she expected Odhran again; it was Rita.

'Saturday,' said Rita. 'Next week. In my house. Can you do it?'

'I think I can.' Lena was careful. She would not say anything about Clare. She hadn't told Rita. She'd texted Caoimhe and Orla; both had answered, OMG. They had no words for it after that. Lena was surprised to find this aggression rewarding or notorious; she had just gone and done it, apparently – betrayed them with a swift incomprehensible decision.

'You,' typed Caoimhe the next day, 'will never get a lease again.' This was true.

And yet the pull to Dublin, the call from Rita, lit her with a dry and hollow but exciting feeling, of dehydration and pep, that was somewhere between stress and something sexual. The city in its noise would close around her and she would be far from Sunny and Odhran. Two to three hours away; nobody looking, the apartment like a clean upholstered shell. It was a dismaying feeling when she looked at it in the abstract and it made her realise the chalet was weighing against her now, a little, in its bittiness and contingency. It was even less permanent then the apartment in Islandbridge. Where would they live, if they could buy here? In some lugubrious bungalow or semi-d at the edge of the motorway or in a greyish and unrendered McMansion beneath a pendant – no, they couldn't afford that, for that you needed land.

There was, she thought, no actual *suction* to the oven hood. It smelt of burgers, grease, extending back in time. She hated that. She wanted to live in a place that she could clean.

Sunny's room, stale and miniature, was dark now. Lena poured a glass of wine and sat on the couch, pushing back collapsing throws. Odhran would be home within the hour; he was driving, headlights forking into the gloom that had got thicker, darker, more persistent over the last week. It was September, it would soon be October and Halloween.

'Something to say,' Aidan had warned her when he'd

inducted her into the chalet, 'is that people love coming down here in the summer, when the river is full and there are tourists and festivals. But the winters are long and cold and people in Clare, you know, *sit in*; they don't go out.'

'We have your mother,' she had chipped in waggishly.

'Oh yes. The Sonia you have always,' Aidan said.

32

The holiday, meandering a concept as it was, persisted for another week. On Friday afternoon, Odhran suffered somewhat. Lena was in Dublin this time; he had been trying to work with Sunny in the chalet all day. He set his laptop up on the breakfast bar so that the cable and charger had to stretch and dip like ugly bunting between a socket in the kitchen and the bar. Breakfast bars made him think of holidays to chalets when they were young, although why they, a country family, would decamp to Kinvara or Killarney or Brittas Bay was difficult to explain. Often they took the housekeeper. She would lie on a towel on whatever outside surface she'd been accorded and ignore them; she would tan with baby oil. It was a memory thoroughly unerotic in wattage – the baby oil, the breakfast bars.

Sunny walked into the charger a number of times, making the jack jerk from the laptop. Odhran lost patience and Sunny lost patience.

'I'm bored, I'm bored,' she shouted. 'I want to see Mama.'

'Tomorrow you'll see Mama. Can't you play by yourself?'

'I want you to play with me.'

They were driving to the farmhouse for dinner that night, and to stay over. He couldn't call his mother so early and show weakness or she might invoke that childminder she'd sourced and briefed without telling them about it, an action he believed suggested some kind of incompetence or overwhelm on their part, a need for *help*.

'Sunny needs friends,' Lena had said. 'I need to find something structured for her.'

He was concerned this lack of structure would begin acting as a deterrent or mark against the plan for remaining in Clare. But he had so much work. Colm zoomed in, serenely. There had been little formal mention of the merger, of the melting of humanities research funding into science, which told everyone that certainly it was being negotiated; we will have, Colm said often and with misplaced confidence, a seat at the table.

Odhran felt work as a highway or a boulevard opening through him – come what may, he thought obligingly. I'm interested.

Lena had phoned at lunchtime from her mother's house in Naul. 'Is Sunny OK?' she pestered. 'Are you playing with Sunny?'

'Well, obviously I've got work.'

'You need to bracket the day off. You need to do as I do when you're not there. You can't do both things at once.'

'Things need to be done.'

'You are not a surgeon,' she said pertly. 'You are not doing anything *life-or-death*.' It was true and insulting at once. But each ping of the email felt like an elbow to the ribs.

He took this whiplash out on Sunny. 'Can't you be good? Can't you let Mama go to work sometimes, and have a break?'

Sonia, the prospect of Sonia, he was sorry to admit, brought reprieve. It was getting darker, bluer, earlier; an early partial moon shyly appearing over the mountain. The long dark winter would be difficult, yes, if they couldn't find a way to get Sunny into a school or a crèche.

At five, Aidan arrived to drive them to Glennagalliagh as arranged. Lena had taken the car to Dublin for the night.

'How are you finding it?' Aidan could not conceal his pride. It was touching because it was also kind of pathetic. In the intervening weeks, the largesse of the chalet had deflated to a crasser, less impressive reality. For Odhran and Lena at least.

'We feel like we're on a kind of shit holiday,' Odhran told

him. He watched Aidan's face fall and said, 'Oh but it's perfect – it's the perfect situation.'

'Are you house hunting?'

'We have places lined up. It's so useful,' Odhran parroted Lena, following her advice to treat Aidan kindly and maximise their use of the chalet. 'It's so, so useful to be down here, you know?'

'That way, you can look at anything,' Aidan was enthusiastic and pedantic at once, 'at speed. Like, instantly. Also you can weigh your options. I know people I can put you in touch with.'

'You know everyone.' It was verging on comical for Odhran. But Aidan beamed. He was not staying for the evening with them because he had a meeting with the Chamber of Commerce in Limerick, or some wing of it, and dinner afterwards. This was a small thing, he assured Odhran, just a few friends. Odhran thought: pink mafia. But he felt fond and, for the first time, dimly proud of his brother's confident implication in the world of their childhood. He was the one who most resembled their father, really. This was surprising.

'I keep my ear to the ground,' Aidan said. 'I'll know if anything comes up, house-wise.'

At the farmhouse, he left them in the broad glow of lighted windows, light doubling festively off the large mirror in the hall.

Through the closed front door he heard his mother's voice, squealing with hospitality. 'Oh don't be afraid of that!' she said. She was still laughing falsely for his benefit, inhabiting conviviality, when she opened the door. 'Odhran,' she said. As if she were pleasantly surprised. She was doing that thing where she acted like various people could call to her, were in the habit of calling to her, at any time, providing plot points and tweaks; she was pretending in front of someone else.

He felt, at the door, irritated by this, but also a wave of almost indecent relief. Sonia would absorb Sunny's energy; she would want to put Sunny to bed. He could have a beer or something, if there was any beer in the house. He should, he thought, have brought some beer.

Sunny blasted past him. Sonia caught her face and kissed it rapidly.

'Who's here?' he asked, unable to avoid sounding defensive.

'A visitor. I'll explain.'

At the kitchen table sat a nervous woman of Odhran's age. She wore a dark stiff chuba of some kind over a bulky roll-neck jumper; she looked cold, or ready for cold. He wondered at once if he knew her and if she was a neighbour, and nodded a greeting to her.

'There is a little boy named Naoise,' Sonia told Sunny, 'in the front room, to play with you.'

Sunny paused and pushed her lips out, thinking prettily. 'Is he one of my cousins?' she asked.

'He's not. His mammy here is Aude. He's older than you – I gave him the Switch.'

'Oh!' Sunny trotted out of the room at once. She was supposed to be supervised with the Switch, but Odhran sank into a kitchen chair instead.

'Not easy minding a kid on a working day,' he said. 'Aude, is that right? I am Odhran.'

Aude extended a hot hand to shake and smiled tensely at him. She hadn't spoken. She was watching him with an intensity that was also ironical; what, he thought, was going on?

'Aude is someone I have wanted to introduce to Sunny,' Sonia said.

She was standing with her back to the counter for ballast, gripping it. The strained suspension in the room struck Odhran as increasingly concerning, though a casserole of something pleasant-smelling on the range suggested life as usual. He felt he recognised the name. Sonia asked if he would come into the parlour and turned to Aude as she walked out, saying, 'Make another tea if you'd like one, help yourself.'

In the damp little room, before the gaping fireplace, she explained. The woman was a medium she'd met at some kind of Steiner fair. She was part of the loose knot of amiable bohemians who lived between Feakle and the eco-village at Cloughjordan, descendants sometimes of the frontier Bavarians and Danish who'd come to live in unspoilt Ireland, growing food on modest homesteads, in the sixties and seventies; he and his siblings had been to school at various times with Einers and Yngves and Indigos. Banbha and Uisce, whose parents went barefoot all year. As a group of people they were sweet and remote and indifferent and tolerated by everybody else like eccentric guests. Aude, it seemed, also made herbal remedies.

'All I want is for her to speak to Sunny for a bit,' Sonia explained.

Odhran was at a loss. If he took Sunny home in a huff, he would lose the warm, enveloping if ersatz return to adolescence the evening seemed to promise. An image of himself back in the overlit chalet, defrosting a mini pizza, tasered through.

'This is not for me,' he tried to protest quietly.

'If you want to leave Sunny out of it,' she offered, 'she could just speak to you.'

'Do I have to do it?' He sighed. He sounded like a teenager now. He did not believe in any of it, so why object? It might encourage Sunny to be esoteric; or worse, Lena. Though not if Sunny didn't know. It said something about him then – it went against his principles.

Lately, the past life stuff had receded, and Sunny had – famously – said not a word of it to the play therapist. When he saw this, Odhran experienced a rush of gratitude to the play therapist, as if this man had taken Odhran's side in the whole thing without even meaning to. Last week Lena had told him she'd discussed dreams and visions and made-up daydreams and so on with Sunny; that they had agreed ghosts were made up, for example, like dreams. Lena had been animated or charmed by the experience and Odhran nodded vigorously, still a little confused but not wanting to undermine her, and said, 'Yeah, that makes sense.'

So it seemed it was over or heading for over, but here they were visiting it again.

'Can you see why I'm interested?' Sonia asked. She had told a vivid anecdote of clairvoyance to underscore, even sponsor, the talents of Aude.

'You are telling me,' Odhran asked, 'that she could see – Dad?'

'She is very sincere. I know it's strange. But there is this quality to things sometimes, this strangeness,' Sonia said. 'And we have to be open to it.'

'I'm not opposed to that,' he argued. 'I just don't believe in it, and you shouldn't have sprung it on us.'

'I had the thought last minute,' she said, lying obviously. 'Do you remember,' she changed emphasis then, and held up a hand to quiet him. 'The eye? The conjunctivitis?'

'Yes.' When he was a child, he had conjunctivitis repeatedly. His father had driven him to a holy well – that was all he could remember – in a burrow of waist-high stone. He remembered the litter of prayer cards and flowers in foil and candlestubs heaped around the little door, and that, inside, there was the circular rattle of water resolving itself into a hollow. His father washed out his eye with the water. Within hours, the conjunctivitis had gone.

'Sometimes they test water in those places,' he told Sonia, 'and find out it contains, like, chemicals. There is a holy well in Kerry somewhere that has lithium in it.'

'So you remember then,' she said.

'I mean, there can be medical explanations for it, not like. Mystical.'

'Oh I know,' Sonia declared. 'Some day, many things will be proven, probably, that we already know of from a holistic perspective.' She was doing the doctor thing now. 'In my career, I've had to keep an open mind,' she reminded him.

Odhran was unnerved by the situation. He wanted to back out of it. He knew she had never been fully convinced by these things but that she kept homeopathic remedies, had sometimes instructed patients to consider Lourdes or Medjugorje, because, she said, if they believed in God, they would believe in his interventionist interest in them. And this would help.

'Never Knock though,' she often qualified, referring to the Marian pilgrimage resort in County Mayo. 'It has to be a sunny place.'

Once she said, with earnestness, 'Knock is what hell looks like.'

'Most of this chronic pain, for instance,' she had informed him, loftily, when he was a teenager, 'and you see lots of this – this *chronic fatigue*. A whole load of that is emotional. You can give people, kind of, *rituals*, to help with it.'

She was flexible. When a man came to her famously in the noughties and told here there was a demon, and not schizophrenia, in his head, she agreed. In a manner of speaking.

'The question, Packie,' she said – she would perform it later for them, as a skit – 'the question is: Packie, what are you going to do about it?'

This man, she then recommended, should be institutionalised. Forever.

'I see no hope of bringing him to understand his condition,' she said. She wrote to a board of directors somewhere and everything. 'I encourage you with compassion to ensure Patrick Doherty remains a ward of state for the rest of his life.'

Odhran, softening since the memory of conjunctivitis, of his practical and affectionate father, and at Sonia's argument for an *open mind*, ran one set of fingers through his hair. He remembered with a jolt that Aidan's tale, the ghost story, had begun in this damp little anteroom, with its empty narrow girlish fireplace.

'You need to give us space,' he said. 'Lena and Sunny and me.'

'I know that.'

'We didn't come down here to be in your pocket.'

'I understand.'

'If you don't back off, Lena will be spooked and turn against the whole thing.'

'Lena is not so precious,' Sonia said, 'but yes. I get it. I've been excited. Sunny is my favourite grandchild. But I understand.'

'I need to see you back off after this. I'll let her speak to me – not Sunny – and this has to be the end of it. I don't want this past life stuff to follow us down here.'

'I understand.' She repeated this and bowed her head. She was pleased.

'Because,' he found himself continuing with a new and slightly self-important energy, 'a lot of that is Lena's stress just rubbing off on Sunny. Sunny has a big imagination. If we encourage anything, she'll keep doing it too, you know; children are like that.'

'The way I see it,' Sonia referred to the Aude experiment, 'it's a case of: what harm?'

'She doesn't talk to Sunny,' he said.

'That's fine. Just you. I've asked her all this way, in the evening too.'

Back in the kitchen, Aude began to stand. 'I can go,' she said.

'No please.' Odhran gestured for her to sit. 'Only, please don't say anything to her directly, to my daughter. To Sunniva.'

'I never would have.' Aude looked back at him, rabbit-eyed.

They ate together, stew ladled over potato, Aude and her little boy – who was funny, with long hair and an elfin little outfit, like Peter Pan, who spoke to Sunny excitedly, making her blush with pleasure and screw up her eyes – and Sonia and Odhran. There was fruit crumble. Sunny, disappointed, pushed hers away.

'Now don't be cheeky,' Odhran said.

'Can I have biscuits?'

'Plenty of biscuits!' Sonia said.

Throughout, he watched Aude observe Sunny openly and eat, as he also observed, very little. The food was over quickly and the children returned to the front room. Sonia and Aude piled together plates and glasses and began to fill the dishwasher. Aude then returned to the table and took out some notepaper, writing rapidly with a kind of half-pen, something you got free in a hotel room. Sonia set up the coffee percolator and watched her keenly from her post against the countertop again. Her posture made her seem as if she was nervous too, or excited, or had entered some situation the vibe of which was at the edge of her own powers of comprehension and control and tolerance. She was not often attentive in this way.

'OK,' Aude said eventually. 'So what I will say you can take or leave, and I understand you are not fully onboard with this, Odhran, but I don't want to offend.'

Odhran was alarmed a little by *offend*. 'Please continue,' he said.

'First off, she is the sunniest little thing, with a perfect aura,' Aude said. She was strangely unsmiling as she offered this information. 'And the aura changes, it moves between shades, yellow and blue for the most part – it flickers, and this is like upgrading, kind of like downloading, you see?'

They nodded mutely. Even Sonia looked afraid of what might come.

'I mean,' Aude placed more emphasis, 'that she is sensitive and reactive to the environment. I mean she can probably adapt well; she can let energies in. This is good and bad.'

'Right,' said Odhran. He wanted to laugh.

'Now, something that kept on coming.' Aude laughed now, breathlessly, herself. 'Is a satellite. Watching a satellite, but a long time ago – the sixties or seventies.'

'Right.'

When he said this, Aude snapped her head towards him and frowned. 'It's hard to explain. I see a satellite, but it's not recent; I see this very clearly. It is hard to put this across.'

'That's OK.' Odhran shrugged. He did not mean to be hostile; he meant, he supposed, to dilute her attention, to push her forward with the halting monologue she was presenting and being, presumably, paid for.

She continued to look at him. Had he ever heard, she asked, Sunny mention a satellite?

'No.'

'You haven't told me anything.' Aude swivelled to Sonia to corroborate. 'You have not—'

'I have told you a little.'

'You have not told me anything about the content, so to speak.'

'I haven't.' Sonia poured coffee. 'Only that she thinks she's lived before.'

Sonia seemed to be aiming for a certain self-control now; she moved calmly, almost seeming beyond this. She was underwhelmed, Odhran realised with subtle glee, by the revelations. They were too non-sequential and thin. A satellite? What did a satellite look for? All anxiety had left Odhran now; he enjoyed instead the rather banal glow of being proven right in a basically low-stakes way. It was like having his fortune told in a hoky booth, at a harvest fair. Like having a girlfriend read a horoscope aloud, severely, over brunch, because it advised one to love harder or appreciate what you've got or something else that might read as romantic admonition.

'Has that content,' Aude asked, 'ever related to someone buried in unconsecrated ground?'

She paused and closed her eyes. She began again.

'I mean obviously she wouldn't say that, she wouldn't use those words, but – anything about burial, burial in some halfway place? Halfway as in unconsecrated. You know, there is lots of that around here, in Ireland generally.'

Odhran's mind had gone blank, pre-emptively. A light swiped off, a refusal to think or accept this information. Sonia stared.

'A little,' she said.

'Right.' Aude continued. 'There is something there, not Sunny but some earlier Sunny, that knows it's in a halfway place. Something unhappy. Not very unhappy, just a little unhappy.'

There was another pause and Odhran echoed, leadenly, 'A little unhappy.'

Sonia shot him a look.

His mind felt offline, he'd willed it into emptiness. He would not reflect on this information. A thought came purely, finally: if it came up a lot, in Ireland, as she'd suggested, perhaps consecrated and unconsecrated ground was just something she *said*; not even maliciously, he decided judiciously, warming slowly to the practice of thinking again. Not even with malice. Just because she herself believed burial, unmarked burial, was a cultural feature. Which it was. Killeens and famine pits and ancient churches. Plenty of those. If you weren't Irish, which she clearly wasn't, it might seem a feature you would note and talk about.

'Anything else?' Sonia asked.

'Lots of people around here have ancestors with them,' Aude said, 'because this place is – how would you say it? Monocultural.'

Odhran, finally, laughed.

'Lots of people.' She was looking at him, confused. 'You see them with these followers. I don't think Sunny has a follower; she is a reincarnation. She is an ancestor and maybe a couple of ancestors. But this is something children grow out of. They forget. Almost always. She has not said anything this evening anyway.'

'It's receded a little,' Odhran said.

'She will forget about it. I can tell you this ancestor is in unconsecrated ground. But there is so much of that, there are so many burial grounds.'

'This soul,' Aude concluded, 'is not alone.' She said this levelly but seemed to have run out of patience with them, to know on some level that Odhran had come to consider her funny – to laugh at the word *monocultural* because it sounded like an accusation, and because his sense of tension and stress at the situation had not been granted relief. Or perhaps she knew on a clairvoyant level, he thought meanly, and imagined joking with this about Sonia afterwards. He did not believe the woman could read his mind, but probably she could read his facial expression, which was now coolly vacant and impolite.

'And now,' Aude said. 'I have to go. I get tired. I hope you are not offended.' She left somewhat stiffly, towing the child by the hand. They heard the station wagon rattle into life outside, reverse like a breath sucked in, depart. Odhran and Sonia drank coffee.

'That was wild,' Odhran said eventually.

'She was not so – vague as that, last time,' Sonia said. There was further silence. It was a disturbing silence. He had begun to forget most of the details already.

'Where is that place, the cilín?' he asked. The dishwasher was humming now. The kitchen was warm and yellow, not haunted nor contingent in any way; the atmosphere was that of the gentle and sustaining membrane provided by habit and love and prosperity, the feeling of home now that he'd forgiven home and gone into the world and come back.

'I don't know if I could find it again. There's a reburial plot though. You might get the archaeological survey still; they'd have it in the county archive.'

'Or online.' He felt the soft light of the kitchen was making him drowsy. He felt like he needed to sleep heavily. They heard Sunny chattering at the television inside.

'Are you going to tell her mother?'

'I will have to think of some way to explain it,' he said, 'that doesn't sound insane.'

'Will I be in trouble?' Sonia grinned.

'Lena is funny like that,' he said. 'She has a lot of capacity.' She would drill him for details though, he reflected now, with a little disquiet. He could imagine her drilling for details avidly and enjoying it a little, like how she enjoyed Tarot readings and horoscopes and serendipitous coincidences, like how she could be superstitious. But I can't remember anything else, he would say. He had already forgotten most of it. There was nothing to it, he would say.

'I've forgotten all the details,' he said.

'The unconsecrated ground though,' Sonia said.

'But it's not unconsecrated, is it? It was just a cilín. They were consecrated once. Isn't that the point of using them?'

'Truth be told,' Sonia was staring glassily at the fridge, 'I don't know.'

She was silent for a moment, seeming wearier. She said, 'I was more impressed with her last time, it must be said.'

'You should get your money back.'

'Don't be smart.' She reached for the coffee percolator.

Odhran thought about Aidan's ghost, about their father pulling on his boots and striding out into the garden, into the afterlife, or into the night, into nothingness – where, after all, did people go? He'd always assumed it didn't matter and was out of his hands anyhow. He found he still believed this now.

'So, the satellite,' he said.

'What's that?'

'She mentioned a satellite. Watching a satellite.'

'Oh I didn't really follow that.' Sonia rubbed her eyes, relinquishing. And then, 'She's being very quiet, Miss Sunniva I mean, isn't she?'

'It's the Nintendo,' Odhran yawned. 'She knows it is *verboten*, so she's lying low.' He stood up and brought his coffee cup to the sink. 'Bedtime soon,' he remarked airily, hoping Sonia would want to swoop in and do it and release him to check emails openly.

33

'I'm coming up to Dublin,' Lena told her mother on the phone. 'I thought I might call out to you, before I go back down.'

'Back down to Clare,' she specified.

'You are staying down there then?' her mother asked. But it was not hostile this time.

'For now.'

'Well, maybe it's good. You want to be able to buy your own place.'

Lena was surprised. 'Thank you,' she said.

It was a silly thing to say. Why thanks?

'Odhran's mother is into the children, isn't she?' her own mother added. 'She has plenty of grandchildren.'

'If you're coming tomorrow,' she changed then, 'there is a removal.'

'Oh. I'd rather avoid that.'

'It's Mrs Tansey. She lived on Chapel Street. She would have minded you.'

'I remember.' A chain-smoker; rolled her own. She had a big Swiss cuckoo clock. She counted coins out of a cracked leather purse for the messages. Dear God. Here it came: antimacassars, the Snoopy ashtray, the chewy phone coil. Nineties kids TV.

'She must be old.'

'She looked old from an early age, I am afraid.' Lena's mother expanded into drollery a moment. 'She was in her eighties. Eighty-five.'

'She called me unlucky,' Lena recalled.

'She what?'

'She used to say I was unlucky. Always, I don't know, losing things.'

'It wasn't easy for you and your brother that I couldn't stay with your father. That was unlucky, in a way.'

Lena froze on the phone at this, and closed her eyes. For pain or shame, she couldn't tell. Her mother could be frank like this, unexamined, but it was relatively rare. There was a quality of emotional openness to the phone call which was rare and not something Lena wished to sustain or feed, the time for openness between them having passed conclusively.

'No, it wasn't easy,' she agreed. Her tone, she hoped, did not invite further inquiry.

'When you are settled in Clare, I'll come and visit you,' her mother said.

'But I'll see you tomorrow, Mam.'

'Of course. Come out when you like. Though come before five. There is this removal; a few of us are going. I worked with her daughter, or one of them.'

She would come well before five, Lena thought. She would avoid all of that. She had the car; she left Odhran and Sunny after breakfast and took her time reversing the journey past the outlet malls and wind turbines and watching Dublin thicken into carriageways into the aerodrome, a field of energy. A field of energy where planes were slanting above morning traffic. When she was small, they sometimes drove to the perimeter and parked by the chain-link fence and watched the planes. There would be men standing about with binoculars. There was a back-channel to Naul, where the land was yellow and flat.

She stopped to buy two punnets of strawberries from a teenage boy at the side of the road. He had a SumUp console and everything.

'Not cheap,' she remarked.

'Not imported, missus,' retorted the boy, which made her

laugh at the *missus*. Her mother put these under the kitchen tap over and again.

'All them cars going by,' she said, vexed.

They sat outside, which Lena's mother preferred to do whenever possible. There was an orange cast coming over the light, but the row of stubby and foul-smelling conifer trees that had always rimmed the garden and marked it apart from the farmland around it was as shady and damp as ever. Her mother asked few questions about Clare but wanted to know how Sunny was doing and Lena, drumming her longer fingernails against the side of a large stripy mug, said at last, 'It's been a funny year for her. She has been saying things; that she is sad.'

'You mentioned that.'

'That she was *born before*.' She wondered if she ought to play the voice note. It had been some time since the voice note was played.

'I don't know,' her mother said, 'if you told me that.'

'She says things like, you know, *I can remember when I died*.'

She was surprised to see her mother so apparently struck by it. The woman tried to smile. 'All children say things like that. Probably you used to say things like that.'

'Did I?' Lena smiled back, forcing it evenly on, and put the mug down. Her mother had purchased a composter: she spotted it, pyramidal and flimsy, just beyond the deck. The air around it was an agitation of midget flies.

'You used to say funny things. You were a great one for imaginary friends.'

'That's funny,' Lena said. 'What kind of friends?'

'I wouldn't remember. You were three or four, something like that.' 'You know who might have remembered,' her mother started to laugh suddenly. 'Poor old Mrs Tansey, who is dead. I remember you copying her with the cigarettes.' Here she mimed a roll-up, worrying tobacco into the hollow, drawing a toke. 'Pretending you were rolling cigarettes,' she said.

Lena pictured suddenly an old-fashioned comb, someone

placing cigarette paper over the teeth and telling her to blow – a musical instrument. There was no context for the memory but a taste in her mouth like sebum and pomade and the faintly fruity cigarette paper.

'Sunny seems to be growing out of it,' Lena said.

'Will you have more children?' her mother asked suddenly

She was surprised by this, but answered, 'Yes.'

'You like it then?'

'I do. Most of the time.'

'I regret that I worked so hard,' her mother said. It did not seem to have to do with anything and sent a signal, Lena felt, that Lena should leave.

'Well, enjoy your party and all then,' her mother said.

Her mother saw her off from the porch, which was heating up and smelling of plastic. She toed thick ceramic plant pots into new arrangements, folding her arms, leaning over, avoiding a hug. Lena told her really she was working, not enjoying the party at Rita's house; *nice work if you can get it*, her mother said.

Lena drove into Dublin, hitting the school traffic foolishly, and had little time to park the car in the underground car park of the apartment block. When she stepped out, she noted a droning sound; a drone, spread level and hardly perceptible, everywhere. She looked about. It was the lights, the fluorescence, the boiler or perhaps the city's murmur, and everywhere. At first, she thought the bike was gone, but then it appeared, like the pattern in a stereogram, from a tangle of bikes banked and locked and tossed together by the communal dumpster.

She picked around these other bikes to free it. She would need to sell it now. Or just, like, leave it leaning somewhere, allow nature to take its course. Rewild my bike. It amused her to say it, she would need to find someone to say it to – rewild my bike.

'When are you back?' Odhran moaned on the phone. 'We miss you.'

'I am hardly gone.'

'We miss you. Daddy misses you. We are going to Granny's.'

'Are you playing with her?'

'I am playing with her. We are here with the watercolours.'

'We miss you,' he insisted. 'Please come back.'

Lena was halfway into town, weaving, when she remembered it was Rita's house, in the suburb of Cabra, and not Essex Street, that she was bound for this evening, and swore. She had to reroute and take the terrible hill past the Rotunda, then Constitution Hill. It was hard to find a specific house in Cabra too – blocks and blocks of thirties stock with blistered lintels over every door, every row identical. Rita's had been painted the colour of mint ice cream. The hallway was dark and hot, closing over Lena like a coppice, but the smell of detergent met her like a dear familiar friend. Rita was sitting in the front room with her husband, a taxi driver.

'I'm off soon,' he claimed, but didn't move. They were watching the news.

'Have a glass of wine, Lena,' Rita said. When she opened the double doors to the kitchen, Lena saw it was decorated with bunches of flowers and looked not only attractive but mystical – like a dream of a kitchen turned inside-out, sprouting flowers and vines and topiary: Lena had, she realised, lately dreamt of a kitchen of flowers and vines and topiary, Gauguin colours, mystical. Like a gift, this spangled before her again, then faded into powder dust. Rita had laid out a round satin shawl on the table and combed each tassel out. In her garden, which they could see in the soft evening light through a single window over the sink, there was a plastic water feature of a cherub tipping back its head to spout water. The plug that powered this feature was visible, snaking dismayingly into a shed.

Lena looked at everything with pleasure. The wine hit her empty stomach pleasantly. After this, she would not come again. She would not work here again. She would stay in Clare; she would find something for Sunny and herself. It was not worth the money to travel up to Dublin like this, nor worth the knot of confusion in her stomach. Things had not just changed but shattered, suddenly and elegantly, as if by the work of a silent earthquake underneath.

It was the sumptuousness of the space, but also its cramped and close atmosphere, which brought forth this sheer and highly satisfying thought. It was like a grotto but also like a slum. The texture and complexity was tiring to her eyes. She pictured – felt, seismically – the *clap* of a field folding out like a heavy bedsheet, smelt dew and chemical fertiliser and watched skies expand insanely over her; she smelt the rain drying out of silt at the edge of the river or the lake and pictured the raging gorse on the hiking route she used to take with Odhran when they were first courting and visiting Clare. It was not a difficult route; the incline was gentle most of the time, firming into a vertical slope at wide-set intervals, and all around them, vegetation clawed across the landscape gaudily. At the very top, there stood a bulky cement cross, as high as a house, onto which you could climb and look out over the little Viking islands, to the Norman towers and American mansions normally hidden by trees on the lakeshore. She wondered how nice it would be to disappear from Dublin.

'What a magic touch you have,' she told Rita. 'This place looks beautiful.'

'Oh give over. Light the candles,' Rita said.

By the time her husband actually left, there were women arriving. They were middle-aged. This is not a hen night, Rita explained; it's a fiftieth. The woman is shy and hates parties.

The woman was large and kept resetting an embellished bolero cardigan over her freckled forearms. She made several toasts in the front room, each time a new woman arrived, to life after toxic relationships and to a mother's sacrifice, and everyone was pretty well on by the time Rita commenced reading cards in the kitchen and penned the women into the front room, shutting the double doors that divided them.

Rita called them in one-by-one. Each time, the selected

woman hesitated, looking fearfully at the others, exhaling, as if it would be a trial to her. They were women so unlike her mother, warm and sometimes sardonic in a very Dublin way, but all of her mother's age.

'Do you have children?' one of them asked Lena. Lena was smiling blankly and sitting politely on the arm of a chair. It seemed impossible that so many people could crush into this tiny space and still seem comfortable, but they did.

'I have one,' she replied. She still felt smugly filled, within, by open space and sky. She told them about Odhran, about Sunny staying with Daddy, conjuring a slightly dishonest but possibly corrective image of him tending tenderly to Sunny – which he did, of course; he was a good father; she loved him with complete abandon in this moment. He had called to say he missed her. She missed him. There were people who needed her and would need her forever; she was of such consequence to them it felt dizzying. Somehow, this power had come to her. She was a powerful person.

'Do I recognise you?' another woman asked.

'I was a singer once. Maybe you saw me sing.' Lena felt ready, benevolent, to discuss this, to tell a neutered version of the story of her success, but no one asked for it.

Instead: 'Jesus,' the woman said. 'Now you have to sing.'

'Paula sings,' another woman shouted. 'Paula, sing!'

The woman named Paula burst into song instantly, shocking Lena. She sang 'Crazy', in the smoky style of Patsy Cline.

'Well done,' everybody applauded.

'Sing yourself,' Paula shot. They were all well on. Lena sat up and sang the very first thing that came into her head, which was 'Desperado'. By the end they were all joining in.

> You better let somebody love you
> Be-fore-it's-too-late.

Great applause. Rita poked her head through. 'We can't hear ourselves think,' she said.

'Shut up, the ghosts,' one woman whooped. 'The ghosts

are trying to come through. They're trying to give Margaret a warning about that dose of a daughter of hers.'

'It's not ghosts, it's Tarot,' another snapped. 'Totally different.'

'What, not ghosts?' The woman pretended to be horrified.

When each woman returned from her personal reading in the kitchen, she addressed the room. Some gave a summary, happily, identifying notes and allusions to new kitchens and grandchildren and relatives who were deceased but watching still. Others were curt and sat quietly afterwards, perturbed. Some tried to recount what they'd been told and failed, shaking their heads. Lena slipped out to a cold space under the stairs and slid wine bottles from a wholesale box and moved about topping up glasses.

At eleven, she put her hands to her face. It was hot and flushed. Her head was beginning to ache. She wanted water but did not wish to disturb Rita in the kitchen. She poured instead a glass of white wine from a bottle that had been sitting in an icy bucket of slush. It was cool and superficially refreshing. She pressed the side of the glass to her face.

'Open a window,' someone suggested, and when Lena did, they listened to the scrambler bikes whining and droning by outside. To the busses, whacking off a speed ramp, turning at the junction and towards town. Town would be busy. O'Connell Street would fill with violence quickly; murky and moody, carved by wandering gangs of men. She would cycle wide of it and pass the Black Church, roll down Parnell Street to the building on the corner that had been broken open years ago, that had always been reclaimed by trees; up the quays, past Elva's gallery and the basement bar where she and Cian and the band had played one of their earliest gigs, to Heuston. These routes were now intuitive to her. She would soon leave the city and whenever she came back to visit or shop or for the kind of medical attention you could not get in Limerick, it would be changed slightly, by inches, new shopfronts and levelled blocks and glassy offices like tidal waves bearing down, albeit always underneath an excess of colourless sky. With time, she would be entirely out of fashion. She would have children, she thought, and this time accept it. The brevity of this release, this sense of passage to a new stage of life, was physiological, like a warm, immanent pressure in her bowels and back.

Lena finished her wine and felt nostalgic. At an interval in the readings, she helped Rita to replenish snacks and glasses and drank a tumbler of metallic tap water breathlessly.

The women swept out quickly after midnight. Rita held on to Lena – saying, in fact, *I am holding on to you* – to gather bottles and handwash glasses and sweep up a litter of cigarette butts from the patio, where she'd been letting the women smoke after readings. They taped a refuse sack to the countertop and tossed everything into it indiscriminately. Rita began hoovering at once, sending Lena around with a rag and some Pledge. By one o'clock, the place had returned to its original state and Lena was nauseous with tiredness.

'Do you want to wait for Jim?' Rita asked. 'He can drive you.'

'I've got the bike. Not to worry,' Lena said. She would have liked a lift with Jim but did not trust him to return home any time soon. By now she was craving the slightly antiseptic emptiness of the apartment in Islandbridge, the dim rooms she could walk through in a mood of pleasant melancholy, missing her family recreationally.

The way back into town was downhill mostly. Lena took the North Circular Road. She should, she realised, have come this way earlier.

Passing the Edwardian houses on Oxmantown Road, those canting fussy freaky bourgeois mansions that were flats now and had always felt like relics, like something wicked, she hit one of the huge new painted speed ramps at an angle and jerked without warning, seizing up with fright, to the side.

But it did not stop there, because there was a car oncoming and a toss of canopies, the trees leaking their streetlight, and the starless silty sky. There was a puddle on the road, too, between the speed ramps, shallow and shattering now like a screen of glass.

It did not come as pain but a gong, a pure lurking reverberation, the first note struck but not weakened not dispersing not followed by any second or intentional or subsequent strike; a drone or the delayed echoes of many bass voices at the very back of a church; a tight smack to the chin – her teeth were broken, how was that? – and at the back of her head; two impacts, that was it, and she was paralysed.

A further impact. That was earth.

Lena's mind raced.

She thought: I was wrong to leave her, I walked out, I didn't wave, I kissed her in distraction, I was wrong, I left her, I walked out, this arrogance, preoccupation, I have left her many times, so many times I lost my temper, I was wrong to leave her, I was wrong to walk out, I was wrong to pick up car keys, I have not thought of her now for several hours, in the annexe with the padded toilet when my labour started, yes I thought: I've changed my mind, I didn't want her then, I was so wrong, so arrogant, nobody stopped me, I was wrong, I can't reverse it, I've seen it, I have been shown before, I've known it, shame and horror, I have known. In labour she'd been shown: this is a reality, you leave your body and your soul just blows away.

Odhran would underestimate her love for him since she had never said it properly, not told him about freezing in the moment of their marriage, saying vows forgotten now, vows they had taped on a piece of paper to the fridge jokingly, the legal ordinary vows: the moment that she froze in love and terror at this love and felt amazed that she could do it, how she meant it, she had never told him: I was happier to marry you than at any moment in my life.

There were no mistakes. But she had gone through life complaining.

She was greatly ashamed of this in the closing moment.

Greatly sorry: pleading, and ashamed.

No one else came to mind as it filtered out. The last thought was of vomit; how the whole world needed to be brought up and expelled from her, she needed to throw up the world, but no one person could throw up the world, no one body had such vastness. What could have such chasmic vastness? I refuse it, she said, to whatever the entity was. I cannot.

The last flex was a reflex, sharp as a sudden sober thought in the midst of drunkenness: no wait no wait you have forgotten something: turn around.

Acknowledgements

I am grateful, as ever, to my agent Matt Turner, for helping to develop this work, for guiding my ideas, and for all his advocacy; to my wonderful editor, Lettice Franklin, who works a kind of wizardry on everything I do; to my colleagues in the faculty of creative writing at UCD; to the Arts Council of Ireland; to Sydney Weinberg, Aoife Frances, and the girls: Lani, Rhea, Íde, Aphra.

Thank you to Nick Packer for explaining how musicians get paid. Apologies to the people of East Clare for scrambling the topography. The art installation on Arran Quay is based on Daniel Tuomey's *Stuck: A Decomposition*, which I saw at Ormston House Limerick in April 2025.

This book is dedicated to my husband, whose belief in my work, long conversations and deep love make it one of the many things we have made together.

Finally: I wrote this novel pregnant, caring for a small child, and against the backdrop of Israel's latest war on Gaza, which has – at the time of writing – resulted in the murder of more than 60,000 Palestinians, including many, many babies and children. It seemed trivial to put such details into a work of fiction, but this has been a constant context, and is an ongoing moral aberration.